Praise for *Time Salvager*

"Chu creates a fascinating world, strange and familiar, infused with humor, sorrow, courage, greed, and sacrifice. This page-turner is a riveting, gratifying read." —*Publishers Weekly* (starred review)

"An utterly captivating time-travel adventure. To put it simply, Chu's world-building is extraordinary." —*RT Book Reviews* (4½ stars, Top Pick!)

"Chu, author of the Lives of Tao series, has penned a thrilling SF adventure." —*Library Journal*

"Time-twisting action-adventure as only Wesley Chu could imagine it. I enjoyed it a lot. Read this book!" —Ann Leckie, author of the Hugo and Nebula Award–winning *Ancillary Justice*

"Chu has taken a simple, brilliant premise and built upon it an epic universe full of thrills and wonder." —Jason M. Hough, *New York Times* bestselling author of *The Darwin Elevator*

"Chu delivers a powerful and compelling search of the past for redemption in the present, by turns thrilling and sweet and gut-wrenching." —Kevin Hearne, *New York Times* bestselling author of the Iron Druid Chronicles

"More than a compelling, innovative take on the perks and pitfalls of time travel—*Time Salvager* is a sharp study of how human nature might prove mankind's salvation, or eventually doom us all. This is world-building that will make you fear for the future. In a good way." —Cherie Priest, author of *Maplecroft*

"A gripping, taut space opera . . . Immensely enjoyable." —Robert Jackson Bennett, author of *City of Stairs*

"A clever, cautionary SF tale with cool gadgets, characterization that surprised me in the best possible way, and multiple cunning twists." —Kate Elliott, author of the Crown of Stars series

"With time travel, force-field kung fu, and a huge helping of wit, Wesley Chu transmogrifies a bleak long-whimper apocalypse into vicious, high-octane fun."   —Max Gladstone, author of the Craft Sequence

"A time-warping science fiction thrill ride."
                         —Jaye Wells, author of the Sabina Kane series

TOR BOOKS BY WESLEY CHU

Time Salvager

Time Siege

TIME SALVAGER

WESLEY CHU

TOR

A Tom Doherty Associates Book
New York

TIME SALVAGER

A Tor Book
Published by Tom Doherty Associates, LLC
175 Fifth Avenue
New York, NY 10010

www.tor-forge.com

Tor® is a registered trademark of Tom Doherty Associates, LLC.

The Library of Congress has cataloged the hardcover edition as follows:

Chu, Wesley.
    Time salvager / Wesley Chu.—First edition.
        p. cm.
    ISBN 978-0-7653-7718-0 (hardcover)
    ISBN 978-1-4668-5454-3 (e-book)
    I. Title.
    PS3603.H828 T56 2015
    813'.6—dc23

                                    2015014555

    ISBN 978-0-7653-7719-7 (trade paperback)

Our books may be purchased in bulk for promotional, educational, or business use. Please contact your local bookseller or the Macmillan Corporate and Premium Sales Department at 1-800-221-7945, extension 5442, or by e-mail at MacmillanSpecialMarkets@macmillan.com.

First Edition: July 2015
First Trade Paperback Edition: April 2016

Printed in the United States of America

D   0   9   8   7   6

TO MY GRANDPARENTS
AND THOSE WHO CAME BEFORE ME

ACKNOWLEDGMENTS

I grew up in a rural part of Taiwan in the back of my grandparents' convenience store. My memories are hazy, but I remember vignettes—lush jungles, swarms of dragonflies, green everywhere, and lots and lots of rain. Some of my sharpest memories include making a bow and arrow out of a kite and shooting it at my brother (totally safe, I'm sure), biting the principal's son's nose until he bled during kindergarten because he took my toy, and stealing instant noodle packages from my grandparents' general store so I could suck on the pepper during nap time.

My paternal grandparents raised me until I was five years old while my parents were in the United States getting their advanced degrees at the University of Nebraska (Go Huskers!). For the most part, it was a good childhood, except for having an outhouse, showering with a bucket, and having chickens nip at me once in a while.

When my parents returned to take my brother and me to America, I remember telling my crying grandmother that I'd stay with her. I didn't, of course, but I always wondered what life would have been like if I had never left Taiwan. On one hand, I probably would have studied harder. On the other hand, I probably wouldn't have become an author.

I reflect on the decisions made by my parents, grandparents, and ancestors that have led to where I am today, writing this acknowledgment for *Time Salvager*. A change of heart, a freak accident, or a seemingly inconsequential left turn instead of a right at some intersection, and everything could have been different. I hope they're all proud of what came from their choices, mistakes, and sheer luck.

My mother's father passed away before I was born; her mother when I was in high school. My grandmother on my father's side passed away eight months before my first book, *The Lives of Tao*, came out. My surviving grandfather, a retired teacher, is now in his nineties. He's still sharp, exercises, and loves that new television I bought him in 2013 when I went back to visit. That may be the last time I see him alive.

To all my ancestors, thank you for leading lives that have allowed me to exist, to be an author, and to present *Time Salvager* to the world.

This book is dedicated to you.

Wesley Chu, Chicago, September 2014

Time Salvager

ONE

END TIMES

A sliver of light cut through the void, shooting toward the center of the battle display. Every soul on the bridge, breaths collectively held, eyed its path as it streaked across space. The room was dead quiet, except for the droning voice counting down to the point of impact. An explosion the size of a thumbnail blinked and flowered to fill half the display, then darkened again.

The bridge erupted into cheers as the Neptune Divinity flagship's holographic avatar disappeared. But the celebration was short-lived. Captain Dustinius Monk's voice cut through the chatter.

"Station status!" he demanded. The grim news of the health of the ship trickled in.

"Shield arms down," a bridge acolyte said.

"Mobility thrusters offline," another added.

"Aft hull breached."

The list of the ship's injuries continued to grow longer as each station confirmed the already perilous situation. It was a miracle and a testament to her crew that the *High Marker*, the flagship of the Technology Isolationists, was still intact.

Grace Priestly yawned, bored. She was usually bored when dealing with the painfully slow mental pace of average humans. She wondered how long she would have to wait for someone to say something interesting.

Then Monk's second in command, sounding close to panic, reported in. "We are not past the termination shock wave, Captain!" The chatter died and the room became dead silent again.

"Can we get any of the shield arms functional?" Monk asked.

"Not without extensive exterior repair."

"Get me just one damn shield arm and I can deflect the blast!" Captain Monk roared, his voice cutting through the tension in the air. The rest of the crew froze in place. "What about engines? Side thrusters? Any way to move her? Anything, for space's sake!"

"We're adrift, Captain." The acolyte standing next to him shook his head. "Power core down to six percent. There must be damage to the Titan source as well."

"Convert more immediately."

The acolyte's face turned white. "Captain, the systems acolyte reports the converter is gone."

"Gone? How is that possible?"

"She is at a loss, Captain."

Monk pulled up a display and stared at the blast wave of the Neptune Divinity flagship. He brought up another screen and scrolled through the data projections. His body stiffened and the blood drained from his face.

He glanced over at Grace, who stared back with cold indifference. Monk began spitting out orders in rapid succession, doing everything he could to prevent the impending disaster. Every hand on deck worked frantically as the ship's clock counted down to the impact of the wavefront barreling toward them.

Grace knew better. They were doomed the instant the fusion missile struck the enemy ship. With the main engine and side thrusters offline and all three shield arms inactive, the *High Marker* was completely exposed. The brunt of the blast wave would carry her away from the solar system toward the heliopause, from which no ship had ever returned.

Grace knew this was a high probability outcome, as did Monk. That's why, with the *High Marker*'s propulsions disabled, he had asked for her authority to execute a planet cracker missile at such short range. Even knowing the potential consequences, she had still ordered it launched. After all, if they were going to die, the least they could do was take out the enemy.

The captain and his crew were fighting to save the *High Marker*, but as far as Grace was concerned, they might as well be attempting to raise the dead. There were definitely enough bodies lying around the ship for them to try.

Still, it amused her that Monk fought so hard against the inevitable. The captain was a smart man, having been a spacefarer for all of his eighty years. If Grace hadn't known better, she would have guessed that the noble captain was trying to do whatever it took to save his ship. But Grace did know better. He was putting on a show for her, because having the High Scion of the Technology Isolationists die on his ship would shame his family line for all time.

Or perhaps Captain Monk wasn't going through the motions and was actually deluded enough to try to pull off a miracle. Grace certainly hoped not. She'd hate to think she had made the mistake of putting an imbecile in charge of her flagship. Well, there were no such things as miracles, and Grace tired of watching their pointless exercise. The *High Marker* was doomed.

The blast wave's impact jolted the ship, knocking those standing off their feet. Half a dozen more alerts lit up the battle display. Grace, sitting in her gravity chair, watched the crew scramble to combat these new problems as the *High Marker* was swept up by the forward force of the blast.

Grace stood up and looked at her pet. "Come, Swails. When the good captain is ready to report, he can call my cabin."

Swails, her man pet, stood and fell in step next to her. Her wrinkled hands caressed his perfect face. The poor idiot was incapable of grasping what had just happened. He had probably never had an original thought in his beautiful head, but then, that was the way she liked her pets. The bridge crew stopped what they were doing and waited respectfully as she passed.

"Oh, do continue trying to save the ship," she remarked, gliding out of the room. Those dolts would work themselves to death playing this futile game. Such a waste. Grace thought she had guided the Technology Isolationists to be better humans than this.

"Come, pet," she said, motioning to Swails again as she walked down the wreckage-strewn walkways. The flagship *High Marker* was the most advanced ship ever built by man. What the Technology Isolationists lacked in numbers and resources, they more than made up for in power and technological prowess. But even then, sheer numbers and resources could overcome that power, and that was exactly what the Neptune Divinities had been doing. There was only so much opposition any faction could muster without proper resources, after all.

The *High Marker* had been set upon shortly after her rendezvous with the research base on Eris. The flagship, her two escorts, and the dozen or so reinforcements summoned from the planet below took on sixty-some Neptune Divinity ships and won. Pyrrhic victories might not be true victories, but they were still better than the alternative.

The ship attrition rate on both sides of this massive battle was near total, save for the *High Marker*, which was now being knocked out of the solar system. Unless they could repair the engine, a feat no ship had ever accomplished without a space dock, they were doomed to die either in the cold of space or upon impact with a celestial object. Grace hoped the *High Marker* crashed into something interesting like a plasma cloud or a black hole, out of scientific curiosity, of course.

She decided to maximize the use of her remaining time alive and have her pet fuck her senseless. Might as well die happy.

They reached a partially collapsed intersection of the ship. A metal beam and several large fragments of debris blocked their path. Grace saw the blackened remains of a leg sticking out from the rubble and carefully stepped over it, trying to avoid dirtying her dress.

"Help me, pet," she said.

He dutifully complied, gently holding the tips of her fingers as she slowly swung one leg over the beam, and then the other. She moved well for a ninety-three-year-old. Grace watched as Swails jumped over the beam and fell in line beside her again. His movements felt wrong. She played that mental image of him over and over in her head. Something had been bothering her since they had boarded; Swails wasn't himself today.

Details were what differentiated the smart from the brilliant, and Grace was the foremost mind of her generation, and one of the brightest to have ever lived. Soon, it wouldn't matter anymore. She stared at Swails's genetically modified face; it was perfect. He looked like her pet and even moved like Swails, but something behind those eyes betrayed him. They weren't quite as vacuous as her pets' usually were.

He was an impostor in all the small ways that most people wouldn't notice, but she wasn't most people. Perhaps he was just ill and had suffered a bout of momentary thought. It happened from time to time, though the breeders did try their best to wean that tendency out of them. Well, no matter. There was only one thing she needed him for anyway.

The lights on the ship flickered and dimmed by exactly 18 percent. No doubt the good Captain Monk was conserving power to sustain the ship on the remote chance that they might be rescued. Grace's mouth cracked upward into a small smile. The foolish man was just prolonging their torture. If he really wanted to do the right thing, he would open all the air locks and instantly kill everyone on board. That's what she would do. But then, she was known for her mind and sexual appetite, not for her heart.

Grace did wonder how the power levels on the *High Marker* could have fallen so precipitously. Like every other modern space-faring vessel, the power source was located at the heart of the flagship. It was almost impossible to damage the power core without destroying the ship, and there were no scenarios where a 94 percent core leak could occur without some sort of catastrophic failure. At a less dire time, she would have been keen to solve this little mystery. Right now, not so much; she had far baser goals in mind.

"Come, pet." She motioned to him again. "Let us retire to my quarters."

Again, she noticed the slight change in his footsteps. They were wider than Swails's usual stride by a few centimeters. His posture was slightly more erect; the pressure of his hand on hers a few degrees less gentle. Swails wasn't acting fully himself today, but as far as she knew, no technology existing today could completely change someone's appearance. And if it did exist, she would have been the one to invent it. Just to be on the safe side, though, she reached out and caressed his face once more to make sure there wasn't a hologram or illusory veil in place. Yes, the perfect face was still his.

They entered the antechamber of her quarters. She looked over at her two blindfolded kill mutes standing in the corner. Those two pets were quite different from the man pet; violent and slavishly loyal, but prone to excitement and hard to control. All the lights and noise on the ship could send them into a frenzy. Leaving them here was for the best. Still, she was comforted that they were now back within earshot.

"A cup of warm water, pet," she ordered, "and fetch my wrap. If we are to die tonight, I wish to do so in comfort." Swails brought her the water as she disrobed.

Grace looked outside her portholes into black space. By the angle of the stars streaking across the window, the out-of-control tumbling of the ship seemed to have worsened. She expected the gravity to be cut at any moment to conserve energy. Monk was predictable, if anything.

She tore her gaze away from the portholes and gestured for Swails to attend to her. This could be her last fuck, so she wanted to enjoy it. Her pet was the finest of his litter; she would miss his tender touch. At least she had tonight.

She lay down on the bed and motioned for Swails to fulfill his duties. He obediently stripped and performed the Slave's Prayer to request permission for the honor of joining a master's bed.

Grace studied Swails's movements; she had seen him perform the ritual dozens of times before. The gestures were correct, but he was missing his usual grace. As he finished the prayer, Swails fell to his knees at the corner of the bed, spread his arms out, and looked up at the ceiling.

Instead of giving permission, Grace crawled seductively to him and placed her palm on his hard, toned chest. She ran her hand down his stomach, feeling all the familiar grooves and bumps of his muscles. Then her fingers wandered up to his heart. She closed her eyes and listened. The beats; impossibly fast for a clone. She cupped his chin with her other hand and lowered his face toward her.

"Who are you, stranger?" she asked.

Swails hesitated for an instant. "You know?"

"I've suspected since this morning. You haven't been Swails all day."

A smile broke out on his face. "You're a rare woman, Grace Priestly. It's an honor." Swails left her bed. He walked to her desk at the other end of the room and began rummaging through her belongings.

"What are you doing?" She stood up and retreated to the corner of the room, alarmed.

Swails ignored her as he picked out papers, scans, and datachips. He tossed aside several rare books and sorted through her personal tab files, generally making a mess. Grace hated messes. Then he pulled out the recently engraved Time Law Charter and lingered on it, his fingers brushing the inscriptions. He had found what he was looking for.

The charter was the culmination and moral principle of the past ten years of her research. The technology was ready. All humanity needed was a force that could responsibly wield this new power. If her new agency was successful, Grace Priestly would be credited with not only saving mankind, but propelling the Technology Isolationists to new heights. That allorium-engraved charter he held in his hands was the guiding law of this new agency, Chronological Regulatory Command, and it would lead them out of humanity's self-inflicted starvation.

"Put that back!" she yelled. "Kau, Trau! To me!"

Her two kill mutes burst into the room with their blindfolds lifted, exposing their glowing cybernetic red eyes. It grated on her sensibilities to resort to violence right before her end. Grace was never one to favor such heavy-handedness, but this thing wasn't her treasured pet. In fact, she was sure he had killed Swails. Now, she wanted answers.

"Capture. No kill. No kill." She enunciated the words carefully. The kill mutes were of low intelligence, and every command other than "kill" had to be communicated clearly.

Trau leapt into action, a dozen small blades extending out of his arms and legs. He charged the impostor, slashing with his limbs, while Kau moved into a defensive position between her and Swails, his own blades exposed.

"Alive!" Grace barked.

It seemed she had given those orders to the wrong person. Trau reached Swails faster than any human could and raked the impostor across the chest with enough force to split an unenhanced in two. Instead, a faint yellow shield surrounding Swails appeared and burst into sparks, creating an electrical backlash that bounced Trau's blades harmlessly to the side.

The impostor retaliated, moving so quickly his body blurred. The two whirled around each other in a deadly dance, Trau's blades and the strange yellow sparks flashing in the air. Just as quickly as the melee had begun, it was over.

One moment, the impostor was next to Trau, the next, he was standing behind the kill mute. With a flick of the stranger's wrist, Trau went flying across the room and slammed into the wall so hard the blast shields on the portholes lowered from the force of the impact. Trau's steel-infused back snapped with a loud crack against one of the structural beams jutting out of the wall. He emitted a mechanical wail and went limp, the red glow in his eyes fading.

Grace gaped at the fallen kill mute. This was impossible. These were class-six cyborgs! They were each designed to defeat a platoon of armored marines. Panic seized her as her gaze went back to Swails, or whatever the thing was that looked like her pet.

Kau continued to keep his body in between her and this impostor. He would attack on her command and most likely die just as quickly. Swails eyed Kau with unworried interest, as if just waiting for this fight to finish so he could continue with whatever task he was here for. Looking closely, she could see a soft, translucent yellow glimmer hugging his skin, and then her eyes trailed to the allorium charter the impostor had left on the desk during the melee.

Then it all made sense.

"Kau," she said, pointing at the door. "Leave the room. Make sure I'm not disturbed."

The kill mute looked at her hesitantly. These cyborgs were not completely stupid after all. They recognized a strange order when they heard one.

"Go!" she repeated.

Eyeing Swails warily, Kau stepped over Trau's body and shuffled out of the room. The impostor ignored the deadly kill mute, seemingly unconcerned. Kau paused just as he was about to leave the room. He looked at the impostor, then, with a grunt, left. Grace noted that pause. Apparently, there were still some kinks in these level sixes that needed ironing out.

"Close the door," Grace ordered.

The impostor raised an eyebrow, no doubt either surprised that she was willing to remain alone with him or that she was still ordering him around. Nevertheless, he complied, closing the double sliding doors. Their eyes met, and for the first time, Grace saw depth in Swails's eyes: awe, sadness, regret, pain. These were all emotions the real Swails should not have been able to feel.

"How far from the future?" she finally asked.

Swails smiled. The shimmer from the strange yellow shield faded, and then his face began to erase itself line by line, as if a recording of someone drawing a face was being played backward. She watched each feature recede until there was nothing more than a bald empty mass of skin where the face should be. Then the entire head disappeared, replaced by a lighter-toned, white-skinned man with an unfashionable display of facial hair.

"Twenty-sixth century, High Scion." He bowed nearly down to his knees. For a second, it gave her hope that the Technology Isolationists had prospered into the future, if her position was still honored. "How did you know?" he asked.

Grace tsked. "Your disguise only fools a few of the senses."

He bowed again, this time not quite so low. "The legendary Grace Priestly. You're exactly as you're revered."

Grace studied him more closely. He was a tad thin for Grace's taste; she liked her men a little larger than perfection standard. He had a handsome face, symmetrical, at least, with features at approximately 70 percent facial ratio of optimum. The intruder had a long thin face, sunken cheeks, and other imperfections associated with a spent soul. Within seconds, those brown eyes, slightly curved nose, and distinctive chin told her everything she needed to know about his background.

"How fares mankind three hundred years in the future?" she asked, studying his every facial movement.

His skin was almost translucent in the light of her cabin. Had this man ever felt direct sunlight? He had the look of a spaceborn: pale, tall, and lanky, typical of someone who spent his entire life between the planets. His brown hair was unruly, leaving him looking dirty and disheveled. Strange, she had assumed someone from the future would be better groomed. By Technology Isolationist standards, he wouldn't look like someone allowed into the communes, let alone her ship.

"If only I could bring good news," he said.

"Of course, you won't be able to tell me anything, seeing how that might change events."

He shook his head. "News of the future wouldn't matter in this case. The charter's second law . . ."

"'Travel to the past is restricted to truncated time lines and within appropriate lengths for the chronostream to heal in event of ripples,'" she recited.

"Yes. You remember."

"I wrote it last night."

"It's the second-highest Time Law."

The realization of what his words meant struck Grace like a physical blow. "The *High Marker* is to be my grave then."

She did something uncharacteristic and ground her teeth. It was a childhood habit she had broken as a teenager. Now, all she wanted to do was make up for all those lost years and grind them to their roots. "I knew we were doomed; the probability of surviving was slim, yet it feels different when all doubt is removed."

Then all the feelings she suppressed behind her cold facade leaked out of her. Grace sat down on her bed, unsure whether she was angry or sad. Her body shook with conflicting emotions. She wanted to laugh, scream, and burst into tears all at once. For the first time in decades, she didn't know what to do next. She closed her eyes and dug her nails into her palms. She was the High Scion! Revered, even hundreds of years from now! That was worth something, yes? Right now, though, the honor felt hollow.

She looked up at him. "Why are you here? . . . Of course. It was you who drained and stole the *High Marker*'s power source."

He nodded. "And the charter. It's a desired relic."

"So this time travel agency I envision exists? It prospers?" Grace's chest swelled with pride.

He hesitated, then gave her a halfhearted smile. "The agency is cherished and loved. It's all that stands in the way of humanity's collapse, High Scion."

A lie, or at least a truth he did not believe. It mattered little. With her death around the corner, Grace didn't care about splitting hairs. "I see. Very well, then. You may take it."

He bowed again. Bowing must be common in the twenty-sixth century. No one ever did that now. Grace kind of liked it. She watched as he strolled to the desk and picked up the charter, hefting it in one hand. For such a supposedly desired relic, the time traveler didn't treat it with what she thought was proper reverence.

He made a gesture with his other hand and a black circle materialized in the air next to him. She watched, fascinated, as he deposited the charter into the hole. Then the circle blinked out of existence.

"How did . . . ?" she asked.

"Inflationary theory applied," he said.

"Alan Guth?"

He shrugged. "I only use it. I don't know how it works."

"I see." Grace looked out the window. "At least science has progressed by leaps and bounds then. I am heartened by that."

"Unfortunately, no. I wouldn't lie to you, High Scion."

She stood up and walked up to him. "Now what? The ship is doomed, you say. You have the charter and have siphoned the power source. Now you abandon the time line?"

"As per your directive." He seemed almost resigned to her fate.

Grace seized on the slim opportunity. "Take me with you," she blurted out, clutching his wrists. The time traveler's resolve wavered; conflict flashed across his face. "Even in the future, there must not be many like me."

"None with your mind," he agreed, shaking his head. "But, the first Time Law prohibits——"

"Screw the Time Laws!" she said. "I wrote the damn things, most of them half-drunk while intellectually masturbating. They mean nothing. Take me with you."

Grace was begging now but she didn't care. For the first time in over half a century, her emotions overcame her. This felt shameful, but her work wasn't complete. She had too much to offer humanity still. She had the entire Technology Isolationist faction to care for. Worse yet, now that her lifelong ambition of utilizing this recently discovered time-traveling technology had been proven successful, there were so many possibilities to explore. She just had to be a part of it. Thoughts of visiting the utopian ages of the twenty-first century made her heart skip a beat.

"Take me." She sobbed and threw her arms around him.

The time traveler averted his eyes. "I . . . I can't, High Scion."

He held her in an embrace for several awkward minutes. Finally, he pushed her away and she noticed his eyes glaze over for a brief moment.

"I have to go," he said. "I've already stayed too long."

She released her grip reluctantly, pulling herself together and regaining her composure. She remembered who she was again. "How much time do I have?" she asked.

"I don't know, High Scion. Historical records indicate the *High Marker*'s last known location was one hundred forty-eight AUs past Eris. Then the ship disappeared."

She wiped her wet face. "Call me Grace."

The time traveler looked at her one last time and gave her one last bow. "It was an honor, Grace. I'm . . . I'm sorry."

There was a bright yellow flash, and then the time traveler that had worn Swails's face disappeared.

TWO

JAMES GRIFFIN-MARS

A burst of light temporarily blinded James Griffin-Mars, and he found himself staring at the dull glow of the sun ninety-eight AUs away, a lone yellow point in black-speckled space. A strange ring of total darkness surrounded it.

It took a few seconds for the lag sickness to subside as James sucked in large gulps of air from his atmos band. He hadn't thrown up from time-travel-induced nausea since his first salvage and wasn't about to make that fresh-fodder mistake again. Smitt would never let him live it down. If anything, this sick twisting in his guts should feel like an old friend by now. The lag sickness had been coming on stronger of late, sometimes even lasting hours after a foray. Maybe it was just this particular salvage, but the pain and bile rising into his throat hit him harder than usual.

James squeezed his eyes shut and counted down from a hundred, using the beating of his heart as a metronome. Floating in the empty space didn't help with the nausea, and his body seemed to have inherited the *High Marker*'s rotation when he jumped back. He was spinning fast enough to wring the liquid out of his body. The atmos band around his wrist managing the environmental shield was the only thing keeping his insides together in the vacuum.

James pulled up the time on his AI computer band: 22:38:44, 05, June 2511, Earth Standard, exactly sixteen hours, fourteen minutes, and thirty-three seconds since he had first jumped back to the exact same date and time in 2212.

A distant voice, like sound coming from the other end of a long thin tube, crackled inside his head. "James, this is Smitt, you back in the present? Come in, my friend." There were ten counts of silence before the voice repeated itself. "James, this is Smitt, are you back in the——"

"I'm here," James answered, his comm band relaying his thoughts back to his handler. "Any ripples?"

"Negative. Swails's body was found back on Eris, but the ripple only affected a three-week stream before the time line healed over it. How's the package?"

James activated his exo-kinetic band and pulled himself out of his spin. The ring of darkness surrounding the sun disappeared into a lone black circle as his body stopped rotating: the dwarf Eris. He stared at its black surface, so different from the glittering display of life he'd seen just a few short hours ago from his point of view. In the past, Eris was a bustling colony, brimming with lights, life, and constant movement. Now, it was an abandoned husk. James opened the netherstore container and checked its contents. Nodding with satisfaction, he raised his head and looked back at the sun.

"Smitt, all packages secured. Pick me up."

"Sending the collie your way. You came back a bit farther out than we predicted. Hang tight. What took you so long?"

James pulled up the tactical from his AI band. Smitt was right. He was twenty minutes late on his return, courtesy of those last few moments with Grace. At the speed the *High Marker* was hurtling through space, that twenty minutes covered a vast distance. Still, it had been worth the delay to spend a few more moments with the legendary Mother of Time.

Sixteen hours ago, he had jumped back to 2212 on Eris and snuck onto the *High Marker* before it took off. Then he had murdered Swails, sent the body back to Eris in one of the cargo containers, and spent the entire day impersonating the pet as he watched Grace Priestly at work. It was a magnificent experience.

Still, he had almost missed his window. If he had dallied another twenty minutes on the *High Marker*, at the speed it was flying out of control, James would be dead by the time the collie got to him. Even now, being twenty minutes off, it'd take the collie over an hour to reach his position. This was the tricky part of ship jumps. Placement and parallel periods were two completely separate variables; both had to be carefully calculated. And no matter what, the present time line continued. The amount of time James spent in the past had to be added to the present during his return jump.

Forty minutes later, James caught a glimpse of a small flickering light traveling from the center of the black circular mass that was Eris. As the collie approached to intercept, the light slowly grew larger. Space had a funny way of distorting distance. While the gleam of the collie started out no larger than the nail of his forefinger, it grew steadily. It was still another half hour before it finally pulled up next to him.

James willed his exo to push him toward the collie until he stepped onto its starboard wing. A few breaths later, he was inside, strapping himself into the pilot's seat. He connected his bands to the collie's power source to maintain his levels, but didn't bother compressing the interior of the collie, preferring to depend on his atmos for air.

Chronmen generally had an unsavory reputation within the solar system, but no one ever called them careless. Careless men in his profession did not live long. At least once every few months, James would hear about someone who knew someone who had deactivated his atmos in an old collie, only to pass out and never wake up because of a slow decompression leak.

The collie, short for Tang Collinear Streaker, was relatively reliable as three-hundred-year-old ships go, but then again, she was three hundred years old. Whatever paint might have been on her when she was first built had long since flaked off from the constant abuse of space travel. Her starboard side was a mismatched patchwork of armored plates that made the collie look like its halves were separate pods welded into one deformed monstrosity.

The interior of the ship looked like the cell of a brig, a plain rectangular box with a metal bunk on one long side opposite the hatch, and a small latrine and storage bin in the far back. The ceiling was barely tall enough for James to stand up, and there was just enough room for a person to pace in circles if he felt like exercising. Otherwise, besides the control panel and seat up front, the bare-bones collie was low-tech in almost every other way. That was what made the ship so desirable. Complicated ships made for complicated maintenance.

James watched as the life support systems came online and reported the ship's status. He didn't bother following the health check. If the damn thing blew, there was nothing he could do about it. Even if he knew what had to be done, he wouldn't know how to do it. Chronmen had enough on their plates just doing their jobs without worrying about the mechanics of their ships. It was up to the nut docs and Smitt, his handler, to deal with the rest. The only thing James knew about this contraption was that when the blinker on the upper right of the console turned green, which it had done just now, he'd be ready to go.

"Smitt, I'm inside *Collie* now," James thought, as he opened one of the lockers and threw on a chem suit to cover his near-naked body.

"Good job, man," Smitt said. "When are you going to give the old girl a proper name?"

"What's wrong with her name?" James asked.

Smitt chuckled loudly with a snort that James had gotten used to and thought endearing. "You're the only chronman who names his collie *Collie*. You've got the imagination of a metal plate."

James grinned. "Saves on paperwork. Anyway, coming home with package in tow."

"Excellent." There was a pause. "How did you pull it off? I mean, did you meet her? Talk to her? Grace Priestly was supposed to be heavily guarded. Does she look just like those vids of her?"

"She was . . . worthy," said James. "Remarkable. Even to the end."

"She knew about you?"

"You're not called the Mother of Time and hailed as the smartest person in history for nothing. She figured it out quick enough. Took it better than most."

"How did you get close to her?"

James grunted. "How else do you get close to a lord during the Warring Tech period?"

"You fucked Grace Priestly?" Smitt's voice went up an octave and cracked. James couldn't have shocked him more by saying he had discovered alien life. "So . . . um, how was it?"

James leaned back and looked out the aft window. The ship had windows only on the port side, as the starboard side was covered in plates. The engines came to life and the collie slid around Eris toward the Ship

Jungle. He thought back to holding the weeping Mother of Time in his arms.

Following the Warring Tech period after her death, the Core Conflicts of the origin planets—Venus, Earth, and Mars—drew in the outlying colonies. Eventually, the wars' resource demands became so great that the outliers—Eris, Pluto, and Mercury—were resource-suffocated until they eventually had to be abandoned. Eris, once a scientific bastion of the old Tech Isolationists, was now a planet of ghosts.

A beep from the console tore James away from the window. The collie was about to enter the Ship Jungle. The space ahead began to clutter as more and more specks of what looked like gray dust dotted the blackness. The vid on the collie's dashboard registered thousands of approaching signals, the carcasses and bones of hundreds of thousands of ships that had fought over the gaseous and chemical resources of the solar system's gas giants—Jupiter, Neptune, Uranus, and Saturn. The Gas Wars, which had taken place seventy years after the Core Conflicts, were said to have been the deadliest conflict in the history of mankind, causing a billion deaths over a span of forty years.

The collie maneuvered into the graveyard, navigating around and among the hulks that had been used by previous generations. There was still good mining here, though the real payday lay in the past. James saw the insignia of the AR Star Fortress, one of his past salvages. He remembered that one well. The Star Fortress had been a mobile base that housed a quarter million of Mars's Flak military and was their launching point to claim Oberon, a moon of Uranus and the home base of the Kuma Faction. In the end, the Star Fortress base broke and three hundred years later, James reaped massive rewards off its power core, which should have bought an entire year off his contract. Instead, he pissed away six months of the buyout on whiskey and whores.

"*Collie*'s responding sluggishly. Might need you to work through some of these controls," Smitt said, static covering much of his words.

"Switching to manual."

He took control of the ship and began to guide her gently through the debris field. The collie had already slowed to a crawl as they neared Neptune. The junk field grew more congested the closer he got to the planet. James was, at best, a passable pilot, and maneuvering through such a dangerous section of space pushed his skills to their limits. Without Smitt's help, there was no way he could have navigated *Collie* through this hazard zone.

An exhausting seven hours later, the collie finally exited the Ship Jungle, little worse for the wear, other than a few scrapes and minor collisions. It'd be another few days before he reached the ChronoCom outpost at Himalia Station. Exhausted, James put the ship back on auto, lay down on the rusty metal bunk in the back, and activated his cryo band. Within seconds, he felt its effects as sleep swept over him. He needed the rest. Time travel was a wearying affair and a strain on the mind. Hopefully, his brain would be too exhausted to dream; James doubted the musings of his unconscious mind would be pleasant.

THREE

HIMALIA STATION

Just as James was drifting off, someone shook him awake. On reflex, he powered on his exo band, expanded his field, and lashed out. The powerful exo-kinetic system—the military-industrial complex being one of the few industries still innovating—practically made him a god whenever he ventured back in time. The yellow glow of the exo sparked to life, expanding outward and slamming the intruder into the interior wall of the collie. A kinetic coil sprouted from it and wrapped around the man's waist. It squeezed.

"Whoa!" the dock engineer gasped and threw his arms up. "Easy there, Chronman. You're among friendlies."

It took James a few moments to realize where he was. He froze, glancing in both directions before dissolving the kinetic coil. He had been dreaming when this poor soul had tried to wake him. Fortunately, the dream had already faded from memory, though it wasn't hard for James to guess what it was about. He only had nightmares these days.

He glanced at the terrified engineer. The man was holding his breath, waiting for James to say something. The fool should know better than to wake him so soon after his return from a salvage. Strangely, James was ambivalent about almost killing the engineer. Not that he took pleasure in harming others, but if the accident had happened, would it matter? He wasn't sure if he'd feel anything either way.

James sat up on his bench and shook his head. "What the abyss do you think you're doing waking a chronman up that way?"

"I'm . . . I'm sorry," the engineer said. "We left you alone in here for four hours. Your handler sent word to wake you and retrieve the marks from your job. Shipment to Earth goes out in a cycle. I need to bag it." His eyes moved down to look at the netherstore band around James's wrist.

James held out his left arm to the engineer.

"Uh, Chronman?" The engineer pointed at the yellow shielding around his body. "You're still on."

James looked down and then back at the hull of the ship. Finally, he powered down his exo and atmos bands, watching the fields waver before flickering off. He felt a rush of stale air and inhaled the heavy odor of oil and metal. The station's filtration generators were on half power again. James flipped the netherstore container's link to the engineer. "Have at it. Two items. Register to S-yi and C-san."

When the transfer was completed, the engineer scurried out of the collie as fast as he could. Chronmen were the second-highest operatives in ChronoCom and also the most feared by the rucks—civilians—for good reason. It took a special sort of person to be a chronman, and it wasn't the good kind of special.

A prerequisite to becoming a chronman was five years of grueling training at the ChronoCom Academy on Tethys. Officially known as time operatives, chronmen had to be intelligent, quick to adapt to changing situations, and be good actors. They also must have short memories of their past assignments.

Good chronmen also shared negative traits. They tended to be antisocial, short-tempered, excessively violent, and borderline suicidal. Needless to say, the life expectancy for people like James was short.

Still, in spite of all their psychological problems and eccentricities, chronmen were considered critical to maintaining the power supply for all of humanity, so nearly everything they did was tolerated. Some even argued that having eccentricities made good chronmen, rather than the job causing such behaviors.

James walked down the ramp of the collie and passed through the crowded docking hangar. Himalia Station was a launching point for mining operations to Jupiter as well as one of the only ChronoCom offices this far out in the solar system. Right now, mining operations were quiet while salvaging operations were in full swing.

James paused as a yellow collie—the *Ramhurst*—one of the newer ships, still sporting its paint job, came in hot on its landing and nearly took out half an engineering crew. Not having seen Palia in several months, he waited and watched as several engineers scrambled to the ship and pried the door open. A few seconds later, they floated Palia out on a gurney and sped off.

James grabbed Kia, Palia's handler, as she ran by. "What happened to her?"

Kia shook free. "Curellan Mining uprising. She got caught during the retrieval. Barely got her back. Sorry, James; talk later." She sped off.

James watched them all disappear down the corridor toward triage. He hoped she pulled through. Palia and Shizzu were the only surviving chronmen from his graduating class at the Academy, and James couldn't stand Shizzu. The rest had either died on assignment or poked a giant in the eye, which was chronmen-speak for steering your collie toward a gas giant and letting go of the controls. Palia dying would make for an awkward reunion between him and Shizzu.

Another group of engineers rushed by, this time toward a collie he didn't recognize. James got out of their way and headed out of the dock. He was supposed to report to Smitt at Hops—Handler Operations—but instead, he headed to the lower levels and toward the Tilted Orbit.

Himalia Station wasn't as large as other bases. Though the largest moon after the four satellite colonies around Jupiter, Himalia was only 170 kilometers in diameter. Still, it had a population of a quarter million, mostly gas miners, military, and ChronoCom personnel, which skewed the gender demographics slightly toward men. More like six to one. The pleasure boys and girls were so scarce and sought-after that they were almost as well respected as chronmen. Even then, most of them were transient. They'd arrive, get rich in weeks from nonstop work, then bail out as fast as they could.

The halls of the station were three sides' metal and the ceiling a layer of natural rock. The moon's elliptical orbit subjected the surface to extreme temperatures, necessitating that the majority of the base be kept underground. This made all the corridors incredibly cramped and dusty, as showers of pebbles and debris continually rained down on the station's inhabitants.

The light flickered, as it tended to do when the power was kept to a third, which these days had become the new norm. James, walking in a hallway barely wide enough for three people abreast, moved with the downward flow into the residential section. Though cramped and claustrophobic, Himalia Station was one of James's favorite bases of operations. Most inhabitants were too transient to bother knowing, and the few permanent residents knew to leave one other alone.

James reached the Tilted Orbit and sat down at the bar. Several of the grease-faced miners sitting on both sides of him got up to give him space. It wasn't that people hated him; they just knew better than to get in his way. No one messed with a chronman. And if one messed with you, you just took it. James didn't abuse his position of power often, but he knew some who did. Since chronmen were all that stood between society functioning and completely falling apart, it was a capital offense to injure one of his kind.

By last count, there were fewer than twenty chronmen on Himalia Station and maybe a hundred on Earth, with possibly three thousand across the rest of the solar system. Three thousand minus one if Palia didn't make it.

"Jobe," James gestured. "Whiskey. Whatever crap no one else can afford, and a round to every soul here."

The bartender nodded, brought over the bottle and a tin cup, and gave him a generous pour. "On your tab, James." He walked away to provide each patron his free drink.

James barely looked up as a few of the other patrons toasted him with their tin cups. It was something he did every time he returned from a job. Some had mistaken the gesture for friendliness. Nothing could be further from the truth. The few who tried to thank him personally were met with a blank stare and a turn of his back.

For the next hour, James sat alone, ignoring the increasing number and the growing cacophony of the patrons as more miners and station workers streamed into the Tilted Orbit. He stared at the bottle of whiskey, the level of which decreased by the pour; it was down to half now. His thoughts wandered back to the whiskey Grace had ordered him to pour for her. Swails's job was also that of poison tester, and the two whiskeys he had tried while in her service were divine. The past had some truly great whiskey, not this crap they had here at the edge of hell.

James looked around the packed bar. There were only two drinking holes on the station, so both were rarely empty. A few other chronmen had walked in, each staking their claim at different parts of the bar. Other than a slight tilt of the head, none of them acknowledged the others. Like James, they sat and drank alone.

Even with this many people in such a confined place, there was still no one around him. No one was willing to take the chance of standing too close to a chronman. James lifted the tin cup and took a sip. Well, almost no one.

"You're supposed to report to Hops before you make your way here," he heard Smitt say behind him. It was better than having his handler's damn voice piped directly into his head.

"I broke a dumb rule; fire me." James shrugged and signaled to Jobe to bring another cup. He poured the so-called whiskey to the brim and slid it over, sloshing a third of it on the counter.

"Easy there." Smitt cupped the whiskey gingerly in his hand. "Just because you're a rich god among men doesn't mean the rest of us are. There's a reason the miners are drinking swill and you're drinking . . ."

"Swill," James muttered, taking another sip. He turned to his only living friend in the solar system. "You want to know what I've tasted before? What I've seen? Remember that salvage during the twenty-first century with the formation of the Luxe Empire? There was this drink they were just handing out like water . . ."

Smitt lifted his drink. "It's called champagne, James, and thanks for rubbing it in."

"Not just that. It seems every time period before ours was better. We're sucking on the dregs of civilization. Frankly, I'm tired of coming back." He slammed his fist on the counter. The bar got quiet. Usually, fights breaking out between the patrons was no big thing, but when a chronman was involved, everyone paid attention. James looked around at the staring eyes, then shifted his gaze back down to his cup. He hated the attention; all chronmen did. They were trained to keep a low profile. "It's like waking up to a nightmare every time I return," he said, eyes focused back on the dark liquid at the bottom of his cup.

Smitt patted James on the back. He was probably the only human being James allowed to do that. "Past is dead. Script's run its course. All
you see when you go back is the illusion of choice." He was used to James's
ramblings by now. It wasn't like these were revelations that had just occurred to James while he was soul-searching over a cup of whiskey. This
rant might as well have served as his debriefing every time he returned
from a jump.

James looked up at the crowd, half of them still keeping one eye
on him. He had gotten into scuffles with quite a few of them, before they
had found out who he was. Once they had found out, though, they had
just stood there and waited for him to beat on them. He never did. That
took the fun out of brawling. That was why he never wore his ChronoCom
insignia.

James slid his hands through his hair and lowered his head to just above
the bar's surface. "I don't know what I'm doing. I need a change of scenery,
to get out of this shit hole."

"You just might," said Smitt, reaching over and plucking the bottle out
of James's hand. He gave himself a generous pour. "As your handler, it's
my job to see to your needs. You have a new salvage. It's an on-book luxury call with a big payout."

James frowned. "What the fuck you talking about? I just got back. I
have mandatory downtime. Not to mention I'm already two weeks late on
my miasma regimen. Listen, the lag sickness—"

"Already got you waivered. You can catch up on your regimen after
the job. Trust me, it's worth it," said Smitt. "Stoph was originally on book
for this but he poked the giant two days ago. ChronoCom is low enough on
experienced chronmen as it is to spare a Tier-1, so I volunteered us for
this little gem. It's a private request from some shiny wig on Europa,
so you know they have fat scratch. Helps keep the lights on, yeah?"

James sighed. "Thousand in the Academy and they can't maintain
chronmen levels. What the black abyss are we doing?"

"You know ChronoCom can't afford to screw up salvages these days,
and the cut rate at the Academy is eighty percent. Death rate for chronmen is what, seventy-five percent before two years? We got maybe five
hundred guys on hand that ChronoCom trusts for Tier-2 jobs and up, and
you remember what happened with that idiot Jerrod swapping in the fresh
fodder straight out of the Academy. Kid died and the entire salvage was

ruined. Eight hundred units of transferable power for a battle cruiser lost forever because the handler assigned a near-ruck."

"Did they at least jump him into the beginning of the scenario to give the time line another shot at a jump?" James asked.

Smitt shook his head. "Nope. Put the fodder smack in the middle of the salvage. That whole time line is too frayed and unstable now for another jump. But those're the rules. Usually only one shot at a salvage. That's why there's only a hundred or so of you Tier-1s, and why you make the big scratch." There was a beep and Smitt's eyes glazed over for a moment. He frowned. "Make that ninety-nine. Palia didn't make it."

"Guess it really will be me and Shizzu at the reunions." James raised his cup to his former classmate. Now they were down to two. He wondered which one of them would be the last man standing.

Smitt grinned. "Just you, actually. Shizzu joined the chain, raised to auditor while you were fucking Grace."

"That fodder Shizzu is an auditor?" James grounded his teeth. He couldn't think of anyone more unworthy of rising up the ranks to become a watcher of the chronmen. "You have to be kidding. What did that asshole do to deserve that?"

Smitt shrugged. "It surprised a lot of people, to be honest."

"Black abyss." He threw back the cup and slammed it down on the table. "Whole agency is going to hell."

Smitt stood up and again patted him on the back. "Get some sleep. You're heading to Earth at the second rotation with the next shipment."

James made a face. "Earth?"

Smitt grinned. "You have to take one for the team once in a while. You said you wanted a change of scenery. You didn't say how nice a one."

FOUR

MING DYNASTY

There was something about the city of Luoyang in northeastern China that reminded Auditor Levin Javier-Oberon of Habitat-C3 Oberon, the colony of his birth. Maybe it was the thick soot in the air, the uneven gray brick streets and walls, or just the sound of the city constantly buzzing at all hours of the day; it was definitely the squalor. That was the thing about poverty: no matter what planet or time period, squalor was squalor.

Humanity seemed to shit itself the same way in 1551 C.E., during the height of the Ming Dynasty, as it did in the present. For some reason, the damn race never learned how to stay out of the gutter. Maybe that was why scientists estimated that mankind would be extinct by the year 3000. Well, not if Levin and the rest of ChronoCom had a say in the matter.

He passed by a small koi pond in the slightly less squalid merchant district and paused to observe the ghostly glassy-eyed fish swimming around in the clear water. He looked at his own image reflecting through the ripples, his paint band doing an admirable job blending him in with the thousands of pedestrians walking through the city.

His gaze moved up beyond the waterline to the stone and wooden building that wrapped around three sides of the pond, to the curved tiles that arced up to the center point of the roof. Behind it, the sun was half covered as it made its daily journey toward the western horizon. It was almost time.

Levin willed the fourteen bands clinging loosely against both of his arms—six on his left, eight on his right—to tighten. He didn't bother masking them with his paint band, instead passing them off as iron rings, commonly used by mercenaries as a blocking bracer. Like most operatives, he preferred to use as little of the paint as possible when on a job. Assuming his paid sources were correct, he would have need of those bands very soon. Levin walked up a short flight of stairs and swung open the red double doors that led him into the Hong Jiu Inn.

It was a busy night, filled with patrons, but not more than the usual that he had observed over the past two days. The eating area was packed with merchants, locals, and soldiers. A group of drunken Uyghers filled three tables on the far left, caravan troops by the look of them. The table adjacent to theirs seated a group of Mongols. The guards kept careful watch over that entire end of the inn. It wouldn't take much to ignite a confrontation.

To the right of the door were at least three of the city's gangs. Levin recognized two of them: the Yellow Snakes and the Dirt Dragons. Levin frowned; none of these people looked like any of Cole's men. Then he noticed a scrawny ruffian walk up the stairs to the second floor and disappear into one of the rooms.

Of course. Cole was a big man now. These grunts weren't worth his time. Levin walked through the crowded area, slipping between benches and chairs filled with toughs, traders, and pleasure girls. Doing this quietly probably wasn't going to be an option, but he'd have to try. It had taken him two weeks just to locate the feared and infamous Fist of the Low Laying River, or whatever the hell he was calling himself here. It'd be another month to find him again if he left this inn without Levin's hands around his neck.

A bouncer standing at the base of the stairs stopped Levin with a hammed fist and shook his head. "What's your business, pig?"

"I have business with big brother up top," said Levin, his comm band translating his words into Han.

The bouncer looked him up and down, and grunted. "A pig like you belongs down here with the other swine. Go away before I beat you so terribly your mother feels it." He shoved Levin on the chest.

Levin caught the shove nonchalantly with his left hand and twisted the bouncer's thumb at an odd angle. He tried to pull away but Levin's exo held his grip like a vise, and he squeezed until the bouncer's knees buckled.

"Are you sure you wish to block my path, friend?" Levin tightened his grip. "The Jiang Hu is vast. Do you know all its masters?" He squeezed even tighter.

The bouncer quivered and bobbed his head up and down several times. "I'm . . . I'm sorry, *Sifu*, Please forgive me."

Levin let the bouncer go. The fewer ripples the better, though he didn't worry much about that here. The odds of a time chronostream self-healing in this cesspool of an inn were high. Still, best not to take chances. That boy had already made enough ripples for both of them, running away from the present. The poor fool knew better. No one ever escaped the auditors.

"Next time, know who you disrespect before you are taught a permanent lesson," he said.

The bouncer scurried to the side and let him pass. Levin continued to the top of the stairs, which opened to a hallway that overlooked the eating area on the right and had a row of doors on the left. He went to the door on the far end, where the sounds of revelry were loudest. Cole would want easy escape routes out of the building, and the window overlooking the eating area below gave him a clear view of people coming into the inn. Not that it would help him much in this instance. Levin's paint made him look like the other thousands of Han walking in the city.

Levin slid the double sliding panels outward and intruded on the private dinner of two dozen scruffy-looking men at a pair of long tables on each side. Two men and a girl sat at a smaller table on a raised platform on the far end. The one on the left looked the part of a Low River gang member, possibly a lieutenant or a second lieutenant. The one on the right was a pleasure girl draped over the man in the middle.

"I seek Ko Li," he said formally.

All eyes turned toward him. Levin stifled a grunt. Of course Cole would make himself look like a god among these men. The real Cole looked ordinary in every way possible, save for a pockmarked face from a childhood disease that had ravaged his body. This paint job he now wore made him look like an Adonis. No wonder he was causing ripples. Vain and stupid. At least Cole had made himself look indigenous enough; just taller, more beautiful, better fed, and built like a giant. Definitely not the best way to remain inconspicuous. Well, if the guy was going to try to live a fantasy, he might as well have gone all the way.

"How dare you?" A skinny bandit at the end of the table stood up and snarled, puffing out his chest. He must be the lowest among them.

Levin kept his eyes on Cole, half-expecting the fugitive to take off at any moment. Instead, Cole nodded at the skinny bandit.

The bandit stomped up to Levin and pointed at the ground. "You address Sifu Li as 'master,' you insolent dog." The bandit tried to slap Levin.

Levin didn't bother using his exo. Doing so could give him away to Cole. Besides, he didn't need to use it against this scrawny thing. Levin slipped forward, spun, and used the bandit's momentum to send him sprawling into the center of the room. The rest of the bandits stood up, cleavers and broadswords drawn.

"I wish to speak with Sifu Ko Li, better known as the Fist of the Low Laying River," Levin repeated, his voice low and measured. He waited for Cole to make his next move.

There was tension in the air, the calm right before hell cracked open and brimstone spewed forth. Levin was content to wait. Cole's next move would determine what the fugitive was thinking. If he fled, then he already knew Levin was an auditor. If he sent his men to attack first, he was insecure of his position here. If he was . . .

"Please join me," Cole said, standing and clapping his hands. "It is always an honor to have another master in the room. Please sit. Sit."

Levin kept his face on his prey as he walked into and through the group of thugs with their weapons still drawn. He stopped just opposite Cole at the end of the table. Once there, both sat at the same time.

"Thank you for your hospitality," said Levin.

"Who do I have the honor of sharing this table with, Master?" Cole asked.

"I am a master of nothing."

Cole chuckled. "How true. Are we not always students thirsty for more?" He gestured to the woman, who picked up the teapot. "So you wish to see a test among skilled students of the world then. But first, my table is yours. Would you like some tea?" She poured Levin a cup before he had a chance to respond.

"They don't have tea where I come from."

Cole raised an eyebrow and his hands froze. The two stared at each other long and hard before Levin finally leaned forward and spoke Solar English in a low voice. "There was some real genius in your plan. Forging your requisitions to obtain a solar charger. Poisoning your handler. Corrupting your jump records so we couldn't pull you back. Fleeing to a time and place where you can mask the use of your bands as mystical martial arts. You had this planned out pretty well."

The blood drained from Cole's face. His gang looked on with interest, no doubt thinking there was some mental battle passing between two masters. They were a superstitious lot, which of course was why the fugitive chronman had fled here to begin with.

"Can't blame a guy for trying," Cole finally said, recovering from his initial shock and pretending to shrug it off.

Right there, Levin knew he had made up his mind and was going to try to make a run for it. He leaned forward. "Tell me. Is it Past-Era Addiction? If it is, we can help you."

Cole threw his head back and laughed. "No, you fool. I'm not addicted. I just hate the present. Any sane man would."

"That's unfortunate," said Levin. It really was. If it was Past-Era Addiction, he could use that to argue leniency for the boy. Instead, Levin would now have to apply the full force of his directive.

"So now what?" said Cole.

Levin picked up the small teacup and took a sip, curious to try it. Bitter but aromatic; he kind of liked it. "Depends on you," he said. "You can surrender, and we can return peacefully, and I'll be sure to note that in my report, or you can try your odds fighting with an auditor."

"If we war, won't it create large ripples?"

Levin shrugged. "Perhaps, but in this time and region, I have little doubt the chronostream will self-heal. The question is, will you survive? Is that something you're willing to risk?"

Cole spat on the floor. "As opposed to die in the present? What kind of a question is that? Listen, Auditor, no matter what you think, I'm not going back. The only thing you're taking back to that shit hole is my dead body."

"Technically," Levin said, "I don't need to care how you are brought back." He took another sip of the tea. He was really getting used to this bitter drink. Maybe he could take some of it back with him to the present. "Tell me, Cole, why didn't you just hide here and keep a low profile? Why did you have to use your bands and make a name for yourself as some master?"

The Tier-4 chronman shrugged. "Tried that for the first couple of weeks. Got tired of being nobody with no money. Couldn't take it anymore. Used a little power. Then had to use a little more."

Levin nodded. A common story among runaways, which was why fleeing into history almost always failed. The path to becoming a chronman was long and difficult. Survivors of the Academy often wielded their power not only as a status symbol but a badge of honor. Power like that was hard to relinquish after a person was used to it for so long.

"But to become a famed master of the east?" Levin chuckled. "That's a little much."

The last comment earned a grin from Cole. "What can I say? Word spreads fast in these parts. Show some power, attract a few more masters to challenge me, and before I knew it, I'm big-time." He leaned back and put his hands behind his head. "I'm so good, even I can't suppress myself."

Levin eyed the two dozen men seated behind him with their hands still on their weapons. He turned his attention back to Cole. "Why don't you send your men away? We'll go find a nice open area with no one around to conclude our business."

Cole stood up and waved his arms magnanimously at his gang. "Now, why the fuck would I want to do that? As long as there are witnesses, I know you'll hold back. I won't have that problem now, will I?" He looked past Levin's shoulder and shouted in Han, "Brothers, teach this dog some respect!"

Levin stood just as the first of the idiots behind him charged in with a cleaver. Levin's exo-powered movements and shield kept him out of danger, but Cole wasn't wrong. It was Levin's duty to display as little superhuman power as possible. It was important to him to minimize the casualties as well. Still, it didn't mean he had to be gentle.

The edge of the cleaver struck his shield, sparking orange stars into the air around him. In a second, Levin had grabbed his assailant by the armpit and hurtled him toward two more of the thugs. The crowd descended on him, swinging bats and blades as Levin joined the fray, using his natural skills as well as his exo to slice through them, seeming to move just out of their reach, dodging their swing as he mowed down three to four at a time.

Cole joined in the melee, powering his exo to full and launching himself at Levin. The Tier-4 had only four kinetic coils active. Levin doubted he could produce any more than that at his capabilities. In this situation, Levin made sure to fight down to Cole's level in order to keep up the pretense of an actual hand-to-hand fight. He sprouted four of his own coils to lock down Cole's and proceeded to beat him down with his exo-powered fists.

Cole struggled to break free even as more of his gang joined in the fight, adding to the chaos. Every time their weapons struck his exo, small sparks glimmered into the air. Levin scolded himself for being so obvious. He continued to fight by hand, kicking any thugs in reach and battering at Cole's shield.

The number of bodies became overwhelming as a surge of the gang distracted Levin long enough for Cole to shake free. The fugitive chronman jumped out of the window overlooking the main room and landed on one of the long tables below, shattering it and scattering the patrons.

Levin gritted his teeth. There went any hope of doing this quietly. He followed suit and jumped out the window as Cole ran from the building. Levin landed with a thud on top of the shattered remains of the table and sprinted after the fugitive. Hopefully, the damn guy had enough common sense not to exercise his exo to its full extent.

Levin ran outside just in time to see Cole leap atop a tile roof and sprint down its length. Well, so much for that. The sooner he got Cole out of this time, the better, regardless of the consequences. He followed suit, shooting up to the roof, to the gasps of the crowds nearby, and gave chase, using his superior bands to catch up.

The game of rooftop cat-and-mouse continued for nearly a minute as the two bounded across the city's skyline. This was the opposite of keeping things low-key, but the trap has been sprung. One way or another, Levin was going to haul Cole in.

He was making ground step by step until they were only half a building length apart. He was just within reach of Cole's coils when he struck, shooting out with two of his own coils, one that tied down the coil Cole used to push off, and the other to grab Cole around the waist. Cole's mo-

mentum tripped him midair as Levin reeled him in. The fugitive chronman sliced off the coil around his waist, only to have six more of Levin's
wrap around his body until he could no longer move. He struggled and
jerked back and forth against the invisible bonds as Levin floated him
closer. As a final precaution, Levin slipped two small coils down the length
of Cole's arms and snapped all eight of the fugitive's bands.

"It's over. We're going home," he said.

"Just kill me then, Auditor," Cole begged. "I can't go back."

"You need to be brought to justice for violating the fifth Time Law."

"Please," tears poured down Cole's face, "you can't take me back. My
uncle is an auditor. I can't shame him like this."

Levin dropped the paint image and stared stone-faced at his prisoner,
ignoring the look of shock on Cole's face. "The only additional shame that
could have been heaped on me is if I didn't bring you back. Come, your
mother will want to say good-bye." A second later, there was a flash of orange light, and the two figures that moments before were dancing on the
rooftops of Luoyang were gone.

Gossip of the two mysterious masters spread over the years, with witnesses swearing they had seen the two fly through the air. Gossip became stories; stories became facts; facts became lore. Eventually, the tales
grew and the actions more fantastic until it became part of the region's
martial arts legend, which to this day could be found in ChronoCom's
databases.

It was the worst blemish on Levin Javier-Oberon's career up until the
day James Griffin-Mars walked into his office.

FIVE

1944

A week later, after hitching his collie to the transport *JE Pheelrite* from Himalia Station to Earth via Mars, James could just make out the circular brown outline of his species's birthworld. Almost every chronman at one point or another had had to run jobs on Earth. Like the majority of people with means, James avoided the planet as much as possible. Luckily for him, most of the times he spent on the planet were in the past, during better days when it wasn't such a toxic mess.

No government or corporation claimed dominion over Earth anymore. Why bother? There were few resources left to exploit, and parts of the atmosphere were so poisonous that it might as well have been Uranus. That left each of the hundred or so remaining large cities to form their own states alongside the few thousand scattered remnants of the population that now lived in the wastelands or deep underground. There hadn't been a census taken of Earth for over a hundred years, but ChronoCom estimated there were now fewer than a hundred million people living on the planet of their origin.

Without a megacorporation based here, the only global entity with any semblance of power was ChronoCom, which acted as a policing force when the situation warranted. Earth Central, their base in Chicago on the Northern America continent, was the largest of all the ChronoCom facilities, because the planet still held the richest quarry of time salvaging in the solar system. Otherwise, much of the agency's administration would have moved off the mud ball to Europa or Callisto years ago.

Smitt walked up next to James and watched the planet slowly grow larger. "They say the water used to be so blue you could see it from space."

James looked at the brown swirling oceans and grunted. "I don't believe it. They say a lot of dumb things. Last time I saw the ocean on Earth was back in the mid-twenty-third century in a place called Tokyo, two days before the entire city sank into it. Even then the water was just a lighter shade of shit. I remember some clown declaring that humans would be setting foot in the next solar system by 2350. Imagine how disappointed he'd be if he was around today."

Smitt's eyes glazed over, and then he glanced at James. "We're running behind schedule. Need to get you into position during Earth's rotation or we blow it. I've just ordered the captain to detour to Europe first and drop you off from the *Pheelrite*. We'll dislodge the collie separately and have her maintain orbit for you. I'll handle a remote link until I get to Hops at Earth Central. This should be a pretty easy smash-and-grab job for you anyway."

"You call zipping down to a burning castle while it's being bombed an easy job? And I have to cut the room apart in how long? Thirty minutes? You're a crap handler if you think this is easy."

Smitt grinned. "I've just got faith in you. Remember, it's a rich patron. Funds you, ChronoCom, and most importantly, me. We can't live without these guys."

"What does he want with the Amber Room anyway?" James asked. "Humanity is teetering on resource starvation and this rich Europian pays for a Tier-1 chronman to risk his life to go back in time for a silly piece of art? Of all the self-indulgent and wasteful expenditures . . ."

"Not our job to ask," Smitt said. "Guy says he's the descendant of the king that built it. Wants it back in the family." He paused and stared at the collie attached to the aft starboard bulkhead. "By the way, I think we should change *Collie*'s name to *Priestbanger*."

"Fuck you. I'm fine with *Collie*."

Smitt rolled his eyes. "Calling a collie *Collie* is dumb. That's like naming me Human."

James eyed Smitt up and down, and grunted. "Barely." A rare smile cracked a corner of his mouth.

Smitt gave him the middle finger. "All right, my friend, go kick some Nazi ass, but try not to kill anyone that isn't supposed to die anyway."

The *Pheelrite* shook as it entered Earth's atmosphere, her portholes turning red from the heat of entry. The vibrations were so rough, James's teeth rattled. Two hundred years ago, ships slipped through Earth's atmosphere without the passengers so much as feeling it. It was a sad indication of how much technology had been lost over the centuries. The red around the portholes disappeared, replaced by a dark brown gel that caked onto the glass. They must be on Earth now.

The hull of the ship pitter-pattered, pelted by rain or hail or whatever it was. The brown gunk was washed away by more brown gunk as the transport vessel sliced through clouds with little grace. Again, the hull began to rock, which worried James some. This ship had obviously seen better days. He wondered if they'd be able to make it to the landing zone in one piece. If the ship exploded in midair, he might survive a high-altitude fall, but Smitt and the pilots would be pretty much screwed.

"Coming in north from the Baltic Sea," the pilot's voice piped over the comm. "Will reach fifty-four north longitude and twenty east latitude in four minutes."

Smitt's eyes glazed over. "Still running late. No time for a landing. Prepare for an airdrop."

James sighed. Go figure. They always had to make it as difficult as possible. "Let's get it over with." He moved to the bay doors. The hatch split open down the middle and a shrill screech blew into the hold. "Hand me the coordinates and timings."

Smitt had to grab on to a handle attached to the wall as he counted down toward the moving jump. James's atmos kept the wind from affecting him. He looked over at Smitt expectantly. "We're still two thousand meters up. Too high to jump."

"Coordinating drop at six hundred thirty. Jump initiates at four hundred. It will hurt and you might be operating at seventy percent power for the mission but that's the best we can do," Smitt said. Sixteen seconds later, he held up his hand and ticked down his fingers. When his last finger balled up into a fist, James leaped out of the transport.

The free fall was short. One moment, he was plummeting toward the brown rubble of what was once Europe covered in gray ash and soot. The next, there was a yellow swirl of light and then darkness. Then James caught himself free-falling again. His eyes watered and his stomach seized, and then he felt the all-too-familiar sensation of bile climbing up his throat. James willed his body past the lag sickness. After all, he was falling at— he checked his AI band—250 kilometers an hour. Now wasn't the time for a bellyache.

James blinked and focused on his continued descent. For a moment, he thought the jump had failed. The ground beneath him was still a landscape of rubble and ruins. Then he noticed the dozens of fires scattered across a broken city that hadn't been there before. He looked up and saw a group of antiquated planes flying in V formation. A line of explosions cutting across the landscape brought his attention back to the surface. He was landing in the middle of a war zone.

A few seconds later, he slammed into the ground with as much impact as any of the primitive bombs being dropped. His exo lit up and redirected the kinetic impact of the force away from his body. The Earth indented three meters deep and created a termination shock wave forty meters out, blowing a plume of dust and debris high into the air.

James fell to one knee and took a few moments to regain his bearings. He pulled up his criticals on his AI band. Nothing broken, no internal bleeding. Life signs and health still optimal. Exo at 67 percent. The high-altitude drop had taken a lot out of it. Even with the exo at two-thirds levels, he was still practically a god and could conquer half the continent if he wanted to.

Paint image 1944 officer: Third Reich SS Hauptsturmführer, he thought, pulling up all the prearranged tacticals that Smitt had planned the day before. The uniform had to be painstakingly detailed for the paint band to draw accurately.

His appearance shifted as his disguise layered itself onto him, each line and shade drawn one by one, changing his facial features and covering his tight bodysuit with the black uniform of a Nazi. Now he looked like a portly midlevel officer of the Third Reich.

James climbed out of the crater and walked down a deserted street in downtown Königsberg, or what was left of it. There wasn't anyone in sight. He scanned the area and saw cratered cobbled streets and houses set on fire. Many of the buildings had only two or three outer walls. Piles of rubble littered the landscape. He could hear the low rumble of more planes passing overhead, punctuated by additional bombs exploding in rapid succession, shaking the ground. One of these blasts was going to hit the castle soon.

"Smitt, you there?" he thought.

"Coming in a little fuzzy, James. Remote link is weak; must be the interference. Damn area is coated with ions. Probably from the AI war; we're basking in the center of where all that went down. Listen up, I barely got you in and we're still off the mark. Get moving. You don't have a lot of time. Remember, you're deep in time so tread extra carefully."

Smitt was right. Most time lines healed over ripples, but messing around certain sensitive periods of time could have catastrophic effects that the main chronostream couldn't heal over. That's why ChronoCom kept such tight regulations over which chronmen were allowed to jump to which tier of salvage. The Second World War was one of those sensitive points in history where only Tier-1 chronmen were allowed to operate, because even small ripples here could cause serious consequences.

James moved at a brisk jog, making sure not to run faster than humanly possible, since he could exceed that by quite a bit with the exo. He left the main road and made his way through narrow back alleys, hugging the walls when explosions shook the ground. He passed through the shell of a bombed-out building, climbed over a hill of rubble, and jumped the fence into a park where the tops of trees were on fire.

He scanned the small park and saw a young boy burrowed in the sands of a playground staring up at him. The boy was either terrified or in shock. James looked up at the sky. The sands here were as good as anything else. He wanted to help the boy, but such altruism was forbidden. What could he do anyway? The boy was hundreds of years dead back in the present. He probably wouldn't survive the week. After all, the Russians and the British blew this damned city to the black abyss before this war ended. Still, James couldn't help but stare back.

He forced himself to look away and continue on. Right as he jumped the fence out of the park, an explosion knocked him onto his chest. He scrambled up onto his knees and stumbled into an alley as bricks and sand rained. James looked back at the park. The playground was now a crater. He clenched his fist.

"You've veered off route," said Smitt. "What's going on?"

"There's a lot of bad shit dropping on my head," James said.

"What, you think one of those medieval arrows is going to pierce your exo? Come on, hurry up!"

"Hardly arrows," said James as another massive explosion knocked him off balance. Armored or not, these primitives knew how to war. Even at full power, he didn't think the exo could take the brunt of one of those bombs. It was no surprise mankind got so good at killing once they were in space. They had gotten a lot of practice on Earth. Maybe calling himself a god here was a bit premature.

It took much longer to cover the three kilometers to the castle than he had anticipated. By the time he stood on the edge of the castle grounds, one of the bombs had already struck the courtyard. Checking the paint of his disguise one last time, James pretended to clutch his helmet and ran across the open field, hurdling over the mounds of upturned dirt and stone. As soon as he got through the side entrance, he was met with three hostile and terrified guards.

"I hope this translator is accurate," he thought to Smitt through his comm band.

"Not like these primates can ding you," said Smitt.

"I'm here to oversee the transport of the Amber Room panels," he said in flawless twentieth-century German.

One of the guards gave him a funny look. "The city is falling all around us and all you care about is the stupid Russian relic?"

James feigned irritation. "Orders from the Führer. Take me there at once."

"Fuck the Führer," one of the guards in the back grumbled. "He brought this down upon us."

His comrade looked wide-eyed at James's SS uniform. "I'm sorry, sir. He does not mean it. We haven't slept in days. The city has been under constant bombardment."

"I mean every word of it," the other guard yelled, and then he hiccupped. He brought out a flask and offered it to James. "To the fucking Führer then, you stick-in-the-ass."

James wasn't sure if he should shoot this guy or not. If he were a true SS officer, that might be the right thing to do. However, he wasn't sure if the guard was supposed to survive the war. While most time lines selfhealed, it was better not to take chances. He did the next best thing.

With one hand, he knocked the flask out of the guard's hand. With the other, he powered the exo just a tad and threw a right cross at the soldier's chin. It was just hard enough to knock him unconscious without breaking his jaw, though this wasn't an exact science. The soldier's knees went noodly and he collapsed into a heap.

James looked at the other two guards. "Anyone else want to speak ill of the Führer?" Both of them shook their heads and stood at attention. "Good," said James. "Where are they? Take me to the panels before this place burns down around us!" His words were accentuated by another explosion.

"James, hurry up. We don't have data on when the castle burns down but we do know both the Allies and Soviets stop their offensive at roughly seventeen hundred hours, which is twenty minutes from now. Get a move on."

One of the guards gestured down the hallway. "It's in the north wing, first floor, northwest corner. I will take you there."

The other hesitated. "Can I see your papers, sir?" he said.

Another explosion, this time closer, rocked the castle. In the distance, he heard dozens of windows shatter.

James pushed past the man demanding the papers. "Lead on."

He was three steps past the guard when he heard the click of the MP40. "Halt!" the guard barked. James wouldn't be able to talk his way through this. He turned around slowly and stared the guard down, ignoring the gun pointed at his chest. "Your papers, sir," the guard said with a harder edge to his voice as he aimed his gun at James's chest. To James's left, the other guard took a step backward, looking unsure.

"He wants to see my papers," James thought.

"Well, we don't have any. Try not to kill them."

The exo sprang to life, creating a hardened kinetic shell around James's body. To the guards, it would look like his body suddenly shimmered and took on a translucent blocky yellow shape. He sped forward before the guard could pull the trigger, slipped past the barrel and gripped the man's wrist. He squeezed until he heard bone crack. Then he swung left, tossing the screaming Nazi like a rag doll at the remaining guard, who was still frozen in shock. The two collided, the impact slamming them against the wall. James walked up to them and checked their vitals. The one with the broken wrist was unconscious. The other was groaning softly. A downward punch to the temple silenced him.

James looked up just in time to see the east wing of the castle explode in a plume of smoke. The window shattered into his face and the shock wave knocked him off his feet. He quickly picked himself up and took off running, speeding through the hallways past panicked groups of huddled soldiers and civilians. He paid them no attention. In a matter of minutes, this castle was going to burn to the ground.

He burst into the Amber Room and startled three plain-dressed workers dismantling the gold and amber panels on the walls. The room was covered in a layer of dust, but James could see the beauty underneath the grime. The workers were less than halfway done taking the room apart. In the center were two crates filled with large blocks of panels.

They withered under his gaze as he pointed at the door and barked, "The three of you. Out. Now!"

The three civilians weren't about to argue with an SS officer and scampered out of the room. He closed the door behind them and activated several coils, kinetically tearing the panels out one by one and floating them into a neat bunch. When he had six floating, he stacked them and activated his netherstore container, expanding the ring until it was large enough for all six panels to slide through.

His power levels dipped. Netherstore containers used a tremendous amount of energy, and his power levels were already down from absorbing the impact of the airdrop. In the distance, more explosions rocked the castle; debris and dust showered from the ceiling. He could hear panicked soldiers running down the hallway on the other side of the door, shouting, "Fire!" Königsberg Castle groaned and his atmos blipped, indicating environmental dangers from the increased heat.

James kept working, slicing and ripping a dozen of the amber panels at once, floating them into neat stacks, and moving them into his netherstore. He moved as quickly as he safely could, but it was a slow process; several of the panels were very delicate. While not a surgeon or a craftsman, he had plenty of experience dealing with Titan generators, which were infinitely more delicate than these indulgent trinkets.

He was almost done when the door burst open and a scared Nazi ran in. The soldier, barely old enough to shave, gaped at the nine panels floating in the air above his head. Then his eyes moved down to the figure at the center of the strange scene. James's exo made the air near his skin shimmer with a yellow hue. He walked toward the boy, his energy still focused on hovering the panels.

The young Nazi's voice broke as he raised his rifle. "It's the work of the devil."

James lashed out with a kinetic swing and knocked the rifle out of the soldier's hands. When he reached the boy, he grabbed him by the collar and, with exo-enhanced strength, threw him across the room. The boy hit the wall awkwardly and collapsed to the ground with a bone protruding out of his leg. He howled and tried to crawl away.

"Damn it, James, hurry up," Smitt urgently crackled in his head.

James turned from the boy and finished his work. He had just completed storing the last panel when he noticed tongues of flames coming from underneath the door to the adjacent room. He glanced back at the boy still huddled in the far corner and saw the stark terror in his eyes, either from the fire or from James. James gritted his teeth, closed the band on the netherstore, and turned to leave.

"Lord save me," the boy soldier cried over and over again. "I don't want to die. I am a good person. I don't want to die."

With a kinetic hammer, James punched a hole into the wall.

"Please, help me!" the boy screamed. "You must be sent from God, an angel. I'm a Christian! Save me! Please deliver me!"

James stopped again. The fire was threatening to consume the room at any moment. That boy wasn't getting out alive unless he did something about it. Well, if that was the case, then that boy was as good as dead. James turned and approached the terrified Nazi. "Your time on this world is over. Make peace with your life. It'll make your final moments easier."

The boy, probably not even sixteen, face shiny with tears, reached out and clutched James's ankles. "Mercy! I follow the Führer. I'm a good person. I'm a good person!"

James stared at the terrified youth and was brought back to his own childhood, when he had lived in constant fear. He shook his head sadly. "You're not, but I'm sorry anyway."

As a final mercy, he brought his fist down upon the boy's skull, crushing it. Then he turned and left the Amber Room as Königsberg Castle burned to the ground. A few minutes later, there was a bright yellow flash, and James disappeared from April 10, 1944.

SIX

DREAMS

James pulled his head out of the glass of whiskey and glanced around the Never Late bar at Earth Central. The Never Late was twice as big as the Tilted Orbit but had only a third of the patrons, and every single one of them—all chronmen, for sure—was drinking alone. At least there were more women here. He counted twenty, which made this joint the best odds he'd seen in the past six months.

Another good thing was that the whiskey was cheaper, not that price ever mattered to him. The swill here was just as bad as the swill in space, but really, everything in the present tasted like crap compared to the stuff from the past. James downed his drink and poured himself another from the bottle.

He never thought he'd feel bad for a Nazi, even if it was just a kid. He had a little Jewish blood in him, though that meant a lot less now than it did five hundred years ago. These days, everyone had a little of everyone else's blood.

Born on Mars colony Brukhim Ha'baim in the Hellas Planitia basin, the old Israel's only colony in the solar system, he had more Jewish in him than most. Still, that Nazi kid was just that, a dumb kid. James raised his glass in salute and then downed it. At least they didn't serve drinks in tin cups here.

He thought of his mother and little sister, Sasha. Mother had died during the Mars Plague Bomb of—James pulled up the date—2490. He couldn't remember when he lost Sasha. They had been in Mnemosyne Station, a refugee camp high up in the orbit of Mars. Barely fifteen at the time, he had kept them both alive for almost a year. James's eyes moistened and turned the same tint as his red drunken face. He had tried to hold her close every night. He gave her whatever scraps he had, and fought off all the adults who tried to steal their meager belongings or lay a hand on them. Then one day, he woke up and found her missing. He never saw her again. She was nine or ten; he hated himself for not remembering.

When she disappeared, he went crazy, killing two of the men who had constantly harassed them and beating to unconsciousness another who had always leered at her. That got him tossed into the refugee prison, which caught the attention of a ChronoCom recruiter. The man pulled James out of certain labor camp slavery and enrolled him in the Academy. Through her death, he owed Sasha his life.

Smitt joined him at the bar two hours later. By this time, James had lost his usual stoic demeanor and was belligerently yelling at the bartender and everyone else around him. The other patrons ignored him. While that was usually fine by him, this was one of those rare instances where he wanted everyone's attention. James bellowed and raged at anyone within earshot.

"Hey, hey, hey," Smitt said, pulling James's arms down and leading him back to his seat. "You're yelling at other chronmen here, not rucks. These guys wouldn't hesitate to throw down with you."

"Good," said James, reaching for his glass and nearly tipping it over. "I'm tired of people treating me like a leper."

"Hardly that." Smitt signaled to the barkeep for a glass of water. "A dick, maybe. A leper, never."

James buried his face in his hands and ran his fingers through his hair, anguish twisting his expression. "He was a little fascist, ya know. Little fucking Nazi, and I smashed his skull in with this." James held up his right hand and powered on the exo. "Like a sledgehammer on a melon. And that's being merciful."

Smitt wasn't very good at being a comforting ear. "Look, James, kid was a goner anyway. You know that. I'm sure in that moment, you wish you could have done something, but that's not possible. You're from their future. You can't change the past. The time line self-heals."

This was all Time Law 101. Smitt and James had attended the Academy together. Smitt had failed to make the jump to full-tiered status, and like many who washed out of training, he stayed on to become a handler, while James had become a chronman.

Every chronman at one point thought about changing the past. The allure of rewriting what had already happened was so great that Chrono-Com created a separate division, the auditors, just to guard against chronmen making that mistake.

James lifted his head and stared blurry-eyed at Smitt. "So, let's have our stupid meeting. Any ripples from my Nazi foray?"

Smitt shook his head. "A few small ones. One of the guards that died actually survived the war and had a son in 1952. However, the family line died by 1961 in a boating accident. The time line effectively healed by 1978."

"Great, prevented a kid from being born. Same as killing him," James muttered, throwing another glass of whiskey back. This time, instead of putting the glass down on the counter, it slipped out of his fingers and shattered on the floor. The bartender shook his head and signaled to Smitt by pointing at the exit.

James stood up abruptly and nearly fell, knocking his stool over. He pointed back at the bartender and raged, "I leave whenever the abyss I please, you fucking ruck."

"That's our cue." Smitt wrapped his arms around James's shoulder and led him out of the bar. "Let's get you to bed. We'll be at Central for a few months; try not to pick too many fights with the locals. They could make life uncomfortable for us."

A few minutes later, an exhausted James lay in bed squinting at Smitt leaving the room. He was so drunk he couldn't see straight. He saw a silhouette of a nine-year-old girl standing by the door.

"Sasha," he called out, reaching for her.

The figure turned around and spoke in a familiar voice. "Sorry, James, what did you say?"

"I didn't mean to let you go. I tried to hold on to you," James mumbled, before collapsing back into bed. "I'm sorry."

Then darkness swept over him.

James woke up in a storage container filled with racks of dehydrated provisions. It took him a moment to remember why this placed looked familiar.

Grace Priestly. This was the container he had stowed away on to sneak aboard the *High Marker*. He had first jumped back into 2212 on Eris hours before the ship had taken off on its ill-fated journey toward Earth. He had hidden in here as the supplies for the ship were being loaded. Was he on the *High Marker* or on Eris? He couldn't tell.

James felt along the ridged edge of the container until he found the hatch to the opening. He put his ear to the wall and listened. Dead silence. He was about to pull the lever down when he noticed his uncovered arms. His bands were gone!

James patted both arms where the dozen bands should have been. He was completely naked! How could this have happened? For the first time in years, James felt panic rise up his throat. Without them, he was just a regular human, one who could be shot or burned or . . . James stared at the latch on the container panel. He didn't have his atmos. If he was in a zero-atmospheric environment, opening the hatch would kill him in seconds. A dozen scenarios ran through his head. He sat back down in the container. What was he doing here anyway?

He couldn't remember.

As if on cue, the lever turned and the hatch opened with a loud hollow echo. He watched warily as someone bent down and looked at him with an amused expression on her face.

"Are you staying in there forever, pet?" Grace Priestly asked.

James tilted his head at her. Somehow, the fact that she was standing there giving him that patronizing smile didn't bother him in the slightest. She looked good for a ninety-three-year-old woman. Especially for one who was dead. She offered him a hand and pulled him up with much more strength than her thin frame should have possessed. He looked around the familiar cavernous room. He was standing in Bay 6 of the *High Marker*, the cargo hold in which he had originally stowed.

What was he doing here?

"Are you coming, pet?" Grace stood at the door, looking impatient. Women like her did not expect to be kept waiting.

Dutifully, James followed, letting Grace drape herself on his arm, though her demeanor allowed no mistaking who belonged to whom. The hallways of the *High Marker* were the same brightly lit cold corridors that he remembered, but now the ship was peaceful. Quiet, eerily so. James looked behind him. The hallways were deserted. Even the humming sound of the Tech Isolationists' famed Titan engine was missing.

"Where are we?" he asked.

"We're where you want to be," she said.

"I don't want to be here."

Grace looked amused. "You only think that."

She led him to the control room of the ship, where the nothingness of space outside the heliosphere of the solar system awaited them on the display. Only a few specks of light pierced the black emptiness.

She turned to him. "We're past the point of no return. What are you going to do about it?"

There was a pause as James glanced up at the screen and then back to her. "There's nothing I can do."

Grace smiled and repeated herself: "You only think that."

She took his hand and led him to the exit. He stepped off the command deck and into the Amber Room. Inside, the young Nazi soldier was staring up at the intricate gold and amber carvings on the wall. The room itself looked different. Gone were the cakes of dust that had smothered the luster, as if someone had polished the entire room to a bright sheen. The walls practically glowed like the sun, giving the room a dream-like flare.

The soldier turned and smiled. Then he pointed toward the shiny wall, which was almost too bright to look at. "Beautiful, no? Now I see why you killed me to get it."

"That's not how it happened," said James.

"Yes, yes." The soldier laughed. "You had no choice. Your Time Laws and everything. More important than my life, ja?"

Upon closer inspection, James realized that the soldier wasn't wearing his uniform, just a shirt and a pair of trousers from his era. He looked every bit a boy and not at all like a mass-murdering fascist. The boy pointed up at a small, intricate gold chandelier suspended from the ceiling.

"You missed that, did you know?" he said. "Forgot to take it with you. Is your rich patron, the one who probably put the Amber Room in his private display, going to mind?"

James shrugged. "Abyss if I care."

The soldier fell in next to them as they left the room and continued down the hallway. "You save the pretty trinkets that you don't care about, yet kill what weighs heavily on your mind. Mixed priorities, ja?"

"It's just my job," said James as they turned the corner toward where he had first entered the castle.

The soldier smirked. "I bet your rich patron is sleeping well tonight."

They passed the three guards whom he had encountered at the castle. They were standing at the window looking out at the courtyard in the center of the castle, where a massive bonfire burned, blanketing their faces with an angry red glow. They turned to him in unison and waved.

"It's all right," one of them said. "We're dead anyway. I hope that lets you sleep better at night."

"Hey," one of them remarked angrily. "I was supposed to live and have a son!"

"Yeah, but you all drowned," the first said. "Dying here is much less painful than drowning. He did you a favor."

"You only think that," the one who was supposed to live said.

James and his two escorts stepped out of the castle and entered a dark hallway littered with refuse. A familiar foul stench wafted into James's nostrils. It was the smell of human misery and death.

James's mind froze in recognition; they were on Mnemosyne Station. Panic seized him and he tried to retreat into the castle, but the way back had disappeared, replaced by rusted gray and slimy walls sprouting large iron tubes running across the length of a hallway.

Grace laughed, ignoring that they were standing ankle-deep in liquid shit. "Oh pet, you can never go back to where we came from. You have to move forward, isn't that right?"

"Another Time Law, ja? The present is all that's important. Fuck the past!" said the soldier.

They continued on down the hallway and James relived those terrible days all over again. In the distance, he could hear the cruel chatter of the gangs, the screams of victims, and the constant banging and hissing of steam pipes. That loud hollow ring, like a cracked bell, echoed nonstop across the station, just as he remembered. James squeezed his eyes shut and tried to push those painful memories out of his head.

"You're no longer the child you once were, pet," Grace said, caressing his face. "Besides, don't you want to see her?"

That "her" snapped James back to reality. It could mean only one person. He opened his eyes and saw a little girl with matted auburn hair and large round eyes. She was barefoot and in rags, with a dirty satchel in her hand. She stood at the end of the hallway and waved. Then she turned and ran.

"Sasha!" James screamed, taking off after her, past the cubbyhole they called home, through the makeshift air-hatch market, and down past the guard offices. No matter how hard he ran, Sasha stayed a step beyond his reach. He continued chasing her, his heart thundering in his chest as his body threatened to fail him.

Every time she turned the corner, he willed himself to go faster. His legs began to feel heavy, but he kept urging them on. Faster! Harder! His desperation increased. Somehow, he had lost her. Finally, exhausted, he collapsed onto the floor, sucking in large gulps of air and retching at the same time. The layers of grime mixed with stagnant pools of feces forced his stomach to tighten and twist harder than any time jump could.

James picked himself up and staggered forward, barely able to stay on his feet. He leaned against the slimy walls for support. Turning the corner he entered a crowded room filled with dozens, no, hundreds of people. They were all relaxed and chatting with each other. As he entered, all of them turned to him in unison and waved.

James's blood froze. He had seen these people before. On his left were a group of pilgrims from 2235 that had suffocated when their life support system failed. In the center was the crew of the battleship *Judas*, destroyed during the Core Conflicts. Behind them were the Luna Base Delta scientists who had caught the asteroid virus 2C-F. The faces and times went on and on. Each of them was a past assignment, people he had left to die.

Then he saw Grace, bouncing Sasha on her knees, running her old wrinkled hands through his little sister's tangled auburn hair. "Such pretty curls you have, dear," Grace cooed into Sasha's ear. She turned to James and smiled that patronizing Grace Priestly smile. "Nice of you to finally join us, pet. Why don't you have a seat and catch your breath."

James took a labored step forward, and then another. He was almost within reach of Sasha when the station cracked, tearing a line across the floor. He stared helplessly as the room drifted away. There was a massive explosion of air escaping into space, and the moisture in his mouth evaporated. He stretched out his arm in a futile attempt to reach his sister.

"Sasha!" he screamed silently in the vacuum of space. Yet he was the only one who couldn't speak.

"Why are you leaving me?" Sasha cried, tears falling down her face.

"Oh dear," Grace said. "Pet, are you killing us a second time? Oh yes, we're already dead."

"You only think that." The Nazi soldier smiled.

"Sasha!" James screamed, bolting up from his bed. His head slammed the top of his sleep pod and he bounced back down on the mattress. Groaning, he flailed out of the opening and dropped two meters down onto the concrete floor. On instinct, he powered the exo and expanded his kinetic field, calling forth four coils ready to lash out. The dark room was bathed in yellow as the energy surrounding his body crackled. Crouched on the floor, James's eyes darted left and right, his still-sleeping mind searching for signs of his long-dead sister.

"James, can you hear me?" Smitt's voice echoed in his head.

James's tightened face slowly relaxed as he realized where he was. He stood up and surveyed the room. "Smitt?"

"I'm outside your door. Your comm band's been on all night. Must have been an abyss of a nightmare. When I felt your exo power up, I ran over. Listen, the first thing you have to do is power down and open the door."

James glanced at his glowing wrists and the mist-like shield covering his body, then stood up hesitantly. The yellow light in the room faded, leaving him in total darkness. He unlocked the door, and without waiting for it to open, walked away and sat down at the table in the corner, where an almost empty bottle of whiskey begged to be polished off. He threw back the contents of the bottle as the door opened with a creak.

Smitt stuck his head in. "Hello?" He turned on the light, saw James with the bottle in his hand, and shook his head. "It's five in the morning." He came in and sat down opposite James. "For once, can you not drink when you're not on assignment?"

James grunted, pulled a glass off the shelf, and offered it to him. Smitt shook his head but accepted it anyway. Then he put the glass to the side. James leaned against his chair and wiped his forehead. His shirt was soaked, and his skin burned and itched as if he had wandered onto the surface of Mercury without a rad band. He touched the bump growing on his scalp.

"That hurt." He felt the burgeoning knot growing on his head. He wasn't sure if he was dizzy from smashing his brain on the sleep pod or from his earlier binge.

Smitt looked concerned. "Maybe we should cut back your bar visits. Third time this month you've had an episode."

James put the empty bottle on the floor and reached up to the shelf above him for a fresh bottle of whiskey. He popped the cap off and brought the bottle to his lips.

"No, I don't think you should," Smitt said, trying to take it away from him. A look from James stopped him. James took a swig and held the whiskey out toward Smitt, who shook his head again.

"Look, James, this is getting a little out of control. I'm saying this as your friend, not your handler."

"You're probably right." James took another swig. "I don't really care. I feel like I'm about to crack any minute, and this bottle here is the only thing keeping me together." He smacked his lips. "What are they going to do? Fire me? Ground me from salvages?"

"You want to get out of ChronoCom eventually, don't you?" Smitt said. "You're doing well. At this rate, we buy our way out in four, five years tops. You really want to jeopardize that?"

James dropped his head. Four or five more years meant a hundred more salvages. How many more dead faces was he going to see? How many more would haunt his dreams? He grunted. Not like it mattered. The dead already numbered higher than he could count. What were a few more?

"You know I have an abyss's chance of earning out, don't you, Smitt?" he said in a low voice. "I won't survive four or five more years."

Smitt leaned forward. "Listen, I didn't want to say anything while you were hitting the bottle, but we just got a choice job. It's a big one, big enough to buy up several years of our contract. It also has an added bonus: a ticket to heaven."

James raised an eyebrow.

Smitt nodded enthusiastically. "Yeah, a golden ticket."

"What is it?" James asked.

Smitt looked James up and down. "Briefing's in a few hours, so stop fucking drinking and sober up."

"I don't have much more left in me," said James. He stared at the liquid swishing in the bottle. "Any day now, I'm just going to fly . . ." He laid his palm down horizontally and slid it forward. ". . . straight into Jupiter's fucking eye."

Smitt shrugged. "I always had you pegged as one of those who just flew off into the heliopause to see what's on the other side." He shook his head. "Anyway, it won't happen. It's a golden ticket," he repeated, "as long as you don't screw it up." He grabbed a towel from the rack and threw it onto James's head. "Get your ass cleaned up."

SEVEN

PLANNING

A painful hour later, James was trying to ignore his raging headache as Smitt and a well-dressed corp in a Europa-style suit went over the next salvage, code-named Sunken City. This job, a high priority Tier-1, had to be very important, because there was a surprising amount of detail to the briefing. James glanced at the half dozen other pale-faced corps sitting at the side, studying him. Few of his briefings included guests and subject experts, much less code names.

James found out just how large and important this jump was a few minutes into the briefing. Sunken City was the salvage for the infamous Nutris Platform disaster of 2097. The year itself, often referred to as the Cliffside of Humanity, was equally famous for being the final year of prosperity before the Great Decay began.

The latter part of the twenty-first century was known as the Final Golden Age, a half century blessed with peace, cooperation, and innovation. During that era, the nations of Earth rose up against the threats of environmental catastrophes, famine, and greed. They ushered in an era of many great technological and cultural wonders. Unfortunately, it was short-lived. The Nutris Platform was one of the last relics of that time.

"Why am I dropping so far away from the platform?" he asked as he pulled up the job briefing. For some reason, the physical insertion point was thirty kilometers farther out than usual.

"There are concerns with the military facility's advance surveillance," said Smitt. "We're just being extra cautious on this job." James grunted in disbelief but continued reading, skimming over the general overview and digging in to his mission parameters. A massive secret military facility off the coast of Russia, the platform had sunk into the Arctic Ocean days after it went online. According to public documents, a faulty experimental power source—the progenitor to the Titan source—was the culprit. Over three thousand scientists, military personnel, and crew were lost.

He frowned. "If a power generator was the catalyst of the disaster, I can't extract the energy source that caused the explosion. Isn't that why Nutris has been off-limits from salvages all this time?"

Smitt nodded and looked over at Sourn, the head suit. Sourn was a representative of Valta Corporation, one of the three largest mining conglomerates in the solar system and majority owner of Europa colony. The company also held 14 percent of Jupiter's mining rights, 21 percent of Neptune's mining rights, and owned outright fourteen of Jupiter's sixty-seven moons.

By the looks of Sourn and how labored his walking was, this was probably the first time he had ever set foot on Earth. James doubted the man had ever been in a full-gravity environment. Europa, where Valta was based, ran only a third of Earth's gravity on the colony. His face was particularly pale, even by spaceborn standards.

"Chronman James Griffin-Mars, we're fully aware of the Time Laws and the limitations of our rights from the purchase of the Nutris contract. We understand that the power core is off-limits. We don't want that." He transmitted several images to James's AI band. "We want these."

One was a stock photograph of a data core, and the other two were drawings of what looked like machinery: one a series of small machines connected by tubes and filters, and the other a circular contraption centered around a crystal in a container. James studied the picture and then the drawings. The images were so basic he couldn't make out what each machine's purpose could be.

"Seems pretty straightforward," said James, bemused, not quite sure what the big deal was. "You want me to obtain industrial equipment from an isolated military platform in the Arctic Circle within a two-to-three-day window?"

"Technically a four-hour window, between when the explosion is first reported and when the platform sinks into the ocean," Smitt corrected.

James's jaw fell open. "After the explosion? Why not the night before?"

Sourn shook his head. "It has to be in that window. There's too much time line risk if you initiate early."

"That makes no sense," James said, looking over the data more closely. "Unless taking these three units would prevent the explosion, I can just grab them the night before and avoid the chaos. I don't see the—"

"It has to be after!" Sourn cut him off. He looked over at Smitt. "Moving on."

"There are concerns about breaking the data core's uplink prematurely," Smitt said.

James wasn't sold on their logic. That was something the time line could have easily healed over, but if this was the way they wanted it done, he would accommodate them.

"Fine. After. What about the layout of the place?"

"The facility was highly classified, so no blueprint survived," Smitt said. "You'll have to scout the platform on-site."

"Small window, zero scouting report, classified military installation?" James ticked off each finger. "This whole thing is literally fucking impossible."

Sourn shrugged. "When we purchased this contract from ChronoCom, we were assured one of their best would be assigned to it. We have every confidence in your ability to carry this out successfully. After speaking with your associate here, we believe our added incentives should be adequately persuasive."

Smitt leaned in. "Remember what we talked about last night? On top of the payout that effectively buys out four years of our contract, Valta is also offering us residency on Europa if we hit all the objectives. You said you wanted out of ChronoCom; this is the way."

Sourn nodded. "As you know, Europa is an exclusive colony; not anyone can just migrate there. If you perform as expected, Valta will gladly extend an invitation and offer employment at a salary commensurate with your status as a ChronoCom operative."

These buyouts, commonly referred to as golden ticket jobs, were extraordinarily rare. The guaranteed pay at his current scale on Europa was just icing on the cake. It sounded way too good to be true. All chronmen's accounts were held and controlled by ChronoCom, and all the funds reverted to it if the chronman died. A chronman could get control of his account only after buying out his contract. And considering that the life expectancy of people in James's line of work averaged less than ten years, it was a long shot for anyone to get a chance to earn out of ChronoCom.

James was pushing fifteen years. He was considered one of the seniors and even then, he still had five more years left on his contract. For Valta to purchase four of his last five years, especially with the recent dearth of Tier-1 chronmen, they would have to be paying an exorbitant sum. James tapped his finger on the table, lost in thought. Something smelled foul here; he just couldn't put his finger on it.

"Why?" he asked finally, arching an eyebrow. "Buying us out must cost Valta a fortune. What's the catch?"

Sourn smiled. "Consider it extra incentive. Valta knows how delicate this job is. We wish to guard against any decisions to abort. Just get us what we ask for and we will deliver as promised."

James looked at Smitt, who nodded. "Central's already confirmed the terms. We just need to come through."

James bit his lip. With this much scratch being offered, who cared about things being off? Nothing else mattered now except for finding the fastest way to escape his current hell. He was exaggerating when he said it was an impossible job; it was just a very difficult one. James had beaten difficult before. This couldn't be harder than surviving Mnemosyne Station, after all.

"Sounds like I have no choice," he said. "Let's get this over with."

They spent the rest of the morning working through the logistics. The more James learned about the salvage, the more uneasy he felt about the job, but he had learned years ago that reservations meant little to chronmen and even less to the megacorporations.

The long briefing ended at ten, giving him sixteen hours before mission got the job. James hadn't had breakfast yet and was starving. He needed another drink too. Both of these issues would need to be rectified before he could begin the rest of his day. His body informed him of its priorities and he headed toward the Never Late. A drink came first; sustenance later.

"Where you off to, my friend?" Smitt said, falling in next to him.

James grunted. Go figure, he'd get handled by his handler even when not on a job. He imagined Smitt being particularly unbearable for the next few days. The success of this job affected them both.

Smitt wanted to get out of here almost as badly as James did. Almost. While handlers didn't have to put up with the trauma of the jumping into the past, they were the lowest tier of the agency and were barely treated better than pesky caretakers. After almost twenty years, some of them could almost get as suicidal as chronmen. Bottom line, both of them could use a change of scenery.

"Whoa, whoa. You are not going to the Never Late right now, James." Smitt jumped in front of him. He spread his hands out as if that would actually bar the way. "No drinking tonight. Not before an important jump. In any case, this salvage is important enough the director wants you to meet with Levin in an hour before even clearing you to go."

"Fuck Levin," James snarled. "Besides, I have an hour to get a couple drinks and lunch in before the audit anyway."

Smitt pointed a finger at him. "Check yourself, James. You want out? This could be it. Just play nice with Levin and maybe you might reduce our sentence from five more years to just one and change. Just smile and be on your best fucking behavior with Levin. Do the job, and we're in the clear, got it?"

James tried to pass him again, but Smitt would have none of it. He kept his arms out and almost tried to tackle him when James pushed through. It would be comical if it wasn't so sad. James saw the desperation in his friend's eyes as he tried to keep him from his booze.

"After my audit with Levin then," he grumbled, turning around. "I'm going to take a nap in my quarters."

"I'll be right outside waiting for you," Smitt said, following him every step of the way.

EIGHT

LEVIN JAVIER-OBERON

evin watched as the prison collie took off from the landing pad and shot toward the sky, a small yellow streak disappearing into the morning, joining the thick caravan of ships constantly streaming through the atmosphere.

The trial should have been short. ChronoCom trials were usually just formalities. After all, the agency never acted until it was sure. Otherwise, they'd just be wasting scarce resources. In this case, though, Levin had a personal stake in the outcome and argued for it until he got his desired result. It took him all night to get what he wanted.

Officially, Levin's role in this audit retrieval was only a moderate success, with the ripples caused by the fugitive an unfortunate but not unexpected aftereffect. The time line was restored, though never fully healed. That would be a minor black mark on his record.

Levin had his own reasons for personally taking on this job. He had restored his honor for having a rogue nephew, his sister Ilana was able to see her son one final time, and Levin had somehow saved Cole from death. That in itself was a minor miracle, considering the ripples caused by his romp through the Ming Dynasty.

The prison transport finally left the atmosphere, its light no longer visible. It would take the ship a few days to reach the penal colony on Nereid, where Cole was sentenced to do hard labor in the gas-processing plants for the rest of his life. Levin had saved his nephew from capital punishment, though in a way, Nereid was a fate far worse.

Levin looked over at his weeping sister. "It's over. We've done all that we could. Will you stay the night before you head back to Oberon?"

Ilana wiped her face with her sleeves and shot venom at him with her eyes. "You should have let him be, Levin. Why didn't you let him stay in the past? He wasn't going to hurt anyone."

"He broke the Time Laws," Levin said. "Bringing him back was the right thing to do."

"Protecting your flesh and blood was the right thing to do," she lashed out, jabbing her finger at his face. "He didn't need to join your damn agency. He had options. Now look what's happened to my baby! I'll never forgive you."

New tears streamed down her face as Ilana fled the landing pad, cursing him every step of the way. Levin watched as his sister disappeared into Earth Central, knowing full well that she was a woman of conviction. He gave himself slim odds of seeing her alive again after today.

He sighed. Bringing in Cole had been the right thing to do. There was no doubt about it in his heart. Still, it didn't make the burden weigh on him any less. He looked up at some of the engineering crews staring at the spectacle of his family grief. Anger burned through his veins and radiated to the surface of his skin—and not a small amount of shame. After all, he might have removed some of the stain on his honor, but Central was still abuzz with talk of this scandal, and every word from these gossipmongers was about him.

Quick, harsh words bubbled up to his lips, but instead, Levin returned the gaze of their judging eyes. He stared them down with a cold rage, daring them, daring any of them to maintain eye contact. He knew his shame was misplaced. It was not he who had broken the Time Laws, only his blood. He didn't bring his own nephew in because he was overreacting; it was because it was the right thing to do. So for that, there was no way in the abyss he would let any of these lower tiers inflict shame upon him.

The engineering crew wilted before him and dispersed, each realizing he or she had something more pressing to attend to than mock the high auditor of Earth. Let them have this one moment where they could feel superior to him. It was likely the last one any of them would ever get.

It wasn't until he was back in his office that he relaxed, and let a few moments of grief pass over him. Ilana wasn't wrong. It was his fault. Cole had joined because of him, because of his uncle who had regaled him with stories of the past when he was a boy. Unlike most other chronmen, Cole did have other choices for careers. Levin, through his work as a chronman and later as an auditor, had lifted his family from the cesspool on Oberon to a better life. The boy could have been something else. Anything else.

Levin went behind his desk and poured himself a glass of bourbon, a rare Pappy Van Winkle retrieved from a salvage back in the late twentieth century. He had been saving it for a special occasion. Today was as good as any, though the occasion was not what he had imagined. He tossed back the glass and poured himself another.

Against the wishes of both his mother and uncle, Cole had joined the Academy of his own volition and had had the talent and skill to rise to the chronmen tier. It was after he began to run jobs that his sensitive soul began to suffer and unravel under the strain. The deterioration was quicker than with any other chronman in recent memory.

Levin blamed the Academy. Someone in psychological analysis should have picked up on his mental frailty early in his first year. Maybe they hadn't dared fail the nephew of a high-ranking auditor. Maybe Chrono-Com, with its depleted ranks, had loosened its strict requirements. In any case, there was failure on every level, and it had paved the way to today. But Levin felt especially guilty. He brought his glass to his lips and sipped the Pappy again.

He gave himself another minute of anger before he pushed it out of his mind. Duty called, and he had wasted enough of his time reminiscing over what had happened. The past was already dead: a chronman axiom that couldn't have been truer.

The vid on his desk began to blink. Levin stared at it for a few moments before sitting down and pulling it up. He had cleared his calendar earlier today to deal with Cole's trial. Whatever it was must be important.

Instead, he received instructions from the director for a last-minute psychological audit on a Tier-1 who was running a jump for one of the agency's largest sponsors. Levin frowned. He disapproved of these sorts of jobs.

The agency was intentionally created outside of the corporate complex, unaffected by capitalistic motivations. After all, ChronoCom was far too important to humanity and to the solar system to be weighed down and tainted by profit and greed. However, with the corporations funding an increasing percentage of their operations, it was becoming more and more difficult to keep corruption out.

"Damned abyss," he swore when the audited chronman's profile came up.

It was James Griffin-Mars. As if his day could get any worse. Levin had banned James from all Earth salvages three years ago because the two couldn't get along, ever since that unfortunate incident with Landon. As high auditor of Earth, Levin was forced to make hard decisions. He had had to make several with Cole, after all. The recent dearth of Tier-1s must have pulled James back. How unfortunate for them both.

Levin grimaced. *Might as well get this over with.* He still had a lost nephew and sister to mourn.

True to his word, Smitt was still standing outside his door two hours later when James received the summons from High Auditor Levin, or Backstabbing Asshole, as he liked to refer to the man. Wearing a scowl, he let his handler lead him through the audit wing to Levin's office door.

"I'll be waiting right here when you're done," his overbearing best friend said. "Behave yourself."

It wasn't that James minded these audits, it was that he hated Levin. Well, no, he felt the audits were a waste of time, too. Passing or failing one of these stupid things didn't really matter. All auditing did was decide the tier of jobs a chronman was allowed to run. With the suicide rate for chronmen so high, there weren't enough Tier-1s these days for the agency to pull anyone off the line regardless, so these audits were essentially a formality.

ChronoCom had commissioned a study a few years ago on the high suicide rates among time operatives. Some of the scientists had hypothesized that excessive time travel affected the brain. James could have just saved them all that time and energy by telling them that chronmen became the way they did because the job fucking sucked. The study became moot when the only recommendation they could make was to offer extended rest to the more senior chronmen. Humanity couldn't afford to bench any Tier-1 operatives.

He knocked on the door and walked in. Levin was busy acting busy and ignoring James, staring at the vid floating in front of him. He was probably the least sympathetic of the high-ranking planetary auditors, which was surprising, considering he was a former chronman.

That was one of the two retirement options for guys like James. Usually, they died on the job, but sometimes, if a chronman was exceptional and kissed the right ass, he became an auditor and tracked the performances of other chronmen and their handlers.

"Have a seat," Levin said after a while. He pulled up James's file on the vid and skimmed it while James plopped on a chair in front of his desk. Levin sniffed at him and raised an eyebrow. "Straight to the bar after breakfast, or was that still from last night?"

"Before, after, does it matter?" James shrugged. "It's something I saw you do often when you were one of us."

"According to Jobe, you were at the bar almost all the time on Himalia Station. Nearly single-handedly keeping the place afloat. He says you buy everyone drinks. You're not saving your scratch. Kujo said you made a drunken scene at the Never Late last night as well. Your account isn't nearly what it should be for a chronman of your status. How are you ever going to save up for life after the agency?"

James snorted. "You mean when I'm dead? Tell me, who has a life after ChronoCom? And don't tell me that shit you do counts."

Levin leaned back in his chair. "What's wrong with what I do? It's my job to make sure our people are operating at peak levels, which you obviously aren't. It's also my job to take corrective action."

"Corrective action like turning Landon in and clearing out half his savings when he was six months from buying out his contract?" James said, leaning forward over the desk, his hands gripping the metal like claws.

"Don't start on Landon again," Levin said. "He deserved his punishment for screwing up three consecutive jobs and then trying to cover it up."

"Twenty years on the job and six months from getting out." James clenched his fist. "He was our mentor and friend."

"Maybe he should have kept his focus on earning out his exit instead of getting drunk before his jumps," Levin said, "a habit that, by the way, you seem to have picked up."

James scowled. "Go fuck yourself, Levin."

"Not if I get you first," Levin said. "I'm supposed to clear you for this corp request. Maybe I won't. Let's start with your last job, shall we?" His eyebrows rose as he read the report. "A six on ripples. A little high for such a minor salvage, don't you think?"

"I got dropped in the middle of a war!"

The meeting went downhill from there, with Levin nitpicking every single decision James had made over the past month. Finally, an exhausting hour later, after both of them had insulted the other countless times, Levin shook his head.

"You're walking a fine line," he said.

"Like I care."

"You might care if your funds dry up, which might happen, at the pace you drink."

"You going to Landon me then, huh? And you wonder why the chronmen hate you."

"No one likes you much either."

"Landon flew his collie into Neptune because of you."

That touched a nerve in Levin. "I'm not at fault for his suicidal actions."

"Keep telling yourself that," James said. "I'm sure you sleep like a baby. You only think that—"

James froze, a thought or memory or dream triggering in his head. He suddenly found himself short of breath. Why did saying that send chills through his body? He clenched his fist and willed his shaking arms still. There was no way he'd show Levin any weakness.

Levin was an observant auditor, though. "Are you all right, James? How are your nerves? You look like you're about to lose it."

"How's your jaw?" James shot back through gritted teeth.

Levin smirked. "Fully healed. Next time you want a go at me, do it while I'm looking."

There was a moment of awkward silence as both men refused to back down. Levin pulled up another set of files and looked them over. "Your last few reports show empathy for the victims of these dead-end time lines," Levin said. "How do you feel about abandoning the Mother of Time?"

Grace's face flashed in front of him. *So how do you feel about abandoning me?* she said.

"The past is already dead." James wasn't sure about that anymore. "You can't abandon dead people." He didn't believe that either.

"And the crew on the ship?" Levin asked.

"Inconsequential. I only went back for the Time Law Charter and the Titan source and convertor. It'll power a million-unit moon colony for years," said James.

Levin made a note in his report. "Good. So the value of the living in the present is still your primary concern?"

James forced himself to nod, and then he paused as a question stumbled out of him. "What happens after we've run out?"

"We salvage more, of course."

"No, I mean out of sources to salvage." He leaned back and furrowed his brow. "During my tenure, I've retrieved over fifteen Titan sources, and maybe a hundred or so lesser cores, converters, and generators. If I remember my studies at the Academy correctly, less than a thousand Titan-powered facilities and ships were ever produced, with only half of them salvageable within the strictures of the Time Laws.

"We've probably already salvaged a third, maybe half of those salvageable sources. We don't have the technology to build anything powerful enough to power entire moon colonies anymore, not since the last of the Technology Isolationists were wiped out. So what happens after we're out of history to plunder? What does humanity do next?"

"That's not really your concern, James," Levin said. "The corporations and the governments will eventually develop new technologies or relearn what was lost."

"The corporations," James scoffed. "All they care about is profit and control. Those shortsighted bastards don't care about the future."

"You're a cynic, James," Levin said. "Always have been. All of us have our roles to play to prevent our extinction. ChronoCom's is to buy humanity time by mining the past."

James looked out the window outside Central. "When's the last time you walked outside?" he asked, his voice low. "Among the wretched people. Breathed the unfiltered air. Lived in the squalor. We're losing."

Levin followed his gaze out the window, and for a few moments, the two stared in silence as the bristling gray winds swirled around the decaying city. Then he shook his head, as if snapping out of a trance, and looked back at James. "We're getting off track. How are you sleeping?"

"Like a baby," James lied.

"What about your lag sickness? Are you up to date on the miasma regimen?" Levin looked at the vid. "Says here you're behind by two months."

James shrugged. "Been busy keeping humanity's lights on. I'll do it when I get around to it."

For another thirty minutes, Levin peppered him with questions about his health and his feelings, asking about everything ranging from throwing up after jumps to his dreams to his drinking habits to when he last bedded a woman. He actually varied it a little bit from the previous time James was there, though not by much.

Finally, a visibly frustrated Levin stood up. "You've given me the exact same answers for three audits in a row, so let's cut to the chase." He walked around his desk. "Don't think I don't see the shakes in your hands. I will call you in after every job until I get straight answers from you. Unfortunately, you're too senior for me to slap you back to running wood recoveries in the seventeenth century, or I would. Now listen closely: next time you get back from a job, you report straight to your handler before you hit the bottle. Understand?"

"Or?" James shrugged.

Levin slammed his fist on the desk. "I'm getting tired of your insubordination," he said, rising to his feet. "I control your fate in ChronoCom. I can keep you here forever, regardless of your credit."

"I've made myself clear on where I stand with your idle threats," James said, standing up as well.

The two glared at each other for several tense moments. Finally, Levin turned his back to him. "I don't think you're stable, but you put on a good act and you get results. ChronoCom doesn't have enough high-tiers to bust you back, but I'm watching you. You slip once and I'll happily Landon you if I get the chance. Now, get out of here and send for Thompson to come in next."

James smirked and started toward the door. "Good seeing you again. Glad we had this chat."

"And get that miasma regimen administered right after this meeting. You aren't green-lit until the medical ward tells me that's done."

James marched out of Levin's office and was about to head back toward the Never Late when he changed his mind and went toward the medical ward instead. Might as well get his miasma regimen over with. That bile climbing up his throat had been getting closer to his mouth every time. Would save him the embarrassment of throwing up on his next jump.

Levin was starting to catch on, and while the man might be a backstabbing ass, he was good at his job. He was right to question James's stability. Frankly, James questioned it himself. He was holding his sanity together by a thread, but he'd be damned if he let a jerk like Levin force him into a corner. That, and he conveniently forgot to send for Thompson.

NINE

NUTRIS PLATFORM

James flew *Collie* north through the Arctic Circle and watched with increasing concern as she struggled against the crosswinds, torrential rains, and fist-size balls of hail continuously slamming into the small ship from all directions. It was a sad testament to the Earth's condition when space debris and interplanetary dust caused less wear and tear on a ship.

The collie sputtered and popped, giving him the impression of a crippled bird about to drop out of the sky. There was also a constant hiss somewhere the cabin. He reminded himself to keep his atmos on at all times.

"James, how's my reception? Gyros are showing a bumpy ride to the north pole," Smitt's voice popped into his head. He was sitting in the comfort of the Hops at Central.

"Just keep her low in case this thing dies," James thought back. "It started leaking cabin pressure an hour after takeoff. Remember to fix that before we head out into space again."

James leaned back in his chair and watched as the collie flew into one of the many electrical storms common in the northern part of the planet. The collie shook even harder, which James had thought impossible. He increased his exo and atmos levels, fully anticipating a midair explosion that would jettison him out into the ocean at any moment.

He was in luck in the sense that he didn't die on the way to the jump spot. A little over three hours later, *Collie* hovered unsteadily over the resting place of the sunken Nutris Platform. He opened the door and looked down at the maelstrom raging below him. The brown raindrops striking his shielding were almost horizontal.

Below him, hundred-meter waves swirled and crashed against each other. With gusts howling at nearly two hundred kilometers an hour, it was so loud, he had a hard time hearing Smitt talking in his head. And to top things off, the radiation was at a dangerous level.

"At the drop zone. Disembarking," James thought. "Get *Collie* out of here."

"Confirmed. Pulling her up into orbit," Smitt said. "Remember your jump window. I'll see you in a couple of days."

James looked down at the five-hundred-meter plunge into the black and brown ocean below. Even though it was water, it was risky. A drop from this height could kill him if he hit something solid. Not to mention that at drop speed, the impact from a crashing wave could be as dangerous as an avalanche of boulders. However, he couldn't risk steering the collie any lower; one large wave could end up swallowing it whole.

He took a deep breath, stepped out into open air, and plummeted down like a rock. He looked up and saw the collie rapidly shrinking in size. Then a large wave struck him and carried him sideways. Immediately, his vision blurred and the clouds above him vanished from view. Another wave hit him from a different angle, and the sky reappeared as he bounced back into the air. He activated the jump band just as a third wave went over his head and crashed down on him, pushing him deep underwater.

James relaxed and let the current drag him wherever it wanted. He just had to let it go and conserve his strength until the force of the current dissipated. Visibility down here was nearly zero and the gunk caking onto the shield barely let him see his outstretched hands.

There was a bright yellow flash, and then the brown gunk began to break apart and clear up. Seconds later, James was left floating in crystal-blue waters. Disoriented, he looked up and saw a shimmering light break through the surface of the ocean, bathing the clear water in a white hue that danced in a gentle swaying motion.

Below him, thousands of fish, almost all extinct in the present, swam together as if one giant creature. They moved in unison, lockstepping back and forth, each a tiny star glittering in the light. In the distance, an impossibly large beast, possibly a whale or some other prehistoric monstrosity, passed by leisurely. James had seen these sea creatures only in pictures, which didn't capture the reality of their size. He watched, mouth agape, as it gracefully slipped by him. After having been in nearly every part of the solar system, this was the most amazing sight James had ever seen.

"You made it through all right?" Smitt asked, voice sounding like it came across a distant funnel. "James?"

His friend's voice in his head snapped James back from the spectacle. "Still in one piece, Smitt. You should see the view. It's amazing."

"You are officially in 2097. Enjoy the scenery, because it all goes to the abyss pretty soon."

James looked up and swam toward the surface. A minute later, his head broke through the water and he looked up at the brilliant yellow light of the twenty-first-century sun. It felt soothing. Peaceful.

James looked east to the horizon and saw the Nutris Platform. He gaped. Any preconceptions he had had about the installation had been completely off. This wasn't so much a secret military research facility as it was a giant floating city. And in a few days, it was going to burn down and sink beneath the waves.

Overhead, a large shadow flashed by, then another. James looked behind him and saw two dozen large craft flying toward the platform. The city's new inhabitants were arriving. Little did they know that they were flying to their graves. James dove underwater and swam after them.

Sneaking into the secret military research base was much easier than James had anticipated. Greenland, the nearest landmass, was thousands of kilometers away, so Nutris security did not seem to bother guarding the perimeter. It took him less than ten minutes after reaching the floating city to find one of the underwater maintenance shafts. After he climbed up to the main level, it was only a few steps to the nearest nexus routing room.

He spent the next few minutes painting on his disguise. He kept his own face, albeit darkening his skin a few shades. Most people in this century seemed to enjoy baking in the sun, an impossible practice in the present. He preferred to keep as much of his natural appearance as possible. It used up less energy and also made it easier for him to talk his way out of being caught without paint.

It had happened only once before, during a salvage on Mercury. The radiation levels had overloaded his paint band, causing it to malfunction. He had been lucky on that jump. The Minos colony usually executed foreigners by putting them in a low-grade rad suit, tying them to a post on the surface of the planet, and leaving them to a slow and painful death.

Satisfied with his appearance, James hacked the nexus and planted his cover. He was surprised. For a military installation, they made it very easy to hack into the central AI. In this time period, just about everything was patched into a distributed artificial intelligence. While his disguise would fool the naked eye, all the systems on the platform would be able to expose him. The AIs at the turn of this century were just coming into their own, and their advancement would grow by leaps and bounds until the AI wars seventy-three years later.

The strength of the distributed AI was that it was very difficult to take offline. The weakness of it, though, was that it was easy to access with an advanced enough intrusion system. All James needed to do was pipe into the stream, which for his advanced AI band was a simple task. Less than two minutes later, James became known to the Nutris Platform AI as Salman Meyer of Prince Rupert, British Columbia. He assigned himself to the central living habitat and proceeded to give himself as much clearance as possible without raising any red flags.

He also uploaded the schematics of the platform to Smitt. They would need to devise a plan if they were going to pull off a triple heist in such a large facility. It would take a few hours for Smitt to receive uploaded data through the chronostream. Until then, James had to find his own way around this maze.

James hated going into assignments blind. One of the reasons he was a long-tenured chronman, as in why he was still alive, was his attention to detail. He did not like surprises. The unknown was death in his line of work. James made a beeline toward the landing hub, where all the other visitors were being offloaded and processed. He became hopelessly turned around when he reached the portion of the platform with taller buildings and lost sight of where the transports were landing.

The alleys were narrow and looked homogeneous, twisting and turning in what seemed like random directions. Twenty minutes later, he found himself at a dead end. His patience wearing thin, James was about to activate his exo and jump on top of one of the buildings when a voice saved him from giving away his cover.

"What are you doing here?"

James saw the shadow of a giant monster on the ground in front of him and jumped, instinctively powering his exo to a low level as he turned to face the perceived threat. He gaped at the massive mechanoid, industrial by the looks of it, of a type that was commonly used around this time period.

Built with four arachnid-like legs and a squat humanoid upper torso complete with four arms and a head, it towered over him. James remembered battling militarized variations of these things during salvages to the AI wars.

He didn't know how this damned thing had snuck up on him. It must have just gotten out of the ocean, since it was still dripping wet. Then the mechanoid laughed, a hollow, echoey giggle that sounded distinctly human. The large metal head with the smooth gray spherical face opened outward, splitting down the middle, revealing a woman inside.

A wide grin spread across her face. "I'm sorry. I find a sick joy in sneaking up on people in Charlotte here. Blame it on having four older brothers with vile senses of humor. Are you lost? New residents aren't supposed to be back here until they've been through orientation."

James caught himself staring at the woman. There was something distracting about her face. He couldn't quite put his finger on it. "I got tired of waiting to get processed," he said when he finally found his voice. "Thought I'd check out my new home."

The predetermined answer seemed to work with her. She flashed him a bright smile. "Well, if you're on the two-year contract, you'll have plenty of time to learn all the nooks and crannies, all two square kilometers of it." Her mechanoid hissed as several panels along the humanoid torso also split open down the center.

The woman, petite, wearing a tight black control suit that covered her entire body except for a small opening for her face, stepped out and jumped agilely off one of the mechanoid's legs. James wasn't tall by present-day spaceborn standards, but the top of her head barely reached his chin.

She walked up to him and stuck out her hand. "Elise Kim, Sector Two, research chief."

James shook her hand. "Salman Meyer, nautical security, Sector Two . . ." He realized his mistake too late.

Elise frowned. "You're on my security staff? I thought I had vetted all the guys personally."

James's mind raced as a graphic console opened in front of her face and she pulled up a personnel report. His information would be there but if she challenged him on any of its validity, he might have to kill her. He couldn't afford the attention. His entry into the distributed AI wouldn't stand up to heavy scrutiny.

Fortunately, she found his name and shrugged. "Ah, no wonder. You were only added three days ago. Here, I'll walk you back to processing. Did you get your habitat yet? Wait, let me park Charlotte."

Elise looked at the mechanoid behind her and pushed a button on the console. The mechanoid churned to life and walked away, presumably to a garage or whatever its holding area was. Satisfied, Elise gestured for James to follow her up a flight of stairs to a floating walkway connecting several of the buildings. The two strolled above the city, bathed by the cool sun and a gentle breeze blowing in from the west. The air felt so fresh it actually burned his lungs.

James quickly learned that this Sector Two research chief was a talkative one. As they walked, she became his personal tour guide. She swelled with pride as she chattered on about Nutris as if she had built it with her own two hands. Several times, she stopped to point down at some of the structures, detailing many of the facilities, including central operations, the science lab, the filtration plant, the cafeteria, and most important, the bar.

She also asked him a lot of questions, which made James profoundly uncomfortable. The woman was far too helpful and way too friendly. His alibi and alias would crumble if she spent more than a few minutes poking at them. The more he talked about himself, the more likely it would be for him to make a misstep. So he did his best to divert their discussion back to her, which Elise was happy to do.

Elise delved into detail about her training at some education center called Berkeley and how she joined the Nutris Initiative after the Third

Central Oil Environmental Debacle, which eventually led to her running this sector's biological research division. It took only a few minutes for her to lose him with her jargon.

James caught himself studying Elise, fascinated. There was something very different about her. For one thing, she was so animated and alive, a far cry from the miners, prostitutes, and sad husks barely living in the present. The other thing he realized that drew him to her was her optimism. She practically glowed at every topic they talked about.

This sort of optimism had long been squelched in the twenty-sixth century. He had to remind himself that the tragedies of humanity had not quite affected this time period yet, though it would happen soon. This year was the Cliffside of Humanity, after all.

He took the time to further examine his perplexing guide. Her tan face was weathered from time under the sun, not from age, and there was a twinkle in her eyes that James rarely saw back home. And now that the conversation had veered away from him, James didn't mind her chattiness. There was something about the sound of her voice. It didn't sound tired. He also decided that he liked her bright smile. It was a good one as far as those went.

James held his disappointment in check when they reached the transport hub where everyone else was being processed. He had hardly spoken five words to her and hoped to find a reason to delay parting ways.

"So, this is it," he said. "Thanks for leading me back out to civilization. I might have starved out there in the iron jungle."

She grinned. "Plenty of fish if you needed." There was a moment of uncomfortable silence. "Well, I need to get back to work. See you around the sector?"

"Maybe grab a drink at the bar later?" he blurted before he realized what he was saying.

Elise winked at him. "Maybe another day. I've got five more hours in Charlotte before I can call it a night. No biggie. We have two more years to get to know each other."

He waved at her as she disappeared around the corner. Then his hands fell to his sides and tightened into fists. "Two days, you mean," he muttered.

When those two days were up, she and everyone else here would be dead. With a grimace, James walked to the end of one of the lines and waited to be processed.

"Hey, James, is everything all right?" Smitt asked.

"Everything is fine," James said. "Why do you ask?"

"Because your heart rate is a hundred forty beats a minute."

TEN

ELISE KIM

Elise had just finished a fourteen-hour shift on the ocean floor and was now slowly heading back up to Nutris Platform for her weekly senior staff meeting. It was a long time sitting in one place but she didn't mind. She had taken a nap inside Charlotte while the mechanoid was processing floor samples around midnight. Charlotte was like her second bedroom. Elise looked out at the clear waters and marveled as Charlotte's high beams pierced the darkness, exposing the beauty of the sea.

It had been a long night, and chances were, it'd be another long day as well. The newest batch of victims, as she liked to call them, had just flown to the platform by transport in threes and fours. By the end of the week, Nutris would be at 80 percent capacity and fully operational. There would be many more sleepless, deep-underwater nights for the next couple of years. Elise wouldn't have it any other way. It actually made her sort of giddy; she was living her lifelong dream, exploring the most remote crevices of the world and healing Gaia from the many previous centuries of abuse.

"Barn Spider, what is your ETA topside?" a voice crackled, almost mumbling, through the radio.

Charlotte's AI, predicting her request, pulled up the depth reading and flashed it in front of her left eye. She radioed back, "Morning, Hank. I'm three kilometers down and rising. I'm going to take a pause at a hundred meters and see if I can say hi to that herd of blue whales lurking in the neighborhood. I want to make sure the foundation cables aren't going to be a problem for them. At the very least, I'd like to snap some photos to send back to my folks."

"So, in fifteen then?"

"Make that thirty."

"You got it, Barn Spider. I'll allocate Bay Two."

"Much obliged."

An hour later, Charlotte crawled into Bay 2 of the mechanoid hanger and Elise stepped out, stretching upward on her tippy toes and reaching for the ceiling with her fingers. Her mechanoid was custom-built for her, so technically, she could stretch while inside, but fourteen hours was fourteen hours, and even someone like Elise, who lived to pilot mechanoids, could get a little claustrophobic. She never did find the blue whales, but got distracted by a family of belugas enjoying the warm morning sun.

Elise stripped out of her control suit and changed into her official Nutris Platform uniform. She hated the stiff, military-looking garb, but the director insisted all senior staff be properly attired when inside the Head Repository. Fortunately, that meant she had to wear this thing only once a week, during his status meetings.

She gave Charlotte an affectionate pat on the leg and relayed some last-minute instructions to the chief mechanic before heading out of the hangar. With a little bounce to her step, she passed by the lower dock corridor and stopped at an intersection, a slow smile growing on her face. This was where she had met Salman yesterday, the new security guy on her staff.

Elise had been floating on the ocean surface a hundred meters offshore when she noticed him wandering the perimeter like a lost puppy. She had slipped underwater and closed in like a shark. She even hummed the *Jaws* theme while she crept up behind him and launched the mechanoid onto her unsuspecting prey. The look on his face . . .

No matter how many times she had done that in Charlotte, it never got old.

Salman was nice. A little weird and awkward, but he seemed like a decent guy. Elise liked her men a little off. Mama always said to watch out for guys who were a bit too on the straight and narrow. The ones who showed a little bend were the good and honest ones. Mama was also a hippie from Portland and Dad was a bona fide weirdo, so all her advice needed to be taken with a grain of salt. Well, she and Salman were stuck on this giant metal raft for the next two years. She would have plenty of chances to get to know him.

Elise continued past the lower dock corridor and cut through Sector Two. Her sector. The idea that some supposedly very smart people decided to make her a sector chief blew her mind. As the youngest chief on Nutris and head biologist, she had an important role, and she wasn't going to let any of her recommendations down.

Just last week, they'd found another of those plague blooms, a tiny one on the bottom of the Caspian Sea. Whatever this thing was, it was spreading. Fortunately, early trials were promising. The world community had caught the plague in its infancy, and the odds were good that they could nip the whole thing in the bud. Thank Gaia. If they hadn't, that nasty mutation would theoretically have killed millions of cubic kilometers of ocean within a matter of years.

Elise had long come to accept that the tedium of the next four hours was just as important as her work four kilometers underwater. From their food reserves, to that new space-age energy generator, to the hordes of new staff coming online, the grand poobahs left very little unturned. Paper-pushing kept the lights on and the labs funded, Director Hammon liked to say. It was still a little soul-sucking but she grinned and bore it. By the time it wrapped up late in the afternoon, an early dinner or nap was in order. That or drinks.

"Hey, Elise," Hugh, the security head from Sector Four, called out to her as the meeting wrapped up.

She motioned for him to follow her into the hallway. "What's up?"

"You remember that security guard you transferred to my sector?"

"The Father Time guy with the long beard? About two weeks ago?"

"Yeah. Thanks for that, by the way. Great having a guard who uses a walking stick to go on patrol."

She grinned. "How's he working out?"

Hugh shrugged. "He's not. The guy was around for a few days and then he went missing."

Alarms rang in Elise's head. They were floating on a giant platform filled with nooks and crannies and hundreds of places to fall accidentally into the middle of the Arctic ocean. She should have known better. Her initial instincts when the man had first approached her to ask for a transfer from Sector Two to Sector Four, on the grounds that Sector Two was too large for him to patrol, were simply to discharge him and send him off to retirement.

However, she had occasionally been beaten in triathlon and marathon races by ninety-year-olds, so she didn't feel right firing someone simply because he was elderly. If the guy thought he could do his job, then by Gaia, Elise was going to let him prove to her that he could. Still, she couldn't help but think she'd made a mistake, and a costly one at that.

"Did you report this to the director? Have you sent out search parties?" she asked. "I can get divers to survey the water under the platform. Maybe he fell and—"

"Already did. We came up empty," said Hugh. "I had my guys go over all of Sector Four as well as his housing module. This morning, I went to go pull up his personnel files and got nothing. He's not in our systems."

Elise frowned. "That's impossible. I saw them before I sent him to you."

"That's the thing," he replied. "I saw them too when he came over, but they're gone now. All of them." Hugh looked behind him at the meeting room, where the director was still chatting with his deputy. "I really don't want to go in there and tell Hammon that I lost a guy who somehow doesn't exist."

"Yeah, I could see how that could be an uncomfortable conversation," Elise said. "What about landside? Can we query his background sources?"

"What sources? I can't find anything."

The two stood in the hallway in awkward silence. "Well," Elise said finally, "part of me wants to say, if you don't say anything, I won't either, but that's probably the wrong way to go about it." She thought for a moment. "Go back to the security recruiting files and match them with our staff counts. He had to have come up through there somehow. If that comes up blank, then we have a problem and can't rule out espionage. Until then, don't raise the alarm until we're sure this ghost doesn't exist and we have all our asses covered."

"Sounds like a plan," Hugh said.

"Keep me updated."

Elise watched him head toward the communications room to make the request. She had a bad nagging feeling about all this. A person disappearing like that was nearly impossible. It could be espionage, but who would want to do that to the Nutris Platform? They were a nonprofit and one of the most open-sourced projects in the world. It made no sense.

Elise needed something to take her mind off the long meeting and the news about the ghost guard. Her nice day had taken a turn for the worse and had put a damper on her good mood. She exited the Head Repository and made a beeline toward the nearest bar.

She looked to her right and her face brightened. "Just what the doctor ordered, Elise Kim. Ask and you shall receive," she quipped. She walked toward a figure lounging against the wall. "First day and already sleeping on the job, huh?"

ELEVEN

THREE MARKS

The morning after James arrived on the Nutris Platform, he got lost again, and this time Elise wasn't around to bail him out. Time was short. Nutris was coming online tomorrow morning and would burn down into the ocean by the afternoon. He had spent the entire night wandering around the sectors, mapping the areas and pathing his objectives. It took him until well past dawn before he was able to verify all three targets and formulate a plan.

His AI band would be able to identify the marks once he got inside, but until then, he had to do all the legwork himself. He had originally thought it'd take just a few hours to trace his steps and have his AI band build a functioning map. Unfortunately, the floating city was even more confusing by night than during the day. Not all the lights on the walkways were fully operational yet. James got lost often and ended up wandering in circles. By the time dawn rolled around, he was exhausted and just wanted to get some sleep. Unfortunately, he had to report for his first day of work.

This had been one of his initial concerns with tying himself to the network, but in the end, the advantages outweighed the risks. That was why he had put himself on a security team. Security work was still security work after four hundred years. Sure, a late-twenty-first-century gun was completely different from an early-twenty-sixth-century wrist beam, but it was still patrol, take cover, aim, and shoot. The philosophy of it hadn't changed since these primitive times.

Scratch that. "Primitive" wasn't the right word. This time period was considered the zenith of humanity's achievements before the Great Decay began. While the present certainly boasted some advances in space travel, the military, and colonization, many more technologies were lost from four centuries of war and famine.

The sector commander decided in the first five minutes that he hated James, which really wasn't a big deal since the guy was going to be dead in a day anyway. Until then, though, the doughy commander, a nearly unheard-of adjective in the present day, put him on patrol on the western blocks of Sector Two. That suited James just fine. It gave him the chance to review the layout in his head.

By his estimate, it would take at least an hour to hit all three facilities. He wasn't sure how much time he had before the entire city sunk, but he wasn't taking any chances. Two of the marks were in this area and patrolling gave him the opportunity to enter all the buildings and pinpoint his intended targets. By the time his shift ended, he had mapped his entire retrieval route for the first two marks.

The only thing left was the data core housed in the Head Repository. He would have to go in on that one blind. Access to that building required the highest clearance level, one that James had not given himself. He had initially been tempted to grab the access he needed, but had decided against it. The only people with access to the Head Repository were senior leadership. They probably all knew each other, and a stranger's name mysteriously appearing on the access control list would raise questions.

James did the next best thing and scouted around the building, looking for someone with access his AI could duplicate onto his band. With his shift over, he leaned against the wall opposite the Head Repository and watched the people coming in and out. All of them had their access to the building imprinted on their badges. He'd need to tail one of them and get close enough for his AI to swipe and imprint the access codes onto his own badge. It was that, hack the access control lists, or break the door down as the city sunk into the ocean. The first option was the quickest and most elegant. He'd need those precious seconds.

"Smitt," he thought. "What's the distress call time stamps on the morning the platform sunk?"

"Three hours forty-six minutes between the initial distress call and when the first craft reached their location. By that time, there were only massive oil fires on the surface of the water and high radiation signatures in the entire region."

Not a lot of room for error; none, actually. His initial assessment had been right. This was a difficult mission. It would be a miracle if he got all three marks out. Still, he had to try. This was his ticket out of Chrono-Com.

"First day and already sleeping on the job, huh?"

James turned toward the voice and saw Elise walking out of the Head Repository.

A genuine smile appeared on his face and he waved. It felt strange. Then he noticed her uniform. Now that she was out of her control suit, he could see that Elise was corporate military and a colonel to boot. He stopped midwave and saluted.

She gave him a lazy salute back. "Only when we're on the job and in the presence of officers, pal. I'm just a civilian they slapped a pretty badge on. It's hard enough to make friends around here as it is."

"For you? Hard to believe."

"That's what I thought," she feigned exasperation. "But two-year stints mean all the civilians they recruited have families. Not many singles sign up for this type of job knowing that they're stuck here the entire time."

"There are at least two of us." He shrugged. Immediately, he regretted saying that. What was he thinking? He had work to do, and less than sixteen hours to do it.

She took her badge off her collar. "Well, I'm off duty now. Guess you can buy me dinner."

Her directness stopped James in his tracks. On the one hand, he'd love to spend more time with Elise. On the other hand, she was a distraction he didn't need on this job. After all, the entire place was going up in a ball of radiated fire tomorrow. Hanging out with a soon-to-be ghost was a sure way for him to screw up the assignment, or worse, get himself killed.

He was about to turn her down when he stopped again. Why couldn't he take this woman—probably the first woman he'd ever been attracted to who didn't make it a business transaction—out to dinner? What was the harm of spending one evening with Elise? It would probably be healthy and help preserve his sanity. He deserved a little happiness, didn't he?

She was a dead person; that's why not. And he had a job to do. His internal struggle continued back and forth for several more seconds.

Elise sensed his hesitation and whistled. "Wow, I totally read all the signs wrong on that one. Color me embarrassed. I'm sorry, crewman. I'll be on my way." She turned away abruptly and sped down the ramp.

James watched as she disappeared around the corner. It was the right thing to do, letting her go. He had a mission. He wasn't from this time. No good could come out of this.

"She's just a ghost. She's just a ghost," he muttered over and over again. "I'll be done with this and be on Europa in a year. Done with all this shit."

He turned in the other direction to leave, and then stopped. Her badge. She had access to the Head Repository. He'd use hers. In fact, it was almost his duty to go buy her a drink to get close to her. James's mouth broke into an almost giddy grin as he chased after her.

"Hey, Elise, hey!" He ran after her and jumped in front of her path. "I didn't mean . . . I'd love to . . . Let me get you a drink."

She arched an eyebrow. "Really? You blew it, pal. I don't need your pity drink. I'll get my own with someone who values my time."

"No, that's not what . . ." he stammered as she walked past him. James bit his lip and cursed.

"Hey, James, is everything all right? Your heart is redlining again," Smitt said.

"Shut up, shut up!" James thought back furiously.

"Don't make me pull you out early. Especially this job."

James watched helplessly as she disappeared around the corner. What was with this place and corners? His mind raced. He didn't have a lot of experience charming women. He hurried after her again.

"Excuse me, Elise," the words hurried out of his mouth.

She turned and studied him coolly. "I believe what you meant to say was excuse me, *Colonel,* or *ma'am.*"

"Yes, ma'am, I apologize for inconveniencing you but I'm new to the Nutris and was wondering if there was a local establishment that served drinks," he said.

"East end of the sector. Three levels up, B15," she said, looking away with an exaggerated expression of indifference. "Now, if you'll excuse me, I have important things to do."

"Could you take me there? I get turned around easily. Last time I got lost in this sector, I nearly starved. If it wasn't for—"

"You're such a dork." She rolled her eyes and smirked. "Fine, I'll take you, but you're buying drinks all night. Before I was going to let you buy me just one, with your pay scale, but now you got a lot of making up to do."

A few minutes later, they were seated in the officers' quarters at the Crystal Proof, one of the two bars in the floating city. Elise, being of proper rank, was allowed to bring James in as a guest. Still, it did earn him a few hard looks, including one from his asshole commanding officer. He guessed there were more single men here than Elise thought.

"So," she leaned toward him, "tell me about yourself. You must have an interesting story."

James watched his words. "Why do you think that? I'm as normal as they come."

She gave him a good-natured look of disbelief. "I don't think so. You look to be in your midthirties, but you don't have anything on you. I don't know anyone this day and age without any mods, implants, or inks. You're as ugly as the day Gaia made you."

James paused. "Why are you having a drink with me again?"

Elise leaned in. "I like a man who's comfortable enough not to get artificial. They just don't make guys who aren't plastic anymore." She reached a hand out and tilted his face left and then right. "There's even scars on your face that you never bothered to have removed. Which conflict were you involved in?"

James's face froze. "Smitt, I need a war. Just feed me something."

"There hasn't been a real war in fifty years. The time period before World War Three was the tail end of mankind's golden era."

"Security," James said. "Private corporate military."

"Ah, you did it for the money."

"Isn't that why we're all here?" he said, taking a sip of twenty-first-century whiskey, which tasted like fine smoke, dirt, and lemons. Obviously, in this century, the art of whiskey-making was at its peak as well. James couldn't remember another moment in his life when he was happier than right now, sitting across the table from Elise while holding this fine beverage.

Elise feigned shock. "What? You're getting paid? Almost all of us here are on stipends."

"What sort of military city puts their people on stipends?" He laughed.

Her face took a turn for the serious. "Wait, you're not kidding? You're actually getting paid? How is it possible that security is getting paid when all the scientists are volunteers?"

James was confused but quickly recovered. "Stipend. Salary. It's all the same thing to me. It is a pittance, though. Now I know why. Didn't realize I had signed up for a silly nonprofit."

He thought to Smitt, "We need to dig deeper on this. Something isn't right. This isn't the military installation we thought it was."

"Checking. Stand by, James."

He spent the rest of the evening admiring her while being a good listener. Elise was very animated when she talked, her small hands gesturing with each word coming out of her mouth. Her head often joined the dance, bouncing her dark red hair—cut just below the shoulders—whenever she was making a point.

What James liked best of all about Elise, though, were her eyes. They sparkled, and he found himself being drawn back to them over and over. The color of her eyes wasn't physically bright, actually quite a dark brown, but she had a way of lighting everything up when she looked at him.

Elise was born in a place called Lincoln in the heart of North America on the border of the Confederated United States. She moved west to Portland in the Democratic Union at the age of nine and lived there until she went to Berkeley to study biology.

By the time her life story got to her twenty-second birthday, his AI band had finished copying her badge. That should have been his signal to retire and get some rest. Historical records showed that the explosion occurred sometime in the early morning. He had to be ready. Instead, James stayed and listened to her for another hour until she finished her life story up to about ten minutes ago.

She had begun her career on the hybrid Eco-Kelp Initiative growing mutant kelp that cleaned ocean water, and eventually moved on to the Ozone Terra-Layering Program, where at the ripe old age of twenty-six she became one of the foremost biological technologists in the world. Now, at thirty-one, she was the head biologist for the Nutris Initiative's Bacterial Assembly Project, and a civilian colonel to boot.

"So what would the military want with bacterial assembly?" he asked, polishing off his sixth glass of whiskey. This stuff was so good he had to drink his fill now before his jump tomorrow, hangover be damned.

She arched her eyebrow. "Are you messing with me? That's the second time you said that. Why on Gaia do you think this is a military base?"

James didn't have an answer. Because Smitt told him so wasn't a good enough reason. Some of the things he'd learned tonight didn't match the briefing, and while bad information wasn't uncommon, it was rarely this far off the mark. But then, this was supposed to be a secret installation, so perhaps the real reason behind the platform had been lost in time. Or maybe this was Elise's cover? James's mind raced in circles as he thought of the possibilities. He didn't like not knowing. At the end, though, he reminded himself, it shouldn't matter. He had a job to do.

It was getting late, though the arctic sun still shone brightly in the sky. A warm orange hue bathed the platform with an eerie luminescent glow that reminded him of a rare pleasant dream. With the way this evening had gone, James doubted his dreams could best its reality.

Elise was a little tipsy, having taken him for his word and drunk her fill, and then some. She wavered a little on her feet, only occasionally leaning on him for support as they walked back to her habitat.

"All right, mister," she said, pointing at the door. "This is where I get off. Let's do this again real soon. Tomorrow?"

James couldn't bring himself to say yes.

She rolled her eyes. "It's all right. I'm getting used to your modus operandi. Not exactly a silver-tongued operator, huh?"

James wasn't sure what "silver-tongued" or "modus operandi" meant, but he nodded. "Well," he said, "tomorrow then."

He turned to leave when she grabbed him by the shoulder, rose up on her toes, and kissed him. James froze. She reached her hand behind his head and pulled it toward her. He tasted her dirty martini on her lips and felt her press his body against hers. They lingered, and for a moment, James forgot who he was and why he was here. Elise Kim was the only thing important in his world.

Eventually, she pulled back and mussed his hair. "For future reference, that's what you're supposed to do." And then with a wink, she disappeared into the habitat.

"James, your life signs are all over the place. Is there a problem?"

"I'm good, Smitt," James said. "Real good."

He strolled back toward his pod, enjoying the cool breeze and the ocean air one last time. Compared to most missions, this one had been magical, and it was all because he had happened to meet Elise. It was just too bad it'd have to end tomorrow. James desperately hoped he wouldn't run into her. There was no telling how he might react.

He was almost back at his own habitat when he crossed a section of Sector Two he hadn't wandered through before. One of his bands signaled an alert. Alarmed, James scanned the area.

"Smitt, something is wrong. Jump band just triggered a warning. The chronostream here is frayed. Someone recently jumped into this zone."

TWELVE

SUNKEN CITY

The explosion kicked off the morning with a thunderous boom that rocked the entire platform. Sometime between when he had dropped Elise off at her habitat and sunrise, Sector Four's hydro plant had overloaded and obliterated the sector, crippling the entire city. Unfortunately, Sector Four was the central hub that housed the main foundation that kept the city together. Years of careful planning fell apart within a matter of minutes.

Soon, the connecting modules frayed as the supports for the facility were thrown off balance. Entire buildings, some almost as tall as skyscrapers, toppled into the ocean. Fires broke out across the adjacent platforms.

James rushed out of his habitat and saw Sector Three crack down the middle, splitting what used to be the cafeteria in two, dumping buildings and throngs of people into the ocean. All around him, masses of screaming people fled toward Sector Five to try to escape on transports.

James powered on his exo and waded through the injured and the dead, mentally blocking out the grim sight. The air was filled with the sounds of a city dying, not unlike when he had worked a salvage through the razing of Carthage, or the rape of the Copernicus Luna Colony during the early days of the Warring Tech period.

James didn't think a platform this large could sink from one explosion, even if it had occurred at a critical structural point. The sinking must have been the result of either criminally negligent engineering or an unfortunate coincidence. James wasn't a big believer in coincidences.

An entire group of people running in front of him disappeared under a toppling building, their cries for help drowned by the screech of tortured metal. Another group was swallowed by the ocean when the platform below them gave. Everywhere he ran, the loud crack of metal tearing followed. James pushed the people out of his mind and continued on. The past was already dead. He was only witnessing the last moments of a historical replay.

A lighting tower squealed and collapsed as he passed underneath. If his exo hadn't been at full power, it might have killed him. James brushed it aside and continued to an underwater test lab on the lower level of Sector Two where the first mark, a subparticle filterer, was located.

Abandoned and unmanned, the lab tilted at a fifteen-degree angle. Water was pooling at one corner of the room. He waded waist-deep through the hallways until his AI band identified the mark, a series of intricate machines connected by tubes and filters in a mostly submerged room. James cut the connections from the floor, ripped the cylinder and the machines out of their foundations, and placed them in his netherstore.

"Great abyss, Smitt." James watched as his power levels dipped. "This thing weighs a couple of tons. It's draining the netherstore faster than anticipated. I'm not sure if I can store all three containers and still maintain enough power for a jump back."

"Make do, James. Reduce power to some of your bands if you have to."

James ran out of the teetering building and sped toward the second mark. Within minutes, his levels were down to 94 percent.

James sped past several groups of people clinging to whatever they could grab for dear life. Others were still futilely trying to reach the transports in Sector Five. He wanted to yell that none of the ships on Nutris would escape the doomed platform. He wanted to tell them to make peace in their last precious moments alive.

James could have sworn he heard a woman's voice calling for Salman. If he actually had, he knew who that would be. Elise Kim was the last person he needed to see right now. He pushed her out of his thoughts and refused to turn around.

The building housing the next mark still had people running around inside. James ignored them as he hurried against traffic toward a giant circular room used as one of the main testing labs on Nutris. He burst into the room and saw two scientists working frantically to dislodge a strange-looking machine from its base. There was a large crystal floating in a glass cylinder at the nexus of an array of machines connected by meshes of strange metal thongs. Several glowing needles attached to circular hoops rotating on axis points surrounded the crystal. James worried that this fragile-looking thing might break if he tore it out of its base.

"Thank Gaia!" one of them shouted, looking his way. "We have to save the bacterial sequencer. Help us get this on the cart."

"You two get out of here!" James shouted, pointing at the door. "The whole place is going down."

The other scientist shook his head. "The sequencer is the key to saving us all. It's more important than our lives. We have to save it."

James's clenched his fist. This he hadn't expected. He powered on his exo, ripped the entire contraption off its supporting pins, and floated it toward the waiting netherstore. The two scientists stared at it, mouths agape. Then they looked at James's glowing hand.

"How did you do that?" the first scientist said, stunned.

"Get out of here before the platform sinks!" James yelled, expanding the netherstore container and pushing the machine inside.

The second scientist stared as the sequencer disappeared into the opened black mouth of the netherstore. "You're . . . you're stealing it! You can't. You don't know what you're doing." She lunged at James.

"I'm sorry," said James as he swung an arm, lashing out with a kinetic coil that struck the scientist in the stomach and threw her against the wall. The first scientist screamed and scrambled toward the exit. James let him go. There wasn't anywhere to run. He closed the loop on the netherstore and made his way toward the Head Repository. The last one was going to be tricky. It was located near Sector Five, and there were bound to be crowds of people in the area.

He was running out of time. James bulldozed through the crowds, knocking anyone in his way off their feet. Between the drain on his netherstore and the platform sinking much faster than anticipated, his window of opportunity was shrinking rapidly.

There was also the matter of the chronostream residue from last night. It hadn't been eight hours since he had detected it. It wasn't a strong tear, but it could still hamper his escape jump. Standard protocol on a detected tear was to clear the tear by any means possible. In other words, abort the mission and leave the area or wait out the tear. But the promise of a golden ticket pushed both James and Smitt on. Right now, James had to be extra careful. He was operating without the safety net of a return jump.

James reached the Head Repository and used Elise's badge to get inside. His mind drifted to her. She was no doubt with the rest of the hopeless masses trying to get on a transport. He hoped she died quickly and without pain. The building was unexpectedly full for a place that was about to sink into the ocean. Men and women ran back and forth, frantically trying to stem the damage and coordinate emergency services. Others shouted into communication arrays, desperately calling for help.

James had to credit them for their dedication to their work. They were still trying to save the platform. Most ignored him as he strolled down to the data center on the lower level. Here were where the critical central databases and control mechanisms for the entire facility were stored.

Elise's access got him inside without any problems. The systems were still online, running on auxiliary power as they tried to upload as much of the databases as possible. James knew that the high radiation would corrupt the majority of the uploads, but the system would stay plugged in until the very last second.

He studied the blinking cores and weighed his options. He wasn't sure if unplugging the systems now would cause a time line ripple, but he didn't have much of a choice. He couldn't afford to wait. If the sector fell into the ocean right now, he could die with it. He ripped the systems apart and moved them into the netherstore. It was near capacity and barely holding the containment field in place.

There was a loud squeal of bending metal and then the room tilted violently. James kept his balance and focused on the task at hand. He floated the last few components that made up the core system into the netherstore. A woman's sharp gasp broke his concentration. James turned around, a coil ready to lash out. He saw Elise hanging on to the railings, staring at him with her hand over her mouth.

"I saw you walk into the Head . . . ," she stammered, her voice hoarse. "What are you doing?"

James froze and dissolved the coil. The smartest thing to do would be to kill her now. He had very little time left to finish the job as it was. The last thing he needed was a distraction. The exo around his hands lit up again. He looked into her terrified face. It was the same look he'd seen a hundred times before. She should be just another in a crowd of ghosts. But she wasn't.

"You have to go," he said. "Get to the transports."

"You just blinked my life's work into nothing," she said. "How did you do that?"

"Go!" He couldn't stand seeing her any longer. He didn't need another ghost haunting his life.

"Not without the core!"

"This place is sinking into the ocean. Just go!"

Elise shook her head. "Security thinks this sector's foundations will hold. This project is too important."

If only she knew how wrong she was. He heard more grinding and another whine beneath his feet as the weakened plates and beams that held up the platform fragmented. The slant of the floor below his feet grew steeper. He had seconds left to finish this job. He moved the last few systems into the netherstore and tied it shut.

"Where did the core go?" she asked again, planting her foot on the floor and crossing her arms. "Answer me!"

"You don't know what you're talking about. You need to—"

The room shook violently, and then gravity abandoned them. Suddenly, they were in free fall. James powered on his exo and braced for the impact. He looked over at Elise, clinging to the railing for dear life. When the tower hit the ocean in a few seconds, she would die. The impact from falling across the room to the opposite wall would kill her. Or she would get impaled by the many jagged metal objects shifting in the room. Or if she somehow miraculously survived all those ways to die, she'd drown in the rising water. There were so many ways to snuff out her life.

Elise screamed, arms flailing as she lost her grip on the railing. She plummeted past him across the room. He gritted his teeth, caught her with a kinetic coil, and enveloped the shield around her. Half a second later, the tower struck the ocean. The entire room seemed to cave on top of them, burying them under an avalanche of electronics, steel, and concrete. Ten tons of debris stood between them and the exit. Then the ocean began to seep in. James prepared to jump. He reluctantly let go of her arm.

Elise looked at him and quivered. "Why are you glowing? What's happening here?"

"I'm sorry," he said. "I have to go."

Tears streamed down her face as the water rushed into the room, creating dozens of small waterfalls. "Go where? We're trapped. All those poor people." She wiped her sleeve against her face and looked at him.

James checked the pressure. They were sinking into the ocean fast. He had held off jumping because of her. He should have left minutes ago.

"Good-bye," he said, trying to convince himself that he meant it this time.

"Smitt, jump me back," he thought.

"About damn time," Smitt responded. "Jumping in five, four, three . . ."

James watched Elise as the water rose up to her waist. She looked terrified but kept her composure. "I guess you're right. Good-bye, Salman. At least we won't die alone." She reached out to him.

She was wrong. James closed his eyes. He couldn't stand to look at her right now. He couldn't even provide her that small comfort. In that instant, he loathed every fiber of his being.

"Two, one . . ." Smitt said.

"I'm sorry to leave you," he said, his voice breaking. "And good-bye."

"Jumping!"

James waited for the yellow flash. Nothing happened.

THIRTEEN

EXPLAINING

James froze in shock as the mesh of metal closed in around them. Both his atmos and exo were straining against the outside pressure caving in on them. "What's the problem, Smitt?" he thought urgently. "Why didn't we jump?"

"Hang on, checking," Smitt responded. A few seconds later: "You're still too close to the tear. You can't jump until you're downstream!"

"Why the abyss were we not informed? I want someone's head when I get back! Is it from an illegal jump?"

"I don't know, James. The tear is weak; you must be on its edge. You just have to hold out a little while longer. Stay alive!"

James checked his levels: 35 percent. He was cutting it close. Elise huddled close to his body. If she got more than half a meter away from him, the pressure would kill her. Should he let go?

Elise closed her eyes and took a deep breath, her chest rising and falling as she struggled to remain calm. Her lips moved as she whispered a prayer. James could feel the rapid beating of her heart. She opened her eyes and looked straight into James's. "Mom said it's useless to waste tears. It was nice knowing you, Salman."

"Hold on," he said, wrapping an arm around her waist and squeezing her tightly. He threw out two kinetic coils and parted the debris, pushing it aside as he launched at the wall. Then with a concentrated burst, he punched a hole through it with a third and escaped into the open water. They found themselves floating deep in the ocean. Wreckage from the surface rained past them in slow motion, disappearing into the darkness below. Above them, an angry red and yellow kaleidoscope of lights danced on the ocean's surface.

Elise touched the edge of the shield. "How is this possible? How are you doing this?"

"Stay close to me," he said as he pushed upward. Between keeping the shield strong against the underwater pressure and maintaining the integrity of the netherstore, his levels were depleting rapidly. He had to get to the surface and lower the drain. If the container failed, this job would be a complete loss.

A moment later, his head broke the surface. They were floating on the ocean in the middle of a firestorm. The water burned from the oil that had ignited on the surface. Explosion after explosion blew more plumes of smoke into the air. The normally clear blue sky was tainted with black clouds that blotted out the sun.

With Elise still clutching his waist, James swam toward a piece of floating wreck. He powered them onto the platform, taking a few cautious steps as it bobbled on top of the fiery waves. Elise let go of him and tried to step away.

James tightened his grip and pulled her back abruptly. "Stay inside the shield."

She looked like she was about to snap back, and then hesitated. The two stood close together and watched the remnants of the Nutris Platform, the destruction stretching out as far as the eye could see. There were still people alive. At least a hundred survivors clung to fragments of the wreckage.

How had history reported this a total loss? First-response teams to this disaster arrived within hours. Surely, some of the people here must have held on until rescue. James checked the readings in the area and then realized why: there was so much radiation, someone might as well have dropped a nuclear bomb on top of them. The poor survivors floating out there hoping for rescue would be dead soon from a fate worse than drowning or fire.

Elise struggled to get away from him again. He held her even more tightly.

"Let go of me."

"Listen, Elise," he said. "There's enough radiation here to cook you to a crisp."

She stopped struggling and looked up again at the glimmering shield surrounding them. "And this thing is protecting us from it?" she asked.

He nodded.

"And that's how we were able to survive underwater?"

He nodded again.

Her mouth fell open. "That's not possible. I mean, technology like this doesn't exist."

"Not in your time."

It took a few seconds for those words to sink in. "That's not . . ."

James shook his head. "Assume for a second, as we're floating on a hunk of metal in the middle of a radiated ocean, that I'm not a liar. Because we're still alive, and unless it's some kind of voodoo magic I'm summoning from the depths of the abyss, it's obviously possible."

"Touchy," she said, a hint of the Elise from last night returning. "So if your glitter bubble is protecting us from the radiation, what about all those people out there?" She motioned at the dozens of people close by, shouting for help. By now, many of them were probably already succumbing to radiation sickness.

James shook his head. "I can't do anything for them."

"Those are people out there!" she said, horrified.

"I can't help everyone, Elise."

"They'll die, Salman! We can't just sit around and do nothing."

"My name's not Salman. It's James."

"James," she said flatly. "James the time-traveling jerk who leaves people to die."

"That about sums it up. Now, stop squirming. We're not out of trouble yet."

"What happened to you not being a liar?"

"I lied."

He pushed her down to a sitting position and took a seat next to her. He checked his levels: 22 percent. It was dropping too fast. At this rate, the shields would fail before he cleared the tear. He could release the netherstore containment; that would reduce the power usage enough to wait the situation out. But then, he would lose the entire salvage and any hope of leaving ChronoCom.

"How is it looking, Smitt?"

"The tear has almost passed but is still close enough to keep you from jumping. I don't think it'll be that much longer. Hang in there."

James looked out at the sea of destruction. He watched as a young woman pulled herself onto an overturned platform—a piece of a roof, it seemed—and looked over at him. They stared at each other for a few seconds, ten meters of ocean separating them, and then she spasmed, spewed blood, and fell to her knees. James's stomach churned as she wasted away before his eyes.

"I can't stand to watch," Elise moaned, burying her head in his shoulder. "What are we doing here? We have to do something!"

"We are," said James. "We're waiting."

"For them to die?"

James's eyes wandered from the woman, who had now collapsed, to the group of six wailing people hanging on to a beam in the water, to a man who swam into the burning fire to end the pain. Death was putting on a fine show today and James had a front row seat. He had seen thousands of deaths in his lifetime, but these were by far the worst. He looked at Elise. His most egregious sins were yet to come. When he jumped, her lingering death would start as well.

He should be merciful and kill her right now. It wouldn't take much. A quick squeeze of his exo-powered arm would crush the life out of her in seconds. It would be more humane than exposing her to this radiation. If he cared for her at all, he would kill her right now.

The young Nazi soldier appeared, standing on a piece of burning wreckage off to the side. The boy waved. James tore his gaze away and looked again at Elise. His stomach twisted into knots.

Elise looked at him, alarmed. "Are you all right? I thought you said your shield would protect us." She gently cupped his cheeks with her hands and studied his face. "Okay, I need to know. Are you responsible for all this? Did you cause this explosion?"

He shook his head. "I had nothing to do with this. I swear."

She studied him for a few seconds and then finally nodded. "I'm not sure I believe you, James the time-traveling liar, but you saved my life. I owe you one. If we get out of this alive, I'll show you around 2097."

That forced a grin out of him. "I would like that."

She still didn't believe who he was, but, except for Grace Priestly, no one ever did. In nine months, World War III would consume the planet, marking the end of the Final Golden Age and killing a quarter of the world's population. Following the war, a worldwide famine would ravage civilization for another thirty years. Then the outbreak of the AI Wars in 2170 would kill another quarter of the population. No, death now would be a blessing. At least, he kept telling himself that.

The Nazi soldier, suddenly standing next to him, murmured in his ear, "You only think that."

James checked his power: 15 percent. Maybe he was losing that option after all, but he wasn't returning to the present without the damn salvage. Might as well just die here. He knew in his heart he couldn't survive another five years. He'd rather fly into Jupiter than endure any more of this. So either he came home with the goods or he died here with Elise. He could think of hundreds of worse ways to leave this life.

"What's the future like?" she asked, leaning against him.

"Are you making fun of me or do you actually believe me?" he asked.

"Little of both," she said. "Anything to keep my mind off what's happening to all the poor people out there. What year are you from, James the time-traveling liar?"

"Twenty-five eleven."

"Snazzy. You guys must be flying to Alpha Centauri by now. Must be grand."

James's response caught in his throat. Maybe it was better she didn't know. After all, was there a point in burdening her with the knowledge that the future was a desolate shit hole?

"It's pretty grand," he choked the words out. "Beautiful and prosperous worlds."

"Unicorns and spaceships for everyone, huh?"

James looked down again at his power: 9 percent. He could lower the shield level to extend it. It would leak a little radiation in, not enough to kill him, but it'd make them sick. It would buy a few more minutes, at least. Or maybe he should give up the netherstore. Give it up to live or risk keeping it and possibly die? The choice was obvious.

"James," Smitt's voice interrupted his thoughts. "You're out of the tear. Just in the nick of fucking time. Your power is about to fail. I'm pulling you out now."

"Give me a minute, Smitt."

"No time . . ."

"Give me a fucking minute. I'll let you know when to initiate the jump."

There was a pause. "All right. On your mark, but hurry up. You're at eight percent."

He grabbed Elise and squeezed her, and she squeezed back. His thoughts drifted back to Sasha and his mother.. He had failed them both. His failure to protect the ones he loved was the one constant, and now this pattern was about to repeat itself. He lifted her chin with his finger and stared into her eyes.

"What is it?" she asked.

He leaned forward, arched her back and kissed her, a gentle touch of the lips. At first, she stiffened in surprise and pushed back, and then she relaxed. He felt the coolness of her wet skin against his, and the warmth of her tongue as she reached up and pulled him into her. At that moment, his heart hammered his chest so hard it threatened to break out. He could hear it screaming at his brain as his brain told his body to let her go.

"James, you're too low. I don't give an abyss what you say. You're coming in now! Jumping in five . . ."

"Damn it, Smitt, wait!"

"Four . . ."

James pushed her away and turned his back to her. Tears that hadn't fallen since he lost Sasha flowed down his face.

"What's wrong?" she asked, confused.

"Three . . ."

Smitt's fucking buzzing. James wanted to strangle him right now.

"It's not that," he said. "I'm sorry."

"Sorry for what?"

"Two . . ."

"Good-bye," James said.

"One . . ."

"I don't understand," Elise said.

The yellow light began to flash. James turned to capture her memory in his mind for the last time. She would succumb to the radiation within minutes of his jump. Another ghost in the long trail of deaths. She was already dead. Just another . . .

There you go again, Grace echoed in his other ear.

What's another death among thousands? The Nazi soldier shrugged.

Sasha looked at him and then turned away, saying nothing.

"Fuck my life!" he screamed, grabbing Elise by the arm and pulling her close.

Then the entire world turned yellow.

FOURTEEN

BUSINESS AS USUAL

Levin was not looking forward to the Auditor Chain Council today. He was sitting at his desk when the surroundings of his room disappeared, overlaid by an image of a large round table with twenty auditors encircling it, a modified paint module beaming each and every one of their images to the rest.

Cole's trial was still fresh in everyone's mind, and Levin could tell that the other nineteen high auditors in the solar system were all walking delicately around the subject. He was grateful for their sympathy but irritated by their consideration as well.

After all, if these seniors of the chain felt the need to dance around him with such care in regards to his nephew's trial, this meant the dishonor still clung to him. Even personally capturing and sending Cole to Nereid, the most severe of all possible sentences, did not seem to fully restore his standing among them. And if he had not reclaimed his respect among the most senior of his colleagues, what chance did he have with the lower of the chains? Or the chronmen tiers? Or even the monitor ranks?

Authority might stem from rank but leadership stemmed from respect; therefore, if Levin no longer held his peers' respect, it did not matter if he was a high auditor or fresh to the chain. In the end, Levin did the only thing he could do: he faced their backhanded sympathies with as much dignity as he could muster, and took his rightful place as high auditor of Earth.

The beginning of the meeting went as planned. High Auditor Lynch of the first chain gave the signal. Each of the high auditors began by providing a status of their region. Levin, as the steward of Earth, was last, given the planet's honored status as the ancestral home of the civilization, with the deepest trove of salvages. It was also the most difficult to manage and the largest pain in the ass for the agency.

It was an important position even though Levin was only of the ninth chain, which was considered low for the high auditor of Earth. In his case, it was doubly unusual because though he was considered one of the most successful stewards of Earth in the past hundred years, he still had not risen up the chain. That was another sore for Levin, one he preferred not to delve into.

When it was his turn, though all his peers were already well aware of Cole's infraction, Levin summarized it once more, priding himself on his passive, unemotional delivery. Whether Cole was his nephew or no, Levin Javier-Oberon was still the high auditor of Earth, and he intended the rest of the Chain Council to be aware that his diligence and dedication were intact.

"Very well." Lynch nodded when Levin finished. "Off to the space sectors. Auditor Rowe?"

The high auditor of Space Sector Six spoke. "A Tier-5 chronman by the name of Bond, less than two months from achieving the Tier, recently tried to jump back to 2377 and prevent the outbreak of the first Gas Wars from happening. Her initial job was to return to 2335 for a minor plutonium shipment recovery, but she changed her jump setting at the last second. Fortunately, her handler caught the violation and pulled Bond back before she could do any harm."

"Consequences?" High Auditor Marn of Ganymede asked. That was what anyone here really cared about. Nobody on the Chain Council cared why the chronmen did what they did. Everyone had their reasons— personal, political, religious, or self-righteous. In the end, the only thing the men and women who dedicated their lives to ChronoCom cared about was whether the time line remained intact, and what was the potential impact of forever losing that chronological location.

"Modest," Rowe continued. "The location was the Dione Skirmish; the sixth one. Affected jump region was the battle between two now-dissolved Pangaea patrol ships and a Valta Corp transport. Anticipated potential recovery of one hundred thirty-one units of recoverable power."

Lynch grunted. "Not insignificant. Root cause action?"

"Bond's ancestral family had significant shares in Pangaea. Seems after they lost that war with Valta, it impoverished the family. We believe Bond joined the Academy expressly to accomplish this coup."

There was a low muttering among the council. This was uncommon but not unheard of. Every year, there were always a few fools who believed they could change history for one reason or another by joining the Academy and becoming chronmen, not realizing the extent the checks and balances the agency wielded in order to prevent such occurrences. Most of these crimes were cut off at Hops. The handlers had the ability and full authority to retrieve their chronman at will if they believed Time Laws were being broken. Still, isolated incidents did fall through the cracks once in a while.

"We need more stringent psychological standards and testing at the Academy," Levin said, memories of Cole fresh in his head. "We should have had issues like this weeded out before these unqualified candidates are promoted to the tier."

Joellen, the Academy auditor, rolled her eyes. "We already have difficulties replenishing our current ranks. You want to make it more difficult to promote to the tier? By the abyss, we *lowered* standards twice now in the past six years and we're still not making minimum quota."

"You put waste on the line and that leaves more cleaning for the frontline auditors," said Levin, knowingly walking dangerously close to calling out her ability to administer her stewardship. To accuse another auditor of waste was as grave an insult as one within the chain could give.

Joellen bristled and laid into Levin defensively. He didn't blame her. The Academy auditorship was a difficult position, probably second only to that of Earth. However, Cole might still be his nephew if the Academy had adequately weeded him out as it should have. And Ilana might still be his sister.

"That's enough," Lynch said, finally interrupting them after allowing Levin and Joellen to have their say. Both auditors immediately became silent and bowed to each other. They were still colleagues, after all. Lynch's gaze drifted from Levin to Joellen. "Joellen is correct. We've had to become more flexible with standards on every level in order to fill our Academy quotas, which we're still not hitting. Those have been deemed acceptable compromises. However, due to recent events, Levin is correct as well. The mental state of our chronmen especially cannot be lowered. Raise psychological standards and mental trials back to the standards pre-2505. Agreed?"

"As you wish, Highest Auditor," said Joellen.

Levin nodded. "Thank you, Auditor Lynch."

"Moving on," continued Lynch.

The next case was a more interesting one. High Auditor Marquez of Mars summarized a situation where Tier-3 Chronman Taylor actually succeeded in preventing the Enipeus Vallis Colony from being destroyed in the 2472 Mars Famine. It seemed many of Taylor's family had lived in the colony. Fortunately, the auditors were able to detect the ripple caused by Taylor's action before that ripple reached the present. Marquez sent Auditor Sykes back to Enipeus Vallis twelve days after Taylor committed the infraction and destroyed the colony himself, healing over most of the time line.

By that time, though, Taylor had smuggled his family members off Mars. It took Sykes six more weeks of tracking him down before he located Taylor and his family on Proteus. He had to kill Taylor and fourteen of his family members in order to fully restore the chronostream. Auditor Sykes was meticulous on that job, and the ripples caused by his actions did not last out that year. Levin had a feeling Sykes, already a fast climber in the chain, would one day join the Chain Council. The man deserved his place among them.

The list of jobs and crises continued. Even though the auditors were vigilant in guarding the chronostream, not everything could be prevented. It was up to the auditors to implement corrective action in the time line before ripples reached the present. If that happened, then that time line became present, the chronostream was irreparably altered, and there was nothing that could be done. The auditors of ChronoCom could count on one hand the number of times a significant event had ever altered the chronostream.

The council meeting wrapped up shortly afterward, much to Levin's relief. He had not felt this nervous about an Auditor Council meeting since his very first one. When the rest of the council disappeared from his office, he stood up and poured himself a drink. It had been a trying year. He lifted the glass to his lips and sipped the golden brown contents inside, savoring the sweet burn at the back of his throat. Then he poured himself another.

It seemed more often than ever, chronmen were trying either to escape from the present or meddle in the past. It was to be expected, of course. Each year, humanity died a little more. ChronoCom's charter was to fight that decline, yet things had never gotten better. Every year, there was a little less power to utilize. People went hungry a little longer. Lived lives a little harder. They were losing this war.

If it wasn't for the agency, all humans would have become extinct a hundred years ago. Only the salvages of the past had kept the species together. Still, it was an uphill climb, one that was getting harder over time. Things were only going to get worse as people became more desperate. It was something Levin had to prepare for. As the high auditor of Earth, he would lead the front line against the bulk of the crimes against the Time Laws. He would have to be ready.

"Auditor Levin," a hurried voice said at the doorway. Levin raised an eyebrow as Handler Hameel, looking nervous and out of breath, came in and bowed. Something important must have happened if the chief of Handler Operations came personally instead of reaching him through his comm band.

"Yes, Hameel?"

"Pardon the interruption, Auditor, but we have a possible first Time Law violation. One of the chronmen just returned from a job. There were two human-size life signatures on the jump."

It took a few moments for the words to sink in. After all, of all the Time Laws broken in the past, no one had dared ever break the first. If this allegation was true, the agency had just sunk to a new low under Levin's stewardship. He looked back down at the brown liquid swirling in his glass, threw it back in one gulp. Yes, this was definitely a trying year.

FIFTEEN

PRESENT EARTH

The familiar flash of yellow blinded James as he fell into the brown ocean sludge. Immediately, the nausea of lag sickness overcame him as he sank into the thick, quicksand-like waves. The rising and falling of the oily brown gunk rolled over and enveloped him, threatening to worsen his already tender stomach. For a second, he forgot about Elise and let her go as he flailed in the top layer of ocean. Without his actively willing her to be contained in his exo, Elise slipped through it and disappeared into the frigid brown void.

When he realized what he had done, James grasped for her again, but Elise had already disappeared into the depths of the muck and shit. Panicked, James expanded his exo and dove down after her, pushing his kinetic coils out and probing desperately for any sign from her. His exo's power was depleted and couldn't handle the pressure of going much deeper, but he had to try. He knew she should still be nearby. Earth's ocean was caked with six meters of grime before it gave way to actual water. Once she hit that, he would lose her forever.

Then, one of the coils brushed against something solid. James turned and latched on to it. He saw a glimpse of Elise choking, stark panic on her face, and he expanded the shield around her body. He grabbed her close as she choked and threw up into the interior of the shield. When she had nothing more to empty, he held her still as she shivered and coughed.

They stayed there, suspended in the midst of a brown maelstrom roiling all around the shield.

"James, I detected the jump two minutes ago. The collie is on its way. Should be to your location any second. Is everything all right?" Smitt sounded unsure. "I read some weird signatures."

James ignored him as he held on to Elise. Slowly, her shaking became less violent and her grip around his shoulders slackened. Her head moved around his left shoulder.

"Wow, this is cool," she remarked, her voice strained behind the nonchalant words, looking up at the sludge swirling around the protective sphere.

"You all right?" he asked.

She nodded. "I think so. Where are we?"

"The question is when are we?" he said. "We're at the exact same place we were four hundred years ago."

She froze. "This brown gunk is the ocean? What happened?"

"James, come in, man! *Collie*'s above you. Get your ass up there. Your bands are almost dry."

Several bands on James's wrist began to shut down. He diverted all remaining levels to his netherstore, and exo, rad, and comm band. Even then, he had less than a minute left.

"It's a long story," he said. "For now, hold on tight. We need to get out of here."

James put his arms around Elise's waist. A second later, they exploded from the caked layer of ocean and sped up toward the sky. They flew past the low-hanging hazy mist and rose up a hundred meters toward the waiting collie. The collie hovered as it tried to maintain its position against the battering, howling wind. Just as his foot touched down on the wing, the exo's power gave out. James gripped the door handle while Elise held on to him as the wind blasted them horizontal, their legs scrabbling uselessly for purchase against the slippery wing.

"Smitt, get that door open!" he thought desperately.

The winds wobbled the craft, causing it to suddenly drop and nearly dumping James and Elise over the side. The collie now hovered just above the water as the waves swept gunk along the surface of the wing.

"Smitt!" James screamed out loud.

"Working on it!" Smitt answered. "There's electrical interference."

Elise gasped and pointed behind them. James turned and froze. A massive wave was rolling toward them. It climbed higher and higher until all he could see was an entire wall of brown. The impact of the wave would kill them before they drowned.

The collie's door opened with a hiss.

"Get in! I'm putting in *Collie*'s route now. She'll shoot once the door closes."

James could hardly hear Smitt's voice in his head over the low rumbling thunder of the oncoming wave. Fortunately, Elise still seemed to have her head about her. She squirmed out of his grasp, grabbed him by the neck, and heaved them both inside. They tumbled onto the floor as the door shut. A wave struck the starboard wing, tilting the collie and bouncing them against the side wall.

"Get us out of here!" James yelled. A steady stream of brown water battered against the cockpit windows. The two bounced around like balls inside a container before the violent rocking finally stopped and everything grew dead calm.

Elise groaned as she turned from her side and lay on her back. James pushed himself from his belly up to his knees. There was a nasty gash across Elise's cheek and blood was pouring down from the crown of her head. He wasn't in much better shape.

All his bands had powered down except for his comm band and the netherstore, which was barely holding on with its embedded auxiliary power. James unhooked his netherstore band and transferred the link to *Collie*.

This was the first time since he had joined ChronoCom that he didn't have any bands running. Right now would be a terrible time for the cabin pressure of the collie to drop. He had never felt so naked before in his life.

Speaking of naked . . .

Elise was pointing at him. "What happened to your clothes?" His paint had slipped off and he was wearing only a pair of undergarments. "And what happened to your face? It's all white, like an albino's!"

He ignored her questions. "Anything broken?"

Elise groaned. "My head, my sanity, my . . ." She wrinkled her face. "My nose. I smell like I just took a bath in the sewers." She sat up. "But

no, nothing seems broken." She paused. "What about you? You don't look
so hot, and your face is turning paler, if that's even possible."

For the first time, James realized the full extent of the crime he had
just committed. He had broken the first and most important Time Law.
Since ChronoCom's birth in 2363, no chronman had ever dared to bring
someone back from the past before. It was one of the primary laws in-
grained into every initiate early on at the Academy. As far as the agency
was concerned, they were both as good as dead. Not only was it a capital
offense, he could have weakened and endangered the chronostream. Fur-
thermore, the Vallis Bouvard Disaster hung heavy in his thoughts.

James clenched his fists as he frantically tried to figure out how to get
out of this mess in a way that wouldn't involve their execution. The monitors might not know about her yet. Maybe he could hide her. Stash her
in one of the distant outposts. Keep her away from the monitors. The solar system was vast enough that maybe this one accident might slip Chrono-
Com's notice. After all, this had never happened before, as far as he
knew. They wouldn't be expecting it.

The collie made a sharp turn toward Central. He leaped toward the
cockpit and punched in several new commands.

"Why did you put *Collie* on manual?" Smitt asked. "Your AI band is
offline. I can't get a read on your life signs. Are you all right?"

"I'm fine," he thought back. "Will report in soon. Just, um . . . need
to check on something."

"All right, my friend. Whatever you say." Smitt sounded anything but
all right. "Listen, about that strange signature——"

"The comm band is out of levels as well," James cut him off. "Going dark
for a bit. Will report in soon." It was a flimsy excuse. The comm band used
so little levels he could have kept the link open. It was against protocol for
any chronman to disengage from his handler while on assignment without extraordinary cause. Well, James had extraordinary cause, all right.

The collie had reached the eastern seaboard of the Northern American continent. Brown sloping oceans gave way to a gray barren landscape
dotted by the devastation of centuries of war, waste, and environmental
degradation. They were currently flying over a large radiation field of a
wrecked city that had been razed by one of the dozen conflicts.

Elise's eyes had widened like full moons as she stared at the devastation below with a hand over her mouth. She looked at him and pointed

out the window. "Is that the Washington Monument we just passed? What happened?"

That name sounded familiar. James had taken extensive history courses while training to be an operative, but he had always been a mediocre student. It took him a few moments to recall his history and geography.

"Razed in the middle of the Third World War," he said. "Both the Democratic Union and the Confederate United States surrendered the next year to the Tri-Axis Alliance of China, Pakistan, and Russia."

"When did this war happen?" she asked.

James kept his face neutral as he spoke. "Two thousand ninety-eight, the year following the destruction of the Nutris Platform. It lasted nineteen years and cost over forty-three million lives. Global GDP——"

"Stop. Please," Elise looked like she was in shock. She sat down on the bench and buried her head in her hands. "My family. My friends . . ."

James hesitated. Unsure exactly what to do, he reached a hand out and patted her on the back, stiffly. "By the time it happened, you were already dead."

He thought the words would provide her some comfort. After all, it meant she didn't have to live through all that suffering of the years that followed. Instead, she just sat there silently, numb, her arms cradling her knees as she huddled in the far corner of the bench.

Embarrassed and unsure how to handle her, James walked back to the console and checked the scanner. They'd be landing in Chicago in a matter of minutes. He'd have to hide her before heading back to ChronoCom. Maybe after he answered whatever questions Smitt and the monitors had, he could retrieve her. If Valta held up their side of the bargain, he could be in Europa in two days. He'd take Elise with him, of course. Maybe they could start a new life, assuming she even wanted to stay with him.

This was all assuming Elise's health wasn't an issue. If the Vallis Bouvard Disaster was true, people moving forward in time were doomed to become mentally and molecularly unstable. James never put much stock in that story, thinking it nothing more than scare tactics from the Academy, but it poked at the back of his mind. Well, he'd have to wait and see. For her own good, he might have to kill her after all.

The slum city of Chicago appeared on the horizon. First things first, he needed to find a safe place to hide Elise. He lowered the collie through clouds thick with smoke and soot and entered the habitat zone just under the skyways of moving vehicles. Collies were larger than regular low-altitude transports, and his entry beneath the sky lanes was bound to draw attention. They'd have to park the collie and proceed on foot. He maneuvered to the western town of Humboldt, an industrial center that processed the majority of the city's waste, to park between several mammoth buildings with dozens of smokestacks rising high into the sky, each stack puffing out noxious plumes that spread out until they faded into the clouds.

Hopefully, the heavy smoke would hide his entry, and there would be fewer people around this more heavily polluted area. When the collie powered down, James went to the emergency storage locker and pulled out two respirators and chem suits, handing one to Elise.

"Put this on," he instructed. The chem suit was overkill and could draw some attention, but it wasn't unheard of. It would attract a lot less attention than the antique clothes she currently wore, which ironically looked much more futuristic than the clothing of his time. Not to mention the attention his being nearly naked would draw.

Elise, still in shock, took the gray rubber suit in her hand and stared dumbly at it. Then she frowned. "Why did you give this to me? Are we heading to town or are we growing Ebola cultures in a test lab?"

"Your body hasn't been immunized or protected. The air will make you sick until you acclimate or we get you a band," James said. "Also, you don't exactly look like a local. We'll need to hide you for a while until this problem gets sorted."

Elise slipped into the oversize chem suit one leg at a time. She looked like a little girl wearing her father's clothes. "What do you mean, get sorted? What problem are you talking about?"

"Come on. Let's go," he said, opening the hatch and ushering her out. "There are laws that prohibit bringing someone to the present day. I'll explain later."

He hurried away from the parked collie, pulling Elise along by the hand and walking down a narrow road with a dozen of the towering processing plants on either side. Elise stared at gray sky, visible through the crisscrossing gaps between the buildings. James kept a hand on her wrist and led her along. A few minutes later, they entered an underground tunnel to the mass transit, and were soon moving deeper into the Earth. Elise, her face covered by the respirator, looked around the train, packed with dirty and tired workers returning from the night shift.

She tugged on his arm. "Are you sure we're in the future?"

"Do they have flying cars in your time?" he said.

"Well, they sure had this same sort of transit system," she said. "I mean, how do you still use the same trains from four hundred years ago?"

"I don't know," he said. "I'm not from around here."

"Then why are we here? Where are you from?"

James leaned in and lowered his voice. "Born on Mars colony."

"Why are you whispering?" she asked.

"Because I don't want anyone to try to mug us," he said, all of a sudden remembering how naked he was without any of his bands.

The train stopped deep underground and James dragged her through the tunnels. They walked for the better part of twenty minutes, past the gray and brown sublevels until they reached the purples. Higher toward the surface, they reached a set of blue tunnels, where the decor was much cleaner than in the previous sections.

"Why would people want to rob you if they think you're from Mars?" she asked.

"Because anyone with any amount of money would have left Earth by now."

They continued down the blue tunnels before eventually arriving at a clean, dead-end street. James led Elise through a set of sliding double doors into a building that was a far cry from the decay they had had to wade through to get there.

The Heights was one of the better hotels in Chicago. It was usually reserved for visiting dignitaries and off-planet corporate executives. The cost of staying here per night was usually more than the employees who worked there made in a week. In the present day, few hotels in the solar system outside of Europa, Callisto, and Titan were considered finer.

Elise wrinkled her nose, clearly unimpressed. "What a dump."

James checked them in to the penthouse and led her by the hand to the unit's private elevator. A few seconds later, they saw daylight as the elevator rose past ground level to display fully the splendor and rot of the city. Elise's eyes stayed glued to the window as she saw the advanced technology and the decay of the present side by side. Dozens of tall skyscrapers rose into the air, their tips lost in the low-lying gray smog clouds that blocked out the sun. More smokestacks rose from the ground, spewing massive columns of smoke that seemed to hold up the clouds.

Hundreds of small vehicles and transports zoomed around the tops of buildings, a swarm of metallic locusts coming in and out of the city over the skyway, which reached out as far as the eye could see. On the ground, those who couldn't afford cars walked, bussed, or trained in huddled masses, like tiny ants.

Everywhere they looked, rust dominated the landscape, from the walls of the buildings to the frames of the cars to the railings of their elevator. Occasionally, a dim pale ray of light would sneak past the thick gray clouds, laying down an orange glaze across a surface, only to be swallowed up seconds later. In the far distance over Lake Michigan, an electric storm sparked and shot long streaks of lightning at the water, puncturing the haze, if only for a moment.

Elise look disgusted as she peered out the window. "Everything looks so washed out. What happened to this place?"

"Not just this place. Everywhere on Earth," he said.

"You sure as Gaia lied about the present when we were underwater, James the time-traveling liar."

The elevator dropped them off at the fifty-sixth level, just below the skyway. James led Elise to the suite. It was a spacious four-by-four-meter room with its own bathroom. A single clean bed occupied the center of the room, and a vid screen was mounted on the opposite wall. Being the most expensive unit available, one of its walls consisted entirely of windows, though the grime caked on several of the panels made it difficult to see outside. At this height, James could see only the brown and black wind as it swirled around the building.

He turned to her. "Listen, stay here. Do not leave the room. Do not answer the door. If the lobby calls up, tell them you're indisposed and do not wish to be disturbed. This is important, understand?"

Elise gasped, momentary panic blanketing her face. "You're leaving? Where are you going?"

"I have to report in. I'll be back; I promise."

"What am I supposed to do in the meanwhile?"

James kept the growing irritation rising up his gut in check. After all, she didn't realize how serious a situation they were in right now. It was all he could do to hold it together and not outright panic. For a brief second, he considered surrendering her. He could tell them it was a mistake, a moment of weakness. Perhaps he could even sell the auditors the story that she clung on to him. There were dozens of scenarios that he could concoct to escape this dilemma. Then he thought about Sasha.

"Fucking abyss," he muttered. He led Elise to the bed and sat her down. "There's nothing to worry about. Get some rest. I'll be back shortly."

She nodded. "What if someone knocks? Room service or something?"

"Don't answer it. If someone does try to come in, run. Hide. It's important no one knows you're here yet. Understand?" She nodded again.

James turned on the vid screen to a channel showing a game of Lok Gull from the Callisto League. That should keep her preoccupied. He got up and walked to the door, looking back at her once more while she sat on the bed, confused and still in a bit of shock. He didn't blame her. She had just traveled from her utopian past to his dystopian present. There wasn't a greater contrast between the two worlds than that. It was a lot for her to take in.

"I'll be back shortly," he repeated, hoping desperately that he was telling the truth and that he was not actually saying good-bye.

SIXTEEN

POWERS THAT BE

The powers that be were not happy when James, about three hours late, finally landed at Earth Central. James watched from the sky as he made his descent toward the landing pad. Smitt was there, flanked by four monitors. From fifty meters away, James could see the worried grimace on his friend's face; he also noticed the fidgeting. The auditors must have really put the screws to him when James went so far off protocol.

James recited his prepared excuses. One of the requirements for being a chronman was thinking quickly on his feet and believing his own lies. During the Publicae Age in the mid-twenty-third century, neural bugs were commonplace and a chronman couldn't even step foot in that period unless he was trained successfully to lie and think through the constant mental surveillance. Still, James had the feeling he had his work cut out for him.

His being gone nearly half a day, especially on Earth, of all places, had to have raised alarms. He wasn't sure how closely he had been monitored, but the fact that they were waiting for him at the landing pad probably meant they had tracked him nearly every step of the way once he hit Chicago's airspace.

James took out the bottle of whiskey he had purchased at the Heights and took a swig, spilling half of it over his collar. Well, he still smelled like sewer, so it might actually have been an improvement. No sooner had he landed and taken two steps out of the collie than all four monitors closed in around him. At least they had the decency not to aim their wrists at him. The fact that he wasn't arrested on the spot was a good sign.

Levin, waiting at the bottom of the ramp with Smitt, somehow looked grim and pleased at the same time. No doubt he was reveling in whatever punishment he was about to dole out to James. The man was finally getting his revenge for that busted jaw. The fool must not know about the agreement with Valta. ChronoCom wouldn't dare rescind a payout from an outside party for a promised contract. If word ever got out that Chrono-Com had done such a thing, the chronmen tier would be in chaos. No, as long as they didn't know about Elise, he was safe.

James walked up to Smitt and Levin, and jammed a thumb at one of the monitors. "Is this really necessary?"

"You went off mission, Chronman," Levin said, "and went dark on your handler."

James shrugged with forced casualness. "Comm band ran out of levels. It was a rough mission. Had to process a few things in my head. I got the job done; went to go celebrate. So what?" He wiggled the bottle in front of them. "Want some?"

Levin's face reddened. "You were drinking on a job during a Tier-1 salvage?"

James held his hands up. "Relax. Calm down before you piss yourself. I didn't start drinking until after the job was done." He took another swig.

Levin didn't see the humor in the situation. "Monitors, take his bands."

James lifted his arms toward the guards as if he didn't have a care in the world. "Go ahead. They're dry anyway." He began to hum.

Levin scowled. "Take him to interrogation. I'll debrief him personally." He turned and stormed off.

James continued to hum and winked at the monitors playfully.

Smitt's face bunched up in a scowl. "You seem to be in a cheery mood for once. I don't like happy you. It feels unnatural. Does your netherstore have all the goods?"

James nodded. He watched as Smitt retrieved the netherstore container from within the collie and handed it off to a tech. The tech checked the content fields against the schematics, probably provided by Valta, and then nodded.

Good riddance, James thought. The instant ChronoCom took control of those items, James's contract with Valta was fulfilled. All he had to do now was survive a little longer and he would soon be free of this nightmare. He could hide Elise for a few months until he finished his ChronoCom contract. Then, with the funds he had saved, he could buy Elise a new identity and they could live out the rest of their days in peace and luxury. James shook his head. How could he think that? He hardly knew her!

He and Smitt walked toward the interrogation room with the four monitors in tow. James could tell Smitt was struggling to suppress his anxiety. His friend wasn't exactly fast on his feet; that was why he had never made tier at the Academy. Still, for him to be this on edge made James uneasy. They were almost at the interrogation room when James decided to probe his handler and see just how bad the situation was.

"What's wrong, man?" he asked Smitt. "I just celebrated a little. Why is everyone so uptight?"

Smitt hesitated. "Monitors detected two signatures during your jump. They think . . ." He was so concerned he couldn't finish the sentence, but the implication was clear.

James's heart sank. If they were able to determine the jump signatures, then he was in trouble. He formulated a new plan. James gazed at his bare wrists. He might even have to fight his way out, though there were some things he needed to retrieve first—a fresh set of bands being foremost. Then, if he somehow escaped, he would need gear to stay alive out in Earth's harsh wastelands. There was no better place to find all these items than here at Central.

James needed time to think. He stopped. "We need to make a quick change of plans."

Smitt looked confused. "Our orders are to go directly to I-Three."

James stepped close to his friend. "I don't know about you, but I think it will do us all a lot of good if I took a shower first. Especially if we're cozying up in an interrogation room for a few hours." He leaned further forward.

Smitt must have finally smelled the bilge on James. He pulled back and scowled. "Shit, man, did you swim in the ocean? Fine, go take a bath first, but hurry."

"Our orders were to escort him directly to I-Three, Handler," one of the monitors said.

James gave the monitor a knowing look. "Come now, I just need ten minutes."

Smitt waved them toward James's quarters. "You guys aren't going to be trapped in a room with him for abyss knows how long. You guys can stand guard outside. I'll stay with him in his room."

After a few moments of hesitation, the monitors agreed and led James to his room. He could hear them chatting about a Lok Gull game right outside his quarters. James hopped in the shower and took his time, humming and chatting with Smitt about starting their new life on Europa while he searched for anything useful in his quarters. Smitt's enthusiasm was a bit more stilted.

"It's probably a blip, right?" James said.

"It's not usual, that's for sure." Smitt sounded worried. "I don't think I've ever seen a dual signature in a jump before."

James kept Smitt talking while he scanned his bathroom. As he changed into a fresh set of clothes, he hid a shaving razor in his pants. It was the best he could do.

"Let's go," he said cheerfully as they left his room.

The monitors closed rank and escorted him to the interrogation room. A few minutes later, James and Smitt walked into I-3, where a fuming Levin scowled from the other end of the table. Levin shot Smitt a furious look.

"He had to take a shower," Smitt said, looking embarrassed.

James shrugged. "I was being considerate. I smelled."

"Let's get down to business," Levin said, his jaw set. "Explain your delay."

James tried to look exasperated. "What's there to explain? Big explosion at Nutris; city sunk into ocean. Thousands of people died. I salvaged the gear and barely made it back." He got up. "Can I go now?"

Levin's eyes narrowed. "Sit down! The monitors recorded a dual signature from your jump. Explain that."

"I don't even know what that means," James said.

"Did someone else come back with you?"

"No. Well, maybe I brought back a couple liters of ocean since I was underwater when I jumped."

"You think Hops can't differentiate between bringing back water and life?"

"I don't know what they don't know," James said. "Maybe some fishes came with me."

"Did you bring back a shark? Because it was a damn large signature," Levin snarled.

"What's a . . . ?" James asked.

"It's a big damn fish!" Levin snapped. He spread his hands out. "This large! Because that's how big it'd have to be for surveillance to register the additional signature."

"I didn't have time to check what type of fish it was," James shot back. "I was busy trying to survive a ground zero radiation blast."

The two stared off. Finally, Levin lowered his eyes to his AI band and spoke in a calmer voice, "Why don't we start from the beginning? And I want every detail. Don't leave out a thing."

With a sigh, James retold his entire job, starting with the explosion and how he had narrowly recovered the three marks for Valta. He continued with the failed jump due to the residual tear in the chronostream and painstakingly detailed the hundreds of slow deaths he saw people dying due to the radiation. Then he talked about his feelings. He followed Levin's orders and reported every minute detail of the mission. Most of them were actually true, but he embellished a little to convey the drama. The only thing he omitted was any mention of Elise.

To Levin's credit, it took almost an hour before he, now completely annoyed, snapped and told him to move on. James gave himself a mental pat on the back. It was a masterful telling. Finally, he moved the story to the return jump to the present, where he began an entirely new narrative. He continued to talk about his feelings, describing in detail about how he felt so completely disturbed by the deaths he saw yet was so relieved he had made it out alive.

At one point, James tried to will tears to drip out of his eyes. His body, however, would do no such thing. He finally finished his story, telling them how he wanted to celebrate the golden ticket by getting a couple of drinks.

Levin raised an eyebrow at that part of the story. "Why didn't you go to the Never Late?"

James smirked. "Because that bar is full of ChronoCom men. I wanted to taste freedom, being so close and all. Feels good to be a ruck, you know."

Levin's eyes glazed for a second before he spoke again. "All right then, tell me about the room you booked at the Heights."

James kept his smile plastered on his face even as his throat closed. Of course Levin checked his transaction records. He had hoped it'd be something the monitors overlooked, but he was prepared for this question as well.

"Whores," he said. "Can't celebrate without them, right?"

Levin looked at the mirror to his left, his head nodding slightly. James turned to it as well and waved. Then he noticed the glimmer in Levin's expression. He'd found something. That couldn't be good.

"You rented a whore to celebrate at the Heights." Levin didn't say it like a question.

James nodded.

"Is she still there?"

James's mind raced. Levin must already know or have something on him; otherwise, he wouldn't have asked the question.

He nodded again. "I did hire her for an entire day. Going to get my money's worth."

"She's the one using your access on the net right now as we speak?" asked Levin.

James's heart sank. Elise must have figured out how to use the vid. "I didn't want her to get bored," he finished lamely.

Levin stood up and banged his fist on the table. "You expect me to believe that you gave a whore your chronman access to the entire vid network?"

It was time for James to double down. He stood up and stuck his face right in front of Levin's. "Yeah? So?"

They exchanged scowls. "Very well, then," Levin said finally. "You might be here a while, so I'm sure you won't mind if we send someone there to bring her back for questioning."

James tried his best to seem nonchalant. "Be my guest, though if she asks for more money, it's coming out of your account." There was nothing he could say to worm his way out of this.

Levin stood and looked at the lead monitor standing guard in the room. The lead monitor nodded and motioned for one of the others to follow him out the door, presumably to pick up Elise. James had to think of something fast.

Before he left, Levin turned back to them. "Handler, escort the chronman to the brig."

Smitt frowned. "Why? Is he under arrest?"

"Not yet."

"Then I'm taking him to his quarters," Smitt said. "He hasn't done anything wrong and is completely unarmed. I can confine his access until then."

Levin shook his head. "To the brig. That's an order. If everything checks out, it'll only be for a few hours and I will be the first to congratulate you both on your soon-to-be new life on Europa."

James and Smitt were quiet as they left the interrogation room. James's mind raced as he went over his options. He would be hard-pressed to beat the monitors to Elise unless he left right now. Fighting out of here without an exo was suicide. They were deep in the bowels of Central, along with the entire garrison. The monitors didn't worry James too much, but there were also at least three dozen chronmen and probably a few auditors here as well. They posed the real threat.

Smitt waited until they were alone in one of the corridors before rounding on him. "Tell me I have nothing to worry about, man. This is our ticket out of here. Tell me we're in the clear and this is just an abyss-wasted exercise."

James hesitated for only a split second before nodding. Smitt, however, had been operating with him since the Academy.

"What happened there, James?" Smitt asked, his eyes opened wide. He had a desperate look on his face. "Look, you can trust me. I've always covered for you."

That much was true. Smitt had never turned his back on him or let him down before. James was going to need all the help he could get.

He leaned in. "I brought someone back."

Smitt's face turned ashen and a moan escaped his lips. "You did what?"

"I couldn't let her die." Now was James's chance to escape. He hoped his friendship with Smitt held. "Listen, I need your help. I need to get to her before the monitors do. Can you help me get my hands on some new bands?"

Smitt look conflicted before he finally nodded. "Your access has been locked out, but mine should be all right. We can go to the armory."

They continued past the holding cells and barracks down to the lower armory level. Smitt punched the security code and opened the main armory doors.

He turned to James. "Listen, James, it's not too late to turn this person in and beg for mercy. Remember, we just got fast-tracked out of this place and into Europa. We got funds saved up. We can get out of here. Think about what you're throwing away."

And for those few moments, James considered it. Elise didn't belong here. She was supposed to be dead. Leaving her with the monitors was assuring her death, but she was already living on borrowed time. It wouldn't be a stain on his soul if he did the right thing, would it? He'd just be following the Time Laws. Righting the chronostream.

Strange, he had used this argument so often when he watched all those other people die. Prior to today, it had always made sense. His absence of action was justifiable. That past was already dead. James was just an observer of their history.

It had even felt right when he left Grace Priestly, the Mother of Time. But now, in the one moment when his entire future hinged on following the Time Laws, it felt like a pitiful excuse. Everything felt wrong.

"I . . . I can't." The words were a struggle to say. He slumped his shoulders. "Not this one. I can't turn my back on these people anymore. I'm sorry."

"I understand." Smitt nodded. He opened the door and led James into the armory. "I'm sorry, too."

Four monitors were waiting for him in the room. "Chronman James Griffin-Mars, you are under arrest for violation of the first Time Law."

"He's harmless! He doesn't have his bands." Smitt yelled, stepping to the side. "There's no need for force. He'll go peacefully. He's harmless."

James wasn't sure what hurt worse: Smitt's betrayal or what he was about to do next.

"I'm sorry too, Smitt," he said.

Then James slipped his hand into his pocket, pulled out the razor blade, and showed everyone in the room just how harmless he was.

SEVENTEEN

ENEMY OF STATE

The two unlucky monitors closest to James were the first to face his wrath. Smitt had barely gotten the words out of his mouth when the monitor to James's right dropped from an elbow to the face. Before anyone else in the room had a chance to react, James rammed the razor into the gut of the one on the left. The monitor stiffened as the blade entered his sternum.

Before the body had a chance to fall, James got behind him and propped his body up as a shield. The odds on a razor blade versus the two remaining armed monitors with wrist beams were poor, assuming Smitt didn't get involved. Fat chance of that happening.

James had faced worse odds before. He surveyed the room. The main armory was square, with shelves lined along the walls and a large workbench in the middle. There was little room for movement and even less cover. The closer monitor, a fodder, judging by his clean-shaven face and textbook shooting stance—one hand gripping the forearm of his shooting wrist—was four meters away to his left.

The monitor farther away, a grizzled veteran by the look of him, stood on the other end of the room. He carried his wrist beam like most other experienced combat soldiers, with one arm extended and the other high-chambered, close to protect his body and face. James went for him first.

He didn't have his bands on him, but against monitors, he didn't need them. Initiates at the Academy didn't even work with bands until their last two years. Before then, combat training was strictly conventional, a field in which James excelled in.

He shoved the monitor in his grasp toward the grizzled veteran and leaped toward the fodder. He slid forward feet first, ducking under a hastily aimed shot. He got close enough to stab the razor down on the fodder's standard steel-tipped boots, reinforced thirteen centimeters from the end. James jammed the razor eighteen centimeters from the tip and felt the blade penetrate the softer plastic right where the ankle met the foot.

Before the surprised fodder even had time to cry out in pain, James pulled the bloody razor out of his foot, and in one smooth motion, flung it at the veteran. The razor missed its mark as the monitor sidestepped and knocked the razor out of the air with his armored forearm. Grizzle was able to get one shot off that went wide to the left before James had covered the distance and was on top of him.

James threw three quick strikes. Grizzle blocked two. The third, a knuckle jab to the solar plexus, right between the protective chest plates of his armor, sent him down writhing on the ground, gasping for breath. One more blow finished him off. James turned to face the two remaining men in the room and barely dodged a wrist beam to the face.

As with many new monitors, this one tended to aim for the head. James attacked. The fodder, having fallen on his back, was able to get off only one more shot before James was on top of him. With one hand, James violently tore off his helmet, and with the other, brought his fist straight down on the poor kid's temple. He watched the fodder's eyes roll up into his head and his body go limp.

James turned to Smitt. As expected, his only friend in the world hadn't moved from his place. His ex-handler was always more brains than fight. In this case, he wasn't much of either. James wasn't sure what to do with him. Killing his only friend in the world, even if Smitt had betrayed him, was something James couldn't bring himself to do.

The blood had drained from Smitt's face. He turned and tried to flee the room by running through the wall. He succeeded in only banging his head against the shelf and growing a welt. Smitt turned back to James, rubbing the angry knot on his head, and begged for his life. "I'm sorry, my friend. It's for your own good. There's nowhere to run, James."

James took a slow step toward Smitt, still unsure how to deal with him.

"You know Levin won't stop going after you." Smitt sounded desperate. As he should be.

James took two more steps, cracking his fists. They throbbed in a way he hadn't felt in years. He wasn't sure but he might have broken his forefinger on his right hand. It has been a long time since he last fought without his exo. His mind wandered back to the first time he and Smitt had met at the Academy.

James had just failed a communication channel construction test while Smitt had failed his first-year physical for the second time. They both happened to wander into the Fresh Fish bar to drown their sorrows, which is where they met. They had agreed to help the other pass their tests and had become fast friends.

The right thing for James to do was kill Smitt right there. Smitt knew far too much about him. The auditors could use him to track down James and Elise. After all, James was a wanted criminal. He had broken the Time Laws he had sworn to uphold. Not just any Time Law, but the first and most important. If any other chronman had done the same, James wouldn't have hesitated to take him down as well, if ordered. He reached out, grabbed Smitt's collar, and slammed him back into the wall.

He wrapped his hands around his friend's neck and squeezed. "Unlock the lockers. Now."

Smitt nodded, a choking sound crawling out of his mouth. "Done."

A dozen security locks behind him switched off. Then Smitt closed his eyes and waited for the killing blow. James reached one hand behind Smitt's head and put the other on his chin. One quick twist and his friend wouldn't feel much pain. A low, guttural cry escaped his lips as he twisted, and then stopped.

Smitt opened one eye, puzzled. "Get it over with, James, and for what it's worth, I'm sorry."

"That means a lot to me," James said.

A little of the tension left Smitt's terrified face. "You've always been my brother, and I'll—"

James punched him across the jaw and knocked him unconscious. He shook his fist as he looked down at his fallen friend. He'd definitely let his hands get way too soft, relying on his exo these past few years. Smitt was going to wake up with a splitting headache and maybe a busted jaw, but at least he'd be alive.

True to his word, Smitt had unlocked all the storage containers. If James was going to keep Elise alive out there, he'd need supplies. He grabbed stashes of survival gear: wasteland kits, including provisions, water containers, med kits. Then he rummaged through the holds and equipped his wrists with all the bands he needed. Not knowing when or if he could ever acquire any more of this technology, James stuffed several extra bands into his netherstore, including extra comm, AI, and atmos bands for Elise. An exo would be too complicated and dangerous for her to learn. Instead, he stowed a stash of standard monitor wrist beams. Elise might need to know how to use one to protect herself. Also, there was always a black market for these items. His account would undoubtedly be frozen after this incident, and he would need to find the scratch somehow.

After he had cleaned out the armory, he checked each of the five bodies on the ground. Smitt and one of the monitors were still unconscious, two were dead, and the last one was coming to. James slammed his head to the ground once more for good measure. He briefly considered using the paint band on one of the monitors to sneak out of Central but decided against it. It would take a paint band too long to accurately scan and duplicate a person's face, and time was of the essence right now.

James took off from the armory at a brisk walk. Any faster would attract undue attention. Luckily, the melee in the armory had occurred so fast that none of the monitors had a chance to sound a general alarm. Monitors weren't issued comm or AI bands, for the same reason they weren't given exo bands. These were high-tech bands that were too resource-prohibitive to allocate to common soldiers. Right now, this worked to James's advantage and bought him precious minutes. However, an operations handler would probably expect the team to check in shortly.

The first thing he had to figure out was a place to lie low. Chicago and any of the large cities would be dangerous to hide in; ChronoCom had too much influence over the more civilized settlements, which wouldn't hesitate to hand the fugitives over. That left the wildland settlements or possibly the wastelands.

James headed off toward the hangar. As usual, Earth Central was lively even late into the evening. Planetary salvages occurred at all times, and the exporting of the recovered materials continued around the clock. This made the hangar the busiest place in the entire base. He kept his face neutral and his gait steady as he made his way down the crowded hallways.

Most of the personnel steered around him as he walked, paying him no more attention than usual.

He estimated he might have ten minutes before someone sounded the alarm and all of Central went on lockdown. James was sure the hangar was already being watched, but he had to take the chance. If it was unguarded or lightly guarded, he could quickly overpower the monitors and escape in the collie. If not, well, there was always Plan B. James reminded himself to think of a Plan B.

He would also want to rethink what was considered lightly guarded. With an exo, James was confident he could take on ten monitors dug into defensive positions. Maybe even fifteen, though he wouldn't expect to come out of that unscathed. If there were other chronmen around, his odds decreased dramatically. James was good at what he did, and maybe he could take on a chronman with a team of monitors, possibly even two. Any more was a guaranteed loss. If there was an auditor there, all bets were off.

He reached the south wing hallway leading to the hangar. The traffic was thick as a constant stream of personnel and shipments passed in both directions. It allowed him to blend in with the crowd, but slowed his progress to a crawl. This delay was unusual and seemed like a suspicious coincidence. James didn't believe in coincidences.

He left the slow-moving line and looked over the crowd still working its way into the hangar. Two monitors manned the doorway, waving people through. On the surface, everything seemed normal. Maybe the alarm hasn't been raised yet. Maybe James could get past the checkpoint and out on the collie before anyone was the wiser. There was only one way to find out.

Not believing his good luck for a second, he pushed his way to the front of the line, preferring speed over subtlety. No one was going to argue with a chronman about cutting. He was now less than fifty meters from his escape. He could be out of here with no one the wiser. And just when he was starting to believe his good fortune, Central decided to burst his bubble.

His face popped up through the emergency channel of his AI band, and he saw several more images of himself appear across several of the security monitors. At first, he didn't recognize the man on the screen; it had been a while since he had looked in a mirror. He didn't look well.

James considered retreating back into the hallway, but he was already halfway to the hangar entrance and had brought too much attention to himself, pushing his way to the front. It would seem conspicuous if he backed out now. Besides, there was nothing behind him except more monitors and auditors. This was his best chance.

James lowered his head and continued walking. The two monitors up ahead wouldn't pose much of a threat if they tried to stop him, but he'd rather not kill them if he could help it. The rest of the personnel in the hangar shouldn't be too worrisome. The hangar chief didn't tolerate monitors and auditors lounging in his domain.

The amount of traffic flowing into the hangar didn't waver with this new security warning. Most people just glanced at it and continued on their business. The two monitors manning the door hardly seemed to notice either. Maybe he could just keep his head low and sneak through. It was his best shot.

James glanced at the monitor on the right side of the doorway and cursed. It was Beaulieu, whom he had run jobs with in the past when he had needed backup. James didn't consider him a friend; he didn't have any friends other than Smitt. Well, Smitt was no longer a friend either, but Beaulieu was one of the few monitors in ChronoCom whom James would greet if he passed him.

He shifted to his left and picked up his pace. Ten meters now. James powered on his exo to a low level, but kept his hands to his sides. He looked through the opening and saw his collie parked on one of the left landings, elevated third row up from the ground level. He quickly formulated a plan. Just as he passed the two monitors and dared to hope he had avoided detection, Beaulieu ruined everything.

"Chronman?" he said uncertainly.

James turned to face him, hoping desperately that the guy just wanted to say hello. "Monitor," he nodded. "What can I do for you?"

Beaulieu frowned. "I'm sorry, Chronman, but there's been an alert for you. Please come with—"

Before Beaulieu could finish his sentence, James lashed out with his exo and struck him across the side of his face. Beaulieu flew into the crowd and barreled several of them to the ground. James spun to his left and speared the other monitor with an exo-powered punch, striking him in the chest and most likely breaking several ribs.

The people around him screamed and scattered, making it easier for him to take off. Most of them were support personnel. They were all innocent; he should do his best to avoid hurting them. But then, Beaulieu and the other monitor were innocent as well. He pushed those thoughts out of his mind. He had to get to Elise. That was the only thing that mattered.

A second later, an alarm blared across the entire base, its scream echoing in the massive hangar. James noticed another monitor rushing toward him from the right, and a chronman flying in from the far side of the hangar. The two would have to be taken care of before he could escape with this collic. A chronman could easily disable a collie.

The foolish monitor got to him first, and was dispatched with ease as James cut him across the ankles with a kinetic coil. He picked the monitor's body up and threw him at the approaching chronman. The chronman made a wide gesture with his hands and deflected the poor monitor's body to the side.

James recognized Tassin, a Tier-4 two years out of the Academy. He was a bit of a hothead and still green, which was clear from his penchant for hand gestures to direct his movements.

"Stand down, Tassin," he said when the younger chronman got within earshot. "This won't end well for you."

Tassin looked eager to engage him. "It was only a matter of time before you cracked, James. Everyone knows that. Guess it's just my luck to be the one to put you down. It'll earn me another tier for sure."

Tassin launched himself into the air and dove downward at him. James adjusted his exo field to allow him to see the chronman's coils, three writhing lines growing out of Tassin's body. He waited as one of the coils swung downward at him. James juked to his left at the last moment as the coil slammed on the hangar floor hard enough to crack the cement.

James knew right away Tassin was inexperienced with exo-against-exo combat. Fighting between exo-powered combatants was not sanctioned by the Academy during training. The last thing ChronoCom wanted was their precious salvagers to injure each other. Only auditors were given military-level exo-combat training. However, during their years at the Academy, most initiates engaged in friendly matches to hone their skills. Trainers at the Academy recognized its learning benefits and tended to turn a blind eye to these underground events. Still, those Academy exo melees were a pale comparison to the real thing.

The only other way a chronman learned how to fight another with an exo was through actual combat. Over the years, James had had plenty of opportunity fighting exo-powered pirates in the Ship Graveyard while Tassin had practically none, though that didn't stop the younger, over-confident man from charging in.

James countered the attack, latching his own coil to Tassin's and snaking it up toward its source. Tassin tried to dissolve that coil but James had locked it in place. It became a match of wills and mental coordination as a dozen kinetic coils grew out of both James and Tassin, each pushing, chopping, and squirming, constantly trying to reach the opposing chronman.

Tassin was quick with his coil creations and his precision was commendable. James had to duck out of the way a few times before he could neutralize Tassin's coils with his own. Still, Tassin's control was raw. All of his coils tended to move in unison, and seemed to waver and lose purpose when he actively controlled only one. None of the kinetic coils seemed truly autonomous.

Not like James's coils.

James created nine coils simultaneously and shot them toward Tassin from every conceivable angle, all seemingly random. Tassin was only able to control five at a time and to direct four of them to block James's attack. He leaped backward to open up space, but then James had superior range control as well. As Tassin tried to slip out of reach, two of James's coils wrapped themselves around his ankle and knee, and slammed him to the floor.

Tassin's shield blistered yellow, protecting him from the brunt of the damage, but the rest of James's coils joined in, slithering around Tassin's body, squeezing until the yellow barrier protecting him cracked and began to break down. James gritted his teeth, pulling the coils tighter, slowly crushing the shield. Once it fell, the soft flesh it was protecting would explode from the pressure.

What's another death? the Nazi soldier's voice echoed. *After all, he's just another poor victim already gone.* There was a pause. *Oh wait, he's not.*

The Nazi soldier was right. Tassin wasn't a ghost. This actually was murder. James stared at the young chronman's terrified face. He couldn't be any older than twenty-three. He probably still believed in Chrono-Com's cause, that he was saving humanity one jump at a time. The young fool probably thought he was just doing his duty. He was an innocent.

With a guttural growl, James released his grip on Tassin, wrapped a small coil around his bands, and tore them apart. Tassin collapsed onto the ground, chest heaving as he struggled for air.

It was too bad James couldn't procure Tassin's bands for himself. All bands were designed to link to their user once worn unless actively released. If the user died, the bands were worthless. This safety precaution was initially designed for when chronmen died on jobs. If their futurist technology fell away during a salvage and someone from the past was able to use the bands, it would be disastrous.

James grabbed the young man by the collar and pulled him up. "You're out of your league. I let you live, boy. Remember this." Then James leaped up to where his collie was parked and pulled out just in time for Levin and a platoon of monitors see it jet out of the hangar.

EIGHTEEN

BRAVE NEW WORLD

Elise waited for Salman or James or whatever his real name was—
time-traveling liar—to leave the room before she let herself succumb
to the grief that had been welling up in her since she first came to this
horrific future. For some reason, she wasn't sure why, she didn't want to
cry in front of him. It was all she could do to hold it together until he was
gone, and then once she was sure she was alone, she allowed herself to
break and grieve properly.

For a while, she stayed huddled in a fetal position on the bed, sobbing, her tears streaming freely down her face. The pent-up horror at what
she'd seen in the past day—from the awful last morning on the Nutris
Platform to the horrific future in which she was now trapped—were too
much for her soul to bear. She wept for the people who had died horribly
on the platform. She cried for her parents and the family she would never
see again, people she loved that were now hundreds of years dead. She
grieved for the Earth and the scarring of this once beautiful planet.

In its place was this worst of nightmares, a poisoned, ugly future that
seemed twisted and dark. The beautiful ocean in which she had spent hundreds of hours was now a tainted pool of sickness. Even the sky seemed
wrong, at least to her twenty-first-century memory. Something was very
sickly about the clouds and the sun. It was all a giant bad dream, one from
which she couldn't awake.

And Elise wept for herself, for all that she had lost in an instant. Yesterday, she had friends and family and a life. Today, it was all gone, and she would have to start over. Oh hell, who was she kidding? There was no way she was going to survive this apocalypse. She might as well have died on Nutris. Except she didn't, and now survivor's guilt overwhelmed her.

She cried until her body couldn't squeeze any more tears out, until she was too exhausted to cry anymore, but her mind was too terrified to sleep. Finally, after an hour, Elise decided that she had had enough of her own stupid little pity party. She sat up on the bed, wiped her face, and took several deep breaths. "Get it together, Elise. You had your cry, now woman up. Crying isn't going to make anything better. You've been in worse spots before."

Elise couldn't even lie to herself convincingly. She ignored the space game on the future television and forced herself to crawl out of bed and look out the window. She gazed at the strange yet familiar new world outside. The view from her room was hazy, half-obstructed by a film of oil that gave the outside an almost dreamy, underwater look.

Still, it presented an interesting and frightening picture of this new world. She marveled at some of the fantastic advances, the flying cars that used the sky as a highway and the tall buildings that stacked on top of each other as if they were all made from giant building blocks. She saw an alien-looking structure seemingly floating in the air. Near the lake, a gigantic ship took off and blasted into space. She was disgusted at the visibly brown and gray winds blowing by, and the giant smokestacks dotting the landscape, shooting up humongous plumes of smoke into the clouds. The walls of the buildings looked faded, and everywhere, rust prevailed, as if everything was slowly deteriorating.

An hour of window-watching and pacing later, when her mind had finished running wild and she had no more despair to let loose, Elise finally got bored. And hungry. Mostly just hungry. She hadn't eaten since the night before, during her date with Salman—no, his name was James—and now her stomach growled. Several times, she looked at the door and considered exploring this new world, but each time, James's warnings echoed in her head and she decided to wait just a little bit longer.

By the third or so hour, she was downright fidgety and starving. She began to wonder if he had abandoned her. Doubt crept into her mind. What would she do then if he never came back? How would she survive? New fears paralyzed her as she suddenly felt very much alone.

Elise turned her attention to the future television airing the strange sports game. It took her a few minutes to figure out how to change the channels with a series of hand gestures, and even less time to realize that television in the future sucked just as much as it did in her time.

When the vid light on the wall began to flash red, Elise was more than happy to answer it, desperately hoping that James had returned, preferably with food. Instead, the attendant down at the lobby appeared, his image floating in the air three-dimensionally occupying a quarter of the room.

The man said something but she didn't quite understand. It sounded vaguely like World English from her time, but with the words condensed into one syllable, each punctuated by an exclamation mark, and spoken in a singsong. A very fast singsong.

He repeated his words. He was obviously asking a question. She shook her head again. Then her view pulled back, revealing two menacing-looking uniformed men wearing cone-shaped helmets standing behind him. Then Elise realized that those men wanted to see her. She shook her head more emphatically. James had told her to let no one in. The attendant looked off-screen and said something to them, shaking his head. Then to her horror, one of the uniformed men reached over the counter, punched the attendant in the face, and knocked him off-screen. The other pointed at her and then the connection went dead.

Elise began to panic. What if they were coming upstairs? She had just witnessed one of them assault the poor guy doing his job. The last thing she wanted was to be in these guys' custody. She bolted toward the exit. The short hallway had only an elevator and an adjacent door. She watched, horrified, as the lights on the elevator began to climb toward her level. Her only other path was through the door. She slammed into the door and entered a dimly lit stairwell. Elise looked over the ledge and realized just how high up she was. It was a long way down.

She gritted her teeth and began to hurtle down the stairs two and three steps at a time. She made it about halfway down the building when a loud crack reverberated through the stairwell above her. She heard men shouting. She quickened her pace and, a few minutes later, burst through the lobby door, where she found the attendant still unconscious on the floor near the desk.

Not knowing what to do, she ran out of the Heights and into the blue-colored tunnels. It was then she realized, in her hurry, she had forgotten to grab the chem suit. She cursed, knowing that it was far too risky to go back for it. She had to press on. Elise joined the flow of traffic moving away from the hotel, trusting that as long as she moved with the flow and didn't bring attention to herself, there should be no way those two uniformed men could follow her in these thick crowds.

Though she had walked down the tunnels just an hour earlier, she had been too frazzled and James too much in a hurry for her to notice her surroundings. Now, as she wandered through the colorfully painted passageways, she took the opportunity to study this piece of the future. The first thing she noticed was how packed everyone was. There were hundreds of people about, some walking, some of whom looked like vendors selling wares and services, and some begging. Heck, she even noticed prostitutes, both male and female. The second thing she noticed was that everything was a sty, with layers of brown and gray residue that seemed to cake onto the ground, the walls, the lights, even the people.

It saddened her. So far in the future, everything was much worse. There were very few places this bad in the late twenty-first century. The world governments had banded together a generation earlier to stamp out poverty and hunger, and were mostly successful in achieving their goals. Money and resources were poured into research for disease cures, new food resources, and reusable energy. Low-cost construction and social safety net plans helped eliminate homelessness and sickness. Countries dismantled their armies and reduced military costs in favor of diplomacy and peace. Everything seemed to be heading in the right direction. Somehow, civilization had taken a wrong turn, and now whatever gains had been made during her time were lost again.

A few minutes after walking into the tunnel, her breathing became labored, reminding her of the first time she had gone scuba diving. No matter how she tried, she couldn't take in a full breath. Thinking it was just the adrenaline of being chased, she continued on, moving through the blue tunnels until she turned right at one intersection and accidentally found herself on the surface, standing under a gray drab sky.

The sun's rays just peeked through the thick, fast-moving clouds that sped across the horizon, Elise was struck by their hazy glow, as if a film of grease covered the atmosphere.

She glanced at her surroundings. It was more crowded up here than below, with lines of people moving in every direction as if on some mad scientist's assembly line. Here and there, pockets of people—those not standing in lines—sat in huddled groups, looking on with resignation as those with places to go passed them by. Elise saw a child, barefoot and in rags, pull on his mother's sleeves and giggle at her.

Elise brushed her fingers against the oddly tinted breeze that seemed to hold subtle but visible dimensions—she could actually see which direction the wind was blowing. Her breathing became worse and her senses began to wither under a barrage of attacks. Her head ached, her nose began to burn, and her eyes watered. When she tried to inhale, she felt as if she were sucking in a mouthful of smoke. She dropped to one knee and tried to steady herself. She felt as if she were drowning.

An old woman—a vendor of some sort carrying a tray of what looked like wilted grass—tapped her on the arm and began to speak, her voice muffled and distant. Elise cocked her head to one side and gestured one hand at her ear. The woman, looking irritated, spoke louder and even faster. Nothing she said made any sense. Elise pointed at both ears this time. She couldn't make out anything the woman was saying. She shook her head and shrugged. Finally, as if fed up, the woman took a pinch of the grass and jammed it into Elise's mouth.

"Eat this," she said, or something along those lines.

Too surprised to protest, Elise obediently chewed. She didn't usually chew whatever someone stuffed in her mouth, but there was too much going on right now for her to protest. Immediately, a wave of nausea passed over her and then everything went numb. First her tongue, then her sense of smell evaporated, and then any feeling she had from her hands down to her toes was gone. All her senses just seemed to dampen.

"You can breathe in again, off-worlder," the old woman said, this time purposely speaking in a slow, drawn-out voice. "The cany weed blocks all the good stuff that you aliens aren't used to."

"Thanks," Elise said, breathing in deeply. The air still burned the hairs on her nostril a bit but it wasn't debilitating like it had been previously. She touched her face with her hand and couldn't feel her fingers.

"Numbness takes getting used to," the woman said. "It's good grass, eh? Good cany weed."

Elise nodded.

"Stuff will wear off before dark, girl. You'll need more. You want?" The old woman held up the basket. "Works good."

Elise shook her head. "I don't have any . . ." What did they even use for money here? "I have no way to pay. I'm sorry."

The old woman looked down at Elise in disgust and snorted. "Alien scum with fancy clothes and no scratch. And you take my sample. Fuck you, off-worlder shit!" For a second, the not-so-kindly-looking old woman looked like she was about to reach into Elise's mouth and take back her cany weed sample. Instead, she turned and stormed off.

Elise watched as the woman disappeared into the mass of people, becoming just another stooped figure in an assembly line of hunched-over shadows. She took another breath and looked around. Whatever this weed was doing, it was working, though Elise wished she knew more about what was going on with her body.

Well, what was done was done. Elise picked herself up and explored the area, making sure to keep the blue tunnel exit within sight at all times. The last thing she needed was to get lost and not be able to find her way back to the Heights. Eventually, James would come back, right? He'd better. If she lost James in this strange world, she was as good as dead. For now, she just had to stay away long enough in the vicinity until those guys were gone.

Elise turned around in a slow circle and scanned her surroundings. She was standing in a vast plaza sandwiched in between gigantic buildings on three sides. Each of the buildings was easily a hundred stories tall, their tops lost in the low-hanging clouds. It was also scalding hot down here. At first Elise had thought that running from those strange men had made her feel flushed. It wasn't until a few seconds later that she realized her face was already sunburned from the brief exposure to the elements, even though the sun was nowhere in sight, hidden by the buildings, smog, and weirdly colored winds.

The fourth side of the plaza was a ten-lane street that had vehicles buzzing by at different speeds. Each lane had a set speed attached to it, from the slowest human-drawn wagons to high-tech speedsters that passed by in a blur.

Using her forearm to protect her face from the sun, Elise explored the plaza, moving with the crowds and checking out the vendors one by one.

She was surprised to find that nothing much had changed. In fact, most of the stuff being sold she could find back in the poorest countries of her time, except she was in a major metropolis. It was as if she had gone backward in time instead of forward. There were people selling vegetables, grain trinkets, small electronics, primitive-looking tools, and even some firearms. To her shock, she even found a stall where people were being sold.

Elise shook her head in disgust and continued on her way, turning down another street and seeing more of the same. This time, she entered what could only be called a beggars' row. Here, hundreds of vagrants sat meekly together, desolate and dirty, begging for food or money. The smell overwhelmed the cany weed and made her queasy. Her work back in her time often took her to desolate places filled with poverty and filth, but this place, in the middle of a major city, was as bad as any she'd ever seen. She turned away and fled in the opposite direction, trying to get as far from the misery as possible. However, there was no escaping this world.

As she stumbled through the crowds, she happened upon the first clean, brightly lit place she'd seen so far. It looked like someone had parked a freshly washed spaceship in the middle of the city. Beams of white lights lined the perimeter of the building and somehow, the colored air wasn't able to touch it. The shiny building called to her. Not able to look away, Elise wandered toward it like a fly lured toward a bright light. She didn't seem to be the only one falling under this building's trance. There was a circle of people standing around it as well, just staring at its glow. Once she got to the edge of the crowd, she was stopped by an armed guard ten meters from the building's entrance.

"That's far enough, Earthgrime," a white-armored guard growled. He shoved her backward with one hand and, pointing his other hand at her, said, "Only corporate-class citizens allowed in this shopping district. The rest of you rabble stay where you belong." At least that's what she thought he said; she was only starting to get the hang of this dialect.

Elise looked over his shoulder and saw a steady stream of well-dressed people leaving and entering the building directly through flying transports so they wouldn't have to mingle with the rabble. The guards around the building made sure that the people surrounding the glowing building did not get too close to the so-called corporate-class citizens.

Elise stayed and watched a while longer, staring almost wistfully as small groups of glamorous futuristic-looking shoppers entered and left. They looked like the people she had in mind when she thought of people from the future. Then finally, as if synchronously on cue, all the guards retreated into the building and then the entire thing took off.

"What in Gaia was that?" Elise asked.

"Damn corps still have to do business here on Earth, but there's no city rich enough to take care of their needs. Mobile corp shopping facilities takes care of them until they can finish their business and get the hell off-planet." The man standing next to her shook his head. "Way they keep us separated from them like animals . . ." He put his hands to his mouth and bellowed, "Hey, you all came from here too!"

Exhausted from the depressing outing, not to mention the tender feeling of the skin on her face from just the few minutes of exposure to the sun still hidden behind clouds, Elise decided to head back toward the hotel and see if James had returned. Maybe she could hide near the entrance and catch him before he went inside, or if he was there, he'd surely wait for her, right? What else could she do? She backtracked the way she had come, through the narrow bazaar back to the plaza, then found the blue tunnel that took her underground.

No sooner did she see the entrance of the Heights at the far end of the tunnel than two black-armored men wearing the cone-shaped helmets appeared on either side of her. One of them said something she couldn't quite understand. Elise shook her head. The other one looked at his friend and grinned.

"Off-worlder, huh?" he said. "That chronman knows how to pick them."

"ChronoCom monitors," the first said. "Come with us."

As if to show her how much choice she had to comply with their demand, he grabbed her by the shoulder and dragged her with them. Elise was about to protest when she noticed the emblem on both their shoulders. It was the same emblem as the half-flaked-off one on the ship James flew. Maybe they were going to take her to him.

"Are you guys with Salman, I mean, James?" she asked.

"Quiet, whore," the first one said.

Elise looked stunned. She heard those two words very clearly.

The grinning one leered at her and spoke to his friend as if she weren't there. "Funniest-looking prostitute I've ever seen. Never heard of an off-worlder one. Look at her skin. Not spaceborn white but none of the surface blems. I wonder how much she costs."

The first grunted. "Probably more than you can afford. Let's hurry back. We've kept the auditor waiting long enough."

"Hey, assholes," Elise snapped, swinging her elbows. She was protesting more at being completely ignored and treated like an object than actually being called a whore. Who did these guys think they were! This was no way to—

The first conehead backhanded her across the face. Elise felt her legs buckle and she fell to her knees. "Stop struggling, whore," was all she heard as they grabbed her elbows and carried her limp body along the ground.

It took a minute for the cobwebs in her head to clear. The conehead had busted open her lip, and the smack stung even more on her sunburned cheeks. James's friends or no, she knew she had to escape these two. She had to think of something.

The two carried her all the way back to the plaza on the surface level. Whoever these guys were, the people in these crowded tunnels gave them a wide berth. The two didn't even acknowledge the masses as they continued chatting with each other, once knocking down someone too slow to get out of their way.

Elise devised a plan to escape; it wasn't much of one, but it was better than pretending to be unconscious and carried like a sack of potatoes. She stayed limp until they reached the far end of the plaza. Just as they were nearing the end of the crowds, Elise leaned in toward the guard on the left—the grinning conehead—and pushed into him as hard as she could. She wasn't a very big person, and the guy probably only stumbled a couple of steps, but it was just enough to knock him off balance and into the crowds.

Grinning conehead had to let go of her to steady himself. As he did so, Elise swung her right arm up and smacked the right conehead in the face. He took her punch with a slight swivel of his chin, and then he looked down at her. She tried to knee him in the groin. Same effect. Were these guys robots?! Just then, the grinning conehead she pushed grabbed her hair, spun her around, and smacked her on the side of the head. The blow knocked her to the ground.

"Easy there," the right conehead said, "we still need to interrogate her."

Grinning conehead spat. "Bitch did that on purpose!"

Elise, facedown on the ground, realized that they weren't holding on to her anymore. She got onto her hands and knees and scampered into the forest of legs. She heard a squawk from one of the two but she continued to crawl forward in desperation, around feet, under carts, pushing between bodies. She turned left and then right and continued to change directions until she wasn't sure which direction she was going anymore. All she could hear was the yells from the two coneheads behind her as they barreled through the crowds looking for her.

Suddenly, she was out in the open and on her own. She got to her feet and took off, running as fast as she could to the edge of the plaza and up a flight of metal stairs, pushing and shoving as best she could, but she was still mostly at the mercy of the flow of the crowds. She had turned back once to see if they were in pursuit and was horrified to see that they were only a few steps behind her.

Elise turned right into a crowded intersection and continued to run, weaving left and right as her eyes scanned for any place to hide. She looked up and saw one of those bright clean spaceship stores landing in a clearing and made a beeline for it. She reached the opening where the ship, still fifty meters off the ground, was slowly descending.

Elise tore through the beams of white lights lining the perimeter, ignoring the cries of alarm from the white-clad guards who were keeping the crowds at bay. She gritted her teeth and hurtled under the landing ship. If she could reach the other side, maybe she could throw off her pursuers, since they'd have to go around the building. The sprint under the building looked like a hundred or so meters. As she ran under the ship, she was almost immediately struck by the heat from its thrusters. She staggered a few steps but continued on, willing herself to get across. The building continued to lower, increasing the temperature around her by the second. If she didn't get out from under here soon, she was going to burn to a crisp.

She barely made it out from under the spaceship store when it landed on the ground with a thunderous boom. Exhausted, Elise fell to her knees, but she knew she had to push herself back to her feet. She had to find a place to hide. Unfortunately, her legs had had enough. They gave out. Elise fell again and this time, she couldn't get up. She rolled onto her back, gasping for air. One of the coneheads, the grinning one, appeared next to her.

"Get up!" he snarled. He held up his foot as if he was going to stomp down on her face.

"Not the head, idiot," the other conehead said.

A crowd had formed around them. The grinning conehead grunted, picked her up by the front of her shirt. Elise lashed out, clocking him on the side of the face. The grinning conehead snarled and punched her in the stomach. Elise gasped and almost fainted from the pain.

"That's for pushing me," he smirked. "And this is for trying to run away."

She continued punching and clawing at him, trying desperately to squirm out of his grip. He held her shirt with one hand and struck her again with the other. She squeezed her eyes shut as the blows rained down on her face and body, her own struggle weakening. Then the blows suddenly stopped. She pried her eyes open and noticed that her attacker wasn't even looking at her anymore; he was staring up into the sky. Elise followed his gaze and saw a familiar ship hovering above them.

"Chronman," the other conehead said hastily. "We appreciate your assistance, but we have this under—"

The conehead was yanked into the air and tossed like a rag doll into the ogling crowd. Grinning conehead dropped her and screamed as he was pulled into the air as well. Then she watched in horror as his body slammed down into the ground with force. Then James dropped from the air next to her and offered her his hand. "I have you," he said, pulling her close, "let's get out of here."

NINETEEN

THE HUNT

Levin Javier-Oberon was having an awful week. Today was memorable, at least. He stared at the Watcher's Board in the hallway outside the office of Director Young Hobson-Luna, head of Planetary Control on Earth. The Watcher's Board was nothing more than a giant framed screen filled with hundreds of small electronically inked names, updated once a day at zero hour. Completely low tech: cheap, easy, and symbolic. The board served only one purpose: to display the current roster count of ChronoCom operatives.

Levin glanced down at the numbers near the bottom: 112,311 support, 2,266 administrators, 42,398 engineers, 3,021 handlers. His eyes moved up the list: 42,953 monitors, 3,341 chronmen. Both numbers had dropped since yesterday. The monitors by twenty-six and the chronmen by two. Levin then looked up to the last list near the top: 224 auditors.

Only 224.

From the tens of thousands of initiates at the Academy every year to the foot soldier monitors to the chronmen tiers and finally to the auditor chains, there were only 224 human beings like him out of a population of twenty billion humans in this solar system.

Levin was an apex, part of a select elite cadre that zealously guarded the chronostream. Only some of the largest corporations could field better military units. Obtaining this status was so rare and prestigious that the name of every person who had ever held the auditor emblem was forever etched in ChronoCom lore. No other rank could boast that. Every significant auditor event was carefully documented in agency records. Because auditors mattered. Auditors were important.

Well, today was a significant day for sure. A chronman had broken a Time Law, and not just any Time Law, but the first law, a cardinal sin that had never been broken in their history. Chronman James Abyss-plagued Griffin-Mars had brought someone back from the past, and he had done it on Levin's watch. On Levin's planet of stewardship. To make matters worse, after he committed that heinous crime, he broke out of Central right under Levin's nose and disappeared into abyss-knew-fucking-where.

Levin gnashed his teeth and his hands curled into fists. It was an unbelievable act of incompetence on his part. If he was in the directorship, Levin would have himself executed for such a stupid mistake. Even if he were able to right this crime, Levin would forever be known as the auditor who catastrophically failed in his duties. James escaping was actually the least of his concerns. He was confident he could hunt down the fugitive and drag him back for justice. The sting of the most important Time Law being broken hurt much more. He would consider honorable suicide if he thought it would clear some of that taint from his name. Hell, he still might have to, once the director was through with him. It wouldn't work this way, though. Levin couldn't escape his failure so easily. Things these days were never that simple.

The double doors at the end of the hallway swung outward with a squeak—the lower hinge of the right door making that noise—revealing a pitch-black interior. A draft blew out of the opening. The director preferred to keep the temperature in his office frigid.

A gravelly sounding voice barked out from within the darkness, "Black fucking balls, Levin, you've fucked up on a galactic scale. In my damn fucking backyard, no less. Get your ass in here."

Levin tore his gaze away from the board and entered the director's office, intent on keeping his dignity intact. If he had to face possible orders to execute himself, he would do so with his head held high and his back straight.

"Have a seat, Levin." Director Young gestured at the chair in front of his desk. "No, stand. Sitting is for those who aren't fuckups."

The blaringly loud and vulgar voice coming out of Young's mouth was a surprise for almost everyone who suffered it the first time. In all the years Levin had worked at Earth Central, he had met the director dozens of times and had never received a kind word from him. Levin appreciated his honesty, though.

Young was a frail, scrawny-looking man, with only a tuft of white hair on the crown of his head and on his chin. His back was stooped and his entire body leaned to one side, like a bent tree. His right arm, cut off at the elbow, hung useless from his shoulder, shattered decades ago in service to the agency.

Before his injury, Young Hobson-Luna was the longest-tenured auditor and second in the chain. He had retired from auditorship after he was no longer able to stand watch, and had moved over to the administrative side. Now, only Jerome, the head of Europa, was higher linked.

"I prefer to stand regardless, Director," Levin said. "How is your shoulder?"

Young looked down to his right and shrugged. "Still twisted and useless. That's what will retire you as well, Levin, assuming I don't tell you to strangle yourself first or the guys in Europa don't order me to throw you out of an airlock without your fucking bands. Or both."

"I will honor your wisdom, Director."

"You are still ninth in the chain?" Young asked.

"Yes, Director," Levin said. Right now he was, but for how long?

Young chuckled. "You think you'll slip down the chain for this."

"That would be the least of my punishments. I expect no less."

"Always willing to take the beam to the chest even when you don't need to. Admirable and fucking stupid. Well, we have more important matters to attend to, so tell your self-righteous honor to fuck off and let's get down to business."

Levin's neutral face broke for a moment. "Pardon, Director? If you're not here to punish me, why was I summoned?"

"Stop trying to get yourself hung, you imbecile. It doesn't mean shit and solves nothing. Now you can sit down. I'm tired of looking up at you. Sit. It's an order."

Levin sat down, though he kept his body as erect as when he was standing.

Young rolled his eyes and his face became serious. He leaned forward. "Do you know what's at stake, Auditor?"

"Director?"

Young leaned forward and rested his good elbow on the desk. "In the one hundred forty-eight years since ChronoCom's official inception, no chronman has ever brought someone back from the past. Not once. Do you know why?"

Levin nodded. "The first Time Law expressly forbids——"

"Screw the laws for a second," Young cut him off. "They're just rules. The real reason that Time Law is the most egregious to violate is because . . ." His voice trailed off and he gestured to Levin.

Levin thought back to his days at the Academy. "The Vallis Bouvard Disaster. Experimental chron lab in 2356 that conducted sanctioned retrievals of humans from the past. They discovered that the subjects were not only severely temporally displaced but caused abnormal ripples that tore holes in the chronostream.

All subjects' physiologies and mental states also became unstable and degenerated at the molecular level within a four-week period. The tears in the stream around Bouvard Base destabilized the area, and a fluke ripple within the power generator caused a solar source meltdown in the cooling reactors, obliterating the lab and surrounding region in a two-hundred-square-kilometer area. This disaster was one of the primary catalysts that propelled all the corporations and governments to create a neutral governing body with jurisdiction over time traveling and the chronostream."

Young nodded. "That's right. So now you see our problem?"

"Yes, Director, whoever James brought back is causing havoc with the chronostream in the present. The consequences——"

"No, idiot," Young snapped. "It means the entire solar system will soon realize that the Vallis Bouvard Disaster was a hoax. It was initially staged by our founders to scare all the governing powers to agree on Chrono-Com's creation. It's now just a bogeyman story we propagate to keep the corporations in line and to squash any ideas chronmen may have about playing god and bringing someone back from the past. Do you understand the ramifications if word of this becomes public knowledge?"

"The Vallis Bouvard Disaster was . . . fake?" Levin was stunned.

"Yes, yes." Young waved it off dismissively. "I was pretty fucking shocked, too, when I learned this. Listen, if we don't capture James and whoever he brought back soon, word's going to get out, and it'll completely undermine the agency's authority. Before we know it, we'll have idiotic chronmen and corporations bringing people back by the hundreds and jumping to whatever time line they want. Black abyss, it'll destroy the chronostream!" He stood up and shook his finger at Levin. "You want to fall on your sword? Well, this is how you're going to do it. You're going to capture James and this temporal anomaly. I'm assigning Geneese and Shizzu to you. Geneese is coming in from Luna and Shizzu just returned from auditor training."

"Newly linked?" Levin knew Shizzu from the man's Tier-2 days. He distinctly remembered an unremarkable but ambitious chronman he thought wouldn't survive that tier, let alone make the jump to Tier-1, let alone to the brotherhood of auditors.

Young nodded. "You'll get a division of monitors as well and your choice of tactics and personnel. Make sure they know how to keep their fucking mouths shut. I want this done quietly. Do you understand?"

"Your will, Director." Levin bowed. "Thank you for giving me the opportunity—"

"Save it and fix the fucking problem, you stiff bastard," Young struggled to stand. "Come with me. There's more. We have more interested parties in this whole mess."

Using a cane, Young hobbled around his desk. When Levin offered a hand, the director shot him a glare that would have killed a lesser man. Levin let the old man be; Young was still a fiery and prideful man. They didn't have far to walk since Young led him to the room next to his office.

They walked into a large room with a long rectangular table. Outside of one wall made entirely from glass, the colored winds battered against the once-clear surface with black specks. The other three walls were barren, except for a small cabinet on the back right. Two people sitting close together at the far end of the table were conversing in low tones, only standing to address them when Young got close.

The first one: male, pale, corporate suit, was someone Levin had seen once or twice on the base. He looked like an off-worlder, though not from Mars or Luna. By the shade of his skin and body type, Levin ventured the man had originated from one of the Gas Giant colonies. The other: female, sleek, dark blue combat uniform—Levin recognized the insignia on her arm as from the Valta Mining Security Forces.

He sensed a dangerous edge in her; she was someone he'd have to watch out for. The woman's hair was cut short to just above her ear, a custom among the military within the Gas colonies. Her face, while not unpleasant, was marred by a perpetual scowl and a cold cruel stare that had not changed since when he first laid eyes on her.

What made him particularly wary of this woman were her eyes; she was sizing him up as much as he was her. Like two predators, they acknowledged each other with a slight tilt of the head. They both recognized the dangers of the other. She wore no bands around her arms. Since corporate technology was different from ChronoCom's and in most ways, far more advanced, he couldn't be sure of her capabilities.

"Auditor Levin," the man glanced at him and said. "The director says you will be leading the search for the perpetrator of this unfortunate incident."

"Levin." Young gestured. "This is Sourn, our Valta liaison with the agency."

"And this is Securitate Kuo," Sourn gestured to the woman next to him, "from our special operations."

Levin nodded. "How may I assist?" This was the first time he'd ever seen anyone from the elite branch of Valta's private army. The corp must have something important they wanted on Earth for Kuo to be here.

"We were distressed to hear about the mishap with your chronman on the recent Valta-sponsored assignment," Sourn said. "It seems the work Valta has recently commissioned with ChronoCom was rife with issues."

"I'm not aware of other incidents, Liaison," Levin said.

"That's beside the point," Young cut in. "A Time Law breach is incident enough."

Levin made note of that. The director was hiding something. There was much more to this situation than Young made it out to be. It was irrelevant, though. It wasn't up to an auditor to question the leadership of ChronoCom.

"We'd like to assign Securitate Kuo to your mission, strictly as an observer and in an advisory role, of course," Sourn said.

Levin frowned. Why would a gas-mining company care about his mission to retrieve a fugitive chronman? "Excuse me, Liaison. For what purpose?"

"Just covering our liability, I assure you," Sourn added.

"The fugitive chronman is dangerous," Levin said. "I cannot assure the securitate's safety."

Kuo's smile was not very friendly. "That should be the least of your worries, Chronman."

"It's 'Auditor,' thank you." Levin returned the smile.

"Very well then," Young said. "See to it that Valta has access to whatever they need." He kept his gaze on Levin. "ChronoCom's relationship with Valta is a priority. See that it is kept close and strong."

"Of course, Director." Something in his gut was uneasy with this arrangement.

"The first thing I believe we should attempt," Kuo began, looking directly at Young and Sourn, "is to see if his handler can get in touch with him."

"Doubtful," Young said. "The fugitive assaulted his handler and gave him a concussion, after all. I doubt he would respond to his handler now."

"Perhaps," she said. "However, Valta is prepared to make him a generous offer that might flush him out."

"You're going to bribe him? Reward him for breaking the Time Laws?" Levin sputtered. "We cannot allow this to go unpunished."

Kuo gave him a dismissive smile. "While the corporation respects the Time Laws, there are more important matters at hand. The fugitive might have something we want . . ."

TWENTY

ON THE RUN

Elise woke up exhausted from a restless sleep. She remembered the craziest things, stuff she hadn't dreamt about since she had smoked excessive amounts of marijuana in grad school. It took a few seconds for her eyes to adjust to her surroundings. It was dark, but there were these goofy shadows dancing on the walls. She inhaled and nearly threw up, her gag reflex kicking in. It smelled like garbage here, wherever here was. And now that she thought about it, the left side of her body was freezing, and the right side felt like she had been roasting over a spit.

She yawned and sat up, and noticed the roaring fire a few meters away. A small part of her sighed; so much for the bad dream. That meant—she looked over to her right—James was actually real and she was in a world of bad juju.

"You're up." His voice bounced around the room. "How are you feeling?"

Elise took a moment and suppressed the first, panicked thought that popped into her head. She forced her body to inhale a few deep breaths and not to say how she really felt because she knew she'd regret saying the words to him later. In fact, she decided not to say anything at all. No good would have come of her flight reflex kicking up full tilt and her running screaming out of the room.

Instead, she waited until her eyes adjusted to the darkness. She was sitting in the center of a dirty floor in what looked like a large husk of a building, with cracks streaking the concrete walls and floor. There were large square openings along the walls where once there might have been windowpanes. Everything was at a slant. She could hear waves crashing in the distance, but other than that and the crackling fire spitting sparks into the air, it was eerily silent.

She opened her mouth to say something and her nerves put new words in her mouth. She groaned and rubbed her bruised jaw. "My face hurts."

"I'm sorry for that. I handled those two monitors."

Elise didn't like the vicious sound of that, but her body aching from their beating told her brain to let that one go. She stretched her arms out and pulled herself to her feet. "What happened? Last thing I remember was lying on the ground, then you showed up, and then the rumbling of your spaceship lulled me to sleep."

"Bringing you back has caused some . . . issues," he said. "I wasn't—"

"Supposed to do that?" Elise said, still massaging her jaw to make sure everything worked. "No kidding, James. I could have told you that when we were at the hotel. Your face had turned sheet white—well, whiter than it already is—by the time we got to the room. Then when you left . . . you really messed up big-time, didn't you, bringing me back from the past?"

He nodded.

"How did you do it, anyway? How is time traveling possible?"

James shrugged. "I have no idea."

Elise was flabbergasted. "Wait, what do you mean, you don't know? You're a time traveler. That's what you do."

"I'm a user, not a builder. I fly the collie. I have no idea how that engine works." He held up his arm. "I use these bands. I could care less what makes the exo power up or how the rad band protects me from radiation. Time traveling is the same way. There are people who build the technology and there are those, like me, who use it. There are not enough lifetimes for a person to know both."

Elise looked around at the moss- and dirt-covered walls, and brushed her fingers along the grimy floor. Everything was damp, even the air. This world had a worn and tired look to it, as if the entire planet was slowly melting. Decaying. Even the rocks at her feet looked sad.

She should be grateful she was still alive; she knew that. However, much to her chagrin, as much as she tried to be grateful, she couldn't find the silver lining to anything that had happened. After all, her beloved Earth was a wreck and she had been assaulted by the authorities on her very first day. She might as well be dead.

"Send me back," she said. "Back to my time. Wouldn't that solve everything?"

James shook his head. "I'm afraid that's impossible. You're considered out of sync with your time period based on your physical and chronological location. Time traveling creates tears in the chronostream that forever prevent anyone from jumping to that time and place again. I'm sorry; you can never return to your natural sync."

"Well, how the hell do you do it, then? And wouldn't jumping back create a tear too?"

James held up his armful of metal bands and pointed at one of them. "My jump band acts as an anchor that keeps me in sync with the present and pulls me back on my return jumps. Tears are only created during initial jumps. We're essentially punching holes into the fabric of time, and the anchor allows me to return to the present by pulling me back through the same hole. You weren't wearing one when we jumped."

"How about you send me back to my time but somewhere else then? I wouldn't want to go back to Nutris anyway, on account of all that radiation, but just, I dunno, drop me off in Mo'orea. Or New Zealand."

James shook his head. "I could do that, but the auditors—the police force within ChronoCom—will detect that you are out of sync. They'll send someone back to eliminate the discrepancy."

Being called a "discrepancy" sounded sort of insulting. Elise mulled things over. Quantum physics wasn't really her thing after all. "Well, that sucks" was her final analysis. Waxing eloquently about being trapped in an awful situation wasn't her thing either.

She could feel the slight angle at which the floor slanted, reminding her of her vacation as a kid climbing the Leaning Tower of Pisa before it actually toppled over. She walked to one of the large square openings and poked her head outside. It was completely dark, but she could make out the faint outline of other buildings. They were in a city that stretched to both sides as far as her eye could see. She looked down. On the ground level, ocean water flowed freely through the streets, crashing against the buildings as if they were in a canal. A sharp, pointy-topped building at the end of the street had completely toppled over at the base and looked like a syringe sticking out of the ground.

Elise turned to face James. "Where are we?"

"A metropolis in the old world on the eastern edge of the continent. Torn down by war. Overrun by the rising tides. I believe it was in the province of Massachusetts."

"Boston?" She didn't bother hiding the shock on her face. "What in Gaia happened to this place?"

James sat her down and then filled in the gaps with the major events that had transpired on Earth since her time, from World War III devastating the planet to the decaying plague that had rotted the planet to the ice caps melting and eventually swallowing 14 percent of the world's landmass. Elise was so stunned that she had to sit down and then stand up multiple times.

"How did you idiots let this happen?" she demanded, waving her arms, feeling the urge to take out her fury on someone from this stupid time period, which was unfortunately limited to the only other person in the room. "When I woke up this morning, the sun was out and the ocean was beautiful. The world was at peace. Hell, there hadn't been a war in twice my lifetime! We defeated hunger, disease, and energy starvation. Humanity was finally fixing the planet and picking itself out of the gutter! Now, now . . ." She sat back down again, speechless and bewildered.

"We blew it," he admitted. "In 2098, nine months after the Nutris Platform's destruction, we fell back into our old ways. World War Three broke out over the colonial rights of Luna, Mars, and the mineral deposits in the Main Asteroid Belt. Famine, poverty, and the planet's taint soon followed. We declined as a civilization, wasting resources on war and losing valuable technological achievements. In a short amount of time, the general population's mind-set changed from one of innovation and prosperity to just self-interested survival." He paused. "It gets worse. I haven't even started on what happened once humanity got off-planet."

"How could it get any worse?" she yelled and pointed outside the window. "Look at this place! I was almost better off dying back in my time."

James rubbed his temples with his fingers. "I'm sorry, but I had to save your life."

Elise took a few deep breaths and collected herself, feeling ashamed. "No, I'm sorry. I didn't mean that. I appreciate you rescuing me, really. I just didn't realize the future was such a dump." She sighed and tried to suppress that mountain of outrage in her head. "All right, what's done is done. What do we do now?"

"Now, you need to survive the present." James looked out the window as the faint orange morning rays bathed the room. He plucked four metal bands seemingly out of the air and handed them to her. "Put these on."

Elise stared at the ugly, dark, thick bands. "Um . . . thanks, but they're not really my style."

He held up his arms and showed her the dozen or so around his wrists. "They're not for aesthetics."

He picked out two of the bands and looped them around each of her delicate wrists. "This one is a rad band, and this one is an atmospheric control band. They will protect you against the radiation and the elements. The atmos will allow you to breathe clean air. Do not take them off." He looped another band around her left wrist. "This one is a comm band. It'll allow us to communicate at all times. I'll show you how to work it later on." Then he took the last band—fatter than the other three—held it up in front of her face, and then looped it around her right wrist. "This one is the most important. It's a wrist beam. You will need to learn to shoot with it and protect yourself. Never take any of these bands off."

Elise recoiled. "Like a gun? I can't even kill a bug, let alone shoot someone." She shook her wrists at him, jingling the loose bands. "Take it off. Take it off!"

James clasped her hands gently in his and sat her down. "Listen carefully, Elise. I've done a terrible thing in bringing you back. I broke some important laws. There are people looking for us."

"Like the ones at the plaza today?"

"Monitors. They're the police force of the time-traveling agency I work for." He paused. "Used to work for."

"What happens if they capture me? Will I go to jail or something?"

James shook his head. "They'd probably just shoot you on the spot. You need to know how to take care of yourself."

A cold wave swept over Elise as she looked at the dark metal bands around her wrists. She was tempted just to shake them off and give them back to James. She was an avowed pacifist, and the very thought of wearing a weapon nauseated her. Still, these were extraordinary circumstances. People were hunting her. Not just any people, but from the uniformed authorities of this time. She was knee-deep in serious trouble.

She held up her arm reluctantly. "Fine, I'll wear them on a trial basis. But if I do decide that I'm all right with them, I eventually want them in another color. These are ugly." Even her attempt at a joke couldn't break the somber atmosphere. James obviously didn't get it.

"As you wish." Still holding her hands, he spoke in a slow, measured tone. "These bands link to your bioenergy and respond to commands in your thoughts. You need to be able to clearly identify each one whenever you activate them." He touched each of the bands one by one, naming them again. "Rad band, comm band, atmos, wrist beam. Identify them clearly."

Elise looked skeptical. "Really? You want me to mentally call each of these hunks of metal by their name and think at them? This is ridiculous."

"Close your eyes," he said and touched the bands one at a time again. "Rad band, comm band, atmos, wrist beam. Identify. Now think at them."

Fidgeting, and feeling stupid, Elise obliged him and closed her eyes. "Okay. Now what?"

"Think at them to close."

Elise did so, and squawked in surprise when all the bands tightened around her wrist. She lifted her arms and gaped at how snugly each band fit, as if it were made for her wrists.

"Amazing," she murmured.

A small smile escaped James's somber exterior, and he gave her an encouraging pat on the shoulder. "Well done. Which one is the rad band?"

Elise pointed at it.

He nodded. "Think at it: 'Activate full spectrum.'"

She closed her eyes again. A moment later, she knew the rad band was powered on. She couldn't explain exactly how she knew, just that it was. She opened her eyes again and nodded.

"Keep that on at all times unless I tell you otherwise. The rad band will protect you from most of the radiation and toxins in the air. Now, do the same for the atmos. Think at it: 'Activate all-coverage twenty-six Celsius.'"

She did, and the air around her warmed up immediately; she no longer felt a breeze. She inhaled and noticed that the air felt clearer. She looked down at these little magic bands. "This is incredible." She sniffed the air. "It still smells like crap. Does the band work on scent?"

James nodded. "It will only filter out identified toxic substances. There are settings to filter out all smells if you wish. We can go over its other settings later. For now, let's move on to the wrist beam."

They spent the next few hours practicing shooting her wrist beam. Elise hated to admit it, but she was having fun with these new toys, especially the wrist beam. In a way, she felt like one of those superheroes she used to read about in the digital comics as a kid. Sure, she was an awful shot and would fail to discharge the weapon more often than not, but that just took practice, right?

She was surprised to discover that James was actually a very good teacher. He was patient and gentle, but at the same time methodical, making sure she knew every step of a lesson before moving on. By the time the sun had climbed up the sky and its rays were coming in through the window openings, she felt comfortable enough with her new bands to practice on her own.

"That's enough for now," he said as she fired off her twentieth round of groupings at the concrete wall on the other end of the room. "Let's move on to the comm band."

Elise lifted her right arm up and stared at it. She didn't have to look at it in order to turn it on, but it helped focus her thoughts. Again, she got the feeling that the thing was on. She wasn't sure how; she just knew.

"Good," James said. "I want you to focus on frequency channel E9V1A55. It's a subchannel I created for personal use. You should be able to communicate with me through it."

She did so and again, felt nothing, but somehow knew it was open. "Hello?" she said. "Anyone there? The sixth sick sheik's sixth—"

"Close down the channel! Close it down!" James suddenly barked in a very loud voice.

Startled, Elise complied, shutting down the entire band. "What happened? What did I do wrong?"

Looking worried, James scanned the room and then glanced out the window. "I need to check something," he said. "Why don't you keep shooting at those targets? I'll be back soon.

Then, without a word, he leaped into the air as if he were Superman and disappeared into the wreckage of what was once Boston, leaving Elise to wonder what in Gaia just happened.

TWENTY-ONE

COMPROMISES

Panic seized James as he hurtled across the half-submerged build-ings to get as far away from Elise as possible, only stopping once he got to the far northeastern edge, where the ocean met the city. It took him several leaps across the rooftops of these ruins, but he soon reached the last building still standing against the ocean's constantly crashing waves. He walked to the edge and stared at the violent dark brown ocean swirl-ing beneath him. He should be far enough from her now.

He lashed out at the source of his anxiety. "What the abyss do you want? Don't even bother trying to trace me. I've already altered—"

"I'm not trying to track you. I'm off-book," said Smitt. James could hear the desperation in his voice. "Hear me out. Please, my friend."

James was going to cut Smitt off right there but he was curious. "How did you know about this subchannel?" he asked. "I've cut off all our pre-vious lines."

"Come on, James, it's me. I've been your only friend since the Acad-emy. I was there when you took three days to set this thing up. Two more than anyone else, I might add. Hell, you might not have ever finished the firewall setup for this thing had I not helped."

That much was true. James was always on the low end of the techni-cal skill sets for chronmen work. Smitt tutoring and helping him cheat was a major factor in his graduating from the Academy.

That was a long time ago, though. James was impressed. "And you remembered it after all these years?"

"James, I've been speaking in your head longer than I care to remember. Just took a few hours to backlog and pour through our old notes. You know it's all recorded somewhere."

"Just a few hours, huh?" James's gut felt queasy. If it had taken Smitt only a few hours to find him on the comm, what other mistakes had he made? Was a squad of monitors coming for them right now? What if they had already pinpointed their camp and captured Elise?

"Sorry, James," said Smitt. "You might be clever, but you're not very creative."

"Isn't that the same thing?"

"I was trying to be nice."

"Well, don't be. What do you want?"

"Listen, you're in a heap. A big fucking pile of shit. Levin's about to bring a blackhole's worth of pressure down on you. The agency is out for your blood."

"I wasn't aware of that. Thanks for telling me."

"No need to get pissy at the guy risking his neck telling you. You're the one who brought this down on yourself."

"Spit it out, Smitt. And I swear, if you somehow found a way to track my location through this subchannel, this will be the last you'll ever hear from me until one night when you're least expecting it . . ."

"Damn it, James. Shut up and stop threatening me. Listen! Valta wants to step in. They're willing to make it all right. They'll fix the shit with ChronoCom. Do you hear me?"

James frowned. Could the solution be that simple? Would Valta just sweep in and fix this mess he'd made? He shook his head; nothing is ever that easy, especially when it came to a megacorporation.

"What are they offering?" he asked.

"Sweeter than the original deal. They're willing to buy out your entire contract. Tack on that last year. You get to go straight to Europa!"

James froze, speechless. This offer, too, was unbelievable. How could they actually offer him a better deal after the mess he'd made? Something was very wrong here. "What do they want in exchange?"

"That person you brought back. Is she one of the scientists?"

"Yes," said James, distrusting where this conversation was heading. "Which one?"

"Why do you care?"

"Valta cares. They're willing to erase this entire event for both of us if Valta can claim indentured ownership of this scientist."

Indentured ownership. Common contract terminology used during the Gas Giant mining rush requiring miners to work their homestead for a certain amount of years in exchange for the mining companies paying for their transportation fare. In other words, Valta wanted to claim Elise as a slave.

"Good-bye, Smitt," James said, this time saying the words out loud as well.

"I see. I'm sorry. For everything. I hope you can forgive me one day."

"I already do. I know you were doing what you think is best." James was about to cut the connection when he stopped short. "Smitt, did you ever find out what that residual tear back on the Nutris Platform was from?"

"No. Been a little crazy here since you got back."

"Find out for me, will you? The entire job felt wrong, especially since I wasn't allowed to make the retrieval until after the disaster happened."

"I'll see what I can find out. Hey, James, keep this encrypted channel open for incoming messages. It's the only way I can keep in touch with you. Keep the subchannel a one-way receptacle if you must, but keep it pingable. Please."

James hesitated, recalling the last twenty years of his life, with Smitt as the only constant. This guy was the closest thing to family he had. It might help to have someone on the inside. Could he gamble with Elise's safety? Had Smitt ever intentionally steered him wrong? Even with the incident earlier today, James believed Smitt when he said he'd stepped in for James's own good. Did he still trust Smitt?

"I'll see what I can do," he said. "No promises, but it'll stay open. For now."

James was left standing on the roof alone with his thoughts. He looked out for several kilometers at the slow-moving ocean waves grounding against the buildings. His eyes followed the smaller chunks of concrete that broke off from the structures and fell into the ocean. Sometimes, the ocean didn't want those pieces and pushed them back against the buildings, hammered them against the crumbling walls until they were swept out again. The process repeated a half dozen times.

There was a thunderous crack as one of the large skyscrapers groaned and pieces of debris slid down its curved side, falling into the dark brown waters below. The dying building wouldn't last another year before it, too, would be swallowed up by the encroaching plague of shit.

The sun was still climbing up the sky, its sick orange glow beginning to scorch the Earth. The radiation haze on the fringe of the city was less severe than where he had left Elise. Speaking of which, he needed to get back to her. He still wasn't confident of her wrist beam skills, and though there was only a small chance she might have blown her leg off, leaving her was a risk he had had to take in case Smitt was tracing the subchannel.

A few bounds later, James was streaking from rooftop to rooftop, throwing out the kinetic coils and hearing the howl of the wind rush by him. He could have just flown directly back to their camp, but he wanted to conserve his levels. After all, who knew when the next time he could recharge would be. He would have to learn to be more efficient from this point on.

James watched the city below him slip underneath his feet. He had been in Boston once while on a salvage. A rich patron had wanted to recover many of the priceless works from the Boston Athenaeum before the war destroyed half the city, and then the Hurricane of 2153 finished the job. There were five million people here the night he jumped in and less than two million by the next morning.

How many ghosts lay here; how many deaths were beneath his feet? James shook his head and pushed those thoughts out of his mind. For the first time since he was a teenager, he had to worry about another living being. After years of being alone, he had someone else to fight for again. He just hoped it didn't end up like the first time. James gritted his teeth. This time would be different.

He reached their camp, a small fifth-floor room on the eastern side of a building facing one of the main streets that was now a slow-flowing river. Elise was gone. The fire had been reduced to glowing embers, and most of the supplies they had unpacked remained untouched, but she was nowhere to be found.

"Elise," he called out.

She's not here, Sasha, sitting in the spot Elise had slept, said. *I guess you lost her like you lost me.*

Grace, who was sitting behind Sasha, combing her hair much like she did in his dream, tsked. *You have a habit of carelessly misplacing important people in your life, pet.*

James's heart seized. What was Sasha doing here? Could it actually be her? When he first saw her with Elise back in 2097, he had written it off as the stress of the moment, but now here she was. He reached out for his little sister, afraid that his hand would pass right through her, but even more afraid that she was actually there. He pulled back just short of touching her. Sasha gave him a sweet smile as Grace continued to braid her hair.

"What is wrong with me?" he muttered.

You're going crazy. Grace grinned. *Possibly too much lag sickness.*

That was possible. Temporal miasma pills, due to their highly addictive nature, were the only things chronmen didn't have free access to. Responsibility for distribution of these pills rested on the medical wards at the ChronoCom bases. James just had his regimen before the jump, but he had missed the previous few, and it usually required several doses to overcome the sickness. That could be affecting his senses. Sasha and Grace must be figments of his imagination from the lag sickness.

And what about Elise? Did she just wander off? Was she captured by monitors? There were always wasteland tribes around, indigenous savages that still resided within the husks of the buildings, using the bones of the dead city as shelter against the elements. Maybe one of them had taken her. James clenched his fist. Black abyss help them if she was injured. Afraid to call out too loudly, he tore his eyes away from Sasha and searched the area. He combed up and down the floors, his fear growing by the second.

Elise didn't have an exo, so her movements would be limited. These buildings had been crumbling for hundreds of years now, and many of the structures were unstable. She could have fallen or a section of the ceiling could have collapsed in on her. Dozens of scenarios flashed through James's head, each more terrifying than the last. He didn't sacrifice his entire existence for her so she could die a meaningless death.

Wait, the comm band! He reached out to her through it, hoping she would know enough to answer back. He cursed when he realized that the channel was empty. He had told her to shut it off before he left her, for fear of the monitors tracking her. Now, he had no way to find her in this massive concrete jungle.

Well, James was determined not to rest until he found her alive and well, or touched her lifeless body one last time. He pulled up his AI band and set the point he was standing on as the center of his hunt, and then he began to tear through this dead city looking for its one living soul.

TWENTY-TWO

AUDITORS

There was a knock at the door and two auditors walked in. Levin spared just a glance their way as both sat down on the opposite end of his desk. The original class of auditors made an effort always to keep an open door for their brothers. Most auditors still remembered their chronmen days and were far too private to follow this policy. Levin was one of the few who held on to this mostly symbolic gesture for the sake of tradition.

He didn't trust the two auditors who had just come into his office in the slightest. The one on the left, Geneese, was a floater—an auditor who, without a permanent station, was used wherever and whenever his skills were needed. Levin had worked with him previously on a few retrieval jobs in the Ship Graveyard. The man was a by-the-books auditor, excelling at orders but rarely creative enough to deviate from directions when the situation required it. This made him the perfect auditor for half the responsibilities of the chain and the worst for the other half. He would have to be leveraged carefully.

Shizzu was even more of an unknown. He was probably the most unheralded Tier-1 chronman that Levin had known in his lifetime. He was surprised to hear of the man being raised to the chain. If a chronman had not been raised to auditorship by his eleventh year, he probably would never make it. Shizzu had been a chronman for fifteen. That made him ancient by auditor standards.

Regardless of what he thought of them, they were his brothers now. Shizzu was just a few years short of earning out and could have just floated his way to retirement. Whatever circumstance allowed him to join the chain, he took the auditorship rather than the easy way out. Levin could respect that, even though he had doubts about the man's worthiness.

"Brothers," he began, eyes still focused on the fast-scrolling vid. "I trust you have reviewed the operational scope?"

"Fugitive chronman hiding in the present," Geneese said. "Should make our lives easy. I'm surprised three auditors are being allocated for this, especially one so high up the chain."

A minor dig at his weakened status; Levin let it slide. "It's the least of my penance for allowing it to happen on my watch." He looked over at Shizzu. "You and James were in the Academy together?"

Shizzu shrugged. "Five years and we barely shared a hundred words. Even less as chronmen."

Levin pulled up the man's records and skimmed through the surprisingly brief transcript. The only real skill Shizzu had that made him stand out from other chronmen was his ambition and ability to kiss the right asses. Other than that, he was an expert tracker and investigator, and a poor team leader.

It still puzzled Levin how he had obtained an auditorship with such an undistinguished career. He found the answer at the end of the transcript. His last mission was completely redacted. It must have been a golden ticket assignment that had elevated him to the chain. Funny, Levin hadn't realized it was for sale.

Against proper decorum, he asked, "Tell me about your last job as a chronman, Shizzu."

Shizzu's spine stiffened. "The auditor files are open to all. You may take a look if you like."

"They're all redacted, brother."

"For good reason, then. Someone of sufficient rank—"

"I'm ninth in the chain. If I can't view it, no auditor can."

"Then the directors see fit to keep it from the eyes of the auditors."

This piqued Levin's interest even more. His instincts told him that it was important to pry, and they were rarely mistaken. It was unusual for chronmen to operate on jobs that kept auditors in the dark. Only directors had this authority, and with the recent occurrences and Shizzu's sudden promotion, there were far too many coincidences here for Levin to overlook.

He approached it tactfully. "You are a new brother working with two experienced auditors. There is a level of trust necessary for us to function as an effective unit. Obviously, your last job elevated you to your auditorship. I need to know what it is so I know if I can depend on you."

Shizzu pondered Levin's demand before finally answering, "It was a corporate-sponsored salvage into the late twenty-first century."

That time period set off an alarm in Levin's head. Where had he read another report regarding this recently? Then he remembered. Levin leaned forward on his desk. "Tell me everything."

The meeting lasted another five minutes before Levin barged out of his office, leaving his two underlings there, confused and unsure if they were excused. Levin didn't care if they sat there until they starved to death. Those two were the furthest thing from his mind as he nearly sprinted out of the auditor wing, causing anyone who saw his stormy face to scurry out of his way. He couldn't remember a time when he was this angry, not even when he found out about Cole's desertion.

No, that wasn't true. He wasn't angry at Cole, just profoundly disappointed. Deep down inside, he knew that he would have to be the one to hunt down his wayward nephew, and that once he did, it would spell the end of his relationship with his entire family. None of them would ever speak to him again, even though it was Levin who pulled the entire Javier-Oberon clan out of poverty. They knew Cole's fate was sealed the instant he poisoned his handler and fled into the past, that Levin had no choice but to hunt him down himself.

Levin guessed that he could have assigned the hunt to someone else; Shizzu would have been perfectly suitable for the task. But no, it had to be Levin, even at the cost of his relationship with his family. There was no other way to clear the dishonor. ChronoCom was all he had left, and those fools in the directorships were endangering it.

Levin barged past the Watcher's Board, taking only a moment to pay it proper respect: 50,373 monitors, 3,479 chronmen, and 223 auditors. A class at the Academy must have recently graduated. The numbers were still below what they should have been but at least they hadn't plummeted precipitously. Six years ago, the number of monitors was below thirty thousand after the ill-fated conflict with the Puck Pirates of Uranus. Four thousand monitors had died in a span of two hours.

Levin ground his teeth and slammed open the double doors to Young's office. The director, face buried in a book—a real bound one made of paper—ignored him, his eyes still focused on the pages as Levin stomped up and pounded a fist on the desk.

"You authorized the Nutris job?"

Young put up a finger to his lips, flipped to the next page in his book, and continued reading. Levin had the urge to reach over across the desk and yank the old man out of his chair, but he stopped himself. There were many ways to be suicidal; assaulting a director was probably the worst. His only recourse then was to tower over Young and wait for a response. Six minutes later, Young seemed to have found a good stopping point and finally snapped his book shut.

He looked up at Levin. "You're still fucking standing? Oh yeah, with that stick up your ass, I forget you won't sit down without being invited. Sit."

Levin stayed standing and jabbed a finger down on Young's table. "Shizzu's Nutris Platform job. The one that elevated him to the chain. Is it true? Who authorized it?"

Young looked confused for a moment before he finally shrugged. "Is that what you're pissy about? For a second, I thought you were going to come and demand I give your nephew a reprieve. I would have given it to you, you know. You owing me a favor would have been worth it. I'm surprised you didn't cash in on it." He rolled his eyes. "Instead, you barge in here demanding to know about a fucking job."

"Time Laws were broken! Who ordered it? The High Director needs to be made aware of this!"

Young chuckled in a raspy voice. He opened his mouth and paused, his eyes glinting. Finally, he leaned back and spoke. "Do you know why? Even though you're a planetary high auditor of the most important planet in the solar system, you're still just ninth in the chain, Levin?"

Levin felt bile climb up his throat as he quivered. "If this is an indictment of my abilities——"

"Oh, nothing to do with that," Young said. "You are the finest auditor ChronoCom has, which is why Earth is in your care, but you will never rise above the ninth. Do you know why?"

Levin kept still.

It was Young's turn to slam his fist against his table as he stood. "Do you really want to know who authorized the Valta job? High Director Jerome did, you fucking inflexible idiot. You want to hang someone for breaking the Time Laws? You better go to the very top!"

Levin felt his stomach twist and a jolt shoot through his body as those words sunk in. "Why would he authorize this? This goes against everything the agency stands for."

"Have a seat, Levin," Young snapped. "No, sit, damn it, and let's talk about your promotion."

Levin reluctantly did as he was told. Most of this information he already knew. It hadn't escaped his notice that his career within the agency, while exemplary by any measure, had leveled out. It had never bothered him much, until now. He knew he didn't play administrative politics as he should, but he had always felt his record spoke for itself. Apparently it didn't.

"You don't know the balancing act all the directors must do against the rest of the solar system," Young said. "Our power and control is delicate. When a powerful corp like Valta wants something, it has to be done. The only thing we can do is extract a high enough cost from them that they will think twice about making a similar demand again."

Levin snorted. "Or we can just cut off their power supply. We hold the keys to keeping these companies civilized and lawful."

Young sighed, and for the first time, Levin saw the hard, confident exterior of the director soften, revealing cracks in his legendary iron facade. "You're a good auditor and even a better man, but there's more to being a director than being a good auditor. This shit we do jumping back in time is the easy stuff." He pointed out the window. "The real dangers lie out there, where all the megacorporations and governments lie."

"I don't understand," Levin said. "We power half the solar system. Without us, humanity will collapse."

Young nodded. "Yes and no. We do hold the fate of humanity in our hands." But the corporations hold our balls in theirs. The agency is at the mercy of every single megacorp's whims. They're the ones that supply us with support: manpower, education, equipment, and technology. In return, we supply them our salvage."

"Seems to me our leverage is as great as theirs."

"That's where you're wrong, son," Young said. "Let me tell you something. Where do you think our jump bands come from? Our exos? All our equipment?"

Levin listed off every piece of equipment assigned to the monitors, chronmen, and auditors in rapid succession as well as all their component suppliers.

Young cut him off halfway down the list. "All from corporations. None of this is proprietary. What is to prevent someone like Valta from obtaining their own jump bands and running their own salvage?"

"The Time Laws strictly—"

"Nothing!" Young finished. "Not a damn thing. We are the only agency allowed to jump because Valta, Finlay, Radicati, and all those other fucking megacorps know that if one of them starts messing with the chronostream, they all will. They all know that it's better that none of them have that ability than all of them do. That's why ChronoCom has that authority, because they fucking give it to us."

Levin was stunned. "If that's true, then why do we still allow them to break the Time Laws?"

"Because that authority is an illusion that they can take back at any moment. If Valta wants something, we can push back only so much. In the end, it's better we do the job right than reject their request and have them flub it going off on their own. We try to stay as true to the Time Laws as possible. Otherwise, those bloodthirsty corporations will simply plunder the entire chronostream for every scratch of profit they can claw out of it."

Levin sat through another ten minutes of Young lecturing him about the way everything in this universe actually worked. He felt numb, but he knew what the director said was the truth. He had seen small signs of this many times throughout the years, but had always had such a disdain for the corporate side of ChronoCom's operations that he had stayed in the dark regarding those matters. It was a somber realization.

For years, he had considered ChronoCom the beacon that stood before humanity and stemmed the tide of collapse. Now, he realized he was nothing more than a referee, a mediator making sure all the corporations didn't play too rough.

"Thank you, Director Young," Levin said finally. "This has been educational."

Young nodded. "Keep this in mind. Make sure Valta and Sourn stay happy. Otherwise, there will be abyss to pay, and you'll find yourself on the wrong side of ChronoCom because we can't afford to be on your side."

TWENTY-THREE

REALIZATION

Much to Elise's family's and friends' delight, she had always been a bit of a neat freak, from something as silly as organizing all her books by genre, alphabetical order, and color, to making sure that the contents of her refrigerator were divided into their proper food groups.

Sure, sometimes that caused friction with her loved ones, like when she continually organized her last boyfriend's stuff to the point where he couldn't find anything. They fought over her cleaning habits for months. He was a slob anyway; their relationship was doomed to fail. She just liked things clean and organized, the way they were supposed to be. It made the world a better place.

This made her situation right now on future Earth doubly horrifying. If she could have one wish right at this instant, it would be to take a massive broom and dust off the entire planet. Maybe toss the whole planet in the wash. She wrinkled her nose. By the smell of it, it definitely needed to be disinfected as well.

Elise was standing on a pile of rubble at the water's edge, watching dirty gooey waves push debris and slop onto the rocky shores. This was the second time James had told her to stay still and she had ignored his command. Well, the first time that hadn't been completely true. She probably would have waited for him at the Heights if those guys hadn't come. This time, though, she got bored waiting for him and decided to stretch her legs down by the river in front of the building. What harm could there be? After all, who knew when James was coming back? It seemed every time he said he'd be back soon, he was never actually back soon.

There was a whole world out there for her to see. She had made a hobby of being an intrepid explorer ever since she was a little girl, often spending days wandering the mountainous forests of the North Oregon coast as a teenager. Twice, her parents had had to call for search and rescue. It never deterred her, though. Her love of discovery of the unknown and learning new things led her to biology and eventually to the Nutris Platform. It had also led her to where she was today. In the ruins of Boston. In some godforsaken dystopian future. And hungry as holy hell.

"I should have picked gymnastics or gotten a puppy as a hobby instead," she grumbled. Her stomach grumbled with her.

She knelt over the water's edge and skimmed the surface with a stick, watching the oily texture gunk and slide off. She lifted it to her nose. The water was stale, even though it was from a river; it lacked oxygen and nutrients. There was a stench lingering in the air, as if she were walking alongside sewers. It smelled of rust, rot, and death. It also smelled familiar.

Perplexed, Elise splashed some of the water onto a concrete slab with the stick and spread the liquid apart, careful not to get any of it on her. She was pretty sure this atmos band thing would protect her from any harmful elements, but wasn't ready to bathe herself in toxic river water yet. She sat there and watched intently as the water dried and left an orange residue stain on the rock. She sniffed it again. The same smells as before, but there was something new. The residue consisted of small bits and fragments of animals and plants, long since dead, but never properly decayed. They just rotted and continued to break apart into smaller and smaller pieces until they eventually formed this brown mush.

"No way," she said, her curiosity making her forget about her dire situation. "This can't be what I think it is. Could it have grown so far out of control?"

Elise wished she could take samples right now and study the brown gunk. If this crap was what she thought it was, then the potency of the virus discovered only a decade ago, in 2087, was much more serious than anyone from her time could have possibly imagined. She went farther downriver and double-checked her findings, taking samples from several different areas.

She climbed into one of the toppled buildings leaning against another on the other side of the canal. There was a balcony she could hang off of to grab a sample from the center of the flowing river. Maybe the substance and texture there would be different. Carefully watching her step and climbing onto the walls to scale over debris and sections of submerged hallways, Elise scrambled through the dark slanted corridors.

She traversed several small piles of rubble and then stopped when she saw light. She approached it carefully and whistled when she came across the embers of a dying fire in the corner of one of the smaller rooms. Beside it, there was a small nest of cloth making up what looked like a bed. Next to that was a small satchel. Someone had been here recently. Were they passing through like she was? Did they live here? How could anyone survive in this place?

What if they weren't friendly? Yesterday's beating flashed through her head and she flinched involuntarily from that memory. Then she remembered her wrist beam. Well, she wasn't going to be that easy a mark anymore. Let those bastards try to lay a hand on her. Wait, did she remember how to shoot this thing? Elise spent the next few minutes practicing with the wrist beam.

As she fiddled with her control, a shadow strolled into the room. Elise stared, mouth agape, a person about her size and height stared back equally with surprise. Almost an afterthought, she raised her wrist beam at him. If this was an actual gunfight—if they still called it that these days—she would have lost that draw yesterday. However, she was lucky they were both taken off guard and she was the only one armed.

The person, human by the looks of it, wearing black clothes splotched by brown sludge, with a face and hair to match, gasped at the wrist beam. He whimpered. Elise then realized that he was a young scrawny boy, though she couldn't be sure about his age. If he was living out in the wilds here, he could just be severely malnourished. He was staring wide-eyed at her hand. Elise looked down at her arm and realized that he recognized the weapon. The split second that she had taken her eyes off of him, he took off.

"Wait," she called, taking off after him. "I'm sorry. I didn't mean to point that at you."

She chased him, not completely sure why she was doing this. Her better senses were telling her to treat the kid like a feral animal and get out of his hunting ground as fast as possible. He knew the terrain and could be dangerous. For all she knew, he could be a cannibal. The possibilities and terrors of this place were endless.

Still, Elise chased the boy. Up a small hill, through several slanted hallways, down a hole in a wall, and down the side of the building. He was quick, darting back and forth around the various objects that protruded from the ground. If he hadn't been so busy zigzagging back and forth, she would have lost him long ago. That was when she realized that he was trying to make himself a hard target so she couldn't shoot him.

"I'm not going to hurt you," she yelled at the top of her lungs. "Come on, kid, stop!"

Surprisingly, she got the child's attention. He slowed and looked back at her. He wasn't, however, watching where he was going. He tripped over a windowsill and fell into a building. She heard a high-pitched squeak followed by a thunk and a cry of pain.

Elise ran up to the square hole and peered over the edge. Unfortunately for the boy, he had fallen into a large room that must have been at least a two-story drop. He was lying on the floor, holding his knee, and whimpering like a wounded animal. Her heart reached out to him; he couldn't have been more than ten or twelve, judging by his scrawny little frame. And this was all her fault.

Determined to help, Elise took the long route down to the child, through a lower-level window, past a flooded hallway, and up through a back stairwell, before she found a way to his room. It took nearly twenty minutes, but he was still holding his knee when she, sweaty and exhausted, with no idea how to get out of here, found him. The boy crawled to the corner, quivering with eyes wide.

"It's all right, buddy," she said, keeping her right arm behind her back and trying to soothe him like she would her dog. "I'm not gonna hurt you."

It took her five minutes to close that distance between them. Finally, she got within arm's distance and reached out to check on his knee, though she could tell by the swelling that it was definitely broken. Just as her hands touched his leg, the boy slashed out with a knife in his hand.

"Ow, you little brat!" she squawked, pulling back.

He succeeded in nicking her forearm, giving her a lovely gash. It was good thing she had quick reflexes, or it could have been a lot worse. Then she remembered that he had busted his knee because of her. Again, she approached cautiously, making what she hoped were reassuring gestures, though this time, she watched for his arm. When he tried to slash her again, she caught his wrist.

"Stop it!" she scolded.

He tried to strike her with his other arm. The two struggled for a few seconds.

"I mean it!"

He tried to kick her with his broken leg and howled when it connected with her shins. They both cried out in pain. Elise had babysat hundreds of times, and the best way to handle a child acting up was to let him wear himself out. However, this child had a knife in his hand and she didn't have the time, so she gave him one measured look and then slapped him across the face.

She shook her finger at him. "I said stop it! Now stay still."

The child was so stunned he dropped his knife. Elise kicked it aside and began to check his leg. It was definitely broken, but didn't seem like a compound break. He should recover from this if he kept his weight off.

"I'll be right back," she said, motioning for him to stay. Not like he could move much anyway.

In a few minutes, she returned with a few pieces of wood and cloth she had found in an old apartment and fixed a small splint around his leg. Then she gave him the leg of a table to use as a walking stick.

"That's the best I can do for now," she said, helping him up. "Where are your parents?"

He shook his head.

"All righty, then, guess we're stuck with each other for a bit."

Finding a way out of the building proved to be their next challenge. They boy could hardly walk, let alone climb, jump, or drop down from a ledge. They began to wander the rooms, making their way toward ground level. Several times, she had to push him up onto a ledge. She half-expected him to try to run off every time they got a few meters apart, but was pleased to find that he waited for her every time. Either he had come to trust her, or he realized that she was his best way of getting out of this sideways maze. By the time they escaped the building, the sun was beginning to set. They must have spent the entire day in the damn building.

"At least we're out now," she said with forced cheerfulness.

Her stomach spasmed and she hunched over. She hadn't eaten in almost two days. At least helping the kid had gotten her mind off food, but now her hunger was nearly debilitating. The child must have heard her stomach growl. He pointed at her, and then rubbed his own belly.

She nodded.

He took out a small wad of dried leaves and handed it to her. She accepted it gratefully and put it in her mouth. This was the second time in a day a stranger had handed her leaves to chew. What had happened to all the food on this planet? The leaf tasted vile, but it was something, at least.

Then, to her surprise, the boy took her hand and pulled her southward, deeper into the city. A few minutes later, she realized that they were entering Boston Common, or what was left of it. He was leading her back to his people. Someplace with food, hopefully. Elise didn't know if she could survive another night without eating. To her surprise, no sooner had they stepped five meters into the park than they were surrounded by a dozen dark figures. Elise counted four spears, two high-tech-looking guns, and a host of other stuff she didn't even recognize.

"Stay behind me," she said, pulling the child behind her. She might be able to shoot one of them with her wrist beam, maybe scare them off.

The child tore from her grip and hobbled toward them. One of the figures came forward and dropped to a knee. He inspected Elise's makeshift splint. There was a rapid exchange of words; the adult seemed to be scolding him. Then the child pointed at Elise.

The adult—an elderly man with a gray mane of hair—approached her and planted himself right in front of her, his eyes looking her up and down as if she were a curious, fantastic animal. That, or a side of beef. He caught sight of the bands on her wrists and hissed. Then he studied her smooth white hands and red hair.

Elise took the opportunity to study him as well. He was only slightly taller than her, though the stoop in his back had a lot to do with it. Like the child, the old man was covered from head to toe by a sort of mud. His clothing was a patchwork of handmade stitching and animal hides but he wore very well-made moccasins.

After he was satisfied looking her over, he spoke. Elise had no idea what he said. It sounded like he had put a bunch of letters in a blender with the top off and just spit them all out.

She shrugged and held her hands out, palms facing up. "I have no idea what you just said."

The old man was taken aback. "You speak Old World?"

She could barely understand him, but she recognized enough of the words to piece together what he said. Elise spoke World English back in her time, and maybe now it was considered Old World. The two sounded somewhat related, enough for her to make out his words even though a lot had changed.

"It's just World English where I'm from," she said.

He frowned, not quite comprehending. "You fix Sammuia?" The old man gestured at his leg and then at the boy.

"Is that his name?" Elise smiled, waving at him. He gave her a shy wave back.

"And you bring home. Th . . . thank you."

"Actually, he was bribing me with food." She emphasized that by pretending to put something in her mouth.

The old man nodded and pointed at his chest. "Qawol."

She did the same, patting her chest and enunciating her name syllable by syllable.

Then Qawol waved his arms at the group behind him. "We Elfreth."

She pointed to herself again. "Just Elise."

He smiled and stepped to the side. "Come," he said, gesturing toward the thickets. "We share."

"Get away from her!" a voice above them roared, and a large shadow came crashing down on top of them.

Qawol, surprisingly agile, jumped out of the way as James dropped from the sky and pounded the Earth, kicking up a ring of dust in all directions.

"Elise, get behind me," James snarled. "Why can't you stay put when I tell you?"

She saw yellow energy crackle around his body. The last time James was like this, he tore through the Nutris building as if it were made of Styrofoam. He would rip these natives apart.

"Wait, James!" she cried, grabbing his shoulder, trying to pull him back. She couldn't budge him, though. Her eyes widened when more armed natives appeared, weapons all aimed at James.

James and now nearly two dozen natives stared each other down, waiting for someone to make the first move. This was her fault. She had wandered into their lands, after all. She saw the boy hugging the old man's leg, too terrified to run. Their blood would be on her hands. She had to do something.

"Stop!" she screamed, louder than she thought possible. "Please."

Both parties forgot they were about to shoot each other for a moment and stared at her.

"Stop," she repeated, stepping in between James and the natives near the front.

She looked back at James, then at Qawol. By now, even more of the Elfreth had moved up behind them. They were surrounded.

"We would love to accept your invitation for food," she said, again putting her hand into her mouth.

Elise glanced at James once more and nudged him with her eyes. He scowled and reluctantly lowered his outstretched arms. She held her hand out to Qawol. The old man, eyes fixed on James, accepted it. Together, they walked hand in hand into the thickets, where presumably, she would either find a decent meal or become one. At this moment, it was a risk she was willing to take.

TWENTY-FOUR

THE ELFRETH

For abyss's sake, how many damn times do you have to wander off and get in trouble before you learn your lesson?" James raged, pacing back and forth in the tent-like quarters they had been given by the Elfreth. "Twice now I've asked you to stay put until I return, and both times you're gone when I do!"

"The first time," she said, sticking a finger up, "I had no choice. The second time, you just took off on me. That's twice now you decide to just take off on a whim and leave me sitting around like a dutiful housewife waiting for you to come home," she said.

"What's a housewife?" he asked.

"Never mind."

"Elise," he knelt in front of her, "you don't know how dangerous it is in this time. By all accounts, these people could have been cannibals. You could have been eaten, or worse."

"I fail to see many more scenarios that could be worse than being someone's dinner."

James held his tongue. He wasn't used to people disobeying him, be it out of fear or respect. He was a chronman, after all. Elise didn't care that he was a chronman; she didn't know what one was. She treated him like she would anyone else. James had to admit, he liked that about her. On the other hand, though, he wouldn't mind striking a little fear in her, so she'd damn listen to him once in a while.

"You need to stop acting like a child!" he snapped.

"Stop treating me like one, then," she snapped back, standing up and putting her hands on her hips. The top of her head almost reached his chin. "And watch your tone, mister. I don't know how you treat other people here in the future, but you don't get to talk to me like that."

"What?" He was taken aback. His plan to strike fear in her wasn't working.

"I mean it. Don't do that again."

"I'm sorry," James said finally. "I didn't mean to be rough, but these wasteland tribes can be dangerous." They weren't going to solve this today, and much as he wished, it wasn't like he could order her into submission. "What were you doing out there, anyway?"

"Was bored, mostly," she admitted. "Starving too. And then I got curious about the sewer you call an ocean."

He shrugged. "What about it? It's been like that as long as I've been alive."

"The ocean is not supposed to be brown."

"Who cares what color it's supposed to be?" James had to make her realize how dangerous things were in the present. Out here in the wastelands, there were hundreds, thousands of things that could kill her. Many of these savages were reputed to be cannibals, and that was probably one of the most humane ways she could have died.

They might have been fortunate to come across what seemed like a friendly tribe, but he was still wary of them. They obviously didn't trust him either. If it hadn't been for Elise and that savage boy she had rescued, James would have spilled all their blood by now. He still might. He didn't trust their motives.

A chronman's bands were valuable commodities on the black market, after all, and these savages had already shown themselves to have somewhat advanced weaponry at their disposal. They could be tech thieves, for all he knew, just waiting for him to lower his guard so they could take him by surprise. James unconsciously balled his hands into fists.

The boy with the broken leg, Sammuia, popped his head into the tent, throwing Elise a shy smile as he limped awkwardly on the splint. He gave James a wide berth. "Deenn. Foue," he said.

Elise looked confused.

"He said dinner," said James.

"How did you understand that?" she asked.

"Your . . ." James smacked his forehead. "Your comm band can translate nearly all spoken languages. Turn it on and think at it to activate global translation."

Elise's jaws dropped as she shook the bands on her wrist at him. "You mean all along I had a frigging universal translator here and you forgot to tell me?"

"I was going to get to it eventually. I didn't realize you were going to go live among the savages as soon as I wasn't looking."

"It would have been nice to know about this yesterday! I spent an entire day playing charades with these people. And while we're at it, don't call them savages. They're people just like you and me."

A few minutes later, with the comm band on and translating like it was supposed to, the two joined the rest of the natives for dinner in a wide open field surrounded by six skyscrapers arranged in a circle. Near the tops of the roofs was a circular bridge that connected all of them together. The six buildings, known as the Farming Towers, formed an easily defensible perimeter for the Elfreth to entrench themselves in.

The field in the center among the towers looked worn; this tribe must have lived here for a while. A large fire burned in a pit in the center. It was surrounded by several increasingly larger circles of benches. Small children sat in bunches along the ground, some playing, some being nursed by their mothers. On two sides of the field, guards kept watch on top of two broken columns.

James took a quick count. There were maybe two hundred of these Elfreth here; this must be one of the larger wasteland tribes surviving in the region. Most of them were just ragtag settlements of a couple dozen malnourished people. The Elfreth actually seemed healthy.

Elise was right about one thing: they weren't total savages. The field among the six large buildings was easy to defend. They had built makeshift barricades that could be easily moved to fill in the spaces between the buildings. Their food stores and supplies were stacked and organized near the entrances of the buildings. There was even a land-bound vehicle at the far end. James wondered if it worked.

Elise seemed to be fitting in just fine with these people. A little too fine for James's comfort. They were curious about her strange dress and exotic features. No sooner had she set foot on the field than she caught the attention of the tribespeople nearby. A group of children approached her shyly, and one of the bolder ones offered her what looked like a carving. For the first time since she had come to the present, he saw her smile, and it worried him.

Over the course of the night, his concern increased, as she grew more comfortable with them. Once the children overcame their shyness, it became a game for them to show off to her. He even heard her laugh once or twice. It was as if she had already become one of them. He hated to admit it, but he was jealous. What if she chose to stay with them? What if he lost her to them?

James ground his teeth and clenched his fist, his anger rising up through his body. He had to check himself. He didn't own her. Just because he had brought her back didn't mean she was his property. That would make him no better than Valta. She should decide where she wanted to stay. If anything, regardless of whether she rejected him or not, it was his responsibility to protect her. Like it had been with Sasha.

His thoughts flashed back to his little sister. She would be roughly Elise's age now. Probably the same height. Sudden grief almost buckled his knees as the memory of his sister overlapped the visage of his new ward. Was he doomed to fail her as well?

And me? Grace asked, sitting next to him and clinging to his left arm.

And me. The Nazi soldier waved, standing off to the side. He paused. *But you don't really care about me, do you?*

"Don't you two have anything better to do?" James asked.

You'd think so, the imaginary Grace replied.

That's a question you should be asking yourself, the Nazi said.

James shook her free violently and stood up. It wasn't the same with Grace and the Nazi. They were already dead. No. That wasn't true. Elise was exactly like them, except with Elise, he had chosen to bring her back. With all the others, he had chosen to let them die. He was a monster, playing God and choosing who lived based on personal whims. He buried his face in his hands. Even when he tried to do good, bad things happened.

Fucking abyss, he needed a drink. He wondered if these natives had anything that would do the trick.

James looked up and saw Elise looking his way, a concerned expression splashed on her face. She held one of the children in her arms and had a gaggle more following closely behind. Their eyes met, and she immediately put the child down and excused herself. She walked over to him and put a hand on his shoulder.

"Hey," she said. "Are you all right? You're looking a little unsteady, and a bit pale. Well, more than usual." She touched his arm. "You're shaking. Are you sick?"

"Chronmen don't get sick," he replied.

"All right, tough guy," she said, snaking her arm around his right elbow and leading him toward the fire. "Why don't you stop moping in the dark over there and hang out with everyone else?"

"You like these people?" he asked, dreading the answer.

"They're good people," she said. "They just have to warm up to you."

Elise sat him down on a stone next to the fire, and made a point to introduce him to the people nearby. He was amazed that she already knew many of them by name. They treated him like almost everyone else in this solar system did, just short of open hostility with a mix of caution, fear, and wariness.

The warmth of the fire felt good. James had kept his atmos turned off in order to conserve his levels. Now, he was feeling an assortment of temperatures, from the chill in his toes to the burning itch on his arm closest to the flames. He sat down next to her and stared at the fire. There was something alive and chaotic about a real fire, how it flickered and danced and spit sparks into the night air. Within a few seconds, the fire got too hot for him and he had to shy away from the heat.

Dinner came next, and it was pathetic. Both James and Elise were given dented metal bowls with a handful of berries, cooked vegetables, some strange blackened bits, and a sliver of meat. James's AI band ran an analysis of his meal: wild berries, mixed leaves, cooked cockroaches, and rat. None of this was new to James. He and Sasha had survived on a diet much like this back on Mnemosyne Station.

Elise made a gagging noise and struggled to choke down the cooked cockroach bits. He didn't have the heart to tell her what it was. He considered offering her his portion, though that probably would be the last thing she wanted right now. Then he reminded himself that he hadn't eaten in over a day as well.

As the two of them choked down their meals, he watched what the Elfreth ate. If they were eating the same thing as they were, then he might be able to put to rest his theory of them being cannibals. Fortunately, it seemed tonight was cockroach and rat night for everyone.

All of them were thin, especially the young. Many of the children reminded James of his childhood. Like he had been, each of them was skinny, tired, and hungry, but still young enough not to surrender to the hopelessness. At least not yet. Each of these kids was strong and resilient. They had to be to have survived this long.

"James." Elise nudged him. "You're bigger than me. Maybe you should have some of my dinner." She pushed her plate toward him.

"You need it as much as I do," he said gruffly.

She shook her head and looked at the children huddling over their small bowls. "Look at these people. They're starving. I've never gone hungry one day in my life. I don't think they've ever gone a day when they weren't." She looked to him. "Is there anything you can do? You have all these fantastic powers."

"I can't just conjure up food, and I think breaking into a food bank might draw some unwanted attention. Let's not forget we're both wanted by probably every authority in this solar system."

"Then go back in time to get it," she said, and brightened. "Yeah, why don't you? Head back to some point in time and bring back food for these people."

James shook his head. "It's more complicated than that. There are rules to follow and consequences to time travel. I can't jump back for small benefits like food and basic supplies. It's not worth the cost."

"Not worth the . . ." Elise looked angry. "Look at them, James! Some of the children don't look like they'll live through the winter. How is that not worth the cost?"

James looked away from her, his teeth cutting on his lower lip. It wasn't her fault. Elise didn't know what she was asking for; she didn't know the consequences. Yet, that earnest compassion on her face . . . . There was this kindness and vibrancy to Elise that James found alluring. It moved him in a way that he had never felt before. He found himself unconsciously drawn to her.

An idea occurred to James. He could accomplish two tasks at once. This was the perfect opportunity to test Smitt, to see if his twenty-year-old friendship had survived this trying situation. If Smitt found a jump point for him, would he have an ambush waiting for James? James could arrive a day early and if ChronoCom forces moved into the region . . . It would be risky, but something he needed to find out. And Smitt, as a handler, would be a valuable resource for him to leverage.

There was more to it, though. James would never admit it, but he desperately wanted to believe that his only friend was still his friend. Finding out where Smitt stood was more important to him personally than getting the food for the tribe. This gave him the perfect cover to test his old friend's loyalty.

"Excuse me," he said, standing up. He walked to the edge of the camp and shot up into the air, bounding on top of several buildings until he could no longer see the spark of the campfire. He landed on the water's edge and stayed still, listening for any signs of activity. With what he was about to do, he couldn't be too cautious. Satisfied that he was far enough away from the Elfreth's base, James sat down at the water's edge, and looked up at the gray and brown clouds that covered the sky.

"Smitt, you there?" he thought. "Smitt, let me—"

"I'm here, James. Have you come to your senses? Are you ready to turn yourself in?"

"No, but listen, I need a favor. It's an unusual request. I need you to dig around the chronostream and find a jump point that won't cause any ripples."

TWENTY-FIVE

Aid

Salih should have listened to Kaela that morning when she told him about her bad dream and begged him not to go out to sea.

"The oceans are angry and a storm dances near," his little sister pleaded, tugging on his tunic. "There might be pirates. A whale might swallow your ship whole."

Salih had laughed at her overactive child's mind, patted her on the head, and promised to bring something back once he returned from the short voyage to Carthage and dropped off the foodstuffs that the city so badly needed. The Romans were on the march toward the city again, and if history proved correct once more, it would be a very profitable summer for Salih and his two modest trade ships, laden with barley, salted fish, and smoked meats. He could charge three times more at a besieged city than anywhere else in the Mediterranean, and the Carthaginians would gladly pay. By the gods, Salih loved war.

Then Kaela's cursed dream came true. Not just part of it, but all. His little sister must belong to the Oracles. First, a sea creature, large enough that Salih could only guess it was a whale, smashed into his lead ship—the one filled with the expensive salted fish—and crippled her. Salih had lost a day tethering his remaining good ship to the crippled one to move the crew and merchandise on board before it was lost. Then, over-encumbered, the remaining ship was too slow to outrun Sicilian pirates who had sensed an easy prey.

Salih, as a last desperate measure to escape, steered the ship into a storm. His risky plan worked, kind of. On one hand, Salih lost the pirates in the storm. On the other, he lost his mast and oars in doing so as well. Most of his men had perished in the storm, and now three days later, the rest were succumbing to the cruel sea one by one. Salih himself hadn't eaten anything for days, except very salty fish.

His two surviving sailors, Adom and Geb, were dying belowdecks, complete invalids suffering from salt poisoning. Salih cursed the gods, his men, and his ill fortune. He cursed Kaela most of all. After all, she was the one who stood to inherit his wealth when he was gone. She must have profaned him to the gods. She was devious, that one, and far too clever by half for a seven-year-old.

Now, huddled under a tarp to protect himself from the ferocious sun, Salih grimaced at the half-eaten salted fish in the wooden bowl next to him. In disgust, he smacked it overboard and watched it disappear into the sea. Why did all his cargo have to be so heavily salted on this trip? The one time he didn't bring fruits! Fruit spoiled in sieges and it was the wrong season; that was why. Still, the gods had played a cruel trick on him.

The tarp fell off and Salih felt the sting of burning rays on his sunburned back. He shook his fist at the gods and pleaded, "Horus, damn your infernal heat. I can't take it much longer."

There was a yellow flash, brighter than the light of Horus. Salih shied away in terror as a silhouette of a man appeared floating in the air, casting a long shadow over him. With the sun to the back of the figure, Salih couldn't quite make out who he was. The very fact that he was floating could only mean one thing, though.

"My humble apologies, mighty Horus." He threw himself onto the deck of his ship. "I meant no insult. Please save me from—"

"Quiet," the dark figure said, drifting down to the deck. As his body moved out from the sun's path, Salih realized that the god looked like any other man, except for his strange garb. He must be divine, though, or at least noble, for his skin was so pale, it was as if he had never stood in daylight before. Of course! How could the sun god's own rays darken him?

Salih stayed prostrated as the figure made a circle around the deck. He checked the broken mast and then knelt down in front of Salih. "Where is your cargo, merchant?"

"Down below, great Horus," Salih said. "Please, it is yours. Just deliver me to safety."

The figure made a chuckling noise, which Salih found strange. Did gods have a sense of humor? He stood up and walked to the starboard side of the ship and looked out toward the horizon.

"Come here, merchant," he said.

Salih obeyed and crawled on all fours toward the figure.

"Oh, stand up, for abyss's sake," the figure said.

Salih dutifully obeyed and stood, though he made sure to keep his head bowed and his eyes on the ground. He had once heard the story of man who stared at the face of the sun god and had his eyes seared off. Salih was already in enough trouble, being stranded out to sea. The last thing he needed was to go blind from—

"Do you see those clouds on the horizon?" The figure pointed at the dark rumblings in the distance.

"Yes, great god. It is the same storm that destroyed my ship and drowned my crew. Mighty Yam must have been displeased with my offerings before I set—"

The figured turned and faced him. "In two days' time, the storm will engulf you again. This time, it will not be as merciful. It will break your ship and you will drown."

Salih's face turned white. "Please save me, great god. I have a family, a sister, an elderly mother."

"I can do nothing for you, merchant, except offer you a quick death. I'm sorry."

The dark figure rose up into the air, and then Salih's deck buckled and cracked with a thunderous bang as if lightning had come down from the sky. The cargo stowed in the hold broke through the deck and orbited around the floating man. He made a strange gesture, and then all of Salih's cargo disappeared.

Salih watched in horror as ocean water rushed through the gaping hole in his ship. It was sinking!

"You have helped many people today, merchant. I hope your next life remembers that." The god gave him a tilt of the head, a small sign of respect that Salih found strange coming from a deity.

"Great god," he cried, reaching his arms out toward the figure. "Save me!"

The last thing Salih saw were the ends of his ship as they folded up and over him, finally blotting out the angry sun that had plagued him for so many days. Then everything went black.

The instant James pulled his haul from the trading ship out of his netherstore, the party began. The savages—no, the Elfreth, he reminded himself that Elise didn't like it when he referred to these people as savages—gathered around excitedly as he stacked bags of barley and meats and fish on one of the tables. James wasn't sure what they were more fascinated by: the fact that he was pulling things out of midair or that he had just brought enough food to last them weeks. He realized a few minutes later that they could care less about this magic trick of his with the netherstore as they mobbed the foodstuffs.

An elderly tribeswoman, her hair tied neatly in a bun, wearing a leather piece on her chest that could only be called an apron, came and inspected one the sacks. A knife materialized in her hand and she slit a small corner off the top. She sniffed the contents inside and her face lit up into giant smile. She waved the kitchen staff closer. The smile fell a bit when her eyes rested on James, but he was rewarded with a slight nod. Then she began to delegate.

More and more of the Elfreth came to see what was going on. Word soon spread all the way up to the Farming Tower roofs, and soon, the entire tribe left their daily work early and a spontaneous celebration exploded in the field.

Elise came a few minutes later with Sammuia, the boy with the hurt leg, leading her by the hand. The boy seemed to follow her wherever she went. She eyed the stockpile, a small smile spreading across her face.

"Did you rob a grocery store?"

"A floating one," he answered. "Originally meant for the fishes. I thought I'd put it to better use."

"Did everything go all right? You were gone for a few days." She paused. "I was worried."

James nodded. The actual job only took a few hours. However, he had gone to the jump site two days early and stayed a day in the region after he returned to reconnoiter ChronoCom's activity when a patrol came to investigate the jump. He was relieved and deeply moved to discover that he could still trust Smitt. If Smitt had wanted to betray him, monitors would have been swarming the general vicinity. Knowing that Smitt was still his friend lifted a great weight off James's shoulder.

Elise and James stood side by side as the tribe broke down the foodstuffs within minutes. James was now inclined to agree with Elise that these supposed savages were anything but. If anything, through the necessity of stretching their meager resources to the limit, they were as efficient if not more so than any of the people in the civilized colonies.

Even the now-emptied sacks were cut down for blankets, clothing, and bandages. Meats were stripped from the bone and then the bones stockpiled for stew and weapons. Dried herbs were mashed into paste for seasoning and medicine. Nothing went to waste. Within an hour, the six pallets of foodstuffs were gone, then a small legion of children moved in to pick up any remaining grain that might have slipped through careless hands.

Elise put her arms around him and leaned on his shoulder. "You did good, big guy. Lots of people are going to have full bellies tonight."

He grunted. "Would have done better if the merchant had a little whiskey with him."

"Did they have whiskey back then?"

James shrugged. "Whiskey, mead, ale, wine? Who cares. I'll drink anything right about now."

One of the Elfreth must have overheard him, because a few minutes later, a young man walked up to them. He eyed James up and down as if about to start a fight, and then tossed him a dented tin flask. He banged his chest twice with his fist and pointed at his heart. "Chawr."

James caught the flask and, with more than a bit of skepticism, uncorked it and took a sniff. Whatever was inside smelled like a dead animal soaked in tar, but it was definitely booze of some sort. James raised the flask to him. "Thank you, Chawr." This was the first time anyone in the tribe had showed him a kindness.

The man stared at James very seriously and nodded. "For food. Fair even."

James stared at the flask and shrugged. In his case, it probably wasn't a bad trade. He was barely fighting off the shakes. He took a swig and nearly spit it out of his mouth. His knees buckled and he almost dropped to one knee.

Chawr howled with laughter. He slapped James on the shoulder and joined a group of his friends watching in the distance. They all looked over at him, whooping and joking as they walked away. James was pretty sure they were now just making fun of him.

"Don't spill a drop," Elise teased. "Wait, you're turning red. Are you sure that's what you think it is?"

"Definitely not," James gasped, in between labored breaths. It was in fact alcohol, though he was sure it could probably run a diesel engine. He bent over, still gasping for breath, not sure if he should thank those young Elfreth or kick their asses. Finally, after several minutes, when he felt back in control of himself, he shrugged and took another swig. It still burned his throat like the abyss but he was ready for it this time.

"You're unbelievable," Elise said. "I can smell that crap from your breath. You stink like a fire-breathing dragon."

"What's a . . ."

"Never mind."

For the rest of the day, the two sat in the middle of the bustling field inside the six towers as the Elfreth prepared a feast. It seemed they had also invited some of their neighbors, as a few other groups of natives James had not seen before came shortly before dinner. The two groups embraced and the festivities approached.

The anticipation for dinner was building. At that very moment, James felt something he hadn't felt in a long time. A small wave of contentment washed over him as he stood in the center of this community, flask of wasteland liquor in hand. For a brief instant, he felt like he belonged. Sure, no one spoke with him, or even looked him in the eye, but he had brought them this gift, and for now, they accepted him. No, they tolerated him a little more. He still saw the distrust in their eyes and their wariness when he was around, but this boon of food, though a terrible and inefficient use of his power levels, time traveling, and health, went a long way for these people. Plus, it got him some liquor, which for him felt much needed. It had been days since he last had had a drop.

James's eyes wandered over to Elise. Since she had come to the present, she had been mostly subdued, often crying in her sleep. Now, being here with these Elfreth, her old self was starting to peek through. It was rare to see her smile like that. It reminded him of the first time he met her on the Nutris Platform.

Their eyes met and he thought she blushed, though it could have been the reflection of the fire. That alone was worth retrieving supplies for these savages. Still, it was a high price. Elise had no idea what she had asked for in making that jump for something as inconsequential as foodstuffs.

Now, a nine-point-three-day or 1,632.2-kilometer radius of time and distance around where Salih died was a dead zone, the chronostream ripped and permanently no longer accessible for someone to jump into. The time and distance varied based on a planet's rotation or whether the jump was in open space, but the impact was still the same.

In a singular case, it could be overlooked, but unregulated in mass quantities, it could devastate the chronostream. That was why the agency weighed the worth of every jump into the past. By now, they would also have been alerted of his illegal jump and sent auditors to investigate. It would be only a matter of time before they tracked him down.

James looked down at his shaking hands. Also, without a miasma regimen, which was carefully guarded by the auditors within ChronoCom, the lag sickness was slowly killing him. He inhaled and felt the sick oily sensation that now seemed permanently stuck in his throat. The twisting in his guts felt natural now, as if the spasms of pain wracking his body were simply a part of who he was. And with every subsequent jump, it would just get worse.

TWENTY-SIX

AUTHORITY

evin tapped his foot impatiently as the search team returned from the Mediterranean Sea. The agency had detected an illegal jump in that vicinity and dispatched the team to investigate hours ago. Unauthorized jumps were rare, since they were serious offenses. There usually weren't more than two to three dozen a year within the entire solar system, and most were caused by chronmen.

At first, Levin had immediately suspected that it was James, possibly fleeing to some time in the past where he hoped to escape from justice. That's what most fugitive chronmen did. However, hiding in the past was dangerous, since any ripples in the chronostream caused by the time traveler could be detected by the agency. No, hiding in the present usually was the smartest way to stay under the radar.

What was even more surprising to Levin was the fact that the monitors detected a return jump as well only a few hours later. It must have been a very short trip back to the past for the culprit. That would mean whoever it was—Levin hadn't ruled out James yet—wasn't trying to hide in the past but had dropped in for a quick salvage. The mystery deepened.

Standing on the roof of the building of the skyscraper ChronoCom had converted into an outpost, he paced back and forth as the search team's collie landed on the roof. He nodded as they filed out, saluting him as they passed by to go down into the building. All the men were accounted for.

Levin had learned from his former mentor early on to always receive your men when they returned. "If you're willing to send men out on a dangerous mission, be willing to see them home," Landon had said. A young Levin had taken that to heart, even if Landon had fallen from his once noble ways.

Several of the savages and settlers who scrounged a living in these wastelands had confirmed sightings of James recently; his hideous collie was easily distinguishable from the rest of the ChronoCom fleet. Any monitor who crossed his path would be hard-pressed to survive the encounter. To be fair, it was not completely unexpected. Regardless of his mental state, James was a skilled chronman. He had been put on the short list multiple times to be raised to the chain. His downfall at every review was his temperament and mental instability. This recent violation of the Time Law only proved that denying him the auditorship was the right decision.

The sun had just disappeared along the western horizon. Levin waited until he was the last one on the roof before heading downstairs as well. Tomorrow, the search would continue. He was about to walk inside when he saw a glimmer of light. It shot across the night sky and turned abruptly. He watched as it grew larger and larger. A ship. Not ChronoCom, by its exhaust signature; agency collies used an older, atomic-spark propulsion system that emitted a whitish-yellow trail. It was a reliable, if not slightly inefficient design that had been used since the twenty-third century. This moving light had a blue tail, and moved with a smaller signature.

"See it?" Levin thought to the night watch.

"Yes, Auditor," Jerkis, the monitor on duty, answered. "Hailing for rights."

"One of ours?"

"Just received ChronoCom codes. Valta signature. Valkyrie class attack ship."

Levin sighed. Corporate bureaucracy was the last thing he wanted to deal with. Levin had hoped to ditch Kuo behind at Earth Central when he began to hunt for clues of James's whereabouts. It seemed she'd found her own ride.

The last thing he needed was interference and delays from soft off-worlders who didn't know how Earth's delicate global community operated. There were different rules down here in the wilds than up there in space.

"Confirm with the director on this ship," Levin said.

"The planetary director had just contacted us about the Valta contingent," Jerkis said.

Valta's contributions to the agency were significant, and with their investment into ChronoCom came influence. Levin was pretty sure his job was about to become much more difficult.

He waited alone on the roof of the building as the sleek Valta ship, looking like it had just left the space dock, came to a hover over the roof. Protocol would warrant that he should call up his senior officers to greet the Valta contingent, but in this case, Levin was going to allow his men the rest they deserved. He watched the ship land and come to a rest in near silence. The blue glow of the ship powered down with a low hum and then the hatch lowered.

Levin noted at least nine pieces of technology that were more advanced than anything ChronoCom used just by eyeing that landing. He wondered about their weapons and shields as well. What else was Valta keeping from everyone else? The corporations were holding out on the agency. He recognized Sourn first, walking in what looked like a deep-space mining suit, complete with placement thrusters and high-rad shielding. And like the ship, the suit looked brand new. The off-worlder must be really worried about his exposure to Earth's toxic atmosphere. Levin's face turned to a grimace when he saw another person follow the Valta liaison down the ramp.

"Auditor," Sourn said, maneuvering awkwardly in his giant suit, "how goes the manhunt?"

"It goes." Levin bowed. "Tracking an elite operative is much like putting together a complex puzzle."

"I'm sure you're very familiar with Securitate Kuo by now." Sourn gestured. "Could we speak inside? I find these wide open spaces disquieting."

"Welcome to Frankfurt, Liaison." Levin gestured toward the door leading downstairs. "Please, this way. You'll find the atmospheric conditions downstairs well within off-world survival parameters." A poor jest, but one that would probably calm Sourn's fears. The conditions downstairs were no different from those on the roof. The space was just more enclosed.

Levin led them down the flight of stairs two levels to a large open room with a circular table. He had commandeered this area as his command center and ran the operation in this region from here.

Sourn looked around, sniffed at the layers of dust caked on everything inside. "Intolerable," he muttered. He looked at Levin's three officers working in the room, and then back at Levin.

"Leave us," Levin ordered. The three men dutifully complied, leaving him alone with Sourn and Kuo.

When his men had left, Levin sat down in his chair at the head of the table and gestured for Sourn and Kuo to do the same. He leaned forward. "So to what do I owe this visit?"

Sourn was about to sit down on one of the chairs, and then thought better of it. Instead, he walked to the map of Europe and studied the markings Levin and his team had made on it.

"The culprit with the woman from Nutris is still at large?" he asked.

"Chronman Griffin-Mars and the individual suspected to have been brought from the past are still unaccounted for," Levin said.

"And the search from that unauthorized jump?"

How much of his operation does Sourn already know about? How deep is Valta's feed into ChronoCom? Were any of his men reporting directly to them?

Levin took a deep breath and checked his anger. "I sent a scout party to analyze the jump. There was an unauthorized return jump as well. Unfortunately, my team did not arrive at the location in time to intercept the return."

"A salvage then?"

Levin nodded. "Originally, I hypothesized that it could be the fugitive chronman trying to escape to the past. Instead, monitors indicate he made a distance jump far back in the past."

"For what purpose?"

"Unclear. Supplies, food, another human? Who knows what a chronman who no longer follows the Time Laws is capable of?" He emphasized his next words. "That's why it is imperative that control of time travel be strictly regulated and controlled by the agency."

Sourn grunted. "Seems you guys cause as many problems as you regulate."

"I assure you we have this under control. In any case, this is a Chrono-Com operation, one that Valta has no authority or vested interest in. If there is anything—"

"Valta has a vested interest in your mission. Do you have any information on who he brought back?"

"Negative, we believe it must be a straggler he had become infatuated with while he was on the salvage. Chronman James has a history of being alone. Perhaps . . ."

Sourn raised an eyebrow. "We could care less about your chronman. We have reason to believe the temporal anomaly that was brought back could be one of the lead scientists from the Nutris Platform. Your mission parameters are now changed. She needs to be captured alive."

"That's not possible," Levin said. "Time Laws are not flexible. Violations cannot be allowed to stain the time line. Our objectives are clear."

"Your objectives are now to support the capture of this fugitive. Confirm with your superiors if you must."

At the same time, a message from Young popped into the queue in Levin's comm band. He didn't bother opening it. Of course Young would back up Sourn. The director and most of the leadership were in the pocket of the corporations. Now, it seemed even the Time Laws could be bought.

"How can I assist Valta?" Levin said, gritting his teeth.

Sourn gestured to Kuo standing next to him. "The securitate has been monitoring your progress and has made some recommendations. There are developments that have elevated Valta's interests in this operation. From this point on, Securitate Kuo here will assume a larger role in this operation. You are in command, but she will be protecting that interest, starting with a direct order to keep the anomaly from the past alive. Follow her direction when she feels that intervention is necessary."

Levin gave Kuo a slight bow. "ChronoCom welcomes your active support in our operation." He emphasized every one of those words.

Kuo's face finally changed just a bit and the corners of her mouth curled up. Levin wouldn't quite call it a smirk since there wasn't much of a smile there. "Happy to be of assistance, Auditor."

"Very well." Sourn nodded. The guy seemed like he couldn't wait to leave this squalor. "I'll leave you two to your work. I want results, Securitate. See it done."

"Yes, sir." Kuo bowed. That was the only sign of deference Levin had seen from her.

The two of them watched Sourn bolt out of the room. Two minutes later, Jerkis sent word that Sourn's ship had taken off. Levin and Kuo sized each other up, both trying to take control of the situation.

Kuo broke the silence first. "From now on, I will need access to all of your communication channels, not just the ones you deem necessary. Inform your men of the new chain of command."

"Since you are officially only functioning in a support capacity, I will be happy to relay the requests I approve of to my men," Levin said.

Kuo didn't miss a beat. "I had hoped not to trivialize your role to that of a gopher, but you may do as you wish."

"Thank you for such consideration."

"Have you investigated the fugitive's personal relationships?"

"Increased surveillance has been applied to his former handler, yes. However, ChronoCom does not feel it is necessary to cast an invasive net over everyone who has ever interacted with him."

Kuo looked disapproving as she walked to the map and studied it. She spoke with her back still to him. "Your resources seem to be stretched quite thin."

"We use what we can, Securitate, and he is only one fugitive, after all."

"Report to the director that you will require three times your current allocation. If you have insufficient numbers, I will be happy to provide Valta forces."

Levin kept his face neutral. Like the abyss he was going to let her take over his operations like this. "I'll see what numbers we can spare."

She pointed to four of the regions that Levin had circled. "These are the high-probability zones on the continent. I see they are all rural."

He nodded. "Every remaining major city has a heavy state presence. His best bet to avoid discovery would be in the wastelands and the scattered settlements throughout these areas."

"The two fugitives, James and the scientist, they have rad bands?"

Levin nodded. "Possibly. He ransacked the armory before he made his escape."

Kuo made a slow circle around the table. "Good. What if we were to filter all high-population zones with trace grayon gas? Valta uses it to trace pirate ship movements in mining operations regularly."

Levin frowned. "Grayon gas is highly radioactive. That would kill off every living person for several kilometers. There could be thousands of wastelanders there."

Kuo turned to him with a perplexed look on her face. "And?"

TWENTY-SEVEN

TRIBAL LIFE

Sammuia appeared in their tent once again just as the sun was rising. This time, he had company with him. A girl, slightly taller, but with his same face, peeked at Elise over his shoulder while he nudged Elise's shoulder.

"Elder Elise," he whispered in her ear. "The sun is up."

James, sleeping on the far side of the tent, bolted out of bed, his eyes shifting back and forth to the two children in the tent. Sammuia yelped in terror. Whatever hopes Elise had for waking up peacefully were ruined by the cries of not one but two children literally climbing over her to get as far away from James as possible.

She gave him a dirty look and pulled Sammuia in for an embrace. "There, there," she soothed. "The big bad monster's only being a jerk."

James looked at the young boy, and then at the flap through which the girl had run for cover, and yawned. "These people obviously have no concept of privacy."

"Is there something you need, Sammuia?" Elise said, turning the boy's head so that he was no longer staring petrified at James. "And who did you bring with you?"

"This is my sister Rima," Sammuia said, puffing out his chest and pulling her back in the tent. "She wanted to meet you."

"Hello, Elder," Rima said, eyes averted and toe digging into the dirt. She held out a single flower.

Elise accepted it and held the girl's hands. "Thank you, dear."

Sammuia tapped her on the shoulder. "Elder Elise, Oldest Qawol would like you to gather with the tower workers."

Sammuia nodded, and then clung to Elise again when James got out of bed. Elise wondered what had happened between the Elfreth and his people for them to be so terrified of him. Even the food he brought them earned him only temporary goodwill. Would they ever learn to trust him?

James scowled. "They're trying to make you one of them."

There was a hint of anger in his voice; Elise wondered why. Did the Elfreth do something to upset him? Why was there so much animosity between them? She had to remind herself that she was a visitor here to this world and there was much she didn't understand. After all, a lot had changed in four hundred years. She looked down at the dust-covered ground, complete with vines and weeds crawling in between what looked like chunks of cracked concrete. Their tent was on what used to be a street.

"Damn straight, a lot changed," she muttered. She stood up and stretched, rising to her tiptoes and feeling her aching joints pop. She was used to surviving in the wilderness back home; she wasn't the lab rat sort of biologist, after all, but what she was going through right now was a whole new level of discomfort.

"Come on, James the time-traveling liar," she said, "we ate their food and slept in their homes. The least we can do is work for it."

Sammuia and Rima, each one holding one of her hands, led them to where the Elfreth had gathered in the communal field. Franwil, Qawol's wife, was in charge and split everyone up into smaller groups. James made a small ruckus when Elise was separated from him, but finally relented when she pinched him on the arm and told him to mind his manners.

"I'm only going to be planting crops on that rooftop," she whispered fiercely in his ear. "If something happens, I'll think to you through the comm band and you can come all knight-in-shining-armor at me. But for Gaia's sake, stop being so petulant. You're scaring people."

James kept that scowl on his face until the very last moment, when his group led him away to help reinforce a dam that kept the rising tides from overflowing into their camp. Elise watched as he looked back no less than three times as he disappeared over the hill, looking like a little boy being forced to go to school.

"Be safe," he thought to her.

"I'm hoeing crops. What could go wrong?"

"I'm still not convinced they're not cannibals."

Elise's group started the morning climb up one of the six towers the Elfreth referred to as the Farming Towers. The six buildings formed a ring and were connected at the seventieth floor by a sky bridge. The tribe had planted crops on the flat roofs of the tall buildings above the low-hanging fog clouds that often covered the sun's rays.

It took half an hour for the entire group to climb the stairwell up to the seventieth floor. At first, Elise feared they would be walking up in pitch darkness. Fortunately, the tribe had taken off the doors on every level and cut direct paths to the outside, so sunlight could illuminate the darkened stairs.

The group passed the tedium of the long walk by singing tribal songs that told the story of their ancestral home in the south along the Delaware River, in a so-called magical alley with tiny houses where the Elfreth received their namesake, and the long journey up through the terrible Manhattan island, finally to this blessed sanctuary here at the Farming Towers.

To Elise, the songs sounded like a combination of old church hymns and yodeling, except everyone was off-key and harmonizing seemed to have become a lost art. Maybe she was being a little critical. After all, these people were all singing while walking up seventy flights of stairs in a stairwell that was basically one gigantic echo chamber. Also, Elise would be the first one to admit she was tone-deaf, so who was she to judge?

As for the climb up the Farming Towers, Elise had always kept herself in good shape—a requirement in her old career—but by the time they had reached the sky bridges, she was grateful for that small moment of rest.

Looking around, she realized how soft she was compared to the people of the Elfreth. They hadn't even begun work yet and she was exhausted. She was probably one of the youngest and fittest looking here, the rest of the group consisting of the elderly and the women, yet she had the most trouble keeping up.

Next, they split into six even smaller groups as Franwil delegated where each group was to work. Elise was one of the last chosen. She couldn't help but flash back to her elementary playground days when she was often chosen last due to her diminutive size.

"You stay with me, girl." Franwil pulled Elise along by the wrist as if she really were a child. They joined a group of six older women, all either short or so stooped over that their hands nearly dragged against the ground, if they just let them hang down.

The small group climbed another four flights of stairs before they reached the roof, where Elise found several neat rows of tall crops that looked not unlike stalks of corn, but with husks of bloodred vegetables buried just under the soil. The stalks of the crops were a pale gray with a strange finish so smooth that they looked unnatural, almost metallic.

"Dig up the husks and put them here," Franwil instructed, pushing a brown woven basket into Elise's hands. "Watch for the stem. Rub your fingers against the grain and you might lose one."

Elise looked over at a pile of the long rod-like stalks, cut up and stacked neatly to the side. "Do I need a machete to cut the stems?"

Franwil shook her head. "One of the other groups will rotate here later in the afternoon to do that. Our job here is to only gather the blood corn."

They set about their work as Elise and the women methodically worked their way down the neat rows, their short height making it easy for them to pluck the husks out of the dirt while simultaneously protecting them from getting lashed by the foilage above them on the stalks that could cut flesh by mere touch. It was backbreaking work that continued for the better part of the morning.

Just as they were finishing up, another group arrived to take their place. This time, it was a group of taller women and men, with straight backs and armed with machetes and gloves. The two groups nodded and traded positions. Elise's people rested while the new group went to work, first using their gloved hands to tear off the leaves and then hacking away at the base of the stalks with the machetes, creating several smaller piles.

"What do you use them for?" Elise asked as she watched the stacks of stalks grow.

Franwil gave her a puzzled smiled. "The body of the blood corn, once shorn, can be used to build shelters that keep the insects away, while the leaves are used for filters to clean the impurities out of the rain." She paused. "This is mother-to-child wisdom. What poisoned life did you and the chronman find us from again?"

Elise pretended not to hear as her small group left their replacements to do their work. James had decided this morning not to tell the Elfreth where she had come from. Even in such a remote place, the wasteland people knew of chronmen and the Time Laws. If the tribe ever found out the truth about her, who knew what they would do? They might end up turning her over to the authorities, drive them away, or maybe even kill her on the spot.

Instead, James had spun a tale of her abuse and how she fled from another tribe, and how he had found her while she wandered the radiated mountains of Appalachia. They had accepted her easily enough, more so than James, whom they avoided and watched at every waking moment.

The group walked down the four flights back to the sky bridge, and continued on to the next building, where they replaced yet another group who had been laying soil and breaking apart the larger chunks of dirt with hoes and pickaxes. There, they planted seeds brought up by even another group, this time younger children who carried the large sacks in twos and fours. Sammuia was in that group. The boy grinned and made a show of holding her hand in front of the other children. Overall, Elise was impressed with this well-tuned operation.

She looked over the edge of the building down at the rest of the Boston Common, where the low-hanging soot clouds swirled, the gray-colored winds dancing around the buildings like wisps. It was a harsh world she lived in now. To survive out here, these people had to work and live efficiently, and rely on one another for things to get done.

The backbreaking work continued until noon, when the scorch of the sun became too much for them to handle. All the crews retreated to safety inside the shells of the skyscrapers to break for lunch. There, children even younger than Sammuia, all under ten years of age, brought up their meals: assorted brown and green mush with salted leaves and small black grubs curled into balls. She was starting to get used to these disgusting meals.

In fact, she was so hungry she didn't even realize she had inhaled it all until her plate was clean. She looked down in surprise. It was as if her taste buds had turned themselves off in order for her body to digest the nutrients without throwing them up. Elise gazed around the room. This was how these people lived, day in and out.

During the hottest four hours of the day, when it was far too dangerous to work, the crews spaced themselves out on the stairwell of the building and passed containers of water, fresh sacks of untainted soil, seeds, and useful farming tools up from the surface. The old soil, with its nutrients used up, was tossed over the side of the buildings. This work continued until the sun began its descent toward the horizon and the temperature cooled. Then the crews went back to the roof and worked three more hours until it was too dark to continue.

When the long day was over, everyone marched in twos back down the buildings. Elise's initial fears about ascending and descending in darkness now came true, since the setting sun no longer offered enough light to illuminate the doorways. Fortunately, the group was prepared for this. The lead and anchor person of the group turned on some sort of light around her wrist, not unlike the kind James used. Elise was initially uneasy with the oppressive darkness, but soon her eyes acclimated to the low light until soon it no longer bothered her.

She had to be helped by several of the children as they made that final trek down the stairwell to the ground floor. According to Franwil, this was their typical day, with only every eighth day saved for rest. By the time they reached the communal field among the six buildings, night had just fallen. Dinner was brought out and, for the next few hours, they sang and told stories around a large bonfire. Most of it was a big haze to Elise. She was so dead tired that she almost dozed off into her dinner.

Franwil nudged her awake and helped her to her feet. Otherwise, Elise probably would have just fallen asleep on the grass. "Get some sleep," the elderly woman said. "Tomorrow is another day."

She signaled to a gaggle of children to help her to her tent. Elise barely made it. She probably wouldn't have without those kids holding her up. To her surprise, James was already sprawled out on the floor inside. He hadn't quite made it to his mattress.

"What's wrong with you?" she asked.

His eyes fluttered open and an "uh" escaped his lips as he tilted his neck so he could see her. "Tired," he said softly, then groaned as he tried to sit up. After one or two futile attempts, he fell back down onto his back. "Just come closer," he mumbled. "I can't quite move my head to see you."

Elise was too tired to smile and instead just lay down on her side next to him. "Standing takes too much energy. What happened to you, tough guy? Shouldn't this be a cakewalk?"

"We were moving mountains of dirt with sticks and shovels. These primitives are trying to change the course of a river by hand, for abyss's sake."

Eyes closed, Elise lifted her hand and wiggled her fingers. "Couldn't you just use your bands and do that hocus-pocus thing you do?"

"Doing hocus-pocus takes energy, and I'm not going to waste it moving mounds of shit to divert a river of the same stuff. Energy is at a premium. Who knows how long I will be able to keep these bands charged? This isn't like your time period, where there's a plug around every corner."

"No roast in every pot, huh?"

"What's a . . . ?"

Unable to crane her neck toward him, Elise grunted and rolled onto her right side, using her left arm resting on his chest to support herself. "Never mind."

James opened his left eye and looked down at her hand resting on his chest, for the first time noticing how close she was to him. It must have given him strength, because he managed to roll left until they were facing each other. He looked a little uncomfortable lying so close to her. To be honest, it made her a little self-conscious as well.

"What I wouldn't give for a bath," she murmured, running her hand down his arm. She frowned at the dirt that caked onto her finger. "Do they exist anymore? Seems like personal hygiene has gone the way of the dinosaurs these days."

James put his right arm on her shoulder and they steadied each other as they lay on their sides, too far apart to embrace properly, but close enough that she felt a tingle shoot up her back. The heat of his presence was comforting. The truth was that Elise didn't know what to think of him. James was still the same Salman she had taken a liking to back on Nutris, but he also wasn't.

The mysterious stranger she had crushed on was even more mysterious than she ever thought anyone could be. There was a broodiness about him, a sadness that seemed to suck the joy out of a room. And now that she thought about it, he definitely wasn't as good-looking as Salman, either.

He must have cheated when he did that illusion thing with the bands. His skin wasn't nearly as smooth and his nose was a little crooked. His eyes were probably a little too close for her taste and his eyebrows were out of control. Now that she thought about it, he kind of smelled too. Wait . . . she probably didn't smell like a bed of roses, either. Nothing in this world did. But even with all his flaws, Elise still felt this flutter in her chest when she was close to him. James wasn't the perfect man, but right now, she could tell he was hers.

She reached out and caressed his face, running her fingers along a faint scar on his right cheek. "What happened here?" Then she noticed the dozens of scars crisscrossing his arms and face, some so faint she noticed them only after close study, but some so deep, they formed ridges along his skin.

"You poor thing," she murmured.

James rolled onto his back again and closed his eyes. "No need to waste pity on me."

Elise kept her arm across his chest and pulled herself in closer to him. The two, too weary and exhausted to do much else, fell into a deep sleep, with neither moving an inch until sunup, when they had to do chores all over again. This one night, though, the first since she had miraculously survived the disaster on the Nutris Platform and then came to this terrible present, she didn't cry herself to sleep.

TWENTY-EIGHT

EARTH PLAGUE

James woke feeling discombobulated. Where was he? The surroundings felt unfamiliar and he was freezing. He scrambled to his feet and powered on his exo, comforted by the fact that his bands were still wrapped around his wrists. In most of his dreams, occurring nightly now, he was often left unarmed and helpless.

The faint, comforting yellow glow of the kinetic field expanded from his body and filled every inch of the tent, every signal and piece of information filtering back into his AI band. His body was shivering, so he willed his atmos on. Why did he turn it off? He never did. Then he remembered where he was and why he wasn't enveloped in his usual environmental cocoon. He was now a fugitive and couldn't afford to waste his levels on comfort anymore. His old life, as hard as it was, was now just a distant luxury compared to what lay ahead. He'd have to get used to freezing like this.

"Fuck," he growled at the thought.

Even though it was so cold that his toes had gone numb, James felt strangely rested. He assumed that sleeping without an atmos would have affected his sleep. Instead, he had woken feeling better than he had in months. Then he realized why: he hadn't dreamt last night. James couldn't remember the last time that had happened.

He closed his eyes and relished his fleeting peace. There was something else. No, someone else. Elise was here as well. Close by, holding him. He remembered her touch on his chest and how during the night, her arms had wrapped around his shivering body. And he had finally slept that rare dreamless sleep, and it was wonderful.

Elise!

Where was she? He clawed out of the tent opening, nearly taking the entire thing down. He was about to call her name aloud when he realized it was not yet daybreak and the camp was still. He swallowed his yell as he scanned the grounds.

The tribesman on guard, perched on one of the tall broken columns, eyed him with suspicion, slowly angling his rifle James's way. The Elfreth still didn't trust him. Of course they didn't; James wouldn't either, not after what the corporations had done to them following the Welfare Exoduses a century earlier.

Keeping his hands out in plain view, and feeling silly for doing it—he had learned it put them at ease when he did that—James walked to the base of the column and looked up.

"Have you seen Elder Elise?" he asked.

The guard nodded and pointed toward the river, where James and the crew had spent the past few days digging. James thanked him and made his way there.

"Elise, are you here?" he thought.

There was a long pause before she finally responded. "Hello? Um. Damn thing. Hello? Is this thing working?"

"I can hear you."

"You scared the crap out of me, James," she said. "Give me a warning before you barge into my head like this."

"What exactly do you want me to do before I talk to you to let you know I'm going to talk to you?"

"I don't know. Knock or something."

"Knock. Knock," he said.

There was another startled stammer, and then Elise laughed, her voice ringing inside his head. She must have been laughing aloud because he could hear her voice downriver, the echo bouncing off the tall black structures rising up from the ground

James picked up his pace. If she were any louder, she'd wake the whole tribe in a few seconds. He found her kneeling at the water's edge, arms elbow deep in the slow-flowing sludge that folded over itself as it ran downstream. He didn't try to mask his steps and she craned her head as he approached.

"Who's there?" She smirked.

"It's James."

Elise rolled her eyes as she stood. "You're hopeless. Do you know that?"

He actually had no idea what she was talking about but he had more pressing matters to deal with right now. He looked at the ominous buildings that shot up into the skies around her, their windows like blackened eyes, all seemingly staring right at them.

"You can't just wander off like this," he said, pointing at the high-rise on the other side of the river. "It's not safe out here. There are more feral inhabitants in the buildings across the city than there are people. In fact, according to the hunters, a nasty nest of wolf variants took up residence right there across the street. If one of them decided you were dinner, I wouldn't be able to save you in time."

They were in an area far too enclosed and with far too many places to hide for his liking. The wilderness filled the night air not only all around them, but above them, in the abandoned buildings a hundred stories tall. Howls, barks, and the constant chirping of unknown creatures continuously emanated from the derelict skeletons of these once mighty structures as nature took back the land block by block.

"This isn't the first time I've worked in a dangerous environment," she said.

"There are also some very dangerous people hunting us as well."

She shrugged him off as she set a plate of the sludge on a boulder. "I'm not going to hide in a cave for the rest of my life, James." She turned her back to him and stuck her arms into the river, this time reaching deep down until the water reached up to her shoulders.

"This is not up for debate." He knelt down next to her and peered over her shoulder. "There's . . . what are you doing? Be careful or you'll fall into the river."

Elise rolled her eyes. "Cut it out, Dad. I have your atmos thing on anyway." She pulled her right arm out of the mud and wiggled her fingers toward him. He just gave her a blank stare. She exhaled in exasperation. "You're no fun."

"Mud's not much of a deterrent, though I think I have enough caked on me as it is."

"Well, if you must know . . ." She pointed at the boulder nearby. For the first time, James noticed the fourteen plates lined up neatly in three rows. He walked over and picked one up.

"Don't touch it," she said, more sharply than he'd ever heard her speak to him.

James put his hands up and backed away.

Elise joined him and shooed at him. "They're all in order." She pointed at the top row. "Two hundred meters upriver before the sharp bend at three elevations." Then she pointed at the middle row. "Immediately after the bend." Then she pointed at the last row. "Four hundred meters down.'

"I don't understand," James said.

"The water is infected."

"How can water be infected?" he asked.

"Like a festering wound. Back in my time, we called it Earth Plague. It was a newly discovered virus that sprung from a combination of environmental variables: carbon levels, pollution, radiation, ultraviolet rays . . . a perfect storm of bad crap upon bad crap happening. We first discovered small blooms of it in the Indian Ocean. And then reports of similar patches sprung up all over the world."

"How do you know so much about it?"

"That's what the Nutris Platform was for. The global governments realized that this Earth Plague was a real threat to our planet, and they all pooled their resources and gathered the most well regarded scientists to destroy the plague." She bowed her head. "Some of the best minds on the planet. I had a lot of friends there."

"I don't remember seeing this Earth Plague when I was in your time," James said, puzzled.

"We intentionally built the Nutris Platform in the Arctic Circle. We needed a clean environment where the virus couldn't prosper. Cold weather hinders its rapid mutation rate."

"I wonder why it was labeled a military installation by ChronoCom." Or by Valta. He wasn't sure who was in charge of that operation anymore.

She shook her head. "I don't know where you got that idea from. It was a cleanser. By the time the platform went online, we were only a few months away from starting trials. All we had to do was refine the particle filtering and sequencing."

James shook his head as a lump sunk into his stomach. "You mean if the base hadn't blown up when it did, Earth wouldn't be this mess?"

"We could have cured her," Elise said. "Maybe I still can."

"By yourself?"

"I can try. It's not like I have anything better to do right now," she groused. "If I had the right equipment, who knows? Maybe I can pick up where we left off. It's definitely something worth exploring, but this place is a mess."

James stayed with Elise for the rest of the night until dawn, acting as her lab assistant and pack mule as she gathered more samples and carried them back to camp. By the time Sammuia found them to gather for the day's work, they had collected over forty plates, each carefully labeled. Elise had to recruit the two children to help move the small trays into cover.

"How is this going to cure the planet?" James asked as they returned to join the tribe for the morning assignments.

"Not sure if I can," she admitted. "Not without any equipment. This is just more out of curiosity right now than anything. It's nice to have something to think about other than this awful mess I'm in."

He leaned in to her. "We still need to talk about what to do next. We can't stay here forever."

She shrugged. "It's not a bad life, James. These seem to be good people and the work is honest. What else are we going to do?"

"I didn't bring you back here for . . ." He paused. Why did he bring her back? It wasn't for her own good; that, he had to admit. He did it for himself, and now that she seemed to be adjusting to life here, he wanted to take her away again.

"Selfish bastard," James muttered under his breath.

He felt the familiar pull of anxiety as they were separated and she was led by both hands by that gaggle of old women back into one of those tall rusted relics of the past. His instincts were to run after her and snatch her from that group of old hens coaxing her away from him, shoot to the underground garage across the river where the collie was parked, and flee to some remote place far away from the searching eyes of ChronoCom and these savages.

Oldest Qawol waved him over and pointed toward the same group he had worked with yesterday. James kept his face neutral and held in his sigh.

The other large party of men was venturing northwest to hunt for game in one of the skyscrapers. He would be much more useful running with them. But that would require a large degree of trust on both sides, something neither had at this moment, which relegated him back to digging ditches and damming rivers, crap work that was far beneath a chronman.

Ex-chronman. Even worse: fugitive.

"Your thoughts are loud, stranger," Qawol said, putting a hand on his shoulder. "I can hear your worry all the way from afar."

"It's nothing," he said.

"Running minds never run nowhere," Qawol said. "Josni says you worked hard with the others yesterday. He was surprised."

"Why would he be?"

"People who have no intention of staying have no need to work hard for the tribe's benefit. I do not anticipate you or the girl staying much longer."

James stopped. The Oldest was right. Why did he break his back for them yesterday? He didn't know. James looked back at the six towers that disappeared over the ridge as his group made its way down to the river, then he looked back at the makeshift dam they had erected yesterday. The whole wall looked ready to buckle. Being in that pit right now was dangerous.

It had leaked in a few areas and the supports—bunches of gray plant stems bound together—were bending and being pressed deeper into the mud. He watched as the first group of men jumped down into the ditch to inspect the braces, probably not realizing the danger they had just put themselves in.

He watched, alarmed, as one of the men knocked on the dam wall and then tried to readjust the slanted stem pushing against it. The wall sagged a little more. Three kinetic coils burst out as the glow of the exo crackled around him. Alarmed, several of the Elfreth nearby jumped back and pointed. Another standing on the far ridge aimed a rifle at him.

James gritted his teeth and jumped down into the ditch just as the stem supporting the sagging wall snapped and a torrent of water came rushing into the ditch.

TWENTY-NINE

CURE

Elise nursed the small fire tucked safely inside the ring of rocks and fanned it gently with a fan made from knitted insect wings that Rima had given her. Sammuia's older sister had developed a fascination with Elise and was now resorting to nothing less than a string of gifts of silly trinkets and useful knickknacks to curry her favor.

As much as Elise had tried to tell the girl that bribery wasn't needed to earn her friendship, Rima was persistent. The rest of the Elfreth seemed fine with the girl hanging around her, even relieved that she was so pre-occupied. It seemed Rima had a reputation as a troublemaker among them.

Some of the gifts were very useful; for example, what looked like a hollowed-out half of an old carburetor that now served as a heating plate for Elise's tests. Others, like this insect wing fan, were just pretty to look at.

Wait, no, she took that back. Elise switched the fan to her left hand, silently thanking it for helping keep the fire alive. It had taken her the better part of the morning on her rest day to get the fire started for the heating plate so watching it finally grow felt she had just climbed Mt. Everest.

Qawol had cut her off from using the tribe's supply of oil, so in order to run her experiments, Elise had to gather her own tinder and figure out how to start her own fires. The first few days, James would just zap something and it would be—presto!—fire. He wasn't always around, though, so she decided it was high time she learned how to make one on her own.

Sitting over the fire on top of a metal grate was one glass and three tin cups, borrowed from the cooks. She wished they were all glass so she could examine how the contents of the sludge from the river broke down, but she had a feeling glass-making was pretty much a lost art around these parts, like just about everything else.

"Should have paid attention to those blacksmithing and glassblowing classes at summer camp, Elise," she tsked. "You'd be all set by now."

She was delusional if she thought this stone age experimentation was actually going to lead to a cure for the Earth Plague, but she wanted to learn more about this exotic new world. She was a scientist after all, and this is what scientists did when they were curious, so she studied the sludge with what she had on hand even if that meant resorting to third-grade science projects. If anything, it helped pass the time.

Ever since the second week James and she had joined the tribe, her routine had become: get up before the sun rises, gather samples until dawn, work the assorted tribal chores, then spend the rest of the evening after dinner playing at caveman biologist. These exercises gave a little of her previous life back to her. They also reminded her of everything she had lost.

"You busy?" James said, knocking on the wall of her lab.

"Lab" was a really loose term. She had commandeered a burned-out residential guardhouse of an old complex downriver from the settlement. It had only two and a half walls, but the roof didn't seem to be in any danger of collapsing. It kept her dry from the rains and offered just enough ventilation so she didn't smoke herself out when some of her less-than-aromatic experiments went awry.

"Hey you." She beamed as he walked in and studied the fire. They didn't see much of each other during the day because of all the chores the Elfreth set them to, so it was always a little thrill when he stopped by every evening. It was strange; he totally wasn't her type, but nothing made a smile splash across her face the way his being around did.

She was also very proud of James. After the incident at the dam when he saved a group of tribesmen from drowning, the Elfreth seemed to have finally thawed toward him. In return, she saw him make a real effort not to be such a statue to them. Now, he stomped and scowled less in camp, and not all of them pointed their guns at him when he passed. She considered that a vast improvement. Most were still uncomfortable around him, but at least both sides were making a little effort.

"The old windbags ordered me to bring you dinner," he said.

Elise made a face. Eating had somehow gone from her favorite pastime to her most dreaded. She had mostly gotten use to the meager sustenance of this land, though some of it still took choking down for her to digest. At least her body had adjusted. During the first few days, her stomach had launched a protest that kept her perpetually cramped.

He passed a hand over the boiling sludge. "Any luck on the cure?" He asked this every time he stopped by. For a guy from the far future with very advanced technology at his disposal, he was surprisingly a knuckle-dragger when it came to certain things.

"This isn't like fixing a mechanoid or curing the cold, James." She shook her insect-wing fan at him. "Look at what the hell I have to work with! Do you know what in Gaia this is made of?"

He paused, his gaze moving from the slurp she was cooking in her little pots to the fan in her hand to the makeshift shelf of scrounged lab tools she'd accumulated over the past few days.

"What do you need, then?" he asked.

"Well, for one, it'd be nice if I didn't have to spend two hours to build a damn fire every time I want to heat something up. Maybe a real filtration device instead of a spaghetti strainer, and how about some real equipment? Holy hell, how about a room with four actual walls?" She laughed as she ticked off half a dozen old comforts of home that she missed. James looked serious as he took in every single one of her suggestions.

"I'll see what I can do," was all he said. "This might take a few days to track." He turned and left her lab.

"What? Wait." She ran out after him. "Do you mean it? Can you really get the stuff for me?"

He must have seen the ear-to-ear grin on her face because a rare smile grew on his. "For a cure for Earth? Sure. For you? If it makes you happy." He looked at the opening in her lab where a wall should have been. "What do you think about moving the lab into one of the Farming Towers? I don't feel comfortable with you working so far away from the safety of the tribe."

She shook her head. "It's pitch-black up there at night. You won't catch me climbing those stairs after sundown."

James thought about it and nodded. "I'll see what I can do about adding power to your lab."

Elise couldn't believe it. She didn't think he was taking her seriously. This was more than she could hope for, and she ran through the list of requests that she had haphazardly shot off in her head. She definitely should have been more considerate with what she asked for. "Hang on, let me think it over and get a real list."

James held her hand with his. "Take your time. Eat your meal before the food gets cold. You know how much worse it tastes once that happens."

Elise was so excited she barely noticed the dead grubs, moss soup, and wilted leaves she inhaled for dinner. She made a detailed wish list and double-checked it like a little girl picking presents for winter solstice. By the time she was ready to turn in for the evening, the number of things she wanted had grown to over a hundred.

Afraid that she was being too greedy, she refined it once more, putting the list of lab equipment she wanted into separate columns, from required to optional to nice-to-have alternatives. Too excited to sleep, she stayed up and tweaked the list until it had been reduced to a trim thirty-six items. Then she decided that the eight semi-optional items weren't actually optional after all, which brought up the final list to forty-four.

"Forty-four to save the Earth," she said and rubbed her hands in anticipation.

Farther upstream in the field, the guard on watch banged his nightstick against the column he was perched on. Fourteen times the ringing of the aluminum tube echoed across the camp. By the time the sun came up, the guard would have banged the nightstick up to forty times, the occurrences evenly divided by an old recovered hourglass that he continually flipped. Each banging let the rest of the tribe know how deep in the night they were, and more important, let them know that someone was still watching over them. Falling asleep while on watch was one of the worst crimes a tribesman could commit. No one knew exactly how long the hourglass was, but if Elise had to guess, she'd say it was approximately ten to twelve minutes.

That was the way with things now in the present. Everything was measured in approximations. These people lived life from sunup to sundown, and measurements were taken based only on the capacity of what they used. Metrics for these people were based on fingers, toes, and persons. Thus, those seventy-seven blood corn stems stacked on the far bank for tomorrow's work on the dam would be three persons, three limbs, and two fingers. It made sense, she guessed. Last month, her team was triangulating core temperatures near the center of the Earth and now she was counting mutant tomatoes with her hands and fingers. Go figure.

It was the middle of the night by the time Elise popped her head into their tent. She had counted at least twenty-seven taps of the nightstick, which meant she had only a few more hours to sleep. Tomorrow was going to suck. Knowing how much of a light sleeper James was, she tiptoed around him toward her side of the tent.

James, who was asleep in his cot nearby, rolled over and suddenly thrashed out, startling the hell out of her. He let out a low guttural moan and both his arms shot up into the air as if he were pushing something away. His head pivoted left and right violently as another groan, painful and heartbreaking, escaped his lips. His hands clenched and unclenched as they drew circles in the air.

Elise realized then that he wasn't pushing something away, he was clutching for it. Cries of "no!" rang in the tent as he thrashed even harder. Afraid that he would wake the rest of the tribe, and worried that they might not understand what was happening to him—half of the Old Ones still wanted to send him away—she tried to wrap her arms around him and hold him down, shushing into his ear. He was terrifyingly strong, and for a second, Elise feared for her safety.

"It's all right," she whispered, over and over again.

Eventually, the cries softened and fell into mumbled whispers. He seemed to be apologizing to people named Grace and "Nazi boy." Then he let loose a stream of names, thirty long, saying that he was sorry over and over again. Elise held on to him, trying to keep him still. Eventually, whatever was happening in his dream passed and his heart rate steadied.

The worst seemed to have passed, but Elise didn't move. Maybe her being so close comforted him, and to be honest, his closeness did the same for her. For the rest of the night, for the last thirteen nightstick bangs until sunup call, she stayed near him, her arms draped around his shoulders. And for the second time in so many weeks, Elise slept well.

THIRTY

CASTING THE NET

The small armada of transports landed one by one in the bombed-out basin of Mt. Fuji on what remained of the Japanese islands. This particular region had been hit hard by the rising tides and earthquakes over the centuries. Tokyo, its last remaining city, had sunk into the sea in 2242. Now, only the land mass around Fuji was stable enough for use, and it was here that whatever remained of this island's population lived.

The armada—nine collies and two Hephaestus-class transports—was all Levin could requisition from ChronoCom. To be honest, he was surprised he even got those. Valta must have had a hand in making sure his team got the additional equipment. Hephaestus-class transports weren't regulars in the agency's fleet. They were massive floating fortresses, large, unwieldy, and far too energy-inefficient for any of their operations. The advanced scanners being leveraged to track down James weren't standard either, but courtesy of Kuo, standing a few meters away on the other side of the Hephaestus bridge.

Levin glanced her way. He would trade all this advanced crap in a heartbeat just to be rid of her. The past few weeks with the Valta lapdog shadowing his every command had been a complete nightmare. She had dropped the pretense of being an observer immediately after Sourn's transport had left Earth, and they had butted heads ever since.

But that wasn't what bothered him about her. He could handle disruptive authority. No auditor achieved his link without having to step over dozens of others, be they chronmen, administrators, other auditors, or even directors. Everyone understood the game to climb up the chain. At the end of the day, it was about defeating your allies almost as much as upholding the agency's laws. There were limits, however.

Securitate Kuo took this venture to an entirely new level. The woman obviously did not know what an observational role meant. With the exception of maybe James, Levin had never wanted to kill anyone so badly in his life. And at least with James, there was a decade of animosity built up. With Kuo, it had taken less than a week of having to deal with her arrogant prejudice before he wanted to strangle the life out of her. Her views on rucks and Earthlings in general, while typical of many spaceborn from the Gas Giant moons, were more extreme than most. Even now, as the two walked down the ramp of the transport to the waiting village nestled in the caldera of the Fuji mountaintop, he worried about what she would do next.

The villagers, descendants of an old Japanese space dock military facility, had lived in relative isolation for the past two hundred years. ChronoCom was aware of their existence, having used their village as a base of operations for the nearby chrono-resource-rich region of Tokyo, and had a productive, if not sometimes tense, relationship with these xenophobic people. Levin himself had run several operations out of here in his younger days as a chronman.

As long as the agency respected their requests, the sides usually had an equitable relationship. The only requests the small settlement of a thousand souls had were for the agency to operate in the southeastern corner of the village, and to have no more than two of their people walking among the villagers at all times without permission from their council.

Levin was careful to walk ahead of her as they came down the ramp of the lead Hephaestus transport. "Greetings, Venerated One," he said formally, bowing low as was the custom in these parts. "We are grateful for your generosity, and offer gifts to repay your kindness."

The old man, flanked by a dozen others, returned the bow. "We welcome our friends to our house." He gestured to the southeast corner of the caldera. "May our guests find their accommodations worthy."

"We'll need a new venue for our base camp," Kuo said, cutting in front of Levin. "The transports can only land on flat zones. Those grounds are at a fifteen-degree slant. Our people will have to cross the entire basin to resupply."

Levin leaned in toward her. "Just a slight inconvenience. It's their land."

But, of course, that didn't stop her. Levin had seen individuals of corp privilege operate before, but none as callously and unabashedly as this woman did.

"We'll take this center area," she said, pointing to the field in the center of the village. "The transports require a seventy-meter clearance for loading operations." She pointed at the nearest row of hutches. "That space will need to be cleared."

The four monitors with them exchanged glances and then looked to him for guidance.

"Belay that order," he said, then turned to Kuo. "Walk with me." He was surprised she obliged. They continued down the hill away from the small crowd. "This isn't necessary," he stressed. "Antagonizing the natives over a minor inefficiency isn't worth it. It's a short walk up a damn hill."

Kuo looked down the hill to where they were supposed to set up camp, then back up to the contested ground, then she gave him a flat stare. "Three hundred ninety-three meters distance, to be exact. Assuming your men are in Valta Security shape, they can cover that distance fully loaded with gear in a minute. Do you know how far a chronman can travel during that minute?" Before Levin could reply, she cut him off. "Assuming a lower tech level of bands, which I believe is the standard for band channelers of your agency, two kilometers. Now do you see why we need to be closer to the landing zone?"

"It's not our land to commandeer," he said.

"Savages living in the mud, beggars suckling off the generosity of the corps." She brushed off his words. "The Earth Regent provides these natives year-round supplies of fuel and food stock during their winter months. Valta generously provides nine percent of Earth's off-planet supplies, so unless these savages wish to have their welfare dry up, they don't get a say in this. They better learn to tolerate the inefficiency of having those four hovels removed." She started walking away, and then looked back at him. "Give the order. It is for the good of all parties involved." She didn't bother holding back the threat in her voice.

Levin watched Kuo walk back to the plateau and disappear into the transport. He swallowed his anger and glanced at the four men awaiting his orders. With a sigh, he joined them.

"Vonder, Linden, clear that row of buildings. Try to do as little damage as possible. You two set up a clearing zone for the transports." He turned to the leader of the villagers and bowed. "Please walk with me, Venerated One. Allow me to explain."

The Venerated One didn't like what Levin had to say, and neither did the rest of the council. They had raised their voices and threatened to throw Levin and his men out of their village. At first, he tried to reason with them, to beg, apologize, and offer bribes of increased supplies, but in the end, he told them they had no choice. Kuo's command would be followed, no matter what any of them said. In fact, by the time they had returned to the plateau, Vonder and Linden had cleared the entire area, flattening nine structures. Levin learned later on that four of the buildings were homes.

Levin's head hurt, and for the first time in years, he turned his atmos off and felt the cold biting wind touch his skin. The chill immediately seeped through his cloak and uniform, causing his body to shiver, something it hadn't done in a long time. He inhaled and felt the icy air seep into his chest. He watched the small cloud of steam leave his mouth and float away. He closed his eyes and took a few more deep breaths. These were trying times and things were only getting more difficult.

"Auditor," Kuo's voice cut through the air. "Your attention is required."

Of course it was. Levin paused for just a moment before he cleared his head and walked with as much dignity as he could muster toward the transport. He stole a glance over at his men, who watched him make the laborious journey to the ship with a mixture of sympathy and uncertainty. For the first time ever, Levin felt shame for his position. However, Director Young's orders were explicit. Valta's contributions to the agency were too important to risk, thus compliance with their requests could not be an issue.

"There you are," Kuo said, not bothering to look up as he entered the belly of the transport. She was leaning over a floating tactical display of Asia and the surrounding bodies of water.

"Your agency collies are too well cloaked," she said, shaking her head in disapproval. "Why is that necessary?"

"Because not all ships are Apollo-class retrofitted battleships that pirates avoid in the Ship Graveyard," he replied dryly. "It's cheaper to cloak our ships from detection than it is to equip them for combat."

"And more troublesome when one decides he no longer wishes to be found," she added. "You are an auditor. Why are your people not tracked and accounted for?"

"They're not cattle, nor property," he said. "Besides, live tracking could affect their jobs. Previous centuries had far more advanced detection capabilities than does the present."

"Pity. All high-profile Valta employees are continually monitored. Cuts down on corporate espionage." She gestured with her hands and a three-dimensional map of the region appeared. Kuo made another quick motion and the view pulled backward to display a larger region. She signaled one more time and half a dozen blue dots appeared on the map.

Kuo turned to Levin. "Due to the failed condition of the planetary surveillance network here on Earth, Valta is generously allocating a cast net system for the duration of your search. Unfortunately, these nets cannot detect your collies. However, they will be more than sufficient to detect chrono jump signatures as well as objects with visual parameters." She pointed at the dots." I will leave it up to you to complete setup of the outpost for this region." She paused. "There will be some necessary integration of your handler operations in order to process the data from the cast net. I assume this won't be an issue?"

Of course. First she takes his command. Now, she takes control of their network. Valta was sinking one claw at a time into the agency, and soon, ChronoCom wouldn't be anything other than a puppet of the mega-corporation. Levin wondered how Young and the rest of the leadership could tolerate this. The agency was neither regulated nor profit-driven for a reason: so that something so powerful could not be abused. Yet Levin was slowly seeing his beloved agency lose its autonomy.

"I am sure this will be very useful," he said through gritted teeth.

"Valta just seeks the common good," Kuo said with a straight face. "We need to catch this fugitive and bring him to justice, and Valta desires to apprehend that anomaly for our purposes. Inform your men. I want this base fully functioning within four hours. In the meantime, I'm taking the second Hephaestus to set up the outpost in southern Africa. We'll flush him out of his hole soon enough." She stopped at the bottom of the ramp and looked back up at Levin. "Inform the entire village that their continuing supply of our generosity depends on their cooperation. And you are ordered to shoot any of these savages if they cause any problems."

Then she turned and disappeared into the darkness.

THIRTY-ONE

DIRECTIVE

An argument broke out the next day between a group of younger Elfreth and the Old Ones. The evening began innocently enough. Food preparation was running late, so several of the Elfreth had started singing stories, passed down by word of mouth for generations, around the bonfire to pass the time. Their songs didn't fully translate through the comm bands, but for the most part, James was able to understand the history of these people and how they came to the Farming Towers here in Boston.

This particular tribe could trace their lineage back from the city of Philadelphia, to the time when the last of the city-states on the eastern seaboard collapsed during the Core Conflicts. The Elfreth received their name from the street they called home until they were driven away by a rival tribe from the south known as the Terrible Eagles. For years, they wandered through the Appalachians until a particularly cold winter pushed them to seek shelter on the Mist Isle, formerly known as Manhattan. Additional conflict with the islanders there finally drove them northeast to Boston a little over a hundred years ago.

The atmosphere was merry until talks moved to the upcoming winter. As expected, the Old Ones of the Elfreth worried that even with the unexpected boon of foodstuffs—they acknowledged James with a nod—the winter would still bring many lean months. It had always been this way, every year seeming a bit more difficult than the previous one.

The tribe had never been this large. Many felt that it was time again to move.

The conversation revealed two camps, one arguing to stay in the city and the other urging the group to head northwest for what they believed were more fertile lands. The arguments became more heated when the group of the younger Elfreth banded together and declared their intent to leave, saying that they would no longer be weighed down by so many elderly and useless young. They even went as far as going back to the storeroom and gathering supplies for their trip.

The argument looked like it might descend into violence when the small group of ten, laden with equipment and sacks of food from the storage room in one of the Farming Towers, tried to leave the communal field. Qawol walked in front of their leader and blocked their path. Everyone knew that if something happened to Qawol, blood would be shed.

"Out of the way, Oldest," the ringleader—James recognized Chawr, the young man who had given him the tar booze—growled. "Even you say there are too many mouths to feed. We will relieve you the burden of ours."

Qawol stared at the ringleader's eyes, then he stepped to the side. "If you wish to leave, young Chawr, so be it. I cannot stop you. However, you cannot take what are the people's supplies."

"These aren't their supplies," Chawr said. "This is the tribe's and we were all part of it. You see my brothers and sisters behind me? We're the ones who lifted the Elfreth on our shoulders. We're the ones who hunt and gather and protect the young. We bled the blood. We aren't stealing this. We're owed this."

An angry muttering erupted behind Qawol as the rest of the Elfreth took offense. The Oldest looked back at them and the sounds immediately died. He turned back to Chawr. "The Elfreth will stay. The land here has been good to us. We will survive as we always have. Together, we are strong. Alone, we die."

"The old and weak saps too much from the strong and there are many old and weak in this tribe," Chawr replied.

James looked at the meager supplies they were fighting over: four satchels' worth of dried meats, half a dozen baskets of vegetables, two stacks of kindling, five power packs, two rifles, three crossbows, and what looked like an orbital radio.

"And then what?" he said quietly, surprising most here who had never heard him say two words. "What are you going to do once the ten of you eat the food, burn the kindling, and use up the power packs? Where will you go? What next?"

Chawr looked surprised. "It doesn't matter. We'll figure something. Maybe head south where it's warmer or north where more plentiful game runs."

"So you're going to just survive then."

"That's all there is to life."

A feeling of déjà vu swept over James. He knew what Chawr was saying; he had lived that way most of his life. In a way, he wanted to be just like these savages and look out only for himself and Elise. He wasn't any better than any of them. Ever since Sasha's disappearance, surviving for himself was all he knew. It was all he'd ever fought for. Then he thought of Elise, how she was different, because she didn't do things only for herself.

James thought about the planet and how Elise might be able to cure it. He didn't for a second believe her, but what if he could use that to keep the people together? She was right about one thing: there was no way they could live without a community of people. He didn't know how to survive for a prolonged period of time without his bands. Using his bands wasn't really surviving anyway. Before, ChronoCom was his tribe. Now, he was alone. As much as he hated to admit it, he needed this tribe.

James powered his exo and launched himself onto the guard column so everyone could see his face. He spoke in a strong, assured voice. "What if I offer you a new purpose?" He pointed at Elise. "My companion and I are on a mission to save the planet. We know how to cure the sickness. We need your help."

"There is no cure for a dying planet," someone shouted.

"You lie!" a girl behind Chawr said, shaking her fist at James.

"The sickness has been this way since before I was born," an old woman said. "It has always been this way."

"That's not true." Elise's voice rang across open space, even louder than James's. All eyes turned to her, and for a second, she shrank from the attention. Then her eyes met his, and he nodded. Elise hesitated, gave a small cough, and after a couple of false starts, began speaking. "It didn't use to be like this. I know. I come from the past."

There was a chorus of gasps, though most just responded with blank stares. Though mostly isolated from the civilized world, some in this wasteland tribe must have been aware of the Time Laws, because they looked horrified. Others just seemed puzzled.

A little girl clinging to her mother piped up. "So what is it supposed to be like, then?"

Elise smiled. "Earth was beautiful. The sun was a brilliant yellow, the ocean a sparkling blue. The air was pure, and on a clear day, you could see for miles."

The little girl gasped. "That's impossible. It's like a magic land."

Elise walked over to the girl and picked her up. "It's not. Let me tell you about Earth the way I remember it."

For the next hour, James listened with the others as Elise talked about the beauty of the twenty-first century. The entire tribe hung onto every word she said. Her voice quivered with a passion and conviction so strong that those listening could not help but be entranced. Like them, he fell under her spell as she described rolling hills, lush forests, and the thousands upon thousands of animals that roamed the planet. He heard oohs from the crowds as she described the ocean and drew murmurs of disbelief when she told them about the many spectrums of the sky and how the clouds never looked as angry as they do now. Finally, she told them about the changing seasons and how every spring, the landscape turned green with life.

When she was done telling her story, the air around them was quiet except for the crackling flames of the bonfire. James had traveled to the periods she spoke of but had never taken the time or effort to notice the beauty she described. Now something had awoken in him that he didn't even realize was dead. He wanted that Earth she spoke of and he wanted to believe that it could happen.

James noticed a change in Elise as well. When she spoke about the past, it seemed as if a weight lifted off her shoulders. Over the weeks, she had struggled to maintain a brave front, but James could tell she was hurting. He pretended not to notice when she cried at night, or looked sad. Yet now, when she spoke of the Earth from her time, something in her blossomed, a spark that he had seen only glimpses of since she had first arrived. Now that twinkle in her eyes had returned, and that luminance that had so attracted him to her back at the Nutris Platform was there once more.

It was the little girl who spoke first. "And you can bring it back?"

Elise nodded. "I think so, but I'll need your help." She looked up at James.

Chawr, who was pacing back and forth in the back of the group, barked out, "It's all just fairy tales. You're just telling us this so we wouldn't leave with the supplies."

James looked at him with contempt. "You think that sad pile of shit is worth fighting over? Take it." Chawr hesitated, his eyes moving from James to Qawol then back to the people around him. James turned to the rest of the Elfreth. "Help us and you will have a new purpose in your lives. You can cure the planet for your children and their children. In return, I will do everything in my powers for the Elfreth and see that you are all cared for with food, shelter, clothing. I am a chronman. You all know what I am capable of. What my powers are." He turned back to the Chawr. "You saw the food I brought. I can salvage more supplies than you could ever use in a lifetime. You will never go cold or hungry again. What do you say?"

There was a long, awkward silence, so long that James thought he had failed to convince them. Finally, Franwil stood up. She looked at those sitting at her feet, and then at the group causing trouble. Their eyes met, and the young people looked away, ashamed.

"Chronman," she said, turning to James. "I do not like you. You smell of death and hurt. Your gifts and services to the Elfreth do not wash away your people's crimes. I do not know if what you say is true, and it would not matter to me if it were. If it were I leading, I would banish you."

Several of the Elfreth nodded in agreement.

She looked to Elise. "But I see and trust her. I believe her words. Can you do what he says you can do, child?"

The blood had drained from Elise's face, and she almost shook her head. She looked at James, stark panic on her face. Their eyes met, and he gave her a small nod of encouragement.

"I believe so," she said. "I just need some time and supplies."

"Then time and supplies is what the Elfreth will provide," Franwil said. "An easy sacrifice for such a boon."

James nodded. These fools might be chasing a silly dream, but at least it gave them hope and kept everyone together. It also gave Elise a purpose. Both purpose and hope were powerful tools that one needed to survive in the present. He was just now realizing that he had lost both a long time ago.

"James," Smitt's voice popped into his head. "Are you there?"

"Can it wait?" James replied, eyes still fixated on Elise.

"No, my friend, it can't. It's about that tear on Nutris."

"One moment." James jumped off the column and walked toward the main Farming Tower's entrance. No one noticed him leave; they were too focused on Elise and listened with thirsty ears to her every word. He nodded at the man perched on the guard column in front of the tower. The tribesman waved with his stick. It was something at least. A little progress.

James entered the Farming Tower's lobby and sat down on a marble bench with its edges long since broken and smoothed over by time. He leaned back against the wall and closed his eyes. "Go ahead, Smitt."

"I hacked into the chron database and went through the documentation. Much of Nutris is redacted, so this means the initial request must have come from high up in the chain. It took a while to parse the blackened files. Finally paired up jump manifestos and came across an earlier Valta contract. Seems you were the cleanup crew. Valta had originally contracted Shizzu for the job."

"If his job was the same as mine, why did he jump back so far in advance?"

"That's what I couldn't figure out either. Then I checked the ripple charts. There was a massive time ripple—a level seven—after Nutris that fortunately was short-lived because World War Three broke out. The war basically reset any existing ripples. I checked the Valta records. James, Shizzu was the one who blew up the Nutris Platform. He planted a bomb sourced from the present. The only reason he left was because he was injured while planting the bomb and had to jump back early. That's when you were sent in."

James froze. These were serious allegations. "Are you sure of this?"

"I couldn't believe it myself and went to go follow up with Curran, Shizzu's handler. Imagine my surprise when I found out that she had somehow earned out and was now retired on Luna. I know for a fact Curran and Shizzu were no closer to earning out of their contracts than us."

Of course Smitt would have checked his sources. He was a Tier-1 handler and James doubted Smitt would come to him with this if it wasn't true. The ramifications of ChronoCom purposely carrying out this job and covering it up meant terrible things. Major Time Laws had been broken, no matter how limited the effect. If ChronoCom was willing to engineer dead-end time lines now, then the possibilities of what they were willing to do was endless.

"Smitt, how exactly was Valta involved in this?"

"From what I can tell, they ordered the contract and supplied the bomb. That's why Sourn ordered you to make the retrieval only after the disaster happened. They knew you couldn't jump back beforehand. You were still caught in the tear from Shizzu's jump."

James swore. They had knowingly put him in a no-jump withdrawal scenario and hadn't told him. That was an incredible violation of trust and was very dangerous for the chronman involved. James had no doubts that this information was highly classified. Smitt must have taken extreme measures to dig it up.

"Smitt, thanks. I'm sorry I doubted you. I put you in a terrible position. You watched my back. You're a good friend."

"No more than you did for me back at the Academy, eh? Listen, I also have to warn you. Valta is actively involved with the manhunt. They want your friend badly."

James curled his hands into fists. "This situation is much worse than I thought if a megacorp is involved." He stood up, took a deep breath, and began pacing the foyer. "And Shizzu, that abyss-plagued bastard. Next time we meet, one of us isn't going to be able to talk about it."

"Are you going to tell your friend?"

Several scenarios ran through James's head and none of them turned out well. Still, keeping ChronoCom's involvement in the disaster from her didn't feel right. She deserved to know, and things would be doubly bad if she found out on her own. In the end, he realized he had little choice.

"Eventually, when she's ready. For now, I need her trust, and she needs to have her hope."

THIRTY-TWO

SEARCH FOR THE CURE

E lise scowled at the column of machines lined up against the stone
wall of her newly assembled lab. Most of the stuff was straight-up
stone age, primitive tools from the nineteenth and twentieth centuries
that wouldn't be fit for a grade-school bio lab in her time. The few modern pieces James had retrieved for her were so high-tech and in that weird
twenty-sixth-century mumbo jumbo, and she couldn't figure out for the
life of her how to make the damn contraptions work.

The problem wasn't so much the actual machines; that stuff she could
figure out with time. Elise's main source of grief was this century's dialect. She never really had a gift for languages and couldn't decipher more
than half the words on these futuristic devices. It seemed the comm band
that allowed her to understand all these people and their different languages didn't extend to her ability to read any of it.

So there she had it. Between the primitive tools used by scientists in
the tenth century and the super-advanced ones she couldn't read, Elise
was stuck, expected by everyone around her to cure the Earth Plague.
Elise looked over at Rima, who at that moment was studying the charac-
ters for World English numbers. At least she had someone to help bring
her food. Rima couldn't read and Elise had a sneaking suspicion that they
had assigned the girl to her only to keep the young troublemaker out of
trouble. The lights in the room flickered. Elise looked up and waited for
them to go out.

The Elfreth had enthusiastically embraced their new mission in life and moved her lab indoors to one of the higher levels adjacent to the sky bridges in the Farming Towers. Now, Elise had a room with four walls and a ceiling, and some pretty decent views from her own private lab.

They even relieved her of her daily chores and assigned Rima as her assistant. The girl had a steep learning curve, though, and Elise had to put aside time to teach her basic math. It was frustrating, to say the least. At this very moment, Rima was sitting on a stool in the corner working her way up rudimentary base-ten math.

James was as good as his word and had surprised her several days later with a roomful of equipment. He pulled literally almost a truckload of equipment out of his never-ending magic hat. In the end, he was able to obtain thirty-one of her list of forty-four items, with promises of fulfilling the rest of the requests once he located them. Chief among the things he obtained was a battery-powered generator hooked up to an array of solar panels on the roof. Now, she had all the lights and fires that she needed. By the end of the week, it was starting to feel like a real lab.

While both James's and the Elfreth's commitment to her research was heartening, the promises and responsibilities that came with it worried Elise to no end. Now, she felt a responsibility actually to succeed in finding a cure for the planet. Before, when it was just her and her three-sided hut, her experimenting was just that. Now that she had sold everyone on the idea that it was possible, the entire tribe had jumped on board and expected her to deliver a clean Earth.

The only problem with her new setup was that she had to climb up those stairs every single time she had to work. Elise was now going up and down the stairs at least three times a day, minimum. At least it was a decent workout. She considered moving her sleeping arrangements closer to her lab and tried that for one night. However, the top of the Farming Towers was pitch black at night and the wind howled through the corridors, so she decided she'd rather sleep in her old tent next to James for the time being.

When the lights from the power generator flickered, she motioned to Rima to pause in her studies and clean the beakers from Elise's last experiment. That was one thing the people in the Elfreth were very good at; they were thorough when it came to cleaning, especially their utensils and food. Any hint of the plague on animals and plants had to be cut out and cleaned before consumption. These people had learned over time how deadly the Earth Plague could be if ingested.

Elise hurried out of the room. James must have just returned. The generators weren't powerful by any period's standards, and they had a tendency to flicker on and off when James's collie was around. Recently, he had taken to parking his ship closer, in one of the abandoned garages on the periphery of the camp. Whenever the collie was flying around, all the power sources in her lab went haywire. Probably something to do with magnetic fields and power drains of energy fields or whatever. Elise could care less; she had never been interested in physics.

She hurried down the stairwell of the Farming Tower and, ten minutes later, emerged from the base of the tower and crossed the communal fields. Her legs and calves had gotten much stronger already. They were sore the first few days, but now she barely felt the climb. She passed by several of the Elfreth, who waved almost reverently as if she were some savior. This made her stomach churn. She couldn't look them in the eyes as she passed them, too embarrassed to acknowledge their faith in her.

In the past few days, James had finally begun to use his abilities and technologies for the benefit of the tribe, something he had been reluctant to do earlier. The collie, like most ChronoCom vessels, was equipped to avoid detection, a necessary technology in the pirate-infested gas mines regions. However, it was still susceptible to visual sightings, so all his movements had to be made late at night.

Elise waved when James walk out of the garage. She saw him smile when he saw her; he was doing more of that these days. She felt her heart beat just a little faster as he approached. There were times when he would be gone for days, and though she knew he could take care of himself, she would worry until she heard back from him.

"How goes the cure? Is it almost ready?" he asked offhandedly.

"It hasn't started yet," she snapped, more sharply than she intended. His constant asking was starting to get under her skin.

James looked surprised. "I don't understand. You have everything you asked for. What's the problem?" He leaned in. "Elise, we made promises to these people."

Elise felt her ears turn red as she put her arm around his elbow and tugged him along until they were out of earshot of some of the younger

Elfreth helping out in the garage. They wandered down to the river so she could speak with him in private. Sure, she could talk to him with a comm band, but it still felt awkward to chat with someone in her head.

"I'm having issues," she said after she was sure they were alone.

He looked confused, worry straining his face. "What issues? You said you could cure the plague."

"First of all, I said I thought I could," she said. "And I still know how to cure it. At least . . . well, I might have been a little optimistic." Elise let her frustration show. Even working long days, she knew she had bitten off more than she could chew. She was flailing. After all, she had had an entire team back on Nutris, not to mention a veritable army of engineers, scientists, advanced systems, and robots.

Now she had a fifth-grade chemistry set and a teenager who couldn't count past nine because she had lost her little finger to an infection when she was young. Elise never realized how much of her supposed science genius was dependent on the tools of her time. This week, it had taken her four days to establish some baselines that she could have calculated in thirty minutes back on Nutris. At this rate, it would take a lifetime before she rediscovered the cure. Some scientist she had turned out to be.

"I need help," she said. "Half of the equipment I have is too old to use, and I can't understand the other half . . ."

He looked confused.

"I'm saying I need equipment from my time." She said with exasperation. "You need to go back in time and pick them up for me." She handed him a piece of paper. "I made a new list."

James looked at it and shook his head. "I can't do that."

"Why not?" She threw up her hands. "It's the tools I'm familiar with."

James shook his head. "I can't just go back in time and retrieve items from the past on a whim. Each jump has to be carefully mapped to a dead-end time line. I can't afford to have time ripples that could change history."

"You brought me back," she said.

"I'm a little surprised you're still alive," he admitted.

That took her aback. "What's that supposed to mean?"

"We've been taught since the very first days of the Academy that bringing living things from the past to the present causes catastrophic tears in the present time line and cellular instability in organic matter. It doesn't seem to be happening with you for some reason."

"So go get the stuff I need then."

He shook his head again. "If we hit a dead-end time line, I'll try. Otherwise, it's too risky. Smitt's been secretly helping me pinpoint supplies for the village. I'll see what he can dig up."

"There's one more thing," Elise said. "I need more help."

"I already told you I will have Smitt—"

"I mean I need more people to help me. It's too much work to do by myself."

"What about Rima?"

"Someone with more than a second-grade education, James!"

He shook his head. "I won't be able to help you. Everyone with any modicum of scientific training in the present is indentured to the corporations already. It's unlikely I can recruit someone, short of kidnapping them. People with scientific minds are valuable in the present. Right now, we're just a loose end they have to tie. If we cross that line and steal resources, the corporations will rain hell down on us."

Elise thought about her alternatives. "Can you go back to the Nutris Platform then? Get some of the other scientists?"

James shook his head. "No one will ever be able to jump into that chronological location again within approximately sixteen hundred kilometers and nine days from the point of the tear. Other planets and celestial bodies will have different limiting parameters."

"James, I don't care who, how, when, or what you find," she grumbled. "Just get me someone. I might be able to make do with some of the tools I have, but I need brain power to cure this plague. That's even more important than the tools. Hey, are you listening to me?"

He had stopped and was staring up at the sky. He had a strange look on his face. "Yes. I was just thinking. Actually, I might know just the person. Let me see if it's possible."

THIRTY-THREE

NOT QUITE END TIMES

Grace Priestly took a few steps back and studied the canvas from the opposite end of her quarters. The tints were off—the whites a bit too dull, the hues in the sky a bit too plain—but then, she hadn't packed that many colors. Maybe it was just because her childhood memories of home were much more vibrant, or maybe it was that her old mind finally was failing her.

Grace tsked. Of course not; her mind was just as sharp and her memory just as clear as the day she had last been on Earth nearly a century ago. Just because she was about to die didn't mean she was dying. She walked to the other corner of the room and looked at the painting from the side.

The fading sun reflecting off the snow was perfect, though perhaps a shade too dark. It was an adequate reflection of home. Certainly nothing she would ever show to another soul—something she wouldn't have any concerns with shortly—but definitely a piece of work she was proud of, considering the circumstances.

Grace looked out the window. The spinning stars had settled and were now just streaming by at a leisurely pace. The good Captain Monk, as narrow-minded and unimaginative as he was, had done a very good job righting the *High Marker*. She didn't think he had it in him. Too bad all that work to stabilize the ship from its out-of-control trajectory toward the heliosphere was a waste of time.

According to the last report, energy reserves were down to 2 percent. The engineers were still baffled with the question of where all the rest of the fusion power went. Over 90 percent of a Titan-class starship's levels doesn't just vanish into thin air. That was enough power to keep Eris lit up for two years.

Grace knew the truth, though, and it was much more fantastic and logical than anyone else in this time could guess. She thought back to the meeting with the time traveler, her own personal Grim Reaper who signaled her impending demise. It was a slight comfort that the foundation she had laid down for this time-travel agency still existed. At least something of her creation would survive, something she had not expected of the Technology Isolationists. The war had gone badly . . .

The ship was rocked by a thundering explosion, and the blast shields protecting the interior of the ship slammed down. That's twice this had happened in less than an hour. This time, though, something was different. Not only did the blast shields stay closed, she could hear additional sounds of other barriers coming down outside her room. The entire ship must be going into a full lockdown as the *High Marker* isolated her structural components. That could only mean a hull integrity breach.

Grace pulled up the bridge through her command console. "Report, Monk."

Monk's haggard face appeared as he yelled off-screen. The floating comm eye must have caught him at a bad time. It followed him as he ran across the bridge and scanned an array of flashing red lights on one of the side stations.

"Focus on that console," she ordered.

The comm eye flew up just behind the good captain's head and zoomed in on what half a dozen of the bridge officers were staring at as well. Grace clicked her tongue; what a waste of manpower. The ship had struck something, and the object, instead of being destroyed on impact, was hard enough to punch a hole straight through the exterior plating of the second level of section three. What was strange was that, according to the console, it had also penetrated the blast shields that had dropped down to cordon off that section as well as the hallway blast shields. Whatever this thing was had destroyed three layers of shielding. Four; the section blast shields had also just gone down. Grace's eyes widened. The object made a right turn . . .

"Oh my," Grace murmured. "So many interesting things. What a terrible time to die."

Could it be? Hours before they were all going to die, had they actually discovered alien life? After five hundred years in space, did humanity just receive their answer about life outside this system? And was the damn thing actually rampaging through the corridors of the ship? She watched as the object or creature continued down different paths, turning left at another intersection, cutting through a common room, and then back-tracking the way it had come.

"It knows how to use the lift," she muttered as her eyes trailed the blinking red dot moving throughout the ship. "Interesting." Monk yelled out orders and waved his hands wildly, almost knocking the comm eye out of the air.

"Pan to the captain," she ordered.

The good captain's face had gone sheet white, as had the faces of al-most all of the bridge crew. Monk barked several more commands off-screen and then focused back on the screen. A few seconds later, a dozen green dots blinked to life on the screen and swarmed toward the red dot.

"Get a security eye in there," he said.

Four additional screens floated in the air above his head, each show-ing a real-time feed of the security eyes zooming down corridors toward the red dot. It seemed the security personnel, the green dots, got to the red dot first.

"Initial contact from Sec Team One with visual says humanoid!" an acolyte said from off-screen.

Humanoid? That was a surprise, though something that could blow through the hull of a warship and blast through impact shielding was def-initely more than that.

"Sec Team One down!" the acolyte continued. "Sec Team Two engag-ing from the rear."

"Back to the console," Grace said. She caught the screen just in time to see the first splash of green dots closest to the red target blink out of exis-tence. She saw another group of green coming up from behind it. Then they too blinked out. Still, Monk sent more security personnel after it.

"Get some Kill Mutes out of stasis!" he roared. "I want them awake and working in five minutes. And get a mech team powered up."

Grace watched as a third group of green dots disappeared. Well, if

Monk was going to use Kill Mutes and combat mechs in the tight spaces of a warship, he might as well just blow it apart now. Those killing machines weren't made to fight in such tight quarters. They would tear the *High Marker* apart from the inside out, though considering what that intruder was doing, did it really matter? She was deathly curious, and deep in thought when she caught the end of one of Monk's orders.

". . . Sec Team Six to escort the High Scion out of her quarters to safety," he was saying.

She checked the console again and realized that indeed, the red dot was moving toward her section. Fascinating. Her patience was rewarded as the first of the Security Eyes reached the corridor and recorded a visual of the intruder. She would at least get to see an alien life before she died, which was definitely worth the price of admission. Discovering alien life had always been one of her fondest wishes, unlikely as it was to be granted. The gods had an interesting way of fulfilling childhood dreams.

"Focus on the upper left," Grace instructed. She had to squint as she stared at the screen within her screen.

She caught the tail end of a fight, where armored security soldiers were flung across the air like rag dolls. One of the bodies almost flew into the Security Eye, which managed to veer to the side at the very last second. Then, hovering close to the ceiling, it moved in toward the target. At first, all Grace could see was a dark figure, something definitely humanoid, with two legs and arms. Then she gasped.

"Captain Monk," she said. "Monk!"

He turned toward the Security Eye. "Oh, High Scion! I was not aware you were there. Please be at ease. Everything is under control. A security team is on their way to see you to safety as we speak."

"I see how much things are under control," she remarked dryly. "The security team will not be necessary. Call all your forces back. Do not engage the intruder."

"High Scion? We must! That thing is tearing the ship apart!"

"Call your forces back or I will order you shot on the spot."

Monk hesitated. "Your will, High Scion." He nodded to someone off-screen.

"Good, keep our people clear of him. Do not impede his path no matter what."

"Him, High Scion? Is there something you know about this being? As the captain—"

She turned the comm off and waited. What could possibly be the explanation for this? It couldn't be because of the ship's fusion sources. They were already depleted. It could be the weapons systems, but why wouldn't he have retrieved them his first time here? Besides, most of them were drained from the battle. It could only mean one thing. Grace Priestly began to pack. A few minutes later, there was a knock on the door. How quaint. He punches a hole in her ship, kills over a dozen guards, yet knocks on her door.

"Come in," she said, throwing on her travel cloak last. It was a good thing she hadn't had much time to unpack when the *High Marker* was attacked. Who knew what awaited her wherever she was going.

The same time traveler she saw an hour ago walked into the room.

She stood up and greeted him as if this were an everyday occurrence. "You're back. I must have left quite an impression."

He nodded. "High Scion."

Immediately, Grace noticed the changes in the time traveler. His skin was darker, red, almost as if burned, and his facial hair, which was bad enough before, was overgrown and unkempt. Disgusting.

The time traveler looked over at the easel in the corner. "Nice painting."

"Was just passing the time by reminiscing, as one is wont to do before she dies."

"Is that what Iceland was like back then?"

Grace smiled. "The Blue Lagoon. You know my history."

"Everyone does, High Scion."

"I told you to call me Grace."

The time traveler looked down at the bag floating next to her. "Are you ready then?"

Grace's heart filled with anticipation. Traveling through time had also been a childhood dream. It was what led her to study the field and enter the sciences. And while the uncertain future was something she feared, it couldn't be any worse than where she was now. Still, he wanted something from her, else he wouldn't have come back. Grace wasn't one to leap blindly into the unknown. If she left now on his terms, whatever leverage she had would be lost.

"Ready to leave for your time?"

He nodded. "You already know where staying on this ship leads to."

"Why the change of heart? What about the Time Laws?"

"I am following the spirit of the Time Laws by disobeying them."

Grace raised an eyebrow.

"High Scion," Monk's voice bleeped over the comm. "Are you all right? I am moving teams to your area——"

"Stay the fuck out!" she snapped. "Comm off. Door lock. My authority." She looked at the time traveler and smiled. "Sometimes, the consequences of the unknown are worse than the terrible ones you do know. I don't even know your name."

The time traveler bowed. "James Griffin-Mars, High Scion."

"Call me Grace," she muttered, mulling over his name. She had expected something fantastic and futuristic, but his name, like his appearance, was disappointing. Still, that tidbit of information told her much about the society he came from. Latin derivative. Old Western civilization. Possibly Christian-derivative religion.

Couple that with his familiar features and his mannerisms, not to mention his language . . . Actually no, he was speaking her form of space-speak too fluently. Language was the most easily mutated of cultural references, therefore logically he must be masking his native tongue. He could be well trained to behave in a fashion nonthreatening to her. By space, this could all be an act. Somehow, however, she believed him, and her instincts rarely failed her. That left only one thing to clarify.

"And what would you need me for in your future?" she asked. "My mind obviously."

James nodded. "Among other things."

Grace smirked. "My beauty? My sharp tongue? My leadership? Out with it, boy."

"Humanity needs your brilliance and wisdom to save it once again."

She harrumphed. "Wisdom is something I never had plentiful amounts of. And what would I do in your time?" There was a brief hesitation in his movements, and then she knew he was hers.

"There is an environmental catastrophe in our time," he said.

She nodded. "Of course there is. There's one in mine too. What's your point?"

"We have a scientist who believes she can cure the plague. She needs your help."

It was Grace's turn to hesitate. This plague, known as the Terravira back at home, covered half the planet, and was said to be irreversible. Now, someone in the future had a cure? Her eyes wandered to the painting in the corner of the room, and saw the landscape that was her backyard as a child. Her family had left with the rest of the Technology Isolationists shortly after her seventh birthday, but she still remembered the beauty of the ice caps, or what little was left of them by the time she left. The Terravira had advanced so quickly in the years leading up to the mass exodus . . . Grace shook her head. Up until now, she had always considered leaving her people her legacy, but perhaps she had a higher calling. Could it be done? Was it even possible?

"I have questions," she said, her voice soft and breaking.

"No time." In a blur, James covered the distance between them and was hovering close to her. "Are you with me or not?"

There was a banging on her door.

"High Scion?" a voice said outside. "Are you all right?"

"I need to know now," James pressed.

"Why the rush?" Grace said. "We have all the . . . we don't have time, do we?"

James nodded. "The ship is moving fast, hurtling through space, not subject to the time and distance delimiters of time travel."

"That's how you're able to jump back here so soon. Fascinating." Grace walked past him and grabbed the canvas and tucked it under her arm. "Carry my bag, James," she ordered as she returned to his side. "Now I'm ready."

"Cut the door down," the muffled voice on the other side of the room yelled.

"Brace yourself," James said. There was a bright yellow flash, and then Grace suddenly felt the urge to throw up her tea. Then everything went black.

When she came to, the two of them were floating in the black of space. Her carryall bag and canvas had disappeared, and looking down, her chest was wet. She had a splitting headache.

"What happened?" she groaned.

"You passed out and then threw up on yourself," James said.

So much for looking dignified. Grace suddenly had a severe case of vertigo and felt like throwing up again. She had had just enough embarrassment for the day and willed her body to stop acting so undignified. She reminded herself who she was.

"Now what?" she asked. "Where's your ship? Or did you discover teleportation in the future?"

"Unfortunately, no," James said. "My ship is on its way now. It will be here in a while. Again, our conversation lasted longer than I anticipated and I miscalculated the path of the *High Marker*."

"How did you know the *High Marker*'s location?"

"Your ship had sent constant distress calls before it was lost. I simply extrapolated its trajectory and jumped into its path."

"Which is why you slammed into it." She nodded. There was a long pause between the two of them. "So now what?" she asked again. Grace hated asking. She was usually the one who knew everything.

James linked his arms around her waist and pulled her in close. "We wait, and then we save the world."

THIRTY-FOUR

MEETING OF THE MINDS

The tension in the air became thick as soup the moment James and Grace Priestly stepped out of the collie. This was the longest he had been away from Elise since she had come to the present and she had come down to the garage to meet him. Her eyes widened when she caught sight of the Mother of Time draped on his arm.

At first, she was friendly to the beautiful and exotic but significantly older woman hanging onto him. She offered Grace a hand and smiled. "Welcome to the Elfreth. Thank you for joining us. I'm—"

Grace must have sensed something between James and Elise, and decided to assert her dominance, or just screw with him. "What a precious child," she exclaimed to James, touching his shoulder in a more than friendly manner. "You didn't tell me you had a daughter."

Elise looked like someone had thrown cold water on her as she shot an incredulous look at Grace, and then a ferocious one at James.

He sighed, and of course Grace decided that this was the opportune time to further flame the situation in. She leaned in toward him and gave him a peck on the cheek, cooing softly. "Pet, I've stepped onto your world for about fourteen seconds and you're already in trouble. I don't think this time period can handle me. Your woman, at least, certainly can't. She doesn't seem very glad to see you. No matter, it's time she learns who is in charge."

James watched as she let go of him, though not before she gave him one last visible squeeze on the arm, and then sauntered down the ramp to greet all the gaping tribespeople as if she were some goddess that had come down from the heavens to meet the primitives groveling in the mud. The looks on the tribe's faces ranged anywhere from fascination, bewilderment, to, in Elise's case, barely suppressed hostility.

His initial concern with bringing Grace back was the elderly woman's adjustment to such a grim place. Now he realized that the Mother of Time could thrive anywhere. It was everyone else who would have to adjust to her. He was pretty sure if Grace and Elise went at it, poor Elise would come out far behind, even though she was a third Grace's age. The two women sized each other up, Elise with her hands on her hips and Grace barely acknowledging her with an upturned slant of the mouth.

"What a precious little dear. Could you call your father for me?" Grace said.

"I'd better bring him to you," Elise countered. "We should probably get you a hover carrier as well. Most of our camp isn't wheelchair accessible."

"I think I'll manage." Grace bared her teeth. "I like to stay in vigorous shape." She looked back to James. "Isn't that right, pet?"

Elise's scowl deepened. James shrank. He should have never listened to that voice in his head telling him this was a good idea. Well, he couldn't change the past—actually, that was more untrue than it had ever been—so now he just had to face the consequences of his actions. Just in case, he stepped in between the two.

"Grace, this is Elise Kim, the biologist from the late twenty-first century who is going to save the planet from the Earth Plague." He gestured to Grace. "Elise, this is—"

"Grace Priestly." Grace lifted her chin. "The Mother of Time, High Scion of the Technology Isolationists, one of the six great millennial minds—"

"And my new assistant," Elise snapped.

That stopped Grace in her tracks, and for a second, James withered, this time under both their glares.

"Is that right?" Grace said, regaining her composure a second later. "We'll just have to see about that."

The two stared each other down. James wanted nothing more than to get back into his collie and hide away for a few hours. Maybe this was a bad idea after all. Grace would never take a backseat to anyone, especially to someone she deemed inferior. He'd have to pull them apart and reason with them separately if these two were ever to get along.

"Why don't you show Grace the lab," James said, hoping to break the tension. "I know you're both eager to get started on the cure."

Elise nodded and gestured for Grace to follow. Grace responded by taking her time. He heard them start up an argument as they walked up the ramp.

"Is the Mother of Technology knowledgeable in World English?" Elise asked.

"Only that and eighteen other languages," Grace said.

James watched them leave, looking bewildered. He hoped they didn't stay at each other's throats for long. Right before they disappeared from view, Grace looked his way with a mischievous glint in her eyes. That woman was without a doubt someone he had to watch out for. She was a slippery one; Elise was going to have to be on her toes, too. Chawr, who was standing nearby, grinned from ear to ear. He couldn't understand the exchange that had just taken place, but he knew enough from their facial expressions to fill in the blanks.

"What are you looking at?" said James good-naturedly. The young hothead and his friends had come to him shortly after the night they tried to leave and offered to help in any way they could if James would teach them how to fly a ship. He agreed and made them the collie's pit crew. "Go charge the batteries," he grinned, "like I showed you."

"Yes, Elder," Chawr said, signaling to his guys to help him plug the solar generator in.

"James," Smitt blurted into his head. "How did the retrieval go?"

"As planned. Thanks for the logistics. A little close on the entry but it saved some travel time. What about on your end?"

Smitt sighed. "They assigned me four new chronmen to take your place. Three Tier-5s and a Tier-4."

James chuckled. "Babysitting, eh? What are you retrieving? Coal? Seeds?"

"Worse. Wood. I'm literally jumping these damn fodders into forests days before massive fires and having them chop wood. It's so degrading. I mean, does ChronoCom realize who I am?"

"A guy who failed his chronman advancement?"

"I'm a Tier-1 handler! And thanks for rubbing it in. Seems you've found a sense of humor since you've been away. I don't like it."

James grinned to no one in particular. "You just don't like me becoming a better person."

"The improvement is debatable," Smitt said. "Listen, my friend, I need to warn you. Your little operation here came up on one of the wasteland surveillance reports. Just a blip. Planetary regency likes to keep tabs on what's happening with the savages, and your region's caused some recent energy spikes. If this continues, you'll either need to regulate your energy usage or disperse the concentration."

That was a problem. The past month had become such an unexpected relief that he had almost forgotten that ChronoCom was hunting them. He'd have to be more careful with his movements, possibly park his collie a day's journey away just to be sure. Anything to keep Elise safe.

"I'll keep that in mind," James said. "And . . . thank you, Smitt. You've been more than a good friend. I'm sorry I ever doubted you."

"You still owe me a retirement to Europa, or a clean Earth to live on. I'll take either."

"You got it."

Smitt left the subchannel and James made his way toward the lab, hoping things between Elise and Grace had warmed a little. He worried about the ninety-three-year-old woman climbing those stairs day in and day out. They would have to figure out an accommodation for her. He reached the camp and spoke with the column guard, who confirmed seeing the two head into Farming Tower One.

He was eleven stories up the stairwell when he saw Grace sitting on the steps braiding someone's hair. He frowned. It couldn't be Elise's. Her hair wasn't that long, though it had begun to grow out, making her look a little more like the other women of the Elfreth. James thought it looked attractive.

"Grace?" he asked, approaching her.

Grace looked at him and smiled. Then she went back to her braiding.

James walked around her and stumbled when he saw that it was Sasha's hair Grace was braiding. He backed up against the wall and saw the Nazi soldier lounging farther up the stairs. Grace continued to braid and fuss with Sasha's hair, humming and complimenting his dead sister about how pretty she was.

"You're alive now," he managed to say.

Am I now, pet? she replied, looking up. *You think it's that easy bringing someone back from the dead?*

Why haven't you brought me back then, James? Sasha asked.

"I . . ." James opened and closed his mouth. He didn't have a good excuse. Actually, he did. Sasha was useless to Elise and the tribe. She would be just another mouth to feed. That was justification enough, wasn't it?

Come back for me too, ja? The German soldier grinned, beckoning him closer. *Put me to use. I have skills. Bang. Bang.* He pretended to shoot at imaginary targets.

James shook his head; they were imaginary people. What was wrong with him? He needed to do something about his miasma treatment sooner rather than later. A mad, raving lunatic would be no good to Elise.

He left the small group and continued up the stairs, fleeing these fragments of his past. Elise and Grace were real, no matter what ChronoCom had taught him about those from the past. They were living, breathing people who could now make new choices, and forge their own futures.

This was the best way for him to contribute to Elise's cause. All these years he had thought the resources he retrieved from the past, the technologies, power sources, and equipment, the most valuable things in history that could save the present. Now, he realized that he had it all backward. The resources ChronoCom should have been farming all this time were the people, not just the stopgap bandages of power reactors and fuel supplies. After all, hundreds of years of salvaging had not deterred mankind's decline toward extinction.

James hurried up the stairs. He caught up with them on the forty-second floor of Farming Tower One, where they were resting on the stairs when he came around the corner. Grace was wheezing and sweating. She looked like she was about to faint.

"Do you know how old I am?" Grace snarled when he came around the bend. "I can't be climbing all these steps."

"How could you make her climb all these stairs?" Elise said, shaking a finger at him.

"What the hell?" James raised his arms, palms up. "How was I supposed to have planned ahead for this?"

"You should have!" both women snapped.

James tried very hard to keep his eyes from rolling. "I'll see what I can do. For now, allow me." He powered on his exo and gently lifted both of them with his kinetic coils, carrying them all the way up to the seventieth floor. The entire time, the two women berated him on his thoughtlessness. Somehow, in the fifteen minutes he had left them alone, they had become friends and decided to combine their powers against him.

When they reached the lab, Grace made one quick circle and came out with a list of demands, most for items which James had never heard of. Still, she had a way of putting words together so that he found himself agreeing to almost everything. Then, she walked over to the ancient elevator bank with one half of the sliding doors torn off. She poked her head down the dark shaft and then signaled to him. "Clear this, and have a fabricator build an elevator. This one isn't a request."

"You mean the things you wanted before were optional?"

"No, pet, they weren't, but this one I need especially. I need a working lift if I'm to work up here. And I'm sure those tribepeople of yours will appreciate it as well."

"I don't even know where I can find a fabricator."

Grace rolled her eyes. "I guess I'll have to do it myself. Only way I know it'll be done right. Pay attention. Take notes, pet."

Suddenly she rattled off a list that was easily fifty items long. James didn't know how she knew all this off the top of her head, but then again, that was why he had brought her back. He had a sneaking suspicion that life was about to get much more interesting.

THIRTY-FIVE

TURNING UP THE HEAT

Levin and Kuo stood in the town square of the village of Pinto waiting for the ancillaries to report in. In the distance, the cratered city of Madrid stretched out for several kilometers in either direction for as far as the eye could see. Madrid had been one of the first major cities to fall during the AI War, a victim to the surprise attacks of the gigantic Mountain Hulks passing through the Strait of Gibraltar on their way to Germany, similar to the second coming of Hannibal thousands of years earlier. A city of millions was reduced to rubble within hours when the land underneath collapsed from the stress of hundreds of vanguard burrowers cutting through its foundation. Now, all that was left were scores of crevices punctured deep into the earth.

The people of Pinto, a settlement of miners and excavators, made a living picking through the remains of this once-great city. Most major cities had similar settlements of scavengers nearby. They filled an important role in humanity's ecosystem.

The difference between Madrid and most other fallen major metropolises was that it had actually sunk into the ground, as if swallowed by a massive sinkhole. Because of the added challenge of being buried underground, the city's bones weren't picked as clean as many other city corpses. New useful raw materials were still being discovered daily and Pinto had prospered as a trade hub. It was here that Levin received his first solid lead regarding James. One that he hoped could take him a step closer to finding where he was hiding.

The agency had been dangling off-planet relocation as a reward for any news of the fugitive chronman's activities, and an abnormally large number of tips had filtered in from this region. Once the information was deemed viable, Levin and his people had swept in under cover of darkness and blockaded the entire village. Currently, Shizzu and Geneese were questioning the local government and merchants of Pinto while three squads of monitors were performing door-to-door searches of the outlying buildings. Levin and Kuo had set up their base of operations in the center of Pinto and were waiting for their findings.

He highly doubted someone as skilled as James would allow himself to be trapped so easily, but Levin wasn't going to allow a solid lead to slip by. He looked over at Kuo, who was staring intently out of their makeshift canopy at the giant crater down the hill.

"How deep does it go?" she asked.

He walked up next to her and peered down into the black pit. "They say it's almost a half a kilometer down. Supposedly, the Machines had giant burrowing worms that ate the earth from underneath. Then when the bombs from the Mountain Hulks began dropping, the entire city fell as one giant piece. Some of the miners say there are entire chunks of the city completely intact down there."

"And these Earthlings eke a living picking the bones of the city?"

"Not everyone can have all their needs synthesized artificially."

"Carrion eaters," she spat.

"ChronoCom picks the bones of our past, do we not?" Levin corrected. "Doesn't that make us carrion eaters as well? And since the corps depends on the energy we retrieve, what does that make you?"

She ignored him as she spotted Shizzu approaching from up the hill. He stopped directly in front of Kuo and bowed. This wasn't lost on Levin. "Auditor, Securitate," he said, "we have received confirmation from two separate manufacturers here that a man matching fugitive Griffin-Mars's description has led a small group, usually two to four individuals, here multiple times over the past few weeks to barter for goods. They were also able to identify the distinct features of his collie."

"Several others?" Levin mused. "He has a posse now."

"What did they trade for?" Kuo asked.

"Solar panels, power generators, lab equipment, and several bottles of distilled alcohol. They traded base goods the first time here: food, clothing, and hemp. The second time they were here, they bartered for fiber fabricators, weapons, fuel, and several more bottles of alcohol."

"Sounds like James, all right," said Levin.

That information painted a startling picture of James and that anomaly he was hiding. They were building something and required industrial resources to do it. What could they be up to? Not only that, who were these others with them? Had James linked up with one of the survivalist groups?

"What did those with him look like? Can those merchants tell us anything? Their garb? Skin color? Accents?"

"The merchants did not notice anything out of the ordinary except that they weren't from the region and didn't look civilized, Auditor," Shizzu said. "However, one of them did overhear some of their exchanges and believed it a Northern American dialect of Solar English. The people with him seemed intimidated by the village and looked to him as their leader."

"Of course he's their leader," Kuo said. "A chronman wouldn't follow a bunch of savages."

Levin ticked off the items Shizzu mentioned. "He isn't running. Interesting. All this time, we thought he had gone into hiding to someplace either remote or back in time. Notice he's actually trading food."

If he was still in Northern America, then there would still be a lot of ground to cover. The entire continent had taken the brunt of the devastation from the Third World War, and now was one complete wasteland, except for the half-dozen cities that still sparsely dotted the landscape. If James were leading a bunch of primitive savages, he could be hiding anywhere.

Levin corrected himself; they were still people. His eyes wandered over to Kuo. The damn woman was corrupting his thoughts. Over the past few weeks, she had shadowed his every movement as he set up the surveillance net around the planet, chasing every unauthorized jump that could lead to James's whereabouts.

The severity of James's defection had climbed all the way up to the Council. Now, there was an ongoing discussion among the administrators about following Valta's lead and chipping all chronmen to prevent an occurrence like this from happening again. Some went as far as to favor disabling the antidetection systems on the collies. Doing either would endanger the lives of every chronman operation out there. Leave it to the administrators to concoct such terrible ideas. To make matters worse, Valta had offered to carry out the service for the agency. Levin scowled. What back door would the corporatation create for themselves there?

"How many times have these savages aided the fugitive?" Kuo asked.

Levin did not like where this round of questioning was leading. The Valta operative saw situations in black and white entirely too often. Given her low opinion of the natives out here in the wastelands, she might consider these people's innocent trading with James to be treason.

"At least three, Securitate," Shizzu said.

Kuo rounded on Levin. "The planetary government must send a worldwide communication of this immediately. All settlements must be banned from trading with these fugitives."

"That is not an easy thing to enforce," Levin said. "All it would serve is to prompt the settlements and our fugitive to be more discreet in the future. That only makes our job more difficult."

"Allowing it to continue only makes our job more difficult."

"Your ability to point out the obvious is startling," he said. "Shizzu, inform the leaders of this settlement that James Griffin-Mars is no longer associated with ChronoCom, and that he is now an illegal fugitive within the planetary government. Any further interaction—trade, business, or personal—will be considered aiding and abetting a known criminal and punishable by sanctions to the settlement and imprisonment to the leaders of the community."

"Auditor Shizzu," Kuo added, "find all the merchants the fugitive had dealings with and have them imprisoned for treason. If any resist, execute them."

"Securitate," Levin said, "these people did not know of James's crimes. It's not like he advertised this knowledge when he engaged them. A warning should be sufficient to discourage future dealings."

Kuo sneered. "You've been with these savages for too long, Auditor. You're soft. This won't deter them or the other settlements that have betrayed the planet in the slightest. They need to be taught a lesson."

"I appreciate the advice, Securitate," Levin said. "However—"

"You are weak and impotent," Kuo said. "It's time you learned how Valta maintains their market share. We do not tolerate such abuses."

"Belay that order, Monitor," Levin snapped, stepping in front of Kuo and facing her. "Valta has no market share here."

The edges of her lips curled and he felt the tingle of an exo powering up in close proximity. Where were her bands? He had never seen any on her person. "Are you sure you wish to challenge me on this?" she asked, taking a step forward.

He powered on his own exo. "Punishing the entire settlement in such a manner is criminal. I won't allow it."

The two stood toe to toe, exos powered up and flaring. The orange glow of Levin's exo didn't quite match the brightness of Kuo's white. The pitch of her exo was different as well. Every military unit used exo technology in a slightly different way. Levin had no doubt that there was a very real chance that her exo—being corporate military—was more powerful than his, but he stood his ground.

Instead of powering his exo on and supporting Levin, Shizzu took several steps backward and slinked away from the conflict. Levin knew where that damned traitor would be if this came to a head.

"How would you like to proceed?" Kuo asked in a low voice. "Right here, right now, in front of your men? Let me ask you: What acceptable exit strategy do you think could come out of this? Did you actually think you could beat me? But let's say by some miracle of the abyss you did, how do you think Valta will respond? Stand down, Auditor, you're not my quarry."

She was right. Levin's pride was the only thing keeping his exo powered on at this moment. This was a lose-lose situation. Even if he stood down, any doubts his men had of what little authority he still had would be erased. He had lost his temper and was now paying the price. Kuo must have read his mind. He powered down his exo and felt her white field— hot and cold at the same time—pass through him until it enveloped them both, showing everyone within sight who was really in control.

"I am not unreasonable," she said, "so I'll save you some face." She turned to Shizzu. "Auditor Levin has a point. Delay that order to execute them. Instead, take inventory of what these people received from the fugitive, and take it out from their stock. Burn the grain, destroy the technology, and kill anyone who tries to stop you." She turned back to Levin. "Satisfactory?"

He nodded.

"Consider this your final warning, Auditor. Next time you power your exo on me, I will finish you."

THIRTY-SIX

BUILDING THE BASE

There was a bright yellow flash and James found himself floating in space over the moon of Hyperion. This time, he threw up, spewing the contents of his stomach out into space, splattering the inside of his atmos shield. He hunched over and watched as the bile floated away and coagulated on the wall of the perfect sphere. Well, from this point on, things were only going to get worse. He looked down at his quivering hands. They were numb; he couldn't feel the tips of his fingers or his toes. He wiggled them. Nothing. Nine times in a span of two months; it was too much. And through all this, he hadn't taken any miasma pills.

"Did you get what I asked for, pet?" Grace's voice popped into his head.

"The entire stockroom, including the magnetic siphoner and gravity converter," he answered once he was done heaving and found his voice. "I'm impressed the Technology Isolationists managed to hide a depot on Hyperion. I'd have thought with the moon's chaotic rotation, no one would put a base there."

"That's why we put it there. We had dozens of these stations all over the solar system. This particular depot was particularly well stocked, since every other faction had written the moon off as useless."

"Someone must have found it. There were traces of battle when I found the ruins."

"The space-forsaken Neptune Divinities had caught on to these depots ten years earlier and were hunting them down one by one. They must have eventually found this one. Tell me there are descendants of those shits. After I cure the planet for your girl, I'd like to spend the rest of my days grinding them to dust."

"A little long to hold a grudge, High Scion."

"Call me Grace. My time with the TIs is over."

In the two weeks since he had retrieved Grace Priestly, he had gone back in three more times: this time to retrieve raw materials from the TI depot, once for a cache of food, and once for someone widely considered the greatest geneticist to have ever lived. Unfortunately for that last run, Zing Ri decided he'd rather stay with his plants than heed the warning of a stranger. His plants ate him six minutes later.

Truth be told, none of these was the actual best option. They were just jumps that Grace and Smitt were able to identify as viable targets that wouldn't cause large enough ripples in the chronostream. Though he had already broken the most egregious of the Time Laws, James really was still trying his best to stay within the spirit of them.

James made sure the containment of his netherstore was still intact when the collie pulled up next to him. Hopefully, this was the last find that Elise and Grace needed for a while. He had to rest, or at least get his hands on some miasma pills soon. The recent continuous trips had taken a toll on him physically as well as mentally. If he wasn't careful, James was either going to lose his mind or have a severe cascading organ failure, possibly both.

Grace had taken over the role as his permanent handler, but hadn't mentioned anything about his lag sickness yet. In her time, the longer-term consequences of excessive time travel hadn't been discovered yet. She had to know something was wrong with him, or at least suspect he was ill. As long as Elise didn't know, he didn't care what the hell anyone else thought.

James entered the collie and plugged the netherstore into the ship's power source. It was still several days' journey back to Earth. He would also have to be more careful with his entry. ChronoCom's surveillance and patrol activities had picked up of late.

The collie kicked on and began to skim through the black of space. Now was a good time to sleep. James had had very little rest recently and even less since he had picked up Grace. In the two months since the Elfreth had adopted their purpose, the tribe had prospered. Several of the smaller tribes had even asked to join. Now, the Elfreth's numbers had swollen to over three hundred, more than any other time in recent memory. It worried James, though. It was just more mouths to feed and more supplies to maintain.

"Pet," Grace asked in his head. "Why are you still so careful with my Time Laws? You've already broken the most important one. Why not just do what must be done at this point?"

"Because I still believe in them, or at least most of them," he said. "The laws are there to protect the chronostream and not alter our natural progression, are they not?"

"Actually," Grace said, "I winged several of them based on best estimates of quantum theory. You have to realize, time travel was still very new, and wasn't as exact a science back then as it is now. I've been studying some of the annals of ChronoCom. I agree with most of it, but there are several theories that seem to defy physics. Like that Vallis Bouvard Disaster. It makes no sense for someone to implode that way."

"Well, that and the fact that both you and Elise haven't melted yet," said James. It was a huge relief, actually. He had spent the first few days half-expecting Elise to one night combust into a fireball. "So there is no danger of that? I was worried about that with bringing you back as well."

"I see no logical reason why. Take many of the Time Laws, both from myself and from ChronoCom, with a grain of salt. I was drinking heavily the night before I came up with the majority of them. Keep in mind that they are mostly there as a precaution. The technology has devastating effects if used incorrectly after all."

James lay down on the bench and stared at the ceiling, his eyes tracing scars and blemishes that lined the interior. Each of them had a history. One particular jagged point on the side panel still had his dried blood on it from an ill-planned ambush by two bandits after a night of drinking on Despina Station. That dent on the floor was from the time he smashed his head when Puck pirates attacked the collie while he was in cryo.

"Grace," he asked. "Why did you write the first Time Law? Why shouldn't we bring people back from the past?"

He heard an audible sigh. "Of all the risks time traveling poses, bringing living beings back from the past is the greatest. The likelihood of a more advanced civilization abusing a more primitive one is high. What's to prevent a government from going back to the day before Vesuvius buries

Pompeii and enslaving the population? What about the Neptune Divinity Savior trying to back his dead son, or the Kuma Faction trying to undo their blunder at the Star Fortress? The Time Laws are there to ensure the integrity of the chronostream."

"But I brought you and Elise back."

"And I say you walk a moral gray line, even if it is for a good cause. There's an old French saying: the road to hell is paved with good intentions."

"I thought the TIs were absolutists when it came to the morality of technology."

"Only fools and sociopaths are absolutists, pet."

James hesitated as he considered his next question. It was something he feared asking, but knew he couldn't talk to Elise about it. He wanted her to hold on to her newfound hope. She needed her optimism far too much for him to bring it up. He knew Grace would have no such necessity.

"I have to ask: what do you think about Elise's research, about the odds of a cure actually working?"

There was a long pause before Grace spoke. "She's on the right track; the theories are sound. The research from her time period did indicate that the scientists were very close to a working prototype."

"So it'll work? You two can cure the entire planet?"

"Not a chance in space, at least not with what we have right now."

"I . . . I . . ." James was speechless. "Why not?"

"Because, pet," she spoke as if speaking to a child, "it's a big problem that requires a big solution. We're two scientists, an alcoholic—don't deny it, James—and a mud-wallowing tribe in the middle of a dystopian wasteland. And I thought my odds were bad during my time."

"So why did you sign on for this? Why are you helping at all if you think it's impossible?"

"I didn't say it was impossible, pet," she said, "it's a slim chance, but at least there is a chance. That, and as far as I'm concerned, I'm already living on borrowed time. I was supposed to die on the *High Marker*, remember? Mortality changes one's perspectives and I feel that I owe mankind a better Grace Priestly than I've given them. Just because I'm one of the greatest humans to ever have lived doesn't mean I left that footprint. Looking back, all I did was lead the Technology Isolationists to a catastrophic war. I would like my legacy to be something more."

"I see. Thanks for the candor, High Scion."

"For the last time, call me Grace."

Fifty-six hours later, flying into the atmosphere under the cover of an Arctic storm and going low over the water to avoid detection, James made it to the collie parking grounds with his latest haul in tow.

Chawr and his crew leaped into action as James walked out of the collie. They were all still inexperienced and prone to mistakes, but they were improving. He still double-checked all their work, but they were dedicated and would become competent eventually. Eventually. They'd almost blown up the ship only twice.

Elise, as usual, called him on his comm band as soon as she found out he had returned. "You got the stuff for Grace?" she sounded eager with anticipation.

"I got you a present." He couldn't help but smile. Something about hearing the joy in her voice was infectious.

"I never thought I'd be so happy about an elevator," she said. "No more seventy flights four to five times a day."

James unloaded the materials out of the netherstore and ordered runners to carry them to Farming Tower One. "The parts are on their way up now. See you at dinner?"

"Afraid we can't, James. Too busy up here. Besides, I want to get Grace cracking on the lift right away. Stop on up when you have a chance."

"Will do," he said. "We can go over the next present you want."

James surveyed the hangar, which was nothing more than a half-buried parking garage, and waited until Chawr and his crew had attached the collie to the generator, which was powered by batteries charged by dozens of solar panels he had obtained through trade with settlements all over the world. Once a battery was charged, Chawr's crew would run down and move the energy to the generator. It was incredibly inefficient and usually took four to five days, depending on the weather, to charge the collie fully for a long voyage. James didn't know what in the black abyss they were going to do once winter came.

Some of the very long trips, like the one James took to pick up Grace and the more recent one to Saturn, required extended power. He had bartered for batteries at Earth's black market in Bangkok. The cost to buy enough power to make it all the way back to the heliopause was most of the extra chronman bands he had stolen from Earth Central, including the two precious exo bands he had obtained from storage as backup. Now, relying mostly on solar panels, trips off-planet were probably no longer possible. He perhaps had enough levels in the extended power sources to make a round-trip to Mars or Venus, and then the collie would be Earthbound until he found another power source.

Hopefully, these new advanced TI items—the magnetic siphoner and gravity converter, according to Grace—would help solve some of their energy needs. The list of her demands had been long and he had given up sifting through her requests to see if each was necessary. He didn't pretend to know her thoughts. Two things became abundantly clear to him after the first two days of giving her the breakdown of their situation: Grace knew exactly what was going on and what had to be done, and some of her ideas were so advanced and forward-thinking that he would have no chance of understanding them.

James nodded his approval as Chawr's guys hooked *Collie* up and went through the diagnostics, though he stayed around and watched them go through the maintenance steps. It wasn't that he didn't trust them; it was just that they hadn't earned his confidence yet. His new engineering crew were quick learners, but tended to be sloppy when they didn't understand why they were doing what they were doing. That would come with experience. For now, it was his responsibility to teach them without blowing his collie up in the process.

After they were done and he had double-checked their work, James yawned and walked up a rubble staircase, through the hollowed-out hull of a building down the block from the Farming Towers, and strolled through a small clearing surrounded by ancient skyscrapers with their tops broken off. He was looking forward to his bed; he hadn't slept in it in over a week.

He walked by a small group of the tribe and waved. One of them, the youngest by the looks of him, waved back. Things were improving daily with them, and as much as James hated to admit it, he wanted their approval. He was tired of being someone most people were wary of.

"Are you there, my friend?" Smitt's voice interrupted his walk. "I have the aftereffect report."

"Give it a go, Smitt. Any ripples from the Hyperion job?" he asked.

"A modest one. TI sensors detected strange energy signatures from your jump in. They thought it might have been a probe. The depot heightened security because of your intrusion, which made the surprise attack by the Divinities nine hours later not so much of a surprise attack. Ended with an additional two Divinity attack ships destroyed and an extra thirty casualties."

"Ouch. That's messy."

"The time line managed to self-heal six years later when the entire Divinity base off of Titan was destroyed.

"What about present blips?"

"ChronoCom outpost on Titan reported an unauthorized jump," said Smitt. "I ran the delays and bought you some time, but they were less than a day off from tagging you. Listen, James, you are starting to cut it really close. They're on to you. You need to cut back on these jaunts."

"Just keep me a step ahead of them," James thought back.

Smitt was right, though. He had been helping James and Grace plan these jumps, making sure they happened when ChronoCom either wasn't in a position to respond or when they could mask the jump. Either way, there was only so much he could do before the agency wised up. James's contribution to the tribe as a salvager would expire once he was caught or, worse yet, tracked back to their location.

"I'm serious," Smitt insisted. "You guys have to cut back, or at least lay low better, especially on Earth. Your Asia decoy only worked for the first week, as did your jig in the Mediterranean. It's only going to be a matter of time before they realize you never left the region."

"Make sure they don't," James said. "Or at least give us an early enough warning."

"Look, James, I've scanned your area. You have enough going on there that it's starting to breed significant energy readings. It's bound to attract attention."

James looked around the open space, or the town square, as Elise liked to refer to it. It was a lot busier than when he last left it. There were several machines running and he saw over a dozen small fires burning in barrel drums. And while some netting might help cover some of the light, it was just a matter of time before they were discovered.

"What else can we do? The tribe is getting larger. Our energy use is only going to grow."

"I've been researching your problem. What do you think about the mid-twenty-third century?"

James made a face. "I think the Publicae Age was a period of fascist cesspools and a death trap for any chronman."

"I hear ya. You didn't do too well during your five jumps back, but that time period was the peak of neural and cloaking technology. What do you think about going back and recovering a stealth hood?"

"I'd think you're trying to get me killed, Smitt."

"While that would solve many of my problems, my friend, I think it's the best solution to your little village's issues. Want to talk it over?"

James cursed. He avoided the mid-twenty-third century for good reason. But if it meant ensuring Elise's safety, he said he'd do anything. "I hate your idea already, but all right, let's hear it out." He sighed. He pulled out a bottle of wine he had pilfered from one of the storage lockers at the TI base and settled in for the bad news.

THIRTY-SEVEN

PUZZLE PIECES

There was a knock on the mushy plastered wall next to the doorway of Elise's lab. She looked up and brightened when James strolled in. His popping up at her door unannounced brought that familiar fluttering in her chest and made her face feel flush. She had been so immersed in her work lately that she was no longer even attending evening meals with the rest of the Elfreth. Rima had taken to bringing up food for her and Grace every night.

She missed evenings around the campfire. That was when the tribe bonded, and it felt a bit like Thanksgiving every night. It was also the only quality time she spent with James. She missed him most of all, but her work was too important now.

Grace, sitting at a workstation across from her, rolled her eyes and chuckled. "I'll let you have him today, lamb."

"Thanks, Grandma. I promise to bring him back in one piece," Elise answered sweetly.

The two of them had gotten off to a rocky start: Grace initially demanded to be addressed as the Mother of Time or High Scion. Elise responded by telling her new assistant that Gaia would wither and die before she called Grace that. Then Grace tried treating Elise like her assistant. When Elise reminded her who was actually in charge, the tension in the lab became thick as molasses. The final outrage was when the so-called Mother of Time tried to steal Rima away from her.

Elise had long since given up trying to mold Rima into anything resembling a lab assistant. That became a moot point when Grace came on board anyway. However, the girl had become invaluable as Elise's personal assistant. Rima still desperately wanted to stay near her, so instead of trying to make her something she wasn't, Elise moved the girl out of the lab and put her natural skills to use. She had a rifle allocated to the girl full-time and had one of the tribesmen teach her how to drive one of the rickety ground cars. Now, Rima filled the roles of her personal assistant, bodyguard, and driver, making her completely invaluable to Elise day to day. There was no way Elise was going to give her up.

To both their surprises, it was James who finally broke the ice, mostly because of Grace's continued insistence on calling him "pet." That pushed Elise over the edge, and the two bickered so loudly that the people working on the roofs could hear them go at it. They arrived at an uneasy truce when Grace agreed to concede the nickname if Elise promised to find another assistant for her.

Since then, their relationship had warmed up little by little as Elise came to appreciate just how brilliant Grace was. In the short time since Grace had joined them, she had displayed a frightening aptitude for picking up research and, for the first time, Elise felt like she was making real headway on this Earth Plague cure. The way Grace was able to slide into her role and propel Elise's work forward right away was uncanny. In return, Elise satiated Grace's thirst for knowledge about the twenty-first century, Grace's favorite period of time. It was also one of the reasons she had originally studied time travel.

Now, the two had settled into an awkward mentor-mother relationship built upon mutual goals, one-upmanship, and more than a bit of snark. Elise wouldn't admit it, but she, after the initial hiccups, had eventually grown fond of the sharp-tongued elderly woman.

Right now, Elise kept the butterflies in her stomach under control as she joined James for a stroll. They had both been busy—James with keeping the lab and the tribe supplied, and Elise with her research. She wasn't ready to admit it to him, or to herself for that matter, but she missed their time together. The two had seen each other very little ever since the tribe got behind her, and every time they did get the chance to spend some time together, she'd feel the tingling, nauseating thrill of her stomach twisting into knots. Not that she'd show it, of course.

They walked side by side, close together but shyly not touching, down the sky bridge paths, making small talk and making the circuit around the Farming Towers. Most of the glass panels on the passageway connecting the two structures were long gone, so the crosswinds constantly pushed her toward the edge. As they strolled across the sky bridge to the adjacent building, they passed several of the Elfreth making their way to the ground level. Several of the older women exchanged knowing smiles. Elise pretended not to notice, but her blush betrayed her.

"I brought you something." James pulled a sunflower from inside his jacket. "I know how much you love flowers and how you always complain there aren't any around anymore. I found this at one of my previous jumps. I thought it was pretty. I was going to save it for your birthday but—" he shrugged.

Elise's face turned crimson as she accepted it. Sunflowers weren't the first thing that came to mind in terms of romantic flowers, but this small gesture meant a lot to her. As she often did when slightly nervous, she began to gab.

She told him about her experiments and trials and how helpful Grace was. She moved on to the gossip within the Elfreth and how all the older women doted on her and tried to match-make her with some of the young strapping men in the tribe. She continued talking about her plans to make Rami her new apprentice and how she wanted to start a school to teach all the Elfreth children. She finally stopped herself when she realized that they had made an entire circuit around the Farming Towers and he hadn't said a word. Elise decided she liked that about him. She appreciated how deeply he listened.

"How's the cure coming along?" he finally broke his silence and asked.

"You realize," she said, "assuming that it's even possible, it'll take years before we find a cure?"

"Years?" He frowned. "We don't have that long. I can't keep us hidden from ChronoCom forever. I thought you said back in your time, your people were already close to a cure."

"We *were*," she said. "Doesn't mean we are now. Back in my day, the Earth Plague was only five isolated blooms in remote parts of the world. The damn thing is everywhere in this time." Elise waved her arms in a big circle for emphasis just as a stiff breeze blew in, pushing her a little too close to the edge of the skyway for comfort. She squawked and latched on to James's elbow.

"Why couldn't you just start where you left off?" he asked.

"Because back in good ol' 2097, we had this something called technology." She hated sounding like a broken record. "Resources and manpower a little more sophisticated than a couple of Bunsen burners and a hundred-year-old lady."

"I heard that," Grace said in her head. "You really should learn how to control that comm band of yours. I'm worth a hundred of your primate scientists, by the way."

"Stop listening in on me," Elise thought back. It was true, though. She was awful with comm band management and tended to blab all her thoughts accidentally to both James and Grace, the only two others with bands in the camp. It had led to several awkward exchanges. She closed Grace's channel.

"Well, resources and better equipment I'm working on. What else?" James asked.

Elise thought about it for a second and decided to go for the big issue that had been plaguing her for the past several days. "The biggest hurdle is that the virus mutates constantly like most ribonucleic acid viruses but is also highly resistant to our environment yet. It mutates at an alarming rate. That's why we need to devise a cure that can adapt constantly with the hundreds of strains that the Earth Plague comes in."

"How did you resolve it back then?" he asked.

"It wasn't an issue back then," she said. "We had a bacterial sequencer that could track and adapt to progressive mutations on the fly. We just don't have that technology anymore. Without it, we're pretty much screwed."

James's face scrunched up. Elise had learned to recognize that look on him when he was speaking with someone on his comm band or was deep in thought. "Back up for a second," he said. "That sequencer. What does it look like and where can I find one?"

Elise shook her head. "Only three prototypes existed. One went down with Nutris, and the second one, the original, was destroyed after it caused a flu-variant outbreak in Poland. The third I have no idea."

James put a finger to his chin and rubbed his now-hairless face, compliments of her nagging. Elise wasn't a fan of sandpaper beards. "This sequencer," he asked. "Was there a crystal with a bunch of sharp needles pointing at it?"

Elise frowned. "How do you know what it looks like?"

He shrugged apologetically. "Um, well, I stole it."

"You did what?" Her eyes widened.

"I'm sorry . . . ," he said.

"No." She laughed. "You being a time-traveling klepto is a good thing. If there's a working sequencer here, we might actually have a chance to cure Earth Plague."

James hesitated. "I don't know if that's possible."

"Why not?"

"I believe it's in Valta Corporation's possession. It will be nearly impossible to retrieve."

Elise held James's hands and moved into his embrace. "Can you at least look into it? Please? It's very important."

"I'll ask Smitt to dig up what he can find on the Nutris items," James said. "No promises. There's a good chance they could already be out of our reach."

"Thanks, James, you time-traveling klepto liar." She stood on her tippy-toes and pecked him on the cheek.

"The other reason why I came to see you," he said, sporting a funny look on his face, "is because I need to leave again in four days. This time, I'll be gone for a week."

"Where are you going? Back into space?"

He shook his head. "I have an upcoming jump to the Arabian Sea. ChronoCom's been tightening their surveillance grid. Smitt believes they've isolated our whereabouts to within this hemisphere. High-altitude travel is now too risky. I'm taking the collie underwater through the Atlantic."

"Is it dangerous?" she asked.

"Just promise me you won't leave Boston until I return."

"I promise," she lied. Elise knew how stressful these jobs were for him and didn't want to worry James. That, and she knew he'd fly off the handle if he found out. However, she had already reserved the ground transport to make a field trip with Rima to Mount Greylock in five days, and she had no intention of canceling. Sure, there were risks involved, but no more than what James did going back in time. Both had their wars to fight, and Elise had no intention of not doing her job because her self-declared protector was too busy risking his life doing something else.

THIRTY-EIGHT

WINGMAN

Smitt David-Proteus massaged his temples and resisted the urge to bang his forehead against the console at Hops in Earth Central. He had never realized how spoiled he was handling a Tier-1 like James. The handler captains, in all their shallow wisdom, had determined that they would chastise him for his recent transgressions by busting him down to babysit crappy low-tier chronmen doing coal runs and solar farming in the medieval ages.

It was beneath him, insulting, and more than a little depressing. He had gone from managing a single Tier-1 chronman to an entire gaggle of wide-eyed fresh Academy fodder filled with big egos, small brains, and even less common sense. He didn't expect any of these idiots would survive their first year.

"No, no, Hurls," he said into the console, his voice resigned. "You have to cut the branches off before you put the tree trunks into the netherstore. Look, the fire starts in nine minutes and needs to burn across the full acreage. The way fire works, it needs something to burn, to fuel it. If you don't leave enough materials for the flames to jump from tree to tree, you're going to leave time ripples."

For a second, Smitt daydreamed about disabling Hurls's jump band and stranding the abyss-plagued moron in 1894 Hinckley, Minnesota. This was definitely one chronman who was going to drive down the tenure averages. He had to babysit for another forty minutes, pulling Hurls out right before the out-of-control forest fire overran his position. The guy had to unload his entire container, strip out all the branches from the trunks—leaves and all—and spread them across the areas he had already cut to make sure the fire still spread like it was supposed to before loading the trunks back into the netherstore. It was a lot of wasted time and, at the end of the day, the jump recovered only 60 percent of the units earmarked for that job.

Smitt unhooked himself from the handler console and leaned back in his chair. The worst part of all of this was he would have to do it all over again with Horner, another Tier-5 scheduled to jump to the nineteenth century in seven hours and run a smash-and-grab on anything of worth from a steamship sinking into the Marianas Trench.

"The damn handler captains are running me ragged," Smitt moaned, covering his face with his hands.

Sitting beside him, Punil, a Tier-2 handler, smirked. "Haven't seen you this pissy in years. All the Academy brats driving you crazy?"

Smitt shrugged good-naturedly. "Just forgot how much of a grind it is and how green we all were back in the day. Fresh fodder, the lot of us. Been taking the Tier-1 experience for granted way too long. Even handling Tier-2s feels like I'm being spoiled. Can you do me a favor and haul Hurls in when he reaches Central? I need to get some rack time before my next babysitting trip."

"No problem," Punil said. "Get some rest."

"Thank you, my friend."

Smitt stood up and stretched, patting Punil on the shoulder as he walked down an aisle half-filled with handlers of various tiers managing dozens of other jobs. In reality, his irritation with these lower-tier fresh fodders was feigned. Being knocked down to the bottom rung of hand-holding was actually the perfect cover to scout potential marks to help James's illegal jumps for that savage-tribe pet project of his.

No one would question Smitt's research into some of the low-tech jump zones, considering all the crud jobs he'd had to run recently. Knowing the auditors were keeping tabs on him, he had carefully covered his tracks, making sure he had reasonable alibis for all his hits into the chron database. For unavoidable queries that could tie him to James, well, he had a secret weapon for that too.

Smitt clicked his tongue against the back of his teeth as he turned toward the exit. James was playing a very dangerous game. By helping him, Smitt was uncharacteristically doing the same. He would even go as far to say that his friend was in way over his head, but in the twenty years that he had known the man, James had always come through. As long as both he and James were careful, they could pull this off. He was a Tier-1 handler after all.

Several other handlers waved as he walked past them. He made sure to acknowledge every one of them. While other Tier-1 handlers acted almost as haughtily as chronmen, Smitt knew better. He wasn't the smartest handler, or the quickest-thinking. Nor was he the best administrator or tactician. He was actually average in every metric that defined a good handler. However, he had something going for him that most other handlers didn't: Smitt was a damn likable guy. In the grim business of salvaging, where almost everyone detested everyone else, the intangible currency of people liking you was as good as a Titan source.

Smitt checked the time. Instead of heading upstairs to his quarters, he headed down toward the lower armory level. A few minutes later, he reached the quartermaster auxiliary and chatted his way past Kiesche, the monitor on duty, to retrieve the gear Horner needed for her job tomorrow. Technically, he wasn't supposed to requisition the necessary equipment until the day of the job but, again, being a swell guy had its perks. A few seconds later, he was given access to the armory.

As Smitt walked inside, he glanced at the spot on the floor where James had laid him out a few weeks earlier. He hated to admit it, but that was probably the best thing that could have happened to him. Sure, it had given him a splitting headache and fuzzy vision for the following week, but it did clear him of some of the auditors' suspicions. That was worth getting his head cracked over. Even better, the events that followed allowed James to escape with the bands he needed. Smitt hadn't planned things out that way, but he felt the results justified his concussion. No matter how the others now viewed him, he was still loyal to his friend of twenty years.

When the two of them were graduating from the Academy, only James made it to the chronman tier. Smitt, with his anxiety and nerves, had completely bombed his final test. He was resigned to packing it up and returning to the processing plants back on Proteus for a life of hard and frigid menial labor. In fact, he had flamed out so spectacularly that he had not only failed to tier as a chronman, but as a handler as well.

James, one of the highest-rated graduates, had gone to bat for him and demanded Smitt be allowed a retest, saying he wanted no one else to be his handler. He even went as far as to offer his resignation from Chrono-Com. Their mentor, Landon, already a Tier-2 chronman at the time, had agreed. That second time, Smitt passed, and was spared a short and miserable life building oxygen replicators. No one ever thought he would make it to Tier-1.

"Showed those assholes," he muttered as he opened the lockers and pulled out the bands Horner needed for the job. Tier-5s, basically apprentices, were not allocated their own equipment and had to be spoon-fed every step of the way, with their bands given and taken from them at the beginning and end of every job. As he put all the bands into his nether-store, he glanced over as another handler walked into the armory. With a practiced sleight of hand, he slipped an extra charged paint band into his container.

"Hey Smitt," Eve, the other handler, said as she went about her own work. "Sorry to hear about what the caps are doing to you. Some bad business all around, giving you those little shits to manage."

"Right? I should be packing my bags for Europa," he complained, waving his arms in an exaggerated fashion. "Someone had to take the fall, and as long as they didn't take anything out of my savings, I'll earn out with these scrubs just as fast. I'll just have to work harder."

Eve nodded and wished him luck. Smitt finished his work and picked up his pace, walking a little faster out of the wing than he'd like. He would have to hurry if he was going to pull off data collection tonight. It was the middle of the night in Chicago, and the third shift was just about to switch over. This was the best time for him to hit up monitors who would be eager to get off duty.

He walked as fast as he dared back to his quarters and activated the paint band, impersonating one of the newer sysware techs he had painstakingly stalked. The guy, only a few months on the station, was a loner with a drinking problem, had no friends, and rarely left his quarters when off duty. He afforded Smitt the perfect cover for avoiding the watchful eyes the auditors probably had on him.

A few minutes later, Smitt, looking darker, bald, and more rotund, made his way to the west wing of Central, slowing down and changing his gait. The new sysware tech walked with a limp, and had a tendency to scratch his crotch and tuck his hands into his armpits. Smitt had spent an entire week following him, studying his every movement and habit, as he had had to do thousands of times before when prepping intelligence for James. Except now, it was Smitt running his own jobs. This was at the same time thrilling and frightening. He had failed the chronman tier for very specific reasons, after all.

Smitt entered the data-housing wing in the sub-basement of Central and inserted his doppelganger clearance hack into the security zone. This, too, was retrieved from the sysware tech when Smitt had found him semi-conscious at the bar one night and helped the guy back to his room. Swell guy, that Smitt, everyone had said. After he laid the guy onto his bunk, a swipe of the doppelganger and a copy of the paint band got all the clearance he needed. He grinned as the doors slid open. He made eye contact with the two monitors guarding a second set of doors and lumbered forward in his awkward gait.

"Another shift, Burke?" the monitor on the left said. "Just got here and already piling it on. You're going to make the rest of the techs look bad." Burke was actually scheduled for the fifth rotation.

"Just trying to double-shift my way off nights," Smitt said gruffly. "Would be nice to see some sun once in a while."

The monitor chuckled. "I hear you. I don't know what daylight looks like anymore."

The monitor on the other side of the door shook his head. "So you can burn under the ozone? Nah, I'm happy with nights. Can't wait to transfer off this shit planet."

The two let him into data housing without another glance. Smitt hurried to the rear terminals where the consoles hard-lined into the gigantic chron databases. No matter how much surveillance and security the auditors wanted to slap on him, all of it would have to be outside data housing. As long as Smitt accessed the information from inside this central core, he could bypass all the outer firewalls, sniffers, and bugs. Short of their injecting a bug directly into his head, he should be in the clear.

He connected his AI band to the console and began to retrieve the list of information James, the scientist, and the fucking Mother of Time herself, Grace Priestly, wanted. From jump locations of natural gas deposits to food granaries to solar panel stockpiles, Smitt went down their shopping list and grabbed it all. What his friend was going to do with that information was up to him.

More recently, Grace Priestly—Smitt refused to call her by anything less than her full name—had started making requests directly. At first, he had balked at taking orders from anyone other than James, but no one said no to the Mother of Time. She didn't seem like someone who took no for an answer. Bringing her back here was insanity. A part of Smitt still couldn't believe James had the audacity to do that.

Smitt began poring over the chron database and operations logs, querying anything that could prove useful to James and that anomaly who was the root of all Smitt's woes. He corrected himself; James had berated him for calling her that. It wasn't her fault he was stupid enough to bring her back. That colossal blunder was all James. She was supposed to save humanity's home world, after all. Smitt grunted. Fat chance of that.

An hour into his sleuthing, Smitt stumbled upon something interesting. "What's this?" He frowned, and dug deeper. His fingers tingled with excitement at the possibility of making a breakthrough on one of James's more difficult requests.

After chasing redacted reports for the past two shifts, he had finally come upon a pretty mundane operations report of a ChronoCom transport commissioned by Valta a week after James's jump to Nutris. The transport's mission was to rendezvous with one of the corporation's ships just outside the asteroid Hygiea.

All this wouldn't ring any alarms, except that the transport captain wrote in his logs that when he first reached the rendezvous point, he had raised his ship's alert level, because he thought they were under attack by a heavily armed giant ship with no identifying signatures.

A week later, the ChronoCom Baligant outpost observed an unmarked Zeus-class warship heading toward the supposedly unpopulated Cassini Regio, the dark side of Iapetus, Saturn's third-largest moon. Now, giant warships weren't common. At least not anymore. A few more minutes of sleuthing showed that Valta had only four Zeus-class warships. Three of them were positioned along the Radicati militarized zone, and all three were marked.

"What's an energy-guzzling warship doing where there's no warring to be had?" Smitt asked, tapping his fingers along the console. He checked the time. "Oh crap." He would have to continue this later. He had stayed too long. Smitt glanced back at the door and his hands began to sweat and shake. The real Burke should be heading down here soon. The longer Smitt stayed, the higher the odds of getting caught.

This had always been his problem, why he had failed to test into the chronman tier: he couldn't handle stress. If someone walked in right now and just did a surface-level trace on what he was doing, it would be over. Add in his connection to James, and the auditors would have him on a rack in seconds. Right now, it was all he could do to keep from hyperventilating and passing out on the data-housing floor.

Smitt didn't think he was doing anything that wrong. It wasn't like he was helping James change the chronostream. Far from it. All he was doing was helping some poor savage tribe acquire some much-needed supplies. He felt justified, even.

Oh, who was he trying to fool? Mining this data for James was outright treason any way he looked at it, and if Smitt was caught, there was nothing anyone could do to prevent him from being sent to Nereid or some other awful penal colony.

In the end, though, the consequences didn't matter. Smitt's loyalty to his friend was stronger than it was to ChronoCom. James was the only person in his life who had ever given a damn about him. As far as he was concerned, loyalty was the only real thing Smitt had left in this world.

Luckily, the doors behind him never opened. Smitt finished covering his tracks and unplugged himself from the console, making sure to get his rampaging jitters under control as he walked casually out the door. In a few seconds, he would be out of the tech wing and in the clear. With his heart slamming in his chest, Smitt lurched out of data housing at a consciously slowed pace, waving at the two monitors as he passed them. He gave them a nod and proceeded down the hallway.

"Burke," the monitor on the left called after him. "Lin over here wants to know if you play Lok Gull. Couple of us night shifts are trying to get some games in. Not quite filling out the roster with enough bodies at the moment. Seeing how we all rise and tuck in at the same time, thinking maybe you play?"

Smitt paused at the outer door right before the stairs and looked back at them. After tailing Burke all this time, he knew that the guy liked Lok Gull, and probably the one thing this ruck could use was some friends instead of his bottle. A social life would do wonders for him. However, that could risk blowing Smitt's cover.

"Oh hell," he muttered under his breath. He'd taken enough advantage of this guy. Smitt nodded to the monitors. "Go ahead and sign me up. I might forget so remind me. Can we schedule it for after the fifth shift?"

"Will do, and welcome to the Earth, Burke," the one named Lin said.

Smitt hid his smile and exited the wing. He'd just have to be a little careful in the future when impersonating the guy. The next task on his plate was going to be a lot more difficult and tricky. James had been asking if there was a way he could obtain some miasma pills. Miasma regimens fell directly under the auditors' purview, and busting into the miasma lab was about as easy as getting citizenship on Europa.

However, Smitt had already been mulling over the beginnings of a plan. He made a mental list of the things he had to gather and the steps it'd take to break into the high-security medical ward. He hated to admit it, but the thrill was starting to grow on him.

"Maybe I could have been a chronman after all." He grinned, whistling as he bounded up the stairs.

THIRTY-NINE

CLOSER

Elise turned down the protection of her atmos and inhaled the thinner air on Mt. Greylock in the American Appalachia half a day by ground transport west of Boston. The entire area had another name now, probably having been exchanged by dozens of governments in the four hundred years since her time. It had taken Rima a fair amount of bartering with some of the neighboring tribes to obtain a map of the region from her era that Elise could read. It was much easier for her to work off of that than to relearn the names of this time period.

The air up here at a thousand meters above sea level was much cleaner than at the base of the mountain. Her hand brushed the trunk of a nearby tree and she rubbed her fingers together. The texture of the Earth Plague was different as well. It was less oily and much smoother. She brought her fingers to her nose. The smell of decay was weaker as well, more earthy.

She wiped her hands and moved a little higher up the path, taking out an instrument James had retrieved from a hundred years in her future known as a geotriangular. Fascinating tech, this thing was. She placed it on the ground and turned it on. A few seconds later, a three-dimensional diagram of the mountain flashed in her brain, almost knocking her off her feet.

Elise turned off the band and blinked away some of the stars in her eyes. She was still not used to the AI band. In the two months since her arrival here, she had one by one added more of these metal bands to the collection around her arms. That computer-in-her-head band, as she liked to call it, was her latest piece of jewelry, and it was by far the most difficult one to get used to.

She sat down and rubbed her sore feet. Locating a good pair of size seven shoes was Rima's next job. Most of the Elfreth had calluses like rhinos. It was times like right now she especially missed some of the luxuries of the twenty-first century. Normally, she'd just be coasting up one of these mountains in Charlotte, her feet completely rested and the air-conditioning turned on full blast.

The memory of her mechanoid made Elise a little melancholy; she missed her robot. Earning her advanced certification on Charlotte while she was still a teenager was one of Elise's proudest moments. While other children her age learned to drive or hover vehicles, she spent countless hours walking the depths of the ocean floor. Part of her was looking forward to finding and piloting an advanced future version of her beloved Charlotte, but it seemed the present had done away with mechanoids altogether. Pity. A lot of things these days were pretty damn pitiful.

Elise took a few more snapshots of the ground beneath her as she wandered up the mountain. Interestingly, the vegetation grew thicker the higher she climbed. The signs of the Earth Plague receded here as well. Elise made a few notes, put a few more samples in tubes, and slipped them into her netherstore container. She continued to climb.

She was making real progress in her research. Some of her testing had produced promising results, though she was still a long way from a full cure. The Earth Plague was a surprisingly simple virus that could have been headed off before it mutated and spread. She was confident that, if the Nutris Platform hadn't blown up and sunk into the sea, they could have nipped it in the bud and created a cure, probably mass-producing it for the rest of the planet within a year or two.

The only problem was replication. Even with a working cure, it had to be cheap to produce, since present Earth wasn't exactly full of resources. Her lab didn't have the equipment to replicate and send the cure out all over the world. With the level of degradation already present on the planet, a cure could take months to propagate across the globe. By that time, the plague would have mutated a dozen times over. No, whatever cure they developed, Elise needed a delivery system that cured the entire planet all at once, or at least in a relatively short span of time. Hopefully, James could retrieve something from the past or Grace could use that big brain of hers for an invention that would address this issue.

Yes, with Grace's help, they were making some progress, though more of their time was spent keeping the lights on in the lab than she liked. Grace had spent the first week designing and rigging a working elevator, much to the excitement of every person who had to work in the Farming Towers. Now, the Mother of Time was almost as popular as Elise. In hindsight, it was time well spent.

There wasn't much of a path up here; whatever traces of civilization that had once remained in this area were long gone. Still, she trudged through the increasingly thick underbrush, eager to see what was near the top. So far, she'd found a direct correlation between the air quality, carbon readings, and height of the vegetation. It meant that the plague's ability to prosper depended on . . .

Something in the trees to her left rustled. Elise froze midstep and waited, slowly moving her arm to shoulder level and pointing at the leaves shaking back and forth. The rustling moved to her left, as if cutting off her retreat. She heard the brush to her right shake as well. Elise spun to her right, her arms swiveling back and forth from the two sources of noise.

"Beam level max. No, level two," she thought to her wrist beam. That wouldn't kill a living creature, but would still be strong enough to knock out a charging elephant.

The rustling sounds in the brush continued, and maybe it was her overactive imagination, but they now seemed to be all over the place. She was surrounded! Her arms began to quiver from the adrenaline pumping through her body. She felt her heart rate rocket up until it seemed like each beat shook her entire body.

"Keep it together, girl," she muttered. "Remember your training."

Something squealed behind her, a high-pitched yipping sound that was distinctly inhuman. That made Elise feel better, if only a smidgen.

"Focus, by Gaia, stupid girl," she said.

The rustling sounds were getting closer. Or maybe it was because they were closing in on her. Whatever the thing was, it could come at her from any direction at any moment. Elise considered making a break for it, but thought better of it. After all, the odds of her outrunning this thing were low, and all that would probably happen from fleeing would be exposing her back and leaving herself completely defenseless. No, she was going to make a stand and give herself a chance.

The seconds slowed and ticked by as she waited to see the predator stalking her. Her arms were tiring, and she was breathing so hard she wasn't sure her aim would be straight even if the thing was standing in front of her. Then it appeared.

A lizard-like creature stepped out of the jungle and stuck its tongue out at her. It made the same squealing sound as its forked tongue flicked the air in front of it. It rambled to the right as if drunk and then flicked the air again. Elise's arm followed its path as it went back and forth, ready to shoot if it took another step closer.

As a biologist, she was fascinated by the creature. Its body was like a snake's, allowing it to stand tall and reach high, the way a giraffe would. Its torso and legs were almost human, and she had missed it at first, but there were two nearly vestigial arms. Their eyes locked and for a second, she saw intelligence in those eyes, recognition of sorts.

To her right, another one of these creatures came out, this one larger, with an even longer body. Elise jumped back and aimed at this new threat, only to see it give her a look almost of disdain as it walked by her. The second creature walked next to the first and their tongues flicked at each other. Then the two walked away from her. The first creature looked back at her one last time before the pair disappeared back into the jungle.

Elise found herself holding her breath a few seconds longer, her fingers tingling from the strain of the adrenaline and from holding her aim for so long. She still detested violence, but this was the new reality of her world now. Her heart wouldn't stop slamming into her rib cage. She sunk to the ground and took a deep breath, trying to calm herself down.

Elise had seen more than her share of creatures since she arrived in this time period, most nonexistent in the past. The ruins of Boston were a hive of different species, and strangely, many of them were like these two creatures, with several human-like features. She didn't know how that came to be, either from biological manipulation or natural progression, but seeing strange creatures like this unnerved her less and less.

"Hey Elder Elise, checking in. Your readings are a little high. Everything blue?" Rima's voice popped into her head. The girl was speaking to her through an old handheld patched into her comm band.

Elise grunted. If what her body was doing was considered only a little high, then they need to recalibrate whatever was monitoring her. "I'm fine," she said. "And stop calling me Elder. I'm not that old."

"If you say so, Elder Elise."

The Elfreth all started calling her that when they decided she was the savior of the planet. As far as she knew, only Qawol and Franwil were called Oldest, while a small group of the more senior citizens among the Elfreth were known as the Old Ones. She guessed being called Elder was better than being Oldest or Old One, which as far as she knew referred to people who were actually just old.

"How is your gathering, Elder Elise?"

"It's beautiful here, Rima. You should come join me."

"No can, Elder Elise. Tribe needs the voom. Can't tie it up for so long. You still okay for two days sun top?"

That much was true. The Elfreth had only three transports, including James's, and he didn't let anyone else fly his collie. That left two rickety four-wheelers to be shared among hundreds of people, which meant these cars were always in need. There was no way Elise could keep this one to herself for three full days, so Rima had to drop her off and drive back right away.

"Sun top is fine. You should try to come early and check this place out. It's beautiful. You know, this planet wasn't always like this. It used to be . . ."

Her voice trailed off when she saw a small black speck in the distance approaching her. She might not have noticed it if it wasn't flying very low over the jungle canopy, the force of its propulsion blowing the trees to the sides. Elise had not seen any signs of civilization since she left Boston. Could this be a coincidence? She doubted it.

"Rima, I have a visual on somebody approaching. Going to hide. Keep this channel open."

"I am too far away already, Elder Elise. Turning around."

"Don't do that," Elise said, lowering her voice to a whisper as she crept into the thickets, her eyes never leaving the growing speck. The thing was definitely heading straight toward her. She wasn't so optimistic as to think that this was just a coincidence. If it was hostile, there was little Rima could do to help. She would just be putting herself in danger.

"Listen carefully, Rima, head straight back to the tribe. If something happens, tell Grace. She can find James."

"But Elder Elise——"

"Do it now! I'm turning the comm off in case they can track it." The channel went dead as Elise waited. James was out on some job, whether jumping back in time to gather supplies or off gallivanting across the globe to trade with other pockets of civilization. He'd been away from the tribe more often than not, constantly running errands for her and Grace. Elise worried that he was putting too much on his shoulders. He'd been looking haggard lately. She'd have to talk to Grace about that. Could all that time traveling be bad for his health? Well, he never complained or said anything about it. Typical James.

Her stomach twisted when the speck turned sharply up the mountain and climbed to her level. Any doubt of whoever it was not knowing her location was erased. Sweat poured down her face even though her atmos was keeping her cool. The ship looked like James's ship, one of those collies that the ChronoCom people used. If it was someone from the agency, she was as good as dead. James had told her how badly ChronoCom wanted to capture her. Now, of all the fool things she could have done, she had exposed herself without any means of escape.

The collie leveled off and the ramp swung open. James flew out, landing dramatically in front of her in a kneeling position, kicking up a circle of dust in all directions.

"What in the black abyss are you doing here by yourself?!" He thundered, looking directly at her hiding place.

Elise felt the urge to laugh and cry at the same time, but she wasn't going to give him the pleasure of seeing that. With exaggerated casualness, she sauntered out of the bushes. "Oh, hello. I thought you had already left. I would have rescheduled my little excursion." She managed to look abashed.

"I delayed it. Change in our jump plans. I won't be leaving until tomorrow. No one would tell me where you went. I dug it out of Sammuia."

That darn boy couldn't keep a secret. Well, she couldn't blame him. He was scared enough of James as it was. "You didn't bully the boy too much, did you?" she asked. "It's not earning you any points with the Elfreth, you know."

James was working himself up over nothing. "I told you not to leave the tribe when I'm away. I can't protect you if something happens!"

Again, that assuredness in his voice as if he knew what was best for her. Nothing got her angry like someone who felt like he had the right to patronize her. It hadn't worked for her parents, and it wasn't going to work for James. He was looking out for her; she appreciated that, but he wasn't anyone who had authority over her.

"Now you look here . . ." she began in what she considered a very reasonable tone.

"Don't argue with me," he snapped. "Where we're at right now is the complete opposite of not leaving Boston."

The discussion went rapidly downhill. James was someone who was obviously used to getting things his way, and at his age—she wasn't actually sure what his exact age was—it was a hard habit to break. Elise admitted he intimidated her when he was angry, but she wasn't going to just stand there and take his abuse.

"I'm a big girl, by Gaia, and I have a job to do." That argument didn't get her anywhere. It never did.

"From now on, I'm going to order the watch guards not to allow you to leave the city when I'm not there."

Elise's eyes went wide. She looked up at him, locked eyes with his, and took a step forward. "What did you just say?" Her sudden intensity made him take a step back.

"I said, from now on—"

"Stop talking right now." She shook her finger at him. "I'm not your kid. I'm not your student, and I'm definitely not Sasha. You don't own me. You don't get to order me around."

"If you're not going to listen to reason . . ."

"Get over yourself, James. Don't tell me what to do and expect me to just agree. I need to go on these trips to collect samples. I'm trying to cure this damn planet from a thousand years of neglect and abuse!" she said.

"It's a simple request," he snarled. "When I'm on a jump, don't leave Boston. Why can't you listen?"

"Because it took me a month to even reserve that car for this trip. I'm not going to cancel it on your say-so!"

"You're not going to cure anything if you're dead. It's my job to protect you."

"No, it's not your job. Your job is to look after everyone."

"I don't care about anyone else!"

Elise stopped in her tracks. There was a long, awkward pause. "You should," she finally said. "They're your family too."

James turned away. "No, they aren't. I have no family. Not for a long time. I could care less what happens to them. I just need to know you're all right." He sat down on the ground and looked out over the mountain to the vast jungle below. "I can't lose you like I lost Sasha. Nothing else matters."

"Oh, James." She softened, and sat down beside him. She wrapped her arms around his shoulder. "I'll never replace your sister; no one can. You have to stop blaming yourself and focus on the present. I need you. The Elfreth need you. And to be honest, you need them as well."

He grunted. "What could I possibly need them for? They're weak and helpless. I'm their protector. I'm killing myself feeding and supplying them. What could they possibly offer me?"

She squeezed his arm close to her body. "What could I possibly offer you?"

He looked at her. "That's different."

Elise shook her head. "No, James, it's not. Open your eyes and let people in. Like you let me in."

She tried to catch his eye, but he was still looking away.

"Listen, mister," she said. "You work way too hard pretending to be a stone golem, but you're a really good guy."

The two sat in silence for a few minutes, looking on as the wind swayed the jungle canopy, a sea of rich life that was becoming a scarcity in this world. Even here, though, she could see the hints of brown on the edges, an encroaching disease that was threatening to invade this still relatively lush land.

James must have been reading her mind. "It's pretty up here, isn't it?" he said.

"It is. It used to be like this all over the world. And stop trying to change the subject."

"And you're going to bring it back?"

Elise stood up. "I'm trying, but we're not going to get anywhere sitting around." She walked a little up the path. "You coming?"

James looked like he was about to protest, and then shrugged. "I guess the city can survive a few more hours without us."

"Sorry, pal," she said, "I'm staying overnight."

"Black abyss you are. Didn't we . . ."

"You can stay with me if you like." She grinned. "You know, so you can watch over me." James hesitated. "Come on, I could use a lackey, and since no one else is here to volunteer, you're it." She pointed at a small clearing halfway down the path. "You can start by setting up camp and cooking dinner while I finish collecting samples. I'm starving."

Elise continued working but stayed within earshot for the next two hours, finishing up her sample collection on top of Mt. Greylock. She was mindful to stay within sight of James. The last thing she wanted was him to go off his rocks again. She'd have to do something about that one of these days; she just wasn't sure what exactly. He meant well but she could tell he lacked soft skills when dealing with people. At least he didn't berate her in front of the Elfreth; otherwise they would have a serious problem.

By the time she returned to where she had left him, James had done more than a passable job with the camp. A small animal—Elise had long learned not to ask what anymore—was roasting in a tin plate above a neat little fire that roared in the center of a circle of stones. James was bent over a pot stirring a spoon in a greenish broth, and a small tent was pitched just off to the side, near the edge of the foliage. The whole thing looked almost quaint.

"Well, look at you." She smirked as she dumped her pack on the ground and approached the fire. "All you need is an apron and we'll be ready to play house."

As usual, her twenty-first-century quips went right over his head as he met her comedic genius with a deadpan stare. "I have food. The rations I found out of your daily pack, and I was able to capture the protein—"

"Uh-uh." She held her hands up. "I don't want to know if I'm eating a rodent. I'm just going to pretend it's all chicken." She looked behind him. "Where did you park the collie? I thought we could just camp in there tonight."

"There's not enough level ground to park it. I sent it down the mountain." He paused. "Would you like me to call it up?"

Elise studied the lone tent on the ground and then James, a wicked smile growing on her face. "I guess we can shack up." She sat next to him and powered off her atmos. She bent forward and inhaled over the pot. "Smells good."

The biting wind immediately soaked through her clothing and into her bones. She shivered and leaned into him. His body stiffened as she huddled close, and she felt his unsure hands drape around her shoulders. It was almost cute, but really, she was getting tired of having to do all the work.

"Do you think you will be ready to leave at first light?" he asked. "I don't like being exposed like this. There are still people looking for us."

"We haven't heard from your ChronoCom folks since we joined with the tribe. They could have given up already."

"They won't stop looking for us, ever." James paused. "Listen, Elise, there's something you need to know. There's more to what happened on Nutris than what I've told you."

Elise felt his hands shake and pulled away from his shoulder. He avoided her gaze and stared intently at a small rock at his feet. His usual stoic facade was cracking as she saw anguish twist his face.

"What is it, James?" she asked.

He exhaled. "I found out who was responsible for the Nutris Platform's destruction. It was a megacorporation from the present named Valta. ChronoCom was complicit in the disaster as well."

The words didn't register in her mind at first. "I don't understand. What do you mean, responsible?"

"Valta arranged to have Nutris destroyed so they could obtain the technology on the platform. ChronoCom carried out the job."

"You?" she gasped.

"No," he pleaded. "It was another chronman. I had nothing to do with them planting the explosive. I was only sent back for the retrieval."

"You told me that it was a natural disaster! Now you're saying it's your people who did it?"

"I didn't find out about the sabotage until afterward," he said.

Something about that sentence niggled at Elise. "Wait, when did you find out about this?"

He hesitated again. "I won't lie to you. I found out that night you told the Elfreth you were from the past. I was waiting for a good time to tell you."

A hundred images of her friends on Nutris ran through her head. Thinking they died in an accident was vastly different from knowing they were murdered. Murdered by people in this very time she was trying to save. By James's former colleagues, in fact.

Elise didn't know what to think. She did know she had to decide whether she could trust him. If she did, then she had to believe that he had nothing to do with Nutris's sabotage. If she didn't believe him, then this should be the last time she ever saw him again. She could send him away from the tribe then. He would do so if told. Maybe that was for the best. But she already knew her answer.

Elise clutched his hands. "You promise me you had nothing to do with it?"

"I swear it upon my sister and mother," he replied in a whisper.

"You promise me you'll find whoever is responsible and make them pay?"

"I'll give you that justice. I didn't . . ."

"Good, now hush. I don't want to talk about it anymore. Stoke the fire, will you? It's getting cold out here."

For the rest of the night, neither said much. Mostly, they both stared at the fire. Elise's mind raced as she clung to the memories of her past life, of friends and places that she would never see again. She couldn't help but compare it with the world she now lived in, and think about how much she had lost.

To be honest, she surprised herself. The first few days she was here, she didn't think she would last. After all, she had lost everything and was now trapped in what was essentially a completely foreign world. Yet, here she was, still trying to be that scientist and still trying to do good.

She looked up at James sitting just a meter away. She owed it all to him. Though he wasn't aware of it, she knew how much he had sacrificed for her. Qawol and Grace had told her not so much about his past, but what his people were. She'd had to go to them because James wouldn't volunteer any information.

Once she realized what he had given up, she was touched. Grateful as well, but more touched, because in the end, she knew where his feelings came from. Sure, he was awful at showing his emotions, but that's just the way he was.

Elise moved close to him and nestled into the crook of his arm. "It's cold."

James put his arms around her and held her close. "I'll get more wood," he said.

"I think we're okay for now," she said.

Of course James didn't get the hint and started to get up. She pulled him back down and put a finger on his lips. "Don't you dare think about getting up again," she murmured, bending his head down and covering his mouth with hers. At first, he froze at her contact, and Elise thought she had misread his feelings for her, that maybe all this time, he just considered himself her protector.

Then he softened just a little and she felt him return the kiss. He put his hands on her hips. Elise linked her fingers behind his neck and pulled herself onto him. James brushed the hair away from her eyes. She felt each of his calluses as his fingers brushed down her cheeks toward her mouth. He continued to hold her as if he were afraid he'd drop her and she'd break. It wasn't enough. Putting both her hands on his face, she kissed him with renewed intensity. If he was going to treat her as if she were some sort of frail china doll, then he had another thing coming. The pressure drove him backward and they found themselves on the ground, still cocooned in James's exo.

"About leaving at first light," she murmured, brushing his cheek with hers as she breathed in his ear and tugged at his shirt. "You might want to reconsider that."

FORTY

TRAITOR

A re you sure," said Levin, a slow burn roiling in the pit of his stomach.

He was sitting in the meeting room next to Young's office. To his left sat the director, Kuo, Hameel from the Handlers Operation, and Buchanan, the medical quartermaster. Levin tapped the metal surface of the table with his fingers in succession as the vid hovering over the center of the table played on a repeated loop. The evidence was there for everyone to see.

There was Handler Smitt hacking into the security net for the east wing, first inserting a doppelganger hack into the system, and then using a paint band to impersonate one of the licensed miasma techs. He hadn't done a bad job; most standard security audits would have missed it if Levin, having anticipated James's need for miasma pills, had not implemented additional security protocols in the medical ward.

"I've tested the entire batch of the miasma pills, Auditor," Buchanan said. "The handler switched several cycles' worth with placebos. Chronmen affected by those batches would only receive two-thirds of their regimen."

"How many pills stolen total?"

"Seven cycles, Auditor."

Eighty-four damn pills. Over a year's worth. What did that mean? Did James plan to continue his romps in time? For what purpose? If he was smart, he would have used his remaining small supply to wean off the lag sickness and fade into obscurity. Instead, he risked increased exposure by leaving jump trails for Levin to track. According to the most recent surveillance, his activity was actually picking up. What was he up to?

Kuo might not think it timely, but Levin and his team were closing in on James's locations. Between triangulating his movements in the present with all his jump points to the past, the team had ruled out all of Asia and Africa, and had pretty much confirmed Europe. Just a few hits more and a little luck, and the fugitive would soon find Levin either at his doorsteps or waiting for him at one of his return jumps.

James's actions were perplexing, though. He still seemed to be trying, somewhat, to follow the Time Laws, except of course for the most egregious ones he'd already broken. All his jumps were short, and to relatively lower-tech salvages, and most of his actions still fit the spirit of the Time Laws. With the recent revelation of Smitt's theft, it was all but confirmed that James had no intention of just lying low. The man was no fool; he must be playing some sort of long game.

The immediate concern at this moment was Handler Smitt. Miasma theft was common. The pills could be addictive if not strictly monitored. Usually, theft was carried out by addicted chronmen or those who sold to them. It usually resulted in nothing more than a slap on the wrist and a requirement that chronman detox in therapy. The problem with Smitt here seemed suspiciously more like treason, which, on the other hand, carried only one sentence. No one in this room believed he was stealing miasma pills for any other reason than to give them to his fugitive friend.

"Our course of action is clear," Levin said, grimacing. "Auditor Geneese, call a squad to escort Handler Smitt to the brig."

"A moment, Levin," said Kuo, holding up a hand. "This situation has value. If this traitor is communicating with the fugitive, arresting him is a waste of this information." She looked over at Levin. "Place a neural bug in his mind."

"Definitely not," Levin said, standing up.

Young scratched his beard and leaned back. "Spying into anyone's mind is frowned upon. It's not our way and can lead to distrust among the ranks."

"It would be stupid not to seize this advantage," Kuo retorted. "We use this on all our high-value employees."

Levin saw Young's brows rise at her choice of words; the director was not used to being spoken to in such a manner.

"I don't disagree," Young said in a slow, measured tone. "But there is collateral damage to the rank and file's morale as it is. If word leaks of—"

"Let me make this clear, Director Young," Kuo said. "Valta feels that this course of action best suits both the corporation's and ChronoCom's interests."

The room stayed very still for several seconds before Young finally nodded. "Very well. Hameel, put a sniff bug on Handler Smitt's person and blanket his sleeping quarters. Make sure he takes it with his morning nutrient regimen."

"This is outrageous, Director," said Levin. This was mind rape. Levin had been a specialist in the Publicae Age during his time as a chronman. He had seen firsthand where this road led.

Right then and there, Levin realized that Young was no longer in control. Valta, Kuo specifically, was in charge. ChronoCom was now just the time-traveling arm of the megacorporation. Levin kept his face neutral, but his heart seized with indignation. Young must have noticed something, because when their eyes met, the director gave him a slight shake of the head.

"What about his past network activity?" Kuo continued.

"The neural bug will be able to track all his communications through his AI and comm bands," Hameel said. "I've grabbed a snapshot of his network activity within the past week. Note this is only limited to his data traffic. An implanted neural bug will allow us to record his active thoughts." He paused. "Filtering out extraneous data. Here we go. Handler Smitt made dozens of queries, including five regarding the Uranus substation disaster of 2411, eleven into the Moon virus of 2077, six on the moon Puck, and forty-three into the Nutris Platform. Yesterday, he had seven queries searching for the location of some salvaged items from a previous job—code name Sunken City—and over nine on Cassini Regio. Today, he had . . . ," he paused, "three queries to the blue sections of the city for prostitutes."

Kuo bolted up from her seat and hovered over Hameel in an instant. "What did you say?"

Hameel was so thrown off by her sudden intensity that he nearly fell off his chair. Geneese and Shizzu had risen and powered on their exos.

Levin kept his hands firmly pressed down on the table. Kuo seemed un-deterred as she slammed her hand down on the table in front of Hameel.

"I'm sorry, Securitate," he stammered. "What are you asking about?"

"What did you say again about Cassini Regio?" she pressed, leaning in close. "Tell me!"

Hameel looked as if he were about to soil himself. "The handler made queries into energy shipments to the colony on Iapetus a few days ago. Then he began to look into the dark side of the moon. It wouldn't have meant much except I don't think the Cassini Regio side has a colony."

"He's mining Valta classified affairs," Kuo said, sprinting toward the door. "I'm going to gouge his eyes out until he tells me what he knows about it."

Before she could leave the room, Levin was there, blocking her path. "You won't touch the handler."

The two stared each other down. Kuo was the only one who had pow-ered on her exo, though. Levin hoped that Young's presence would deter violence from the securitate. Or if it didn't, the director would realize how unstable she was and pull her off Levin's command.

To be honest, he wasn't sure if Young had the spine to defend his au-ditor. After all, it had been a long time since Young was one of them. Once, Levin would not have questioned where Young stood, but now, as an administrator, the director saw things in a different light. Would stand-ing with his own men be advantageous for Young and his view on what was best for the agency? In the end, as in other situations where Valta was involved, Young sat on the sidelines and said nothing.

"You're the one who wanted to use the handler for information," Levin said. "If you burst into Handler Ops right now, what do you think will happen with James and the girl? My guess is we'll never hear from them again. Wait until we've captured James. You'll get your answers then."

Levin half-expected a kinetic coil to tear a hole through his chest as Kuo pondered her options. Finally, she nodded. "If any sensitive infor-mation from Cassini Regio leaks, I'm holding you responsible. There will be consequences." She looked over at the rest of the room. "Excuse me while I report this. I need to increase our security diligence on that moon."

Levin watched her backside as she left the room and walked down the hall. He turned back to Young. "How much longer are we going to have to tolerate this?"

"Finish your fucking job and you won't have to tolerate this much longer, Levin." Young sighed. "Valta's commitment to Nutris is significant. They've been on the losing end of a four-way power grab over Saturn and Jupiter for the past ten years. They're desperate."

"What could they have retrieved from Nutris that could change their fortunes?" Shizzu frowned. "I was there. There was no military technology on it. It was a just a biological research facility."

Young grunted. "Isn't it obvious? How else do you weaponize cures?"

The rest of the room was quiet as those words sunk in. There had not been a significant use of biological weapons since the AI Wars, when the machines had tried to use a nano-variant of the Ebola plague. The results were terrible.

"It's not our business," Young said. "ChronoCom only polices the chronostream, not the behavior of the corps that pays our bills. As auditors, I expect all of you to work toward the agency's interests, and I'm telling you right now that Valta's interests parallel ours. Hameel, how soon can you get the neural bug functioning?"

Hameel looked uncomfortable. "It will take time to replicate. Neural bugs are rarely used, for obvious reasons. Once it's in the handler's system, it will take time for it to latch on to his synaptic nerves and transmit his thoughts. Director, I have to officially protest—"

"I expect word as soon as Smitt's morning regimen has been dosed," Young said, struggling to stand. "I want that detector removed as soon as we receive word about the fugitive's location. Not a word outside this room. Now get out of here."

FORTY-ONE

BIG BROTHER

There was a bright yellow flash followed by James hunched over puking up his lunch. He exhaled as a second surge of vomit crawled up his throat and dribbled out of his mouth. He counted down from ten and exhaled, and then added another ten-count. When his mind and stomach cleared, he stood up and took a deep breath.

Everything looked much different than it had just a few seconds ago. In the present, the city had long been abandoned, a giant metal relic half-sunk into the brown ocean. He was standing in a park, except in his time, all the soil, grass, and trees had long since washed away. In their place, several meters of dried ocean mud caked the ground, angled at a thirty-degree slant.

The dome above him now was clear with the sun just appearing in the northeast. In the present, the glass was shattered, with only a few jagged edges still remaining. The sun in the present was too weak to penetrate the heavy soot clouds that perpetually covered this entire area.

"Are you all right?" There was a note of concern in Grace's voice. "You're reacting worse to it every time you jump."

"Don't worry about me," he said through gritted teeth. "Remember, keep the chatter low. The neural bugs here can't detect you, but my brain waves might react in a way they can detect."

"I do pay attention to the briefings, James."

James was standing on the grass in a large park with a row of perfectly trimmed hedges on one side and a grouping of evenly spaced trees on the other. A marble path to his left cut through the center of a sea of green grass and made a right turn at the far end. He jumped into the hedge and nestled deep into the vegetation. Being caught on the grass was a level-two offense. He had fifteen minutes to prepare for the next few hours.

James checked the time: 5:43 A.M. Seventeen minutes until the night curfew lifted. He'd have to stay in hiding until then. Jumping in thirty minutes before the curfew lifted was optimal for a chronman in this time period. Jump any earlier and he would be moving through curfew, where the security eye patrols were highest. Coming in any later, during operating hours, carried a high risk of being seen. The city was crowded with people who would report him in an instant.

James cleared his mind and steadied his breathing, putting his body through the mental exercises he had learned at the Academy when acclimating to the specifics of this time period. There was a mental calmness that a chronman had to maintain when moving through the Publicae Age. James stayed very still in the bushes and breathed in and out in an almost meditative state. When he felt prepared, he opened his eyes and stared at everything in his field of vision, making sure each identified item filled up his entire active thought.

The blade of grass was green. Green and symmetrical. Symmetrical and trimmed. Trimmed to the edge of the walkway. The walkway was clean. Clean like the air. Purified air was life. Life was the morning. Morning was the sun. His thoughts continued on, occupying his mind so that stray thoughts that could betray him would not be detected by the neural bugs.

"It's six A.M., James," Grace said, her voice evenly measured and monotone.

James stood up and jumped onto the grass. Standing on grass was being wrong. Being wrong was undesirable. Undesirable was committing offense. Offense to society was violating the social contract. Social contract was Adonia.

James walked down the path. He saw the first neural bug perched on one of the light poles off to his right farther down the walkway. By this time, he had calmed his heart rate and cleared his mind. The AI band would pass along the proper forged identity to the system, but there was no way to mask an active brain scan, and in Adonia, there was no escaping those.

He felt a slight buzz, as if an invisible hand had just brushed his hair as he walked nonchalantly under the neural bug, its flickering blue light following him like a watchful eye. James kept his thoughts empty and his emotions suppressed as he turned the corner. In the distance, roughly forty meters away, was the next neural bug.

The path led to a statue up on a small grassy hill overlooking the entire park. To any of the security eyes, he was a devout Adonian making his morning pilgrimage, which, while not necessary, was a common and approved-of behavior.

Behavioral approval is important. Importance is proper. Proper is good citizenship. Good citizenship is devotion. Devotion is pilgrimage.

The statue was of two robed men, mirror images in every way, studying each other for discrepancies. The plaque below them read:

HAPPINESS IS UNIFORMITY OF MIND
AND ACTION
2253

"Whoever said the Technology Isolationists were the precursor of these carbon-copy idiots were morons," Grace grumbled. "Twisted and stupid."

"Both of your factions believed in isolationist superiority."

"Yes, but that's the extent of it. We understood that intelligence and creative differences went hand in hand."

"Hush, please, High Scion, or you'll give me away."

"Don't hush me, boy."

The streets began to fill as the morning crowds, filtering through the narrow corridors of the city, came out single file along the moving walkways, standing uniform and straight as if duplicately dressed doll figures moving down a conveyor belt. The only way to tell them apart was by their height and faces. All else that could be controlled—dress, hair, accessories, clothing—was exactly the same. It occurred to James that it was fortunate the Adonians never perfected cloning, or he imagined he'd be looking at hundreds of the exact same people moving down an assembly line. Here and there, one of the Adonians would move out of line and proceed by foot along his or her way, while others still would join in and take his or her place. It was very orderly. The moving walkway never stopped.

James, at a steady pace, walked out of the park and joined in and stood still while it carried him toward the center of the city. He noticed the neural bugs perched on their poles every fifty or so meters, scanning away with their blinking blue lights, zapping at each person, reading minds and checking mental thought processes. One passed over him and he felt the static buzz as it brushed his brain.

This time period was by far the most difficult for any chronman to operate in. No one less than a Tier-1 was allowed, and even then, most Tier-1s were required to undergo rigorous mental testing and an audit before every jump until they could work this era. It was a salvage-rich zone, but one ChronoCom always had trouble fulfilling jobs in. With a dearth of Tier-1s, the agency would eventually have to tap into this period with less-qualified chronmen. Then they'd start seeing the body count climb.

So far, so good. By now, James was an old pro in the Big Brother time period. This was his sixth jump here, making him one of the more experienced Tier-1 in ChronoCom. There were only four to five other chronmen still alive who had had more. Still, though, he had to be careful: one missed thought could give him away. And unlike with most other jumps, there were very few places he could escape to if detected. If a security alarm ever tripped, the entire city would go on neural lockdown. There would be no place he could hide that the bugs couldn't detect him. He kept his breathing regular and his thoughts a steady stream of nonsensical connections.

Morning stream steady. Steady is stability. Stability is work. Work is contribution. Contribution is whole. Whole is perfection. Perfection is . . .

James stayed on the moving walkway for ten minutes, his neighbors in front and behind changing often as they joined and exited this everlong conga line. Though he was completely aware of his surroundings, he kept his head facing straight, just as all his neighbors did. In this city, standing out was considered undesirable and tended to attract the wrong sort of attention.

Finally, he reached his destination near the center of the city, where the Adonian Dome Defense was based. Being a floating city had its advantages; Adonia had the ability to move all over the oceans. This was an unfortunate necessity for the Adonians, since none of the nations of the world tolerated this city's presence in their maritime waters for fear of Adonia spreading its influence. And, without the resources for a strong military, Adonia resorted to developing exceptionally advanced stealth technology in order to survive. At the time of this jump, there were forty-six of these Adonian cities on Earth and 319 generational ships in space.

In terms of the ripples in the time line, James knew he was on shaky ground. Adonia was currently parked in the middle of the Arabian Sea, cloaked and secretly siphoning oil reserves from the nearby Saudi Emirates. In six days, an underground earthquake near Sri Lanka would birth a tsunami, causing a small change to the water levels filtering in through the city. That in turn would cause their stealth hood to temporarily overheat, forcing the Adonians to reset the shield. All in all, the disruption would be six minutes long.

The neighboring four emirates and three countries in the area would launch forty-two rocket strikes in those six minutes, crippling Adonia. Over the course of three more hours, the bombardments would continue to hammer the floating city until every living soul was dead. Today, James was going to steal that advanced stealth technology and hasten the city's death by a few days.

James left the walkway and joined a small line of people heading into the Dome Defense building. That was one of his annoyances with the Big Brother cities; there were lines all over the place. But with so many people packed into such a small space, it was the most efficient way to keep the city running. It took him another fifteen minutes, one blood test, and two neural bugs to traverse the final fifty meters before he made it into the building.

James continued moving deeper underground through the building's thinning lines, each one getting shorter and shorter, like capillaries diverging from main blood vessels. Eventually, he would arrive close enough to the stealth hood's location. He knew, however, that the fighting would start before he even got close.

His fake security clearance wasn't strong enough to make it all the way to the highest clearance. In four levels, his free ride would run out and he'd have to get through by other means. Right now, he just wanted to get close enough and do the least amount of damage, kill as few people as possible, and cause the smallest time ripple before he made off with the stealth hood.

I don't remember you being so careful around me. The young Nazi had appeared. *You seemed content to crush my skull.*

Oh hush, Grace shushed the boy. *He's busy at the moment.*

Of course you'd tell me to hush, the Nazi soldier snapped at her. *He came back and rescued you. You get to be alive again.*

Maybe if you had a useful ability . . .

James blinked. These two were bickering right in front of him. In the past, James could always tell they were just figments of his imagination. Now, a part of him wasn't so sure anymore, as if his mind couldn't separate what he was seeing from what he believed. This wasn't even the real Grace, just an apparition. She was back in the present. Why was she still haunting him? How in the abyss was this possible? The two continued to fight, their voices getting louder. He tried to ignore them, but couldn't as they continued to distract him.

"James?" Grace's voice popped into his head. "Are you all right? You're showing some strange signatures."

He stopped dead in his tracks and closed his eyes, trying to will all the voices in his head to be quiet. Unfortunately, he was in one of the deep capillaries' hallways where the moving walkways were no longer being used. Stopping in the middle of the hallway immediately caused a small traffic jam. A small woman squawked in surprise as she bumped up to him, then a man made a similar sound when he bumped up to her.

"Are you all right, citizen?" she asked.

James paid her no attention as he fixated on Grace and the Nazi soldier, who continued to argue in front of him. Then there was also the Grace talking in his head. How many Graces were there? And where was Sasha? He always looked forward to seeing his sister. Maybe if he believed hard enough, she would actually become real.

"Citizen?" The woman frowned, peering at his face from the right. He vaguely recalled a man staring at him from his left.

"We have an erred man," the man said, looking up at one of the neural bugs. "Correct and remove."

Two light sources blinked blue over James's head, bathing him, Grace, and the Nazi soldier in an eerie glow. The two became translucent as they continued arguing, completely ignoring their surroundings. He felt the now-familiar buzz of something brushing against his scalp as the lights shone on him from either side. Then the light on the top right neural bug turned red, soon followed by the one on the left. The man on James's left gasped and hesitated, taking a fearful step backward. The woman on his right seized his arm.

"You have been marked with impure thoughts, citizen," she said. "Move to the side and fall upon your knees."

James slowly turned to her. The woman was actually trying to arrest him. She was so small it was comical. The woman tugged at his elbow.

"You are resisting arrest," she grunted. "Comply or things will go badly." She felt like a gnat pestering him. James tried to shake her free, but she latched on to him more tightly, jerking back and forth as if she thought more tugging would wiggle him loose from where he stood. James looked up, and saw that Grace and the Nazi solider had stopped fighting. They were standing there staring back at him.

Oh, just kill her already, the Nazi said. *They're all dead anyway.*

Grace rolled her eyes. *Of course they're all dead. He's from two hundred fifty-eight years in the future!*

I meant they're all going to die in a few days anyway! the Nazi snapped.

"James, what is going on?" Grace spoke to his head.

"Citizen," one of the two red lights spoke in a clear woman's voice. "You are committing Adonia Law Violation 3A-C: impure thoughts."

"Obey the law, citizen!" the little woman screeched.

At least the man to his left wasn't saying anything. He just stood there, frozen in place, too unnerved by James's presence even to move. Suddenly, the upper red light that was pointing at James turned on the man.

"Citizen," it chirped. "For impure thoughts of community and failure to act, you are committing Adonia Law Violation 5-A, failure to uphold order."

That woke the man up. He yelped in fear, turned and fled. A metallic gray cord burst out of both red lights, one aimed at James and the other at the fleeing man. James's exo burst to life, knocking both the woman and the linked metal cable aside. The man, however, was not so lucky. The cord wrapped itself around one of the man's legs and tripped him. He began to writhe around on the ground in pain.

"Snap out of it!" Grace screamed in his head.

More red lights shone on him and several more cords shot at him. Fortunately, his exo responded to them. James took off, running through both the apparitions of Grace and the Nazi. Where was he going again? What was he trying to do? For a minute, he felt confused and disorganized.

"Make a left at the next intersection, pass through the fourth door on the right," Grace yelled in his head.

Red and blue lights were blinking all over the place as more lengths of steel cord were shot at him. James turned at the intersection and ran into six white-uniformed guards. James leaped into action, throwing himself forward until he was in the center of the group. Right when they focused on him, he expanded his exo and slammed them all into the wall.

"Are you with me, James?"

"I'm fine now," he thought back.

"Well, hurry. The lockdown is spreading and you have a hundred men converging on you as we speak. I'm starting to detect a widening ripple. Smitt says ChronoCom has detected the signature of the initial jump. If they catch the ripple, they can pinpoint you anywhere you go in the past to your present."

James cursed. Between his initial jump here and the large ripples he was making, the auditors should be able to track him no matter which direction he fled. These ripples would continue until the time line self-healed from the city's destruction. His best course of action was to grab the hood and just get out as soon as possible. He charged to the set of double doors and blew them off their hinges. He found himself in a garage armory.

"Other end of the room. Second door on the left," Grace instructed.

James continued to the end of the room and went down a long flight of stairs where two guards tried to pin him down with small-arms fire. He reached out to both with kinetic coils and threw them into the walls.

A few minutes later, after having dispatched four more squads of guards and a small horde of rucks who fanatically threw themselves into his path, James found the stealth hood. It was a humongous machine, two stories tall and half as wide, with dozens of cables attached to it. He wasn't sure if his netherstore could maintain a field this large. There was only one way to find out. James began to cut all the cables from the machine.

Suddenly, the entire room became whisper-quiet as, deep down in the recesses of Adonia, everything came to a standstill. The low, imperceptible hum of the stealth hood became noticeable in the silence. A new sound, sirens seemingly a world away, began to scream.

"Adonia has been detected," Grace thought to him. "The Emirates have launched two warheads. They are up in the air now! Pakistan is showing four rockets! The ripples you're causing are huge. You need to leave now!"

James gritted his teeth and sliced through the base of the hood, tearing it off its supports. He willed his exo to lift the massive contraption, but it was too heavy.

"Impact in forty-six seconds!" Grace barked to him. "Forty-five, forty-four . . ."

"I don't need a fucking countdown!" he growled, shooting himself into the air on top of the machine. There, he opened his netherstore wider than it was safe to do so, until it was large enough to cover the machine. Then, he jumped off and slowly lowered the netherstore over the stealth hood. It was slow going as the netherstore struggled to adjust and take in such a large item.

"Fifteen seconds, James."

James ignored her and continued to float down slowly. If he dropped it too quickly, the netherstore might fail, either destroying the contents in its storage or containing the hood improperly, making it useless upon its retrieval.

The door below him burst open and another swarm of guards entered. They opened fire, striking him several times. James checked his levels: 31 percent and dropping by the second. Well, he had ten seconds to half a dozen warheads' impact, or he would die by bullets once his levels failed. He gritted his teeth. He wasn't going to do anything about either scenario as long as he got this stealth hood. Elise and the tribe needed it.

The first cluster of warheads hit the city before the squad of soldiers' bullets cut through his exo. Luckily for him, the city, suddenly tilting a sharp twenty degrees, threw the squad off more than it did him, sliding them toward the far wall. James reached the floor and tied the netherstore container closed. He checked his levels: 5 percent.

"Jump now!" he yelled.

The second set of warheads struck the city, this time cracking the city and shaking the ground so hard the squad of soldiers ricocheted off the walls and floor like rag dolls. An avalanche of fire rolled from the hallway and spilled into the room, eating everything inside in an instant, enveloping machinery and climbing up the dangling cables that whipped about the room. Within seconds, all life in the room, with one exception, had been snuffed out. And if James didn't get out soon, it would be his life as well.

"Grace!" he yelled. "Levels at three percent. Container about to lose integrity!"

The familiar yellow flash came and he felt the pull of the jump suck him in, then everything went black. After the light faded, everything was still black.

FORTY-TWO

THE LONG SLUMBER

James found himself floating, the fiery light and the intense heat of the fire now replaced by pitch-black darkness and the feeling of crushing pressure pounding at his body and dragging him down. Then the lag sickness hit, and for a brief instant, he succumbed to the pain and passed out.

"James, are you there? James!" Grace's voice screamed into his head.

He woke to her voice, and instantly choked on a mouthful of water, his lungs spasming as he swallowed another gulp of the ocean. In a panic, he threw on his shields and spewed what little he had in his stomach out of his body. He gagged and clutched his chest, heaving spittle and fluids that dripped down his chin and neck. The pain this time was overwhelming and he hunched over, incapacitated by the feeling of his entire body being shredded from the inside out.

"You're under three percent, James. I've sent the collie toward you on the western edge of the city. Go!"

He wiped his mouth on his arm and saw a long red streak. His nose leaked blood. No, his mouth as well. Well, it didn't really matter what he bled out of, as long as he got what he came for. James checked his AI band for orientation, found west, and shot through the wall of the now-submerged room, puncturing holes through this underwater coffin as he followed the pull of the collie's signal out into open water. It was going to be close. The netherstore and exo were draining his levels too quickly.

James sucked in one last breath and then turned his other bands off, including the atmos, and waited again for the ocean pressure to squeeze into him. He had no choice. He reached the edge of the city and saw the collie floating a quarter of a kilometer away. He was fortunate that Grace had had the foresight to summon it this close; otherwise, he would not have made it to where he had left it.

He reached the collie with seconds to spare and slipped into the hold just as the exo's power faltered. Within seconds, he had latched his netherstore container to the ship's charger and pumped the water out of the ship.

He collapsed onto the floor, gasping for air as the last of the water filtered out of the interior. He struggled to flip onto his back and waited while his eyes focused on the ceiling. The pain from the jump was still there, the lag sickness as strong as it had been right when he made the jump. He struggled to his knees and threw up again.

"James," Grace buzzed in his head, her voice filled with worry. "I'm recalling the collie. We need to put you in cryosleep immediately. You're not well."

"I'll . . . I'll be fine," he managed to say. "I could really use a drink right now."

His head felt like one of the Farming Towers had fallen on it. Even thinking hurt. His body couldn't handle much more of these jumps without a miasma regimen. It took him several more minutes to get to his feet. He checked the *Collie*'s autopilot and then collapsed onto the bench.

The ship wasn't built for underwater travel so the trip would take three days, but it couldn't be helped. It didn't matter. James intended to use that time to catch up on some much-needed sleep.

"Charge your bands now," Grace instructed. "I'm turning your cryo band on."

"No," he said. "I'd rather sleep naturally."

"Not taking the chance," she said. "Don't fight me. You know I'll get my way in the end, regardless."

That much was true. In the weeks since she had joined them, James had yet to win one argument. In this case especially, he knew he was just being stubborn.

"Fine." He lay down on the bench and plugged his bands into the collie's system. "It's three damn days anyway. I'll probably end up just getting bored."

"You know, in my time, the TIs could get to Saturn in less than three days."

"In your day, you guys got your ass kicked by the equivalent of cavemen in space," he replied, "so I wouldn't puff up your chest that much."

"Being outnumbered ten to one does have its disadvantages."

"Technically, it was only six to one, and the Neptune Divinities were fighting you with a hundred-and-fifty-year technology handicap. The reason you lost was because your people spent more time thinking about doing something than actually doing something."

"Hindsight is always smug and unbecoming."

"One of the advantages of being from the future, I guess."

The collie began to coast, swaying back and forth in a lulling and comforting motion. James shut off all the nonessential systems, relying on his atmos for life support as always.

He activated the cryo band and filtered its readings to his AI band. It wouldn't be as good a sleep as a natural one, but he hadn't had much luck with those lately anyway. He was actually looking forward to a nice long rest.

Smitt had last reported that he was able to smuggle out a batch of the miasma regimen without being detected. That would have to be James's next priority after he set up this stealth hood for the Elfreth. It would be good to see Smitt again. The two of them hadn't spent more than two weeks apart since they were teenagers, and even those two weeks were only because of a salvage he had to run in ancient Mesopotamia for a shipment of gold that had to be spun into circuitry.

"You ready to turn in?" Grace said. "Keep your atmos at sixty percent, your comm band open, and make sure I can monitor your vitals and thought patterns."

"You're not going to watch over me the entire time I sleep, are you? Feels a little creepy, Grace."

"In your current state? Every single second."

James made a face. "As long as you're not poking around in my skull while I sleep. I know how inquisitive you geniuses get."

"Don't worry about that. We geniuses have better things to do than look into your brain. You're just not that smart or interesting, to be honest. Sleep well, James."

"Good night, High Scion,"

James's eyes grew heavy as the effects of the cryo band washed over him. He felt himself sinking into the metal bench as the interior of the collie grew darker and darker. Then, just as he felt blissful sleep sweep over him, he heard a loud bang that spasmed his body, every muscle tightly clenched.

"James?" Grace yelled into his head. "Your brain scans just spiked. Is everything all right?"

James tried to think to her, but his mind couldn't formulate the words. He tried to say something, but his mouth wouldn't open. It took all his effort to open his eyes, but when he did, all he saw was the night sky falling on top of him. His last thoughts before everything went dark was wondering just where all the stars went.

The first thing that touched James's senses was the sound of lapping water as it splashed onto the deck and receded, again and again. Then he felt the tingling of heat against his face, followed by a breeze that made the hairs on his arms stick up.

He thought about opening his eyes; that would be the smart thing to do. After all, he had no idea where he was, or when, for that matter. The latter was an important question in his line of work, after all. Still, these sensations shouldn't be possible. He should be in his collie, passed out and resting. Heck, shouldn't his atmos be filtering out these sensations? These were all questions that needed answering, but damn it, he was so comfortable right now.

"Are you going to spend the entire day thinking to yourself?" Elise's voice asked somewhere off to his left.

James opened one eye, then the other. He was immediately struck by the brilliant glow of the sun on this impossibly clear blue morning. He shielded his eyes with his hand and blinked away the stars exploding all around him. Then he turned to the side and saw Elise, sporting that control suit she wore the day they first met, which split apart down the front, exposing half her naked body underneath.

She poked him playfully. "About time you got up. Come on; there's a lot to do before it happens. We'd better get going."

She stood up and walked away, looking back once seductively, urging him to follow. By the time he picked himself off the ground, she was already an impossible hundred meters away, standing at the top of the stairs leading to the main section of a glistening platform, backgrounded by silver buildings rising up into the sky. She beckoned him again.

James's eyes followed the tallest spire until it seemed to touch Luna. He was on the Nutris Platform, and he must be back to 2097, or at least a time before the platform exploded. But even then, he didn't remember the platform glistening as it was right now. He looked over to the water below. Visibility was at least sixty meters. Schools of fish swam in circles below him as if trying to cause a water funnel right below where he lay.

Wasn't he supposed to be wading through an ocean of shit right now . . . ? Of course. He was in a dream. A blissful three-day dream in paradise alone with Elise. Part of him hoped the cryo band malfunctioned and he never woke up. James couldn't think of a better way to die.

Not quite alone, pet. Grace smiled, sitting up on his other side.

James scowled.

Assuming this was a dream—James wasn't sure yet—if Grace was here, that would mean there might be more ghosts here. He looked up at the top of the stairs, where Elise was still waving.

You going to keep her waiting much longer? Grace said. *"She might decide that you're not worth it. After all, you're just a pitiful wandering soul; why would she tolerate having you around? You and that false sense of control."*

James stood up and heard an "ahem" and saw Grace, hand raised, looking expectantly at him. He helped her up and, together, they walked down the path toward the stairs, with her draped over his arm.

"What do you mean, I have a false sense control?" he asked. "Of course I'm in control. I'm . . ."

Alive? The Nazi soldier appeared on his other side, chuckling. *Haven't you learned anything yet?*

He has a point, Grace said, leaning into him.

The three of them walked up the stairs to where Elise waited. She nudged in between the Nazi soldier and James and took his other arm. Together, they continued down the impossibly bright pathway toward the heart of Nutris. The platform was quiet, without any other signs of life nearby. Not even birds dotted the sky. James remembered quite a few floating on the winds while he was there. The only thing he could hear now were the waves splashing against the platform's supports.

They turned the corner and ran into a group of people huddled next to a building. James remembered some of the faces from his dreams; a building had collapsed on them. He wanted to apologize, to say sorry for not doing more, but they didn't acknowledge him..

He turned to Elise. "Can they see us? Are we invisible?"

"They're dead," she said. "They have no choices."

"I don't understand," James said.

You're replaying what's already happened, pet, Grace murmured, stroking him on the arm. *What is it you're so fond of saying? 'Their story's been told. The past is already dead'?*

"It's different here," he said.

How?

James didn't know how to answer that. Their small group continued on, passing through a pristine sector of the platform, turning down a ramp on the left and continuing along the water's edge. James wasn't sure who was driving this train, but obviously someone here was leading. Just then, he realized that they were retracing his path from the morning of the disaster.

He looked to his left, where another path led down to where the first mark was located, expecting to see the entrance tunnel that led to the underwater lab. Instead, he saw a pile of floating wreckage marring otherwise perfectly blue waters.

"What happened?" he said. "Why is it destroyed here but not anywhere else on the platform?"

Elise frowned. "The subparticle filterer must not be here. I wonder where it went."

Haven't you learned anything yet? Grace said.

The odd group continued retracing James's path. More and more of the poor souls he had encountered before appeared along the way. Most just stood around chatting with each other, completely ignoring James's group. He had an urge to wave his hand in front of their faces or bump them, just to see how they'd react.

They passed by the building where the bacterial sequencer had been stored. Again, like the first mark, the building was leveled, though all the other buildings around it looked shiny and new. Along the way, he ran into several members of the tribe. Qawol, his arms around Franwil's waist, waved and beckoned him to join them. Always shy Sammuia, hiding behind Rima, peeked at him over her shoulder.

"Why are you all here?" James asked. "You don't belong here. None of you do."

They laughed.

"You brought us here, Elder Chronman," Sammuia said.

"We belong here more than you," Qawol said.

Now a full entourage, the group continued until they reached the Head Repository, which also wasn't there. He thought they would stop there, since the next place he had gone in 2097 was straight down into the water. Instead, the group turned up a side path he had never gone down before and continued walking to Sector Four, a lively, talkative group of ghosts passing by other groups of ghosts, yet seemingly unaware of the others.

Finally, they reached the heart of the platform, where a massive turbine spun, making rising and falling humming noises. James walked over to the railing and looked down over the side to see hundreds of blades churning in the water.

"Is this what destroyed the platform?" he asked.

Grace chuckled her high-pitched chuckle. *Of course not, pet. Don't be absurd.*

That's what destroyed the platform, the Nazi soldier said, pointing at a gold cylinder sitting on the ground. The cylinder was plain, except for a large red V on its side. And in case it wasn't obvious enough, the name Valta Corporation was displayed in equally bright red letters below it.

James squinted at it. "Is that really what the explosive looked like?"

Elise rolled her eyes. "Of course not, silly. This is your dream, and since you have no idea what it looked like, you imagined it."

Grace chuckled. *Of course, being such a kill mute, even your psyche had to spell everything out for you.*

A vid appeared over the cylinder and began to count down from sixty.

"Oh dear," Franwil said.

"Do something," Rima urged.

"I . . . what do you expect me to do? I don't even have my bands." James looked down at his hands. Where his arms had been bare seconds ago, two exo bands now wrapped around his wrists.

I guess we're dead. The Nazi soldier sighed. Always dying over and over again.

You can only die once, Grace said. *The rest is just an illusion.*

"I haven't died," Elise said. "James, do something! Save us."

He has no choice, Grace said.

Danger.

But he did have a choice. The timer was down to fifty seconds. James ran to the bomb and lifted it up. It was heavier than it looked. He peered around wildly, trying to think of a way to disable it. How could he prevent this accident from happening again? Should he even try? Was he disrupting the chronostream, or was he actually righting it this time?

He looked over at Elise and Grace, the two dead women he had saved. Standing behind them were Qawol, Franwil, the Elfreth, and all those dozens of people now following Elise's fool quest. They were in danger. Maybe Elise and Grace were better off dead in the past. Maybe the tribe might live longer, more fruitful lives without his interference. No matter what, it seemed he always interfered with others; he destroyed their lives. He had to do something, but everything he did caused more deaths, one way or another.

Danger.

The timer was down to forty. James wrapped his arms around the cylinder and hugged it to his chest. He looked up at the clear blue sky above his head and launched himself straight toward it. He rocketed up until seconds later; the platform was only a tiny circle in a vast sea of blue. The wind whipped and slapped his face, obscuring his vision. He found himself breathing hard. Still, he hung on to the cylinder. The timer was at five seconds now.

James wished he had his atmos right now. He was reaching the portion of the atmosphere where the air was getting thin. He felt his consciousness ebb away and wondered if he was high enough for the explosion to clear the base. He had to be. Well, passing out was a good way to die, wasn't it? At least he'd feel no pain. The danger to Elise and his newfound friends had passed.

Danger.

James heard a long beep and then everything became still. His vision darkened, and then, right before he passed out, the cylinder exploded, tearing through him in a flash of blazing heat that burned through his skin and melted his bones. Every nerve in his body screamed from the terrible pain, and for one brief moment, he saw Elise, Grace, Rima, and little Sammuia. One last thought came to him: Where was Sasha? Why wasn't she here? Well, it probably was for the best. At least she was out of . . .

". . . danger. Wake up, damn it, James!"

James bolted off the bench and expanded his exo, pushing his shield out until it filled the insides of the collie, threatening to buckle the interior of the ship. His breathing was so uneven and his vision so blurred that his AI band was detecting both a heart attack and a stroke.

"James, are you there! Your vitals are exploding."

It'd just take a little push, just another notch more, and then the exo's shielding would burst out of the collie, free at last. Freedom from these nightmares, from the pain. Knees curled up to his chest, he sat on the bench and huddled into a ball. Just a little push more and the collie would break. Already, the ship was groaning under the pressure.

"Damn it!"

In his head, there was a rustling of someone shouting incoherently, as if far away at the other end of a tunnel. The sound of clapping, of footsteps, of people speaking too fast and too far away for him to understand. It was all going on in his head, and he couldn't filter it out.

James grasped his head in his hands and screamed until his throat was hoarse. He waited, feeling his exo bulge and pulsate against its constraints. He nudged a little harder, and was rewarded with the shriek of metal. The console near the front of the ship began to blink red. Red was never a good color. The warnings were always of bad things, things that were going wrong. James was that blinking light. He appeared in time only when something was going wrong. Just one more push and it'd all be over.

"James, focus on my voice!" Grace cut through the cacophony.

James grasped at her voice as she repeated his name over and over again. He squeezed his eyes shut and moaned his own name along with her until his heart rate calmed and the tension all over his body washed out and away.

James fell to his knees, then pulled himself up to the console. He looked at the readings and blinked. This couldn't be right. According to the navigation, he had just passed the Southern American continent and was still a day out from Boston. Why was he up?

"What happened?" he finally choked the words out.

"I had to pull you out of your cryo sleep abruptly and your body did not react well to it. Listen to me, James . . ." Grace sounded urgent.

The dream rushed back to him, and he remembered every detail as if he had just relived it a hundred times over. "I think I get it," he said. "I know what I have to do now."

"For space's sake, James Griffin-Mars, listen to me!" Grace screamed those words in his head so loud James reacted to it as if he'd been slapped.

"What is it?"

"You have to get back to Boston now. Smitt sent warning. They're on their way."

"Who——" He didn't need to finish that thought; there was only one "they" whom it could be. He leaped to the controls and aimed the collie straight up out of the ocean. A day by ocean was less than an hour by air. He had to get to Elise before it was too late.

FORTY-THREE

THE RIGHTEOUS WAY

Levin stood at the launching pad of Earth Central and watched as the sixteen collies hovered in formation overhead. The Hops had been abuzz all morning about this impending attack. If Smitt was going to fall for the ruse, this is when it would happen.

The neural bug had gone online a few days ago and had already put to rest the question of the handler's guilt. Within a matter of hours, Levin had learned that James was currently making a salvage in the Publicae Age. They were too late to act upon that information. Instead, they planted a trap that Levin was now about to spring. So much for brotherhood.

Part of Levin had hoped that they were mistaken about Smitt. He and Levin had once been friends, back in the day when Levin was still friends with James. Smitt's arrest would heavily impact morale. Though of low rank, Smitt was a longtime colleague in the agency and was popular and respected by many. The other handlers would sympathize with his loyalty to his chronman.

"Your plan worked, Auditor," Shizzu said, approaching from behind. "We just intercepted a subchannel transmission from Handler Smitt regarding the attack force."

Levin bowed his head. "Where to?"

"East toward the ruins known as Boston."

"You know where to go, then. I will join the attack shortly."

"Your command, Auditor."

Geneese and Shizzu shot up to one of the collies, and Levin watched as the small fleet headed east. His eyes followed the departing fleet until it was nothing more than small specks swallowed up by the darkening horizon. The fleet would reach Boston in less than thirty minutes. Sure, Smitt might have gotten a message to James's base there; that couldn't be helped. It was a small price to pay for discovering the location of the base. In the end, that small warning would do little to affect the outcome.

The fleet was a significant ChronoCom force, far too large to expend on one fugitive chronman, but Levin was not taking any chances. The ruins of Boston were vast, and a wasteland tribe, with unknown firepower and knowledge of the terrain, could wreak havoc on any invader. Overwhelming force was a sound decision. Levin wished he were going there right now with his men, but he had one more duty he had to oversee before he could join them.

"Monitor Kormin, arrest Handler Smitt and take him to the brig," he said to the man he had assigned to watch over Smitt at the Hops.

"Apologies, Auditor, but Securitate Kuo ordered me to take him there the moment the traitor sent out the transmission. They're both already in the brig."

"What is she doing?"

"She is interrogating the traitor."

"Stop her! That is a private matter."

"I . . . I can't, Auditor."

"Black abyss," Levin growled.

Of course Kuo would supersede his authority. If Smitt had spent even a few minutes in the room with her alone, Levin feared he might already be too late. He rushed back into the building, his hands balled into fists as he pushed his way through the crowded corridors, bowling down anyone who was too slow to jump out of his way.

Levin considered calling in squads of monitors in the event the situation escalated, but thought better of it. No monitor or auditor, for that matter, could stand up against her; he would be placing his people in a dangerous position. No, better he address this on his own. In any case, the confrontation had been coming to a head for weeks now. He should have managed Kuo from the outset. This was his failure. The burden of stopping her should rest squarely on his shoulders.

Levin reached the holding cells, and through one of the viewing screens saw Kuo in a cell with Smitt, who was strapped to a chair with his hands tied behind his back. Sweat glistened on the handler's shirtless body, and his head lolled forward, swinging like a pendulum. His left eye was blackened and blood dripped out of his nose as he hacked and coughed.

Smiling, Kuo caressed his chin, causing Smitt to jerk backward violently, either from pain or terror. She pressed her palm on his chest and he spasmed, his back snapped erect, and his face pointing toward the ceiling in a silent scream. Then he collapsed, unconscious. The lone monitor in the room with them pulled Smitt's head back by the hair and checked his eyes. He looked over at Kuo.

"Wake him," she said, circling the room as if a shark sensing blood.

Levin's nostrils flared as the monitor slapped Smitt awake and the torture continued. Kuo gripped Smitt by the chin and turned his face toward her. "Let's try this question again," she said. "You've already given me the location of the fugitive chronman's base. I appreciate that. Your fate is sealed, so why don't you make things a little easier on yourself? Where is James? Where is the anomaly? What were you searching for in Cassini Regio?"

"I told you already. He's dead," Smitt mumbled, drool dribbling down his chin, "I don't know anything about a damn scientist, and I was just doing research for a Tier-2 job."

Kuo looked at the monitor standing next to Smitt, who stepped forward and stuck a pain rod into Smitt's ribs. He screamed as smoke drifted up from the wound.

"You have no jobs on record in that region. Dead men don't need miasma pills," she said. "Yes, we know about those too."

"He's dead," Smitt moaned, staring fearfully at the pain rod hovering close to his face. "Died in the past."

Kuo signaled again, and Smitt screamed as the monitor jabbed the rod into the base of his neck, this time behind his collarbone.

She caressed his face again and snapped his chin up to make him face her. "How did he die? Where's the body?"

A white glow shifted from her body and wrapped around Smitt's waist. It lifted him into the air and stretched him out, slowly separating his limbs from their sockets.

"He's hundreds of years dead already," Smitt screamed. "I don't know where. Please, please!"

Levin detested this sort of treatment and rarely found it effective. As an auditor, he had had to do many terrible things, but torture was where he drew the line. Sometimes, the death of an enemy was necessary. It had rarely been his experience that torture ever was.

Levin cherished his place in the chain. However, this was too much. For Kuo, a corrupt outsider, to feel that she had the authority and the right to torture one of their own, regardless of guilt, was not only barbaric, but went against the honor of all that Levin held dear. At that moment, he didn't care that the director had ordered him to cooperate with this Valta corporate scum. The director's orders could not be rightfully followed. Levin was going to put a stop to this right now. He slammed open the door and stormed into the holding room.

"This ends now," he said. "Monitor Qem, take Handler Smitt to the medical ward. Place a guard at his door. No one is allowed access to him without my express permission."

"No, he won't," Kuo said. "In fact, Monitor Qem will use that pain stick and jab it into the traitor's neck until he falls unconscious." She sauntered around the room and stopped in front of Levin. "Leave the room, Auditor. You're not needed here." To his credit, Qem did nothing, though for a second, he wore the same terrified look as Smitt.

"Hands off my operative," Levin growled, stepping up to face Kuo. "This matter is not your business."

"It became our business when someone in your agency spied on sensitive Valta intelligence."

"Where is your evidence?"

"You are not privy to it." She turned her back to him and hovered Smitt to her.

"James is dead . . . ," Smitt groaned again, and then his body stiffened as Kuo pinned him against the wall. Her hands glowed white and spread to Smitt's chest. He began to thrash as the sickening smell of burned skin filled the room.

"This is your final warning, Securitate," Levin said, his voice deadpan. Levin clenched his fists and cursed his indecisiveness. There was only one person here who was possibly powerful enough to stop her. However, Young's orders rang in his head. The consequences to the agency weighed heavily on him.

Kuo, so confident of her authority, ignored Levin and kept her back to him. "This is your last chance, Handler. Why are you protecting him? I fail to see value in that misplaced allegiance."

For a brief moment, Smitt looked resigned, and then, finally, defiant. He lifted his head close to hers and managed a smile. "You're a fucking monster, you know that? James is my friend, that's why." Then he spit in her face.

Kuo wiped the spit from her face with an incredulous look. Before Levin could power his exo and stop her, white light shot up through Kuo's arm and into Smitt's head. For a split second, his eyes glowed and he screamed silently, releasing a beam of light as his mouth opened. Then the skin on his face began to smoke and peel. Smitt's body convulsed until his clothes burst into flames. The room smelled of burnt flesh.

Upon seeing Smitt's blackened body, something in Levin snapped. He snarled, "You'll pay for this!"

Kuo turned to face Levin as he barreled into her with the full force of his exo. "You dare," was all she managed to say. They both lit up as the borders of their exos touched, the orange glow of his hammering against the white of hers, causing static to flare up into the room. Monitor Qem, the only other person in the room, was thrown into the opposite wall as the two opposing power sources expanded. The wall behind Kuo melted and Levin's momentum carried them both through the entire section of the brig, leveling half a dozen walls until they exploded into the hangar, finally landing and smashing the top of a parked collie.

Levin scanned their area to make sure none of the scattering engineers nearby were in danger. That momentary distraction, however, proved costly. Kuo had recovered from the surprise attack just enough to roll under Levin's forward force and flip him over to the front nose of the collie, where he bounced off and fell onto the ground. He landed on his feet and retreated to the open space. He eyed Kuo as she took her time and casually followed, jumping off the ship and strolling to the center of the hangar. The two stalked each other like two predators going in for the kill.

Several squads of monitors ran into the hangar and quarantined the area, wrist beams raised. He wasn't sure which of them they were aimed at; he was unsure of many of the loyalties in the agency these days. Still, this wasn't a fight any of them should face.

"Stay back. Do not get involved," he barked. "Clear the hangar."

The glow of her exo was different from his: whiter, with a bluish tint, compared to his angry orange field, energy more electric and lines more jagged than the smooth curved arches of an auditor's. Her shield also surrounded her in a sphere, unlike his, which hugged his skin. It offered her more protection while at the same time being more unwieldy and inefficient. Levin's skin-shield, on the other hand, was much more maneuverable and power-conscious, but could not take as many attacks as Kuo's shield.

Their expanded exo fields touched briefly and Levin immediately felt the surge-back of her field repelling his. He threw himself into the air and sprouted nine coils, expanding them out in all directions and then focusing them straight at her.

Kuo sprouted only one massive thick trunk that was as wide as she was tall. As his coils snaked around it, her trunk shot out toward him and somehow sucked his coils into it as if by some sort of magnetism. Levin threw himself to the side as her trunk punched the air where he had been moments before. He cut his connection with his coils and regrew another half dozen, pushing them into the ground to sweep up around her feet.

Kuo responded by leveling the ground she was standing on, and expanding a spherical barrier around her that melted the floor away. Every coil Levin shot out fizzled as it touched the white sphere with blue tints arcing and jumping across its surface. Her large trunk hammered down on him again, forcing him to take evasive maneuvers as he ducked and juked, trying to stay out of her range. She was pushing him further and further back, which would soon put her beyond the range of his own attacks.

Levin continued to dodge, waiting for an opening. He had dealt with exos of this sort before, commonly used in space battles where range and power were more important than finesse and versatility. Still, the levels of Kuo's exos were far beyond anything he had previously encountered. The energy drain needed to generate the trunk had to be massive. Perhaps he could drain her levels and outlast her.

A sudden jolt from the side knocked Levin out of the air. His vision swam as the ground and sky switched places and the landscape became a blur of colors. He careened into one of the transports, smashing through the front portholes and into the cargo hold. Levin wiped the blood off of his chin. His exo had cracked from that last blow. He wasn't sure how many more of those he could take.

He picked himself up and was knocked down again by pieces of the ship as it began to cave in on him, the metal walls buckling and crinkling as if balled-up paper. Levin steadied his exo and pushed himself upward, only to slam into Kuo's trunk and fall back again. He tried once more, this time shooting to his left. Again, he was stopped by her energy field. The ceiling and walls continued to close in, and soon he was left with hardly enough space to stand.

Levin shot out a dozen small coils in all directions, probing for an escape. It seemed, however, that Kuo's trunk had completely enveloped the transport, and she was intent on crushing him inside. He was trapped. He dropped to his knees as the ceiling came closer, frantically searching for a way out. What was left of the transport was shaking as its skeleton failed to keep its form. He placed his hands on the metal grating of the floor to steady himself, and stopped. He peered down at the flat ground beneath him. It would take a tremendous amount of levels but this could be his only chance.

Levin focused his remaining levels and concentrated them on a single point beneath him. He drove straight down into the ground, through the hull of the ship, into the dirt, rock, and underground piping. He descended six meters and burrowed eastward. One thing he knew about these trunk exos was that, due to the tremendous inertia created from their focused attacks, unless their wielder were fighting in open space, they required him or her to hold a solid base to ground the exos's inertia and thereby maintain position.

He ascended right below Kuo and produced an eruption of earth as he struck her from underneath. She was so taken aback by the attack, her trunk disappeared. This was his chance. That last maneuver had sucked his levels down to 16 percent.

While she was disoriented, he rose into the air and dove straight toward her again, slamming into her with the hopes of piercing her shield for the kill. Her exo flared against his attack and, for a moment, seemed to crack. Then it held. He felt a burning sensation as her white field momentarily receded, then surged forward. It overwhelmed his shield and began to cover his body like a film. His nerves burned and his atmos screamed to his AI band that his body was frying. And then he was through her shield and past the perimeter. Levin reached for her, but suddenly found that he couldn't move.

"Nice try, Auditor," she panted. "You almost had me."

The two stood close together, their noses almost touching. Their exos meshed like oil and water, pushing against each other, small crackles of energy shooting out and producing bursts and arcs. Even without checking, Levin could feel his exo weakening and losing its integrity. He couldn't match her raw energy output, and now that he was inside her field, she had effectively imprisoned him.

"I warned you not to challenge me," she continued. "Consider this your official retirement from Chrono—"

A blast from the side knocked Kuo to the ground, and her exo shield flickered. She spun and lashed out, catching one of the monitors in the chest and throwing him back against the far wall ten meters away. The man crumpled to the ground in a heap. Then, another blow struck her, causing her to stumble. Then another. Before Levin realized what had happened, one of the monitors was picking him off the floor.

"You are injured, Auditor. Allow me to assist you," she said, face grim and determined. "We apologize for disobeying orders, and submit to your judgment after this issue has been resolved."

Levin watched, eyes moist and pride bursting from his heart, as three dozen monitors beat Kuo back, peppering her with wrist beams. He even saw a few of the engineers joining the fray with more conventional weapons.

Kuo lashed out with her trunk, leveling monitors three and four at a time, but not even her powerful exo could handle the sustained barrage.

Levin was about to join the fight and help his people when that same monitor held him back.

"Auditor, you're injured. We have this situation under control."

For the first time, he realized his left arm was broken, probably from when Kuo was squeezing the life out of him. The monitor pulled him to the back of the hangar, to five of the engineers, and ordered them to keep Levin there. At first, he was startled that a mere monitor dared order him around. He reminded himself to find that woman's name later on. Certain monitors' real mettle came through in moments of crisis. The monitor left to join in the fight. When Levin tried to leave again, the five engineers blocked his path.

"Fine," he grumbled. His levels were drained anyway, and he would just be a liability. Levin understood the difference between bravery and foolishness. He became a spectator in his own fight with Securitate Kuo, watching as the monitors who saved his life wore her down, taking heavy damage in the process. Kuo was becoming desperate and tried to take to the air to escape. The monitors were ready for that. One of them brought out an exo-chain, most often used to contain fugitive chronmen. The chain hit her exo and latched on, preventing her from escaping its pull.

Eventually, they cracked her exo and pulled her down to the ground. The group of monitors closed in, dozens of wrist beams aimed at her exposed body while four held her by the arms and pushed her down to her knees. The monitors parted as Levin limped—it seemed he had hurt his leg as well—toward her. He stopped and surveyed the hangar. Evidence of their battle was everywhere. At least ten collies were destroyed, and the bodies of dozens of his people lay motionless on the ground.

"It seems your army of ants had to do the job you couldn't," she spat, twisting back, lunging at him. "You will pay for this. All of you will."

One of the monitors standing to the side punched her in the jaw and aimed his wrist beam at her temple.

"No," Levin said, pushing the monitor's arm away. "This isn't our role. We send her scurrying back where she came from."

"She killed our men, Auditor," the monitor gasped.

Levin shook his head. "There will be a price to pay for what just has transpired. Be sure that I'm the only one that will pay it. For now, take her to the brig and see that she can harm no one else." He looked over at the men crowding around him. "We have injured brothers. Get them to the medical ward." He swung his arm in circles and tested his aching shoulder. It would have to do. His work wasn't done yet. "Prep a collie and get me a set of fresh bands."

FORTY-FOUR

DISCOVERED

The warning came just as the Elfreth were coming together for their evening meal in the communal field. Elise had made the journey down the Farming Tower to sit with Franwil and Qawol to discuss her progress. Well, that and to ask for permission to assign Sammuia to be Grace's assistant.

Currently, without someone officially at her beck and call, Grace had made a habit of expecting Elise to run errands for her, which was an unacceptable setup. That old witch—today was one of their more terse days—was being downright ornery. No sooner did she see Franwil, and beamed her a smile, Grace yelled—she also sometimes had trouble remembering to use her inside voice—into her head.

"Child, they've found us. Warn the others. Get everyone underground. Now!"

"Who? Wha—oh no!"

Elise took off in a sprint, narrowly avoiding bowling over a group of children who were playing volleyball with a fish-hide ball. She had taught them the twenty-first-century's most popular sport out of boredom, and now they played it every chance they got.

"Get inside," she called to them as she ran up to Qawol. "Oldest, chronmen come!"

Qawol, looking anything but hurried, nodded and laid a hand on Franwil's arm. "Gather the Old Ones to the shelter. Have each recall their purposes. Make sure McIlel's purpose is to cover the escape of the others. I will call the guardians." Without a word, several of the Old Ones nearby began to corral the children east toward one of the underground tunnels. He looked back at Elise. "How many and how soon?"

"What are we looking at?" Elise thought to Grace.

"Within the hour and according to Smitt, a shit many. I've already woken James. He's still an hour away. The chronmen will be here before he arrives."

Elise relayed the message and again, Qawol took the news in stride. He barked out a message that was repeated by everyone in earshot. Within moments, the tribe was a hive of activity as the fit men and women appeared with weapons, the elderly grabbed children, and everyone else stowed what valuables they had into buildings or the deep underground tunnels that ran for kilometers under the city.

At the same time, even more assembled with weapons ranging from ancient bows and spears to old projectile rifles to energy pistols. There were even a few wrist beams. She was amazed at how quickly the tribe armed themselves. She guessed they would have to in order to survive so long out here in the wastelands.

It seemed like only seconds had passed before she heard a horn coming from one of the guards standing watch atop one of the Farming Towers. She saw a small speck in the distance, and then she saw another. Within a minute, the sky was littered with them, all growing steadily larger.

The first explosion came a moment later when the bridge over one of the many river tributaries cutting through Boston exploded into a column of wood and dirt. The dam near the common area was the next to go and soon, Elise found herself wading ankle-deep in rushing water. A wave of the flying ships zipped overhead and she saw them turning around to make another pass.

A streak of red flew up from the ground near her toward one of the fast-moving specks and trailed a ship that tried to zigzag left and right to shake it. Their chase ended with the ship exploding and crashing into one of the derelict buildings, shaking the ground as chunks of the building rained down nearby. Fortunately, none of the Farming Towers, where dozens of Elfreth were hiding, was hit.

It then began to rain men, and not in the good way. Dozens of the same black-armored men who had attacked her at the plaza jumped out of the collies, landing around the edge of the communal fields and forming a perimeter around the Farming Towers' grounds. Scratch that; some of the attackers were women as well, and they were every bit as aggressive and dangerous as the men. All of them looked dangerous and seemed to be shooting at anyone who moved, the remaining women and children included.

The dried-up water fountain in the center of the common area exploded, sending chunks of concrete and debris flying into the air, tearing through the closest group of tribesmen. Another explosion followed. Then a chain of explosions erupted, a line of earth and rocks cutting through the camp as four attackers flew by overhead. She didn't know they could do that. Elise saw two more groups of black-armored people charge in from opposite sides. Six more dropped in from the sky. Within seconds, the entire encampment was a battlefield.

The tribesmen returned fire, pulling together their awaiting barricades, forming small squads of twos and threes, and retreating to cover from the clearing in a surprisingly orderly and tactical fashion. Well, no. Nothing the Elfreth did surprised Elise that much anymore. They even fought as a cohesive unit. Still, they were outgunned. Several of the tribe, if not all, would fall before the night was over.

Elise was in a dangerous spot and stayed huddled behind one of the broken columns, too terrified to move. Instead of retreating underground with the children, she had stupidly stayed above and watched the attackers sweep over them. Now, she was caught in the cross fire as the advancing attackers moved in on all sides while the members of the Elfreth defended from assorted barricades, desperately trying to keep them out of the communal fields.

Rough hands pawed at her and lifted her off the ground. Elise screamed for a second until she realized that it was Chawr dragging her toward the first tower. She looked up and saw dozens of the Elfreth shooting from all levels, either at the air, at the ships buzzing about, or at the encroaching invaders at the ground level. It was chaotic. People were dying everywhere. One thing was clear, though; the tribe was slowly losing ground.

Chawr half-dragged, half-carried her back to one of the larger barricades and dumped her at Qawol's feet. The Oldest looked as calm in the midst of this battle as if he were just going out on a stroll. He was study-ing the enemy and giving orders like a seasoned general, every once in a while pointing at certain places he wanted his people to be.

"Qawol," she urged, "You shouldn't be here."

He smiled. "There is nowhere else I should be. You, child, should be with the children. You are too important to be wasted as weapon fod-der." He was interrupted by one of the younger guardians—barely four-teen by the looks of him—reporting in from the far side. Qawol gave him a few orders and then looked at Chawr standing next to Elise. He tilted his head toward the Farming Towers entrance. The young Elfreth grabbed her by the arm and dragged her from the battle.

A line of black-armored soldiers stormed the clearing, overrunning some of the outer barricades. Several more of the Elfreth charged out of the Farming Towers and met them in the center of the fields, using their primitive spears and rifles in whatever ways they could. Before Elise re-alized what had happened, the guardians were fighting close with them on every side. While they still outnumbered the enemy, the guardians' ranks were falling. Everywhere she looked, she saw the brave guardians taking on the chronmen, their weapons often ineffectual. But still, they fought.

It soon became apparent to Elise that several if not all of these attack-ers were looking for something. Someone. Without a doubt, it was her; she was their objective. Part of Elise wanted to give herself up to end the fighting. Another part of her knew her surrender would do nothing for the Elfreth.

Elise and Chawr reached Farming Tower One's entrance and ran across the lobby toward the stairwell. It was a large building with many floors. If they could find a place to hide, they could wait out the attack. She felt ashamed for fleeing, but she knew she wasn't worth a damn fighting. The few shots she had fired with the wrist beam were well off their marks. She was a scientist, not a fighter, and her nerves were not prepared for the cacophony and chaos of the battlefield.

Just as they reached the stairwell, something smashed into the lobby with such force, a cloud of dust blew Elise and Chawr off their feet. She spit the grit out of her mouth and looked behind her, and for a moment, hope sprung up. She saw a dark figure with a glow surrounding him. James had returned! He would know what to do.

Then she noticed that something was wrong. Every time James used his exo, it was yellow; this one was orange. The figure, nothing more than a silhouette against the blinding lights of the fires and explosions outside, stood up and walked toward her. She realized then that there were others with James's sort of powers, and they were on the enemy's side.

"Oh no! Oh no!" she gasped, scrambling on all fours and crab-walking toward the stairwell. He was coming for her.

"Run, Elder Elise," said Chawr. "I will take care of this man."

"No," she cried, grabbing for his arm. "He'll kill you."

He picked her up off the ground and grinned. "No one can kill Chawr. Just you see. Now, go! You run. Hide!" He pushed her into the stairwell, turned, and then charged at the black silhouette, armed with only a hatchet.

Elise helplessly watched as the figure casually swept the young man aside with a gesture of his hand. Chawr picked himself up and attacked again, hacking at the shield, cursing at the top of his lungs. The figure stopped and faced him, shaking his head. There was a burst of light and Chawr flew into one of the walls and crumpled in a heap to the floor. She saw him rise one more time. Their eyes locked and he waved her away. Then Chawr raised his hatchet and charged at the glowing man once more.

Tears streaming down her face, Elise turned and sprinted up the stairs two a time. Now, she had to get away, not for herself, but for that boy— that young man who decided that her life was worth more than his.

She scrambled up the stairs, her steps echoing through the long hollow vertical corridors. As always, the Farming Towers were nearly pitch-black, save for the natural light from the outside that shone through the exits on each floor. Fortunately, there was just a sliver of sun left, which offered enough light for her not to stumble through complete darkness.

Thirty floors up, Elise tired and slowed her pace. As she stopped to rest for a moment, she heard another set of steps. She paused and listened. Elise had missed hearing those steps earlier because, she now realized, they had been matching hers.

"Damn it," she cursed under her breath.

She tried to take a few soft steps, but their faint echoes betrayed her, and she soon heard the second set of footsteps follow suit. He was stalking her to see which floor she got off on. She changed up her pacing, going up three steps at a time or alternating loud and quiet steps to throw off her pursuer. It didn't matter; every time she rounded a stairwell corner, it gave her position away. The bastard stayed on her, and he was getting closer.

Finally, at around the fiftieth level, she decided to hell with it and ran has hard as she could. If she could reach the sky bridge, she could try to lose him in one of the other buildings. Elise scrambled up the remaining flights to the seventieth floor as fast as she could.

Once there, she rounded the corner and ran directly toward Farming Tower Two. No matter what, she had to stay away from the lab where Grace was hiding with all their research and equipment. If these guys got ahold of that, then everything would be lost. Elise sprinted across the sky bridge connecting the two towers and entered the ruins of an old office, where a maze of cubicles and small rooms made for good hiding spots.

She sped down the hallway and jumped into a side corridor, where she found a small closet whose door was mostly obstructed by a ceiling cave-in. It was a tight fit even for her small body. She climbed inside and passed through to an adjacent room. She huddled in the corner and tried to steady her hard breathing. A moment later, she heard approaching footsteps, and a deliberate *tap, tap, tap*. Then a pause, and then another *tap, tap, tap.*

"Wrong move, little mouse," a voice said. "You think hiding here will keep you out of my hands?" There were two loud crashes that sounded very close by, and then metal groaned as a cloud of dust swept past her hiding place.

"If you were wondering what that was, little mouse," the voice continued, "it was the bridge and stairwell. I guess it's just you and me all cozy-like now, eh?"

Elise's nose itched and she pinched it as hard as she could. Sneezing now was certain death. If she made any noise, it was over. She aimed her wrist beam at the small hole she had crawled through, where a sliver of light from the outside beamed in. She was grateful that the sun would soon set. The Farming Towers' exterior walls were all windows, though more than two-thirds of the panes were long gone.

She wouldn't be hard to find then. This guy didn't know about the remaining bridge on the other side. Maybe once it was dark she could sneak off this floor.

"Hide if you like; it makes the hunt more enjoyable," the voice continued. "You're lucky the dust kicked up, little mouse, or this hunt would
be over right quick. No matter, though. It'll only be a small matter of time
before old Shizzu gets ahold of you."

FORTY-FIVE

LATE

James saw the battle from kilometers away. At least half a dozen collies hovered above the city. Pillars of smoke billowed up from the area where the Farming Towers were located. His concern rose as he pulled in closer. This was a major attack.

"Black abyss, there's so many," he said, fear gripping his throat. The scope of the attack still amazed James. Levin must want him pretty badly to commit such a large force just for him. He was surprised to realize that his worry extended not just to Grace, but to the rest of the Elfreth as well.

This was a large operation by ChronoCom standards. Between the six ships he saw floating in the air, the two burning wrecks—one on the ground and one that had crashed into a skyscraper—and at least forty or so monitors with flight bands he saw flitting around, not to mention who knows how many on the ground. ChronoCom must have committed nearly a hundred operatives to this attack. All for a wasteland tribe of a couple hundred ill fed, badly armed men, women, and children. And him and Elise. That's who they were really after. Maybe he could lead them away and buy the Elfreth time to escape.

He desperately wanted to call out to Elise through his comm band, but it was far too risky. He wasn't sure how many of their channels were compromised. Still, there had to be a way he could reach out to her and let her know that he was here, that he was coming for her. Even if he was too late to rescue her, at least she would know that he had tried.

He decided to take a risk. He activated his comm band to every channel in his spectrum. "To all tribes monitoring this, stay off channels. You will be tracked. Emergency ping only."

Only Elise and Grace had comm bands, so they would be the only ones to receive it. Well, those two and everyone in ChronoCom monitoring the channels. Hopefully, they were smart enough to understand his message.

His plan worked. He saw all six of those collies peel off their positions and move to intercept him. Now, he had to worry about surviving the next minute. His collie wasn't armed, and he had little doubt that that wasn't case with those approaching him.

Bright beams shot out of the lead ships and streaked toward him. His collie didn't stand a chance against ship weaponry. It would be torn to shreds and his exo wouldn't hold against weaponry of that level. He opened the door and dove out a second before *Collie* exploded, the blast tossing him out of control as he plummeted to the ground.

James watched his ship of fifteen years explode into a ball of flames, and for a brief moment, he mourned its loss. While he had always thought of *Collie* as the vehicle that took him to the jobs that he hated, the truth was that she had never failed him, even when everything and everyone around him did. Aside from Smitt, she was the most reliable part of his life. Seeing her destruction hurt. Then he remembered that he had left the netherstore attached to her as well.

He slapped his forehead even as he plummeted to Earth. "Fuck me."

James took another second to mourn and then turned his attention back to the battle. He had to manage his levels carefully if he was going to win this fight. Who was he kidding? The odds of him dying today were high. They were assured if Elise didn't make it. His only solace was knowing that Valta and ChronoCom intended to capture her alive. If that were the case, he had to stay alive long enough to rescue her.

James landed hard on the ground two kilometers away from the Farming Towers and took a tumble, sliding and rolling on broken pavement. He was swarmed right away by fourteen monitors, who dropped down from the sky after him. One of them carried an exo-chain and tried to lock James down. James batted him away with a kinetic coil. He grew ten more as they came at him from all sides. Nine were in the air and a squad of five came in on the ground from the east.

James continued moving, pushing himself and sliding in all directions to minimize the stream of wrist beams from burning his shields down. He struck, lashing at monitors unfortunate enough to be within range of his kinetic coil or ramming into others who gave him a direct line of sight.

He was already fighting with eleven kinetic coils, the most he had ever controlled. Because his energies were so spread out, each coil lacked the power and strength to be completely effective. Yet it wasn't enough. At one point, all the coils were in use and he was still fighting hand-to-hand, grappling with the arm of a young monitor and struggling to keep from getting a hole blown in his head.

He looked over just in time to see another monitor charge him from the side. He sidestepped and used the weight of the monitor he was struggling with to throw the second off balance. Two bursts struck the monitor while the third grazed James on the shoulder. Pain flared through his body, and he dropped to one knee, momentarily losing control of all his coils. He looked up just in time to see the monitor aim another shot. Then the man fell as a white beam tore him apart.

James looked up at a window where the white beam had come from and saw a wasteland warrior he did not recognize wave at him. "You are known, Chronman No More," the man shouted out. "Oldest Qawol calls you worthy."

James waved a quick thanks. Now he wished he had spent some time making an alliance with these warriors. They could be a formidable force if organized. It was too late now. No, it wasn't too late. If James and the tribe survived this fight, he could still gather these people together. They had already shown that they were efficient and resilient. They just needed direction and a purpose. His thoughts wandered back to Elise. Right now, James had to fight, or he'd lose his purpose.

As the fight escalated, James noticed that others had joined in. They weren't from ChronoCom, nor could they be from the Elfreth. Some of the other wasteland tribes living in the Boston area must have engaged the monitors as well. These survivors in the wasteland were proud, even of the little they had. For the first time, James felt a camaraderie toward them as they all fought against overwhelming odds. Even with their help, though, it was a losing battle.

Those odds climbed even higher when James saw an auditor, Geneese, land in the thick of the battle. The auditor made his presence felt as his exo tore through an entire fifth level of a building that housed some of the tribesmen pot-shotting the monitors. Once Geneese engaged him out in the open with a dozen monitors at his back, he was doomed.

James reassessed the situation. He was far too exposed in the open to continue this fight. He took off into the air. Lashing out with half a dozen kinetic coils, he was able to take out four monitors before he felt the attack of an exo. Geneese slid toward him at a frightening clip. Auditor's exos were so much faster and more powerful than chronmen's. The impact knocked James off course and he lost control and fell tumbling through the air. He recovered just in time to dodge another attack as Geneese, with momentum on his side, slammed into him again.

His levels were down to seventy within a matter of minutes. James was at a distinct disadvantage against Geneese in the open field. That, and Geneese, like most auditors, was much better trained to fight with exos than he was. Still, James had experience on his side as well, and he had picked up a few tricks along the way. He shot a thick coil straight at Geneese. As expected, the auditor met his coil with an even stronger one. Right before the two sources impacted—a melee that James would definitely lose—he split that coil in two.

Geneese had only a second to react. He was able to slice down on one of James's coils, but took the brunt of the other in the chest. His shielding crackled and held, but the force knocked him back several meters. James took advantage of this momentary opening and lashed out, striking at three more monitors within reach. Then, with more monitors closing in on him, he sped away from the clearing and bounded toward the roof of the nearest building.

His levels were now under 65 percent. He couldn't sustain a long fight with an auditor. The Elfreth had gotten their distraction, though. There had to be thirty monitors on him at this moment. Hopefully, that would dilute the attack on the communal fields enough for the Elfreth either to mount a defense or escape to safety.

James reached the rooftop of the nearest building and was bounding away a second later. Geneese and a dozen monitors followed close behind, not bothering to land as they gave chase. They didn't have to worry about conserving their levels. Whether he was going to get away remained to be seen, though the odds were not in his favor at the moment.

Midbound, James changed course and zoomed downward toward one of the taller buildings. He entered through a window and ran across the floor to the far side. He heard monitors land behind him a few seconds later. Chances were that they would send only a few in to flush him out while the rest surrounded the air space around him to cut off his retreat.

It was a large building and James had options. He turned a corner and ambushed the first monitor, who had pursued too aggressively. A quick strike to the neck with his fist, followed by an elbow to the face, finished him off. James continued on, running two levels down the stairwell and turning south. There was an adjacent building nearby, and if James could jump into it without attracting attention, he could throw them off his trail.

Unfortunately, there didn't seem to be a window along the entire southern wall of the building, so James had to make his own. He crashed through the wall of the building and broke through the wall of the next. Above him, he heard several barks of alarm as the nearby monitors gave chase. Well, it had almost worked.

James continued running through the building, zigzagging through hallways, randomly running down stairs, making his way toward the ground level. The monitors had air superiority, but if there was a way to get underground, he could lose them and hurry back to the communal fields. There were simply too many nooks and crevasses in this jungle for them to locate him. It would buy some time for the Elfreth, at least.

He encountered another monitor and finished her off with the same brutal efficiency as with the first. He wondered at their foolishness for spreading out their forces like this, and then he realized that Geneese was probably using them as feelers. Every time James engaged and killed one, the auditor could pinpoint his presence.

James continued south, jumping through windows when the opportunity was there, making his own when they weren't. He flew across city blocks, juked through side buildings, and finally came to a stop to assess the situation. Sometimes, staying in one place was better than running, after all.

According to the AI band, he was nearing the southern edge of the city and was quickly running out of tall buildings to hide in. At this moment, it was quiet, with only the sounds of the ocean waves crashing into the otherwise dead city.

He saw a shadow creep into the room across the hall. Another monitor, maybe. He slipped to the doorway and leaned his head in. It was a large room with the remnants of a rectangular table in the center. Assorted smashed chairs littered the floor alongside parts of a caved-in ceiling. The monitor was on the far end, moving toward the door on the opposite side.

A thought occurred to James. He powered on his exo and threw himself at the monitor, slamming into him from behind and breaking his neck. He immediately launched himself through the caved-in ceiling, powered down, and became very still. Minutes later, Geneese came in, exo powered up to half. He walked toward the fallen monitor and turned him over.

In a split second, James powered up whatever remained of his exo's power and launched himself straight down on top of Geneese's head. He missed his head, but at this range and power, it didn't matter. The focused energy of a single thrust blew through Geneese's shield and sliced him in half. Geneese only had a moment to look surprised, then he keeled over.

As a safety precaution, James linked his coils around Geneese's bands and broke them. It was too bad he couldn't procure the auditor bands for himself. Auditor bands were so much more powerful and had a much larger energy level reserve, but the same security precautions that applied to his chronmen bands applied to auditor bands as well. Once Geneese died, those bands were worthless.

James checked Geneese's body for any other useful items and prepared to finish off the rest of his stalkers. Levin was going to fly into a rage when he realized that James had killed an auditor.

James's levels were now under 40 percent. The rest of the monitors he would have to defeat without wasting any more power. He had a feeling he'd need as many levels as possible once he got back to Elise. James crept out of the room and bided his time to set up his next trap.

FORTY-SIX

STALKED

Elise huddled in a fetal position in the corner of the small, half-collapsed closet. The jerk was taunting her. Elise didn't know if this Shizzu guy was toying with her or not. His voice came from all directions. One moment, it seemed to be coming from down the hall, the next, close by in the room beyond her. Then it would fade again. Twice, she saw his shadow pass by the small opening of her closet, and each time her heart beat against her chest so hard she thought he could hear it.

When his voice came close, she'd begin to sweat, her hands would shake, and it would take all of her focus to stay still. When his voice was far away, she had to fight down the urge to run out of the closet and make a break for the adjacent tower. Neither of these seemed like a good idea.

She wished James were here. She heard his voice briefly when he got to the battle. At first, she thought she had hallucinated it, that it was wishful thinking. Then, when she heard his words, she realized he couldn't just find her like he usually did. He had warned her and Grace to stay silent because anything they said through their comm bands could be tracked. Not being able to reach out to him made the situation even more difficult, since there was nothing she could do to bring him to her. He had said in that message to use the emergency channel as a last resort. What emergency channel? She felt more alone than ever.

"You know, little mouse," Shizzu said, "I know more about you than you think. You see, we've met. I remember you. We've spoken before."

How could that be possible? Elise didn't know what the hell this guy was talking about. What did he mean they'd met before? There was no way they could have met before unless he was one of those two assholes who tried to grab her at that hotel right before James saved her. It wasn't as if she'd even seen their faces. They'd had those cones on their heads, after all.

Had he been hiding as one of the Elfreth? She gave a start; maybe he was a time traveler as well. James did tell her that there were others involved in Nutris's destruction. Then it hit her; maybe he was the guy who planted the bomb that destroyed Nutris!

Elise bit her lip as she quivered in rage. This was the guy responsible for all her friends' and colleagues' deaths. Worst of all, if it wasn't for him, the Nutris Platform team might have been able to cure the Earth Plague. She fought back the urge to stalk this jerk and shoot him in the face. Chances were, if he was anything like James, he would have that stupid force field around him that made him invincible. Or worse, with her terrible aim, unless he was in point-blank range, she would miss by five body lengths, and the only thing she'd accomplish would be giving away her location.

Be smart, girl, she thought to herself. She settled down and waited.

Shizzu's footsteps and voice faded, and after a while, Elise lost track of the time. The sun was setting and it was getting chilly. The evening breeze was wont to blow through the many openings of the building. She had turned off her atmos as soon as this Shizzu guy started stalking her. She wasn't sure if he was able to track her through her band use, so she was afraid to turn any of them on.

As the minutes passed, she became restless. It had been a while since she had last heard anything other than the high-pitched whistle of the gray winds that blew through the corridors. There were still sounds of fighting off in the distance, punctuated by occasional explosions and screams, but little else.

A nearby crash broke the stillness. Elise froze. There was another crash, this time accompanied by the groan of metal and the sound of drizzling debris. Then another. The far wall of the room Elise was hiding in collapsed, kicking up a swirl of dust. Elise huddled into a ball and held her scream inside. This guy must be punching holes into walls and leveling the floors in order to flush her out. Elise's first instinct was to flee the room and make for the bridge. But then she would fall right into this Shizzu's hands. If she stayed, she risked being discovered or shot. There weren't any good options. The crashes continued.

Elise decided then that she wasn't going to stay there until he found her. She'd rather run and have a chance of escape than stay in place for him to scoop her up. Crawling one slow limb at a time, Elise inched out of her hiding spot and got her bearings. The last orange hue of the sky bathed the entire floor, and only a thin slice of the sun was left as it sunk into the horizon. Shadows from every corner grew by the second.

Staying low to the ground, she pawed her way through the darkness, slipping from cubicle to cubicle. There was no sign of Shizzu. Maybe he was tired of looking for her and had abandoned his search; maybe he was recalled to do something more important than hunt for little ole her. In any case, Elise was confident that if she could sneak across that bridge, she could get to another floor and get away. She reached the end of the room and peeked around the corner to her left. The hallway seemed deserted. Then she looked to her right. The path to the bridge was clear.

Elise took a deep breath and crept down the hallway. Behind her, two more explosions rocked the building. She reached the bridge between Farming Tower Two and Farming Tower Three and picked up her pace. The wind was strong enough here that it would mask her footsteps. She was also completely out in the open so the sooner—

The left wall of the bridge exploded in a shower of debris, knocking her off her feet. Elise turned and saw a dark figure in the hallway behind her. She took off and sprinted as hard as she could across the bridge, but she had no chance. There was no way she could outrun his bands. She was two-thirds across the sky bridge when an invisible force tripped her. Elise tumbled to the ground and felt something wrap around her ankles. It lifted her up by her feet until she hung suspended upside down.

"Emergency channel," she thought furiously. "Anyone in the emergency channel?" She switched to the subchannel she and James shared. "James! This is an emergency!"

She stayed hanging in the air while the figure approached. She tilted her head and looked at her assailant. He looked a lot like James when they first met: bald, pasty white, and in good shape. However, instead of the sadness she often saw in James's eyes, this guy looked damn proud of himself.

"Hello, little mouse," he said. "Now do you remember me?"

"No," she spat, squirming like a fish on a hook. "I would have remembered someone as ugly as you."

Shizzu chuckled. "That's not what you said when we met. You complimented me on my vigor. I was flattered. You were quite fetching wearing that tight black outfit of yours."

Then it dawned on her. He was the old security guard who disappeared back on Nutris two weeks before it exploded. He had begged to transfer to Sector Four, the smallest sector requiring the least distance to patrol. She had taken one look at him and decided to authorize the transfer.

"I was just being nice, you asshole," she growled. "You looked like you were pushing eighty!"

He mocked her and bowed. "Some people, like your boyfriend, who by the way is a dear comrade of mine, prefer to play it straight. I enjoy a bit of theater with my work. Did I tell you that James and I go twenty years back? He was a brooding prick then as well. Now me, I'm a whole lot more fun, little mouse."

"So you pretend to be an old hobbling man to get what you want? That's sick."

He grinned. "Whatever gets the job done, little mouse. Going into the past requires an understanding of that period. I like to think of myself as an actor studying for a role."

"You're the one that sabotaged the platform and killed all my friends," she said. "What kind of role is a mass murderer?"

"Perhaps a little simplistic, but yes, guilty as charged." Shizzu shrugged. "Your friends were already dead, as were you. I just bent the rules and helped you all along. By the way, I am shocked that you are still alive and sane. I would have thought you would have exploded by now, or at the very least become a raving lunatic. Obviously, we need to revisit some of the theories of time travel."

"How can you sleep at night, you sociopath!"

"Such a mouth." He lifted her face to his eye level. "Maybe I should teach you a lesson."

With a casual swipe, he struck Elise on the side of the face, swiveling her head to the side and rocking her entire body. Elise was disoriented as her head rung. Her vision blurred and she struggled to stay conscious. Still hanging upside down didn't help matters either. When her eyes finally focused again, she saw Shizzu gazing off to the side, his eyes carrying a distant look that James often had when he was using his comm band. She squawked and flailed at him with her hands, managing to scratch a long gash across his cheeks.

With a snarl, he smacked her again, making her head ring. He pulled her in close, cupping her chin with a hand. "One more outburst out of you and I'll cut your arms off. You hear me, bitch?"

She could feel his hot breath as his calloused hands clamped around her mouth. She ignored his snarling and tried to clear her head. Her legs were still tied together by invisible bonds, and blood was rushing into her head. She wouldn't be able to stay conscious long. Squirming to her left and right, she suddenly realized she was with him inside his shiny orange shield.

Elise did the only thing she could think of: she lifted her arm and shot him in the face. Either he was overconfident in his abilities or didn't realize she had bands hidden under her long sleeves. Regardless, he wasn't ready for the attack and took a blast in the face. Unfortunately, even at point-blank range, her aim sucked.

Elise thought she had pointed the beam at Shizzu's nose, but either her aim hanging upside down was off or he had moved at the last possible second. The beam grazed him on the left side of his face, burning his cheek and left eye. Interestingly, his hair caught on fire as well.

Shizzu screamed and fell backward. He must have lost control of whatever it was holding her up. Elise wasn't prepared when she suddenly felt herself falling. It was at least a two-meter drop upside down onto concrete. She barely had time to brace herself with her arms and was only partially successful in protecting her head.

Elise groaned as she bounced off the floor. Everything went fuzzy and she struggled to stay conscious. She forced herself to keep moving, even if she didn't know which direction she was going. She crawled on all fours and tried to blink the hundreds of little stars away. She regained her senses just in time to see Shizzu run up and punt her midsection like a kick ball.

"You fucking bitch," he growled.

The blow knocked the wind out of her, and her body slid like a rag doll across the floor. Elise bit her lip and held the moan trying to escape her. She lifted her arm and fired at his general vicinity, but her vision was blurred from the tears.

She fired again, but this time, Shizzu's shield, an orange translucent glow, appeared and absorbed the beam. It didn't seem to faze him at all and he continued to advance. She shot three more times, twice hitting and each time having no effect on him.

"I'm going to rip you into pieces," he grunted. "Valta just wants you alive. No one said with arms and legs."

He flicked his finger and an invisible force pinned Elise's arm to the ground so she couldn't shoot at him anymore. She struggled against these unseen bonds, but it was hopeless. She watched as he approached, his orange shield glimmering and reflecting in the night.

"Maybe I should burn your face off too," he said, "I'll enjoy—"

A yellow streak slammed into Shizzu from behind, carrying him into Farming Tower Two, where he crashed with a thunderous crack into the building and down through several floors. Elise's bonds disappeared and she scrambled to her feet.

She saw James standing over a large hole with murderous rage on his face. He looked back at her and yelled, "Stay back." Then he jumped down into the hole. Yellow and orange bursts of light filled the air, followed by several more loud crashes.

As always with James's instructions, Elise ignored them and crawled to the hole and peered over the edge. She saw James and Shizzu locked in a strange fight. They stood in front of each other, neither moving an inch.

The aura of light around them danced, ebbing and flowing. She could see lines of yellow and orange streak back and forth, each time cut off and pushed back by other lines. Within seconds, she could see how the battle was progressing—James was losing. Every time his yellow lines pushed at Shizzu, the orange lines would cut him off and do the same. James would be able to repel them, but it seemed Shizzu's were getting closer to James than James's were to Shizzu.

The battle continued for another minute, their lights moving back and forth. Slowly, James lost ground, and at one point, one of the orange lines reached him and cut him on the thigh. He fell to one knee, and more and more of those orange lines grew closer to him.

"I wish I could help," she muttered under her breath, feeling powerless. "I need to—"

James screamed, his voice guttural and filled with pain.

His cries snapped her back to reality. Of course she could help. She cursed her stupidity in being hypnotized by the battle. She scrambled around the large opening until she was behind Shizzu. Knowing how bad her aim usually was, she wanted to make sure she didn't accidentally shoot James. Once she was sure she could make the shot, she aimed her wrist beam at Shizzu's back, gritted her teeth, and unloaded with everything she had.

With his shields already up, her wrist beam seemed to have little effect, but with nothing else she could do, Elise kept her aim on Shizzu's back and continued to blast away. She saw his orange shield flicker as it now tried to protect him on two fronts. Then she saw James's yellow field gain ground on him. Elise walked closer, shooting continuously. Shizzu tried to move out of the way, but James seemed to lock him in place with his yellow field. Soon, the orange shield around his body began to crack and disintegrate.

"This is for Nutris, you homicidal bastard!" Elise screamed as the beams blasting from her wrist finally penetrated Shizzu's shield.

FORTY-SEVEN

THE END

James checked his levels one last time: 14 percent. He powered down his AI band along with his atmos, cryo, jump, rad, even his comm band . . . They were now all off. He looked over at Elise, who was preoccupied with bandaging his bloody hand with a rag torn from her shirt. He especially wouldn't need the comm band anymore as long as she was close by.

"What a damn bloody mess." She grimaced, wrapping it up so many times his arm looked like a stump. "I'm surprised your fingers are still attached."

He held up his club hand and inspected her work. It was sloppy and would probably unravel in an hour, but it'd have to do. She was right, though; he was lucky not to have lost any fingers when Shizzu's coils pierced his exo. The burn was severe and he had almost lost consciousness. Well, it was either his hand or his heart. If it hadn't been for Elise beaming Shizzu full in the head, James wouldn't have made it.

She helped him to his feet and together, they limped toward the edge of the building. A stiff breeze hit him full-on, nearly sweeping him off his feet. With his atmos now off, he was taking the full brunt of nature.

James had channeled all his excess levels to his exo. He was going to need it. He looked at the ground seventy stories down. The random ticking of primitive gunfire and the lights of wrist beams still played out

below in small bunches. The Elfreth and their neighbors were still fighting, though they probably couldn't last much longer.

"We need to get out of here," he said in a low voice, looking up to the
sky, still dotted with the silhouettes of several collies hidden behind clouds.
"The ships patrolling the skies will prevent us from escaping by air, and
once the monitors clean up on the ground, they'll go looking for us."

Elise shook her head. "I'm not abandoning the tribe. We brought this
upon them. Besides, all my research is here."

James sighed. There was no dissuading her. Still, he had to try to make
her see reason. "We'll go get your things at the lab. Then we'll hide. That's
what the rest of the tribe should do as well. We can't fight ChronoCom.
We'll rebuild elsewhere."

She nodded and wrapped her arms around his waist.

James aimed for Farming Tower One and shot straight toward it, covering the diameter of the ring of buildings within a second. Time was of
the essence now. He had enough levels to make low-altitude jumps in between the buildings. They could head northwest and possibly lose Chrono-
Com in the wilderness. He had already mapped an escape route the
second night they stayed with the tribe. They could recover in the ruins
of Toronto and possibly rescue the survivors of the tribe in a few days.
That is, if the Elfreth even wanted their help.

Elise ran to the lab with James trailing close behind. She went to her
workstations, confusion and concern on her face. She ran to the other
side of the room and checked the shelves. She began to open cabinets and
drawers. "I don't understand," she gasped. "The notes I keep. I can't find
them."

James scanned the empty hallways, and then the rest of the lab. Something was wrong. She always kept a clean lab, and this place looked ransacked. "Where's Grace?" he asked.

Elise froze. "She was hiding here during the battle. I thought . . ." She
became even more frantic as she dashed to the adjacent room, calling for
Grace. She was nowhere in sight.

James waited for her, slumped across a table to rest his exhausted body.
He wouldn't show weakness to Elise, but he could barely stand. Killing
two auditors was unheard of, not to mention the dozens of monitors he
had cut through. If he wasn't the most wanted man in ChronoCom, he
would be soon. His job wasn't done yet, either. He had a feeling there

would be more killing before the night was over. Maybe even another auditor. He hoped not. If he ran into another chronman, let alone an auditor, the only death left tonight would be his.

James trailed after Elise as she continued to search the floor, using the walls or furniture for support to drag himself along. He looked over at the edge of the building and saw the Nazi soldier, his face half-hidden in the shadows, looking out the window. The boy glanced his way and grinned.

Someone has to keep watch. Who better than a ghost?

To his left, Grace and Sasha were sitting in chairs at his feet, playing some sort of game with their hands. James reached for his sister. He touched her hair and felt the strands run between his fingers. He began to shake, his eyes moistening as he felt the warmth in her cheeks. Sasha shrugged him away.

Stop poking me, James, she said. *I'm not a baby anymore.*

Isn't that the beautiful thing about being dead? Grace smiled. *Especially for children. They stay young and innocent forever.*

James's throat closed at those words and he shook his head. "No! It's not beautiful. There's nothing worse. They don't stay young, because it's not real. Once someone dies, they're gone forever." Except it wasn't true. James rubbed his temples trying to clear his mind. He didn't know what was real anymore.

"You know," a new voice cut across the dark room, "I would call you crazy if I hadn't seen you drunk before."

A figure appeared at the doorway with the translucent orange glow of an exo surrounding his body. James recognized the voice right away and moved toward the window. At his levels, there was no way he could fight Levin, not in this condition.

"Don't even try, James," Levin said. "You've escaped justice long enough. It's time to do the right thing."

James chuckled and shook his head. "You know, Levin, you are the one constant damn thing in this universe that will never change."

"Do it for the people below," Levin continued. "Give yourself up, give up that anomaly, and all those savages below guilty of harboring you will live. It's as simple as that; no more people need to die tonight."

Out of the corner of his eye, James saw Elise freeze in the adjacent room. She needed to run and hide. Escape. Anything but be here with him. He tried to gesture casually with his left hand, giving her the shooing motion, telling her to get as far away as possible. Instead, she held up her wrist beam and aimed it at Levin.

"You should leave," James spoke in a loud voice and shook his head emphatically. He meant those words for everyone within earshot. "Just go. Please."

"Civility?" Levin remarked. "This is a new side of you."

The two circled each other like predators. Well, one of them was a predator and the other a cornered prey who could barely stand. James had to keep Levin's back to Elise. Every second he bought here was one she could use to escape. He just prayed she got the hint.

He saw his three hallucinations off to his right stop what they were doing and watch the events in the room unfold. They were no longer jovial as their eyes stayed fixed on Levin. Little Sasha walked right up next to him and tugged on his arm.

"What are you looking at?" said Levin.

I don't like him at all, Sasha said, tugging again.

"Let's deal, Levin. Mistakes were made," said James, eyes focusing back on the auditor. "I'll concede that I've broken the Time Laws. I'll give myself up, but everyone around me is innocent. Let them go."

Levin chuckled with no trace of humor in his voice. "You don't get to negotiate, James. We're way past that. You need to hand over the woman as well."

"They were wrong," James said. "ChronoCom. The Vallis Bouvard Disaster. It's all a lie. There are no consequences for bringing someone back. I didn't hurt the chronostream. The time line wasn't affected."

"Irrelevant. You broke the most important Time Law."

"Don't you get it? We've lost. Look around you! In the hundred and fifty years since ChronoCom has been around, what have we accomplished? How have we saved humanity? Now, we have a real chance to fix things."

"You brought someone back from the past. There is nothing more forbidden."

"Listen, the scientist I brought from the past . . . she can help," pleaded James.

"You don't get to choose who to save and who to bring back!" roared Levin, fists clenched as he took several steps forward. "We don't make those decisions. You're not a god." He took a step forward. "Now, drop your bands and come with me."

James had to keep Levin talking as long as possible. Elise had to realize that it was now time to abandon him. As a last resort, he dropped his hands. "We both know I can't beat you."

"So unlink all your bands and surrender. Explain your case before a tribunal."

James sneaked a look to his left again. She was still there. Damn girl. Now he had little choice. "I won't," he said, resigned. He powered on his exo.

"Don't throw your life away like this." Levin's exo pulsated and expanded. "You won't stand a chance. I'm not Geneese or Shizzu."

"I have to." James gritted his teeth.

He charged, focusing his levels at a central point in Levin's shield. If James had to die for Elise to realize that it was time to abandon him, then so be it.

Or maybe James would get lucky. Perhaps Levin's exo was drained from the battle. His left arm was in a cast, after all. Maybe James had a chance. In any case, it was too late to second-guess his actions.

The first thing James noticed when his exo smashed into Levin's was that the auditor's exo was near full power. James's already wavering and weakened shield was a shade of the auditor's. He bounced off Levin's exo and crashed into the wall.

James picked himself up off the ground and felt a force smack him from the side, this time throwing him through the far wall. He got up and extended eight kinetic coils, the most his exo could create in its current state. He attacked, weaving his coils back and forth, through the ground, and in random waves designed to throw off defending chronmen.

Levin wasn't fooled in the slightest as he countered with sixteen of his own coils, tying up James's strands and striking him with the others. James felt his exo crack as he flew backward through a windowpane and fell off the side of the building. He closed his eyes and accepted his fate. He didn't have the levels to fly anymore. Falling to his death was as good a way to go as any.

Suddenly, he stopped in midair and was pulled back to where Levin was standing. "You don't escape justice that easily," he said, wrapping

James up and holding him captive. The bastard had even robbed him of a good death.

"Can you just cut it out with this talk of justice," James said, resigned. He snuck a peek at Elise's hiding place; the foolish girl hadn't moved. "Do you even know what your precious ChronoCom has done? We've been sold out, Levin. Our past is for sale to the highest bidder. This agency you cherish so much is just a figment of your imagination."

To his surprise, Levin pursed his lips and nodded. "I'm aware, and my decisions will have consequences that I will pay once I bring you in. However, whatever taint the agency now has in its heart, it doesn't change the right thing to do; in this case, it's to bring you in."

The auditor actually seemed remorseful, his usual stoic facade cracking as if he had his own demons to face. James grunted; he knew better. Levin wasn't the type of person to second-guess himself. However, the pain on his face was unmistakable. It was the same James had felt every day since Sasha had disappeared.

Then he realized: Levin knew about ChronoCom breaking the Time Laws. He knew that the agency he held in such high regard was nothing but a sham. It was eating him up inside, but he still obeyed their orders.

"You're a fucking hypocrite!" James spat.

Levin floated James close. "I assure you; I derive no pleasure from taking you in. We used to be friends, James, and I mourn that loss. You used to like my rigid morality."

"Yeah, until you stabbed our friend in the back."

"Obviously, you don't know what rigid means. No matter—"

Elise appeared just behind Levin's left shoulder, and though James shook his head to ward her away, she ignored him, quite unsurprisingly. She raised her arm and unloaded her wrist beam on the unsuspecting auditor. His exo flickered as it took a millisecond to compensate for her attack. It managed to block the brunt of the point-blank shot, but Levin's back took the rest of the blast. He stumbled forward and dropped to one knee.

James had one chance. He charged forward. An exo would automatically catch any of his coils but it wouldn't block flesh unless actively directed. Elise had forced his hand. He had to try. A raised knee caught the downed Levin straight in the chin, and then a downward punch cracked him on the side of the head.

Levin tumbled backward onto the ground, and James pounced. If he could knock Levin unconscious, they might have a chance. He threw himself into the air and slammed his fist toward the auditor's face. At the last second, Levin moved his head to the side and James hit nothing but cement. James followed up by collapsing his lead elbow and pressing it down on Levin's neck, trapping him in place. He cocked his free arm back and threw it with everything he had at the auditor's stationary head.

James roared as his fist hammered down and came to a stop a few centimeters from Levin's eyes. He struggled and pressed down, but an invisible force stopped the killing blow's momentum. James growled and squirmed, desperate to will it forward, knowing that small space between his fist and Levin could cost Elise her life. No matter how hard he tried, though, he couldn't move.

"No," he cried. He had been so close. Now, it wasn't only his life that was forfeited, but Elise's. His hands clawed at Levin's face as a kinetic coil lifted him off of Levin and floated him in the air. Then he was flying backward, and the room became a blur as he spun out of control. James smacked into a concrete wall and blacked out.

When he came to moments later, he was lying facedown, his body a mass of throbbing pain. He was groggy and his eyes couldn't focus, and black abyss, it hurt to breathe. He saw a blob across the room and blinked, trying to make out what was happening. A woman yelped and that snapped James back to reality.

Elise was floating in midair, her body stiff and her arms close to her sides. She looked terrified as Levin spoke to her in a soft voice.

The image of them so close together terrified James. What was he doing to her? Was she still alive? Was he as helpless to watch her die as he had been with his mother and all those victims from his jumps? Was James about to lose Elise like he had lost Sasha?

"No," he moaned. "Leave her alone, you fucking bastard."

James tried to get up but felt his knees buckle. He pawed at the ground and inched his way closer, first getting back to his knees, and then unsteadily to his feet. His hands, still dragging along the floor, found a slab of rock; it would have to do. He picked it up, held it over his head, and charged in one last moment of defiance. Who knew? He got close last time. Maybe he might get lucky once more.

It didn't happen. Levin stuck one hand out behind him and the rock dropped on James. It rose in the air another two meters and planted itself between the two men. When James lunged for Levin again, the rock smacked him one more time. Blinded with pain, James tried to stumble forward. The rock continued to pummel him on the head every time he tried to move closer to Levin. Finally, dizzy, James felt his knees gave way, and he fell on all fours.

Levin turned around, shaking his head. "Stay down, James, damn it. I don't want to kill you, but I will."

When James tried to get back onto his wobbly legs, Levin shook his head. "You really do never learn, do you?" He flicked his finger and the rock shattered over James's crown. He collapsed for the last time, his face bloody.

"It's over." Levin said, wiping the blood from his own mouth. He sounded angry, one of the few times James could remember him this way. "You don't know what you've cost me with this fool's errand. It would be in my right to rip out your throat now, but it would be a mercy to spare you the trial and a lifetime on a penal colony. As for this anomaly"—he looked over at Elise—"I won't give Valta the satisfaction of their victory either." Levin raised his hand at her. "I'm sorry. It's not your fault. This should have never happened." His hands glowed orange.

"Nooo!" cried James, his fingers stretching toward her, his mouth no longer able to enunciate the words as the blood congealed in his mouth.

He couldn't quite focus on anything he looked at. Raising his head hurt as he looked for the only thing that mattered. He found her on the other side of the room, still floating in the air, caught in Levin's kinetic coils. Their eyes met, she nodded encouragingly, and for the third time since he was a child, tears ran down his face.

"Stop this immediately!" Grace's strong voice thundered over the howling wind outside. All eyes turned toward where she stood in the doorway, hugging a stack of papers to her chest. She must have been hiding, because she was covered in dust. Her face was smudged, and her hair was mussed and unkempt. There was no mistaking who she was, though. Grace still carried herself as if attending her own coronation.

Levin shot his other hand out at the new voice, another orange killing blow ready to strike. Then he stopped. His mouth fell open and he backed away. "It can't be."

"Put your toy down, you jackass, before you hurt someone." She slammed the stack on the floor and walked across the room to stand between Levin and Elise. When he didn't comply, she put her hands on her waist. "By the fish-eyed look on your face, you know who I am then, right? I don't have to introduce myself to you?"

He nodded.

"Good. Hate wasting my time." Grace pointed at the floating Elise. "Now put her down."

When Levin still didn't move or release Elise from his exo, she jabbed his chest with as much strength as a ninety-three-old woman had. She must have been quite strong, because he stumbled backward and fell onto his butt. "You can't be here," he mumbled, stunned. He shot James a furious scowl. "You sacrilegious shit. You brought back the Mother of Time."

"Don't talk about me when I'm in the room," she snapped. "Listen, boy, we've been doing this all wrong. It's time to make a change."

"You can't be here," he mumbled. "The past is already . . ."

"Stop saying that." Grace pointed at James. "That lug over there's been trying to convince me of that for weeks."

Levin looked confused. "I've spent my life following the Time Laws. The chronostream has been kept whole. The Time Laws forbid—"

Grace threw her hands in the air. "Those space-forsaken Time Laws. What a mistake it was for me to make that shit up. How was I supposed to know there'd be a goddamn religion built around me? Obviously, I'm a lot more brilliant than I give myself credit for," she mused. She softened a bit and put a hand on his shoulder. "What's your name?"

"Levin Javier-Oberon, Mother of Time."

"Call me Grace. That title is so clunky. Tell me, Levin, do you know why I invented time traveling?"

"To save humanity."

"Yes, but it's not working, is it? Do you know why?"

Levin shook his head.

"I was shortsighted, using the Technology Isolationists' situation as a template. My entire faction was always resource starved, so I created the agency to fill that need. I was wrong. That's not what humanity really needs."

"I don't understand," said Levin.

"We keep trying to stem the bleeding, plugging holes and patching the cracks. No matter what we've tried, things got worse. Every successive generation only looked at what was in front of their nose without seeing the big picture. The Technology Isolationists were guilty of this then, as is ChronoCom now. We've never examined the root of our problems. One day, and that day seems to be approaching, no amount of mending will work. Humanity will be beyond repair and our fire will burn out."

Levin bowed his head. "All we can do is fight against the inevitable."

"Perhaps, or perhaps it's time we fix what's broken." Grace pulled him to his feet and led him by the hand toward Elise's lab. "Come, I know just the place to start. Help me pick up these papers, dear. They're quite important. Now, have you ever heard of this old Earth saying about teaching a man to fish?"

FORTY-EIGHT

AFTERMATH

James stood at the edge of the building overlooking the other six Farming Towers. He pointed down at the ground where the fighting had continued well into the night. "Stop the massacre." He looked up at Levin. "Only you can do it."

Levin closed his eyes and spoke in a clear voice. "This is High Auditor Levin Javier-Oberon, steward of Earth. All forces pull out immediately. Release all prisoners. We're going home."

The sound of fighting immediately ceased, and James could see groups of monitors stopping their advance and beginning to emerge from the towers and underground tunnels.

"Thank you, Levin. You're doing the right thing," James said.

"Being civil again? It suits you, James. You should try it more often." Levin stepped off the building and floated in midair. He turned around to face James, Elise, and Grace. "Need a ride down?"

A few minutes later, the small group, now on the ground, watched as teams of monitors, many of them looking worse for the wear, most injured to one degree or another, stepped onto the waiting collies. Several of them had to be floated out on stretchers.

The so-called savages had bloodied ChronoCom's nose and given as good as they got. James swelled with pride as he watched his former colleagues retreat. The overmatched Elfreth had accounted for themselves admirably against a vastly superior force.

Several of the monitors glared at him as they walked by. He heard mutterings of "traitor" and threats of retribution, but James didn't care. These weren't his people anymore. In truth, they never really were. Joining ChronoCom had always been a matter of survival, a way to escape Mnemosyne Station. Now, he was escaping ChronoCom by joining the Elfreth. He looked over at Elise. The difference this time around was that he wanted to be with the Elfreth and that there was something here he believed in. Maybe it was the same way with her.

"Quit looking at me like that," she said, slipping a hand into his. "You're making me nervous."

The three of them watched until a lone collie hovered in the air, waiting for its last passenger. "There's one more thing you should know," Levin said. "Handler Smitt was discovered hacking into the chron database and stealing miasma pills. I assume they were for you?"

James nodded. "When will he go to trial? Is there anything you can do for him?"

Levin paused, regret hanging across his face. "The Valta operative Kuo got her hands on him. I failed him. I'm sorry. Smitt was mining information on your Nutris job. There was classified Valta Corp data on it. Look to Iapetus; Smitt died for that information. I pray what's there is worth his sacrifice."

The pain James felt right then was worse than anything else he had suffered that night. If it wasn't for Elise holding him up, he might have collapsed. His hands shook as he fought to stay upright. Elise, looking worried, wrapped her arm around his waist and squeezed tightly. Before Levin could take off, James called out to him, "You sacrificed a lot tonight. I know; I won't forget."

"Just succeed," Levin replied, "and it won't matter."

James knew that he would probably never see him again. Maybe it was finally time to bury the hatchet. He put his left hand on the auditor's shoulder and held out his right. "Look, all these years. About Landon. I held the grudge for way too long. I forgive you."

Levin turned and stared at the extended hand, and then at his face. "Fuck you, James." Then Levin Javier-Oberon flew up to the waiting collie and disappeared into the night sky. The three of them stood there and watched the sky long after the last of the ships had disappeared.

"What did you mean by 'sacrificed'?" Elise asked.

Grace exchanged a knowing look with James. "Come, there's been enough death today. Let's find the living."

The three of them ventured deep into the tunnels, searching for signs of the Elfreth in hiding, checking several of the known spots to little avail. It wasn't until an hour later, as they wandered through an abandoned subway tunnel, that they made contact. Two guards, perched in a hidden alcove above a passageway, hailed them.

Minutes later, half a dozen more guards approached, and James noted that all the weapons were leveled at him. So much for all the trust he had built up over the past few months. Not that he blamed them. These people had been living in relative peace until he and Elise came along and brought a war to their doorsteps. Who knew how many of their people were dead? He corrected himself. Now they were his people too. He owed them his complete loyalty after tonight.

The group led him down through twists and underground intersections, through hidden holes, abandoned buildings, once wading chest-deep through a submerged facility.

They were all exhausted by the time they reached the survivors holed up in a long cavernous underground train station. The entire camp was one large triage, with dozens of the injured and dying lying in neat rows. The air smelled of oil, sweat, and death. Random cries and groans, and the occasional wail, pierced the air. Still, it was very organized. On the left side of the entrance, James saw children, some as young as ten, working in teams of three or four, dragging the bodies of the dead to a crevice and rolling them in. Sadly, there was no other way to take care of the dead.

To their right, a pile of supplies was hastily stacked in the corner. One of the surviving Old Ones kept watch over it and doled out what little the Elfreth had to those who needed it. Again, it was the children who took the brunt of the heavy lifting. It didn't take James more than a glance to know that most of them were going hungry tonight. If that small stockpile was all that they had left, all of them would probably be dead within a few months.

James walked past the makeshift hospital, looking down at the rows of the injured lying on blankets, some bleeding badly, others with broken limbs, and more than a few near death. The attack had been brutal. He had been in enough battles to recognize the extent of the injuries. More than half of the people lying here wouldn't survive the night.

His eyes strayed to find Rima frantically trying to bandage a woman with her sides gashed open. James recognized it as a kinetic coil wound. The woman coughed, blood pouring out of her mouth and her seeping wounds. The girl grabbed another spool of precious gauze and wrapped it around her waist even tighter. Moments later, the eyes of the woman rolled up in her head, and she stopped moving.

Sobbing, Rima moved on to the next body. He realized then that these people had no idea what they were doing. Any trained medic would have recognized that the woman could not be saved. Rima had wasted precious supplies on a lost cause. Supplies these people didn't have much of.

James looked around the room. There were five elderly tribespeople standing around, trying to keep the people organized, and approximately ten children younger than fifteen. Most of the able-bodied were dead or injured. The elderly were too few and slow to control the people while the young were clueless. There was no one in charge. Where were Qawol and Franwil?

They saw Chawr lying against the far wall, an ugly red gash running from the side of his face down to his waist. He held his right arm with his left as a little boy tended to him. His face, contorted in pain, brightened when he saw them. He waved. "Elder Elise, I told you no one could kill Chawr." He grimaced when the boy tried to set his broken arm.

Elise ran and embraced the young man, her eyes wet. She returned a few moments later, seemingly overwhelmed by the sight of so many injured people laid out in lines along the floor. She closed her eyes and gathered herself. She took a deep breath and knelt down next to Rima to tend to one of the injured near the center of the cavern. She looked up at James to let him know that she was going to remain there. James let her be and moved further down the tunnel, stepping over the rows of bodies that filled the room.

Grace leaned into James. "This place is so disorganized. It's the headless leading the dumb out here." She tapped one of the children on the head and spoke in the Elfreth's language. "Excuse me, child, where is Oldest Qawol?"

The child's face fell and she looked away at the small crowd gathered around a body nearby. There, Qawol lay bloodied, taking in short quick breaths as he struggled to speak. His long gray hair was singed off and half of his body was badly burned. James's first thought was that the towels and manpower being spent on Qawol could be better spent on the rest of the injured who might have a chance to survive. A small group of natives huddled around Qawol, holding vigil as they continued to place wet towels over him.

He saw Sammuia among them, clinging to Qawol's hand. At least the boy was alive. Elise had taken a liking to him. She would be devastated if he had died. James immediately felt ashamed, as he realized that he valued the boy above any of these other injured and dead because of selfish reasons. His thoughts wandered to Smitt and how no one else grieved for him. His friend had followed him and paid the price for his loyalty. There was a lot he had to make right here. James closed his eyes and took a deep breath. He collected his thoughts and made a silent vow. The world needed a better James Griffin-Mars, and he intended to give it to them.

"What happened?" he asked in a low voice.

"The Oldest wouldn't leave the field," one of those keeping vigil said, her voice bitter. "Insisted on being one of the last to retreat into the buildings. An explosion nearby threw him across the commons."

"Old fool," James muttered. "You're the leader of your people. Their general. You shouldn't be putting yourself in harm's way."

James knew there was more to it than that, though. Qawol was not only their leader, he was their symbol. He kept the Elfreth together by standing alongside them. Being on the front was the only way he knew how to lead.

The tough old man held on until dawn, and then he passed away, with nothing more than the stilling of his shallow breathing marking his passage. Some of the natives had hoped he would wake at least once more, perhaps to name a successor or just to say good-bye. The old man had been with them longer than anyone alive could remember. And now he was gone, and the entire encampment fell into a deep sorrow.

James found Elise grieving alone in the corner, sobbing with her face in her hands. He watched her quivering body, once more unsure of what to do. He had seen this pain only once before, in Sasha when their mother had died. His little sister had been inconsolable for a week, unable to eat or sleep. James had cried the first night with her, and then he had told himself he had to be strong for them both. That was the last time he had let his guard down like that. Until this year, when he finally cracked.

He went to console as he could. She grabbed his hands and cried into his palms, soaking them with her tears. Together, they stayed in the corner, leaving the rest of the tribe to their private grief for their fallen leader. Eventually, Elise fell asleep, still leaning on him, her hands still wrapped around his.

Franwil came to see them later that night. The old woman's eyes were red with grief, but she looked calm and strong as she spoke. "Today was a day of many sacrifices. Oldest has fallen and most of the strong are dead or too injured to lead. You were the ones who gave us hope and you were the ones who brought this down upon us. It is up to you to fix this."

James frowned. Did she just ask him to lead them? He was ready for them to direct their anger at him, possibly expel him and Elise from the tribe, but this was a turn of events that he never anticipated. He couldn't lead these people. Black abyss, he'd been about to suggest to Elise that they consider going off on their own.

He stood up and addressed the group. "Look, I'm sorry this has happened, and I'm honored that——"

"Not you, Chronman," she cut in. "You still have not earned my trust. I speak to her." Franwil pointed at Elise.

Elise gave a start. "What? You have to be kidding."

Franwil nodded. "No one will follow the chronman, and the rest of the Old Ones are too weary. The strong ones too few. All we cling to now is that dream you fed us. We wait for the day when you can cure the land, so it is only fitting you show us the way."

Elise looked at James, stark panic in her eyes. "James, say something. Tell her what an awful idea this is!"

It was a terrible idea. There could be no one less qualified to lead a wasteland tribe than someone from the past who had never experienced the cruelty of this world. Elise, however, had something none of them had. Goals. Optimism. Hope. Those were traits that had been long drained out of the people who lived in the present. They were the rarest commodities in this century, resources not easily gotten. Maybe it was what they needed. Franwil saw that.

"I don't know anything about surviving out there," Elise said.

Franwil smiled. "Many of the Elfreth have that knowledge. That will not be why you lead."

"She will have help," James added. "From you. From myself. All of the Elfreth."

"A good Oldest knows when to dip into another's well of wisdom. She will have many to drink from." Franwil looked to him. He nodded. For the first time since he had arrived in Boston, an understanding passed between them. "It is settled. The first thing that must be done is to find a new home for the Elfreth. I have suggestions, Oldest Elise." She smiled when she said those words.

James looked over at the Nazi soldier, Sasha, and Grace sitting over to the side. They waved. This time, he waved back. He turned to Elise. "I agree. I'll need to locate another collie and then I can start scouting for a new home. I saw some of the monitors' wrecks. Maybe we can salvage one or two of them. Once I have wings, I can make a few jumps back to get the supplies we sorely need."

"No, you won't, James," the real Grace said, walking toward him. "I tracked your life signs over the past several jumps. Your body can't take it anymore. I give you a sixty percent chance of surviving one more jump, and a twenty-five percent chance of surviving two. You're on the edge of a massive stroke every time you go back, and it's been getting progressively worse. Your time-traveling days are over."

"I have no choice," he said. "We Elfreth need my salvaging more than ever."

Franwil's face took on a perplexed but curious look when he said those words. She nodded in approval and the ends of her lips curled slightly upward.

Grace turned to Elise. "Talk sense into the idiot."

Elise looked surprised, then worried. "Grace is right. I didn't realize. We'll find another way."

Stunned and speechless, James just stood there. In a way, this was what he'd always wanted. To stop being a chronman and not have to face the tragedies of the past. However, this was the one time he wanted to travel back in time. He finally had a cause worth fighting for, with people who were important to him.

Something else occurred to him.

He turned to Grace. "I can only survive one more jump?"

"Sixty percent isn't exactly odds I'd gamble with."

James nodded. "I can live with that. There's one more jump I have to do. I don't care about the odds of survival. It's worth the risk."

FORTY-NINE

CONSEQUENCES

The tribunal was a spectacle, a scandal that spread across the entire solar system like Academy gossip. Every senior of the chain made the trip to Earth to see his shame. Levin thought he could keep his dignity intact as the day progressed, but it was hard. Rumors became gossip; gossip became facts; facts became accusations. By the time he was brought up on charges, Levin had all but committed genocide against the human race and destroyed the entire chronostream. It was all he could do to keep his back straight and not wither from the onslaught of blame and judgment being piled upon him.

Thank the abyss the tribunal was mercifully short. There was no reason for it to have wasted anyone else's time and gone any longer than the three hours it did for the entire leadership of ChronoCom to find Levin Javier-Oberon guilty on all charges. After all, he had pled guilty to every single one and offered no defense for the crimes of not upholding the Time Laws, of willingly letting a known fugitive escape, of attacking a valued Valta operative ally, and of high treason. That last stung Levin the most, but he kept his head held high and face stoic as the charges were read.

To his left, the vids broadcasted his shame, as billions tuned in to the entertaining reality drama of a high auditor's fall from grace. High Director Jerome, the head of ChronoCom, personally recited his crimes and continued at length for all the universe about the stain Levin had caused on the agency's honor and how every other member of ChronoCom would have to bear the weight of his shame.

To his right, Kuo, along with an entire delegation of Valta suits, smirked as the light shone onto his humiliation. Levin had to admit; her presence there hurt him as well. He could feel her smugness all the way from the center of the room. At the very least, she had a broken leg for all his efforts, thanks in large part to the many monitors who had stood with him that day at Central.

They were the one thing Levin defended in this trial: his people. He passionately argued for leniency for all the monitors who had saved him from Kuo, citing their loyalty to the agency and his direct command as the cause for their attacking this so-called valued ally. He had ordered all those monitors not to counter his false claim. In this case, the little white lie saved dozens of them from the fate he was about to endure. In the end, his sentence was the same as that of many before him.

"At least I'll get to see Cole one more time," he muttered as his life sentence of labor until death on Nereid was pronounced. He wondered if Cole would be glad to see him, or whether he would stab him in the back while he wasn't looking. What surprised and stung him a little more was when Jerome announced that his name would be stricken from the Watcher's Board and from all ChronoCom records. He would effectively never have existed. To be cast off from the tiers . . . that broke Levin's stoic facade, his iron will shattering. He had earned the right to be on that board. It shouldn't have been something they could take away.

Yet, Levin had no regrets about his decision. If what the Mother of Time had said was true, then Levin embraced this fate gladly. He looked out the large dusty windows where the gray winds swirled, continually layering more grime on the glass until the view was nothing more than dark shadows passing by. If what she had said really was true, then why not? One life was a small price to pay. He just hoped that James and the girl came through with their promise.

"Do you understand your charges and sentence, Levin Javier-Oberon?" Jerome said as the trial wrapped up.

Levin tore his gaze from the window and addressed the court in a clear voice. "I do, Director."

"Do you have any final words before it is carried out?"

Levin looked over at Kuo, her eyes glinting in the light. She was dar-

ing him to break, to show that he had lost his faith. In the end, he supposed he had, at least with this current iteration of the agency he had
grown to admire and then come to loathe. But then again, he had learned
something new as well, and though he was powerless from this point on
to see it through, he'd like to think that he, Auditor Levin Javier-Oberon,
ninth of the chain, had played a small part in saving humanity. No one
here could take that away from him.

"I do not, Director," he said.

Kuo, Jerome, and Young stood with hundreds of others at the launch pad
and watched as the transport disappeared into the night sky as it began
its journey to the penal colony on Nereid. Kuo sent a signal through her
AI chip to the rest of her team. The effect should be dramatic, after all.

"Bad business." Jerome sighed, looking at Young. "Watch the men
closely over the next few months. Morale will be low; keep them in line."
He turned to Kuo. "I trust the results are satisfactory for our allies at
Valta?"

She nodded. "Valta feels that this is the only way justice could have
been served, and we are satisfied that the proper sentencing has been
handed down. I'd also like to convey a message from our board that
your request for a space station at the Ship Graveyard has been accepted,
and Valta will gladly finance its construction."

"Valta's generosity is legendary, Securitate," Jerome said, heading back
into Central. "Very well then. The media will have a field day with this, and
then it'll blow over next month when something equally loud and stupid
happens."

"There's one more thing," Kuo remarked, remaining in place.

Both Jerome and Young turned back to face her.

"We still have the matter of the Nutris scientist at large. You still have
a problem while this temporal anomaly is free, and we still expect to receive what we paid handsomely for."

"We will mount another operation once this blows over," Young said.

Kuo shook her head. "No, we tried it ChronoCom's way first. Now,
Valta is going to do it our way."

Behind her, a row of parked Hephaestus transports opened their bay
doors and disgorged their cargo. A squad of six securitates and sixty Valta

shock troops marched down the ramp, joined a few seconds later by four combat mechanoids. Kuo looked on in approval as her task force saluted in unison.

She turned to Jerome and Young. "I also have a squadron of Valkyries en route. They will be here within the week. We'll accomplish the mission correctly this time. Clear residences and hangar space for my forces. I expect all your resources at my disposal beginning right now."

EPILOGUE

Sasha Griffin-Mars woke to the distant banging of pipes. She hated them. They always came on when she tried to sleep. She crept out of the small cubbyhole where she and her brother made their home. Home base, it was called. A place to run to when playing tag from the bad people who roamed the big space station.

She was hungry and thirsty. Well, she was always hungry. She couldn't remember the last time she wasn't. That couldn't be helped. She could quench her thirst, though. The dispenser was just down the hall. She wasn't supposed to go off on her own, but James was tired. He had come back from playing tag late last night, bringing home a little piece of bread and three fruits he had found at the market. He gave her the fruit because he hated it, he said. She was more than happy to take it from him. James was funny not to like fruit. It was so delicious. In fact, he was funny not to like food of any sort. Sasha was more than happy to take it all off his hands.

She crawled out of the cubbyhole and stretched her thin arms and legs. She should wake James up to take her to the water dispenser, but he was tired. He needed to go play more tag tonight, so she let him sleep. She had sneaked out for water many times anyway. She was nine years old, after all, big enough to take care of herself. Soon, she would be able to play tag with James.

Sasha looked down both sides of the hall and moved toward the dispenser, her bare feet moving nimbly along the metal grating. There was a heavy stench of refuse in the air, but she didn't think anything of it. Everything smelled like this on Mnemosyne Station.. Besides, she couldn't remember life before here.

Her faint memories of Momma were barely more than faded little sketches that she couldn't quite make out. Momma had pretty hair, and she was tall. Momma was also very sad. Then momma was gone. Sasha remembered crying when she was gone. That was all. She remembered nothing except for coming to Mnemosyne Station and being hungry. Always hungry.

There was the dispenser. Sasha grinned. She was very quiet and sneaky. Soon, she was going to play tag with James and then he wouldn't have to leave her for so long every day. She reached the corner of the station and peeked around the edge. There was no one there. James said it was very important that no one was around. Don't trust anyone but him, he said. They could all be bad.

She pulled the chain and waited as the pipe near the ceiling rattled and then the metal tube with the many holes began to leak water. It drizzled on Sasha's face and she opened her mouth as the water splashed down. The pipe made more banging sounds as it shuddered, the water coming down, then stopping, and then coming down again. She closed her eyes and drank her fill.

When she finished, she turned to sneak back again, but saw two big men blocking her way. She jumped back and squeaked, freezing. Her eyes darted for a cubbyhole to run into.

"Hello, little girl," one of the men said. "What are you doing out and about by yourself?"

"Out for a drink," she mumbled, looking down at the floor and twisting her toe to the grating.

"Where's your momma?" the other asked.

"Gone," she said.

"Aw, poor girl has no family," the first said. "Do you have any brothers and sisters?"

Sasha shook her head. "My brother is with me."

"I have a daughter," he said. "Would you like to meet her, girlie?"

"My brother says I shouldn't talk to people who don't know my name."

"Well, why don't you tell us your name then," the second one said. "Then we'll all be friends."

"I have to go." Sasha tried to walk in between them down the hall. Maybe they'd just let her go and pretend she wasn't here.

The second one blocked her path with his beefy arm and put his hand on her shoulder. "Can't let you go off on your own, girl," he said. "Why don't you come with us? You can meet some girls your age."

Sasha tried to wriggle away, but the man's grip tightened. She tried to cry out, but he put his other hand over her mouth.

"Now, now," he cooed. "Let's just take it easy. This won't last too long, knowing Pael over there. I might be a little longer."

"Hey, fuck you, Bach," the first replied.

The one known as Bach grinned. "Come on. This one likes to squirm. Go up front and watch the path for the guards."

There was a yellow flash of light and Sasha didn't know what happened, just that the man with the smelly hand covering her mouth suddenly flew through the air and slammed into the wall. The other man, mouth open and eyes wide, was staring at something behind her. He tried to take off in the opposite direction.

He fell forward and then started sliding toward her. He screamed as he clawed at the grating, his legs and hands flailing. He flipped over onto his back and began to blubber for mercy. Something covered Sasha's mouth and eyes so she couldn't see anything. There was a loud thunk and then everything became quiet.

The veil lifted over her eyes and she saw both men lying at her feet.

"Are they dead?" she asked, her body trembling.

"No," a voice behind her replied. "Only sleeping. They will wake soon enough with very bad headaches."

Sasha turned to see a glowing man standing next to her, sort of like one of those old pictures that Momma used to bow and make wishes to. Sasha remembered asking Momma what she was doing. Momma said she was praying to Yahweh to take them away from this place. Sasha had spent many days praying like Momma did when she and James first came to Mnemosyne Station a little over a year ago, but no one ever took them away. She hated it here. The Yahweh never came. Or maybe he was just late. She looked down at the floor and twisted her big toe back and forth on the metal grating, shyly sneaking a peek up at the man. He was so bright. Most of the station was always so scary-dark.

The man knelt in front of her and extended his hands palms up. "Hello, Sasha," he said in a soothing voice.

"You know my name," she whispered, her heart welling in her chest. No one on the station knew her name except for James.

The glowing man nodded, his voice cracking. He must be sick, because he was sniffling. "I know a lot about you. I've been missing you for a long time. Will you take my hand? I want to take you away to a better place."

Sasha hesitated. This man seemed nice, and he kind of looked like that man in Momma's picture that she liked to look at a lot. James liked to stare at that picture now. "Are you my papa?" she asked.

The glowing man smiled. "No, I'm not. No one can replace your father. I miss him, too."

Sasha looked at the bodies of the two bad men who had tried to take her, and then back at the glowing man. He knew her name, and he had saved her from these bad men. The glowing man couldn't be bad then.

She took his hand. The yellow glow seemed to wrap around her, tickling her nose and skin, and she felt all warm. She hadn't felt this nice since Momma was around. The hallway around her began to light up and everything in sight turned yellow. Just before everything became too bright, Sasha saw James run to the far end of the hallway, screaming her name over and over again.

"I'm here!" she yelled, extending her hand toward him. "James!"

Then her stomach felt funny and everything went dark.

Turn the page for a sneak peek
at Wesley Chu's next novel

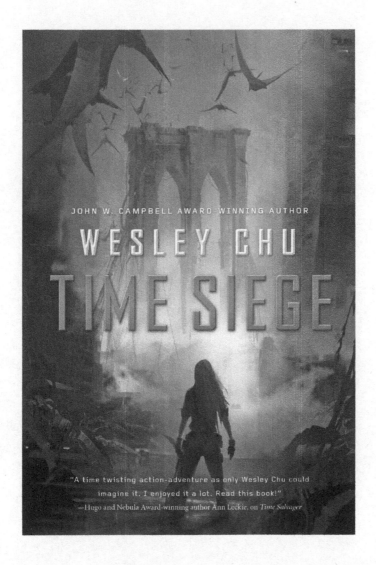

JOHN W. CAMPBELL AWARD-WINNING AUTHOR

WESLEY CHU

TIME SIEGE

"A time twisting action-adventure as only Wesley Chu could
imagine it. I enjoyed it a lot. Read this book!"
—Hugo and Nebula Award-winning author Ann Leckie, on *Time Salvager*

Available July 2016

Roman struggled to keep his footing in the ankle-deep slog of the muddy riverbank. The tainted water, mixed with rubble, dirt, and debris, had been accumulating broken bits of the ruined city for centuries. The resulting mixture was a slow-moving speckled brown mush that folded over itself repeatedly as it flowed down the steep slope.

He slipped on a metal plate embedded in the goo and fell onto his belly, sliding several meters and losing whatever small progress he had made climbing up the hill. He spat out a mouthful of the gunk and cursed as a mushy tide swelled, rolling over and caking him in its grime.

Black abyss, he was going to smell like shit until his next shower. Unfortunately, his next hygiene maintenance wasn't scheduled until the morning after tomorrow. That meant he was going to stink like a latrine until then. Probably meant he was going to have to rack outside of quarters tonight as well.

Someone above him laughed. "Chaki, you bunking with Roman right? Have fun."

Chaki's face appeared at the top of the hill as Roman tried to reclaim his footing. "Damn clumsy fodder. Stop playing in the mud. The collie's here."

Roman looked at the green metal plate that precipitated his fall and scowled. There were some letters on it in an archaic form of solar

English. He wiped the gunk off with his sleeve and read it slowly: New London.

"Are we on the right continent?" he asked in a loud voice. "I thought we're on one of the Americas."

"What kind of a stupid question is that?" Renee called down.

"I don't know," Roman said. "This is my first tour on this planet. I just thought London was a city in Europe. Or was that Africa?"

Overhead, a gray box-shaped ship struggled to fly around the many obstructions to their position. On top of the hill, fallen poles, loose wires, hanging vines, and building fragments jutting up and out were scattered all over the landscape, often making it difficult for the collies—already known for their lack of maneuverability—to reach their landing zones.

They were near a river mouth, and the soft ground had sunk so much that many of the buildings on both sides of the river leaned in over the water until they formed a triangular roof over it. Several of these buildings looked ready to collapse and probably wouldn't stand much longer.

"Why is our extraction point always on top of hills," Roman grumbled. "Why can't it just come down to us for once?"

He renewed his efforts, using his hands to claw his way up. His arms sunk elbow-deep into the muck, getting even more of this shit onto his now completely filthy uniform. Not that it mattered anymore; he couldn't get any dirtier.

Roman and the other half-dozen jackasses with him were just finishing an eight-hour patrol of a region southwest of the city of Boston. Surveillance had picked up movement from what could possibly be the wastelander tribe they have been searching for over the past six months, and of course, his was the unlucky squad sent here to investigate.

The Cooperative Forces, or Co-op, was created after the failed attack on Boston to retrieve the temporal anomaly to fulfill the agency's contractual obligation to the megacorporation. It was supposed to be a joint operation by both Valta and ChronoCom.

However, those Valta assholes—their leader Securitate Kuo specifically—did not seem to know what "joint" meant. Almost all the heavy lifting was carried out by ChronoCom monitors while Valta's troopers just sat on their collective asses all day. Kuo had even had the audacity to tell the lead monitors to their faces that the Valta troopers were too valuable to waste. Black abyss, everyone in the agency hated that woman.

Ever since they cleared out all of Boston and realized that the savages had fled, the patrols had had to expand their search perimeters to include the areas surrounding the city. Now, Co-op troops were forced to blindly chase the hundreds of random energy signatures that popped up in the hopes that one of them was the tribe of savages they were after.

Roman finally reached the top of the hill and was helped to his feet by Renee and Caud. Chronman Mong sniffed him irritably as he continued to eye the collie making its way to their position. "Next time, be more careful, you fool. If the collie pilot insists we clean his ship, you're the fodder doing it, you hear?"

"Easy for you," Roman muttered. "Not every asshole gets exos to fly around."

Roman wouldn't dare say that aloud. Mong was a Tier-5, fresh out of the Academy, and like most chronmen, thought he was a big deal. If Roman had to guess, the guy was probably nineteen years old. Definitely green and inexperienced, but already as arrogant as a Tier-3. Still, even the lowest chronman outranked the most experienced monitor.

The squad brushed themselves off and waited as the collie lowered itself to the ground. Fortunately, this patrol had been uneventful, though part of him wished the damn savages would just show up so they could end this hellish mission working under those corporate Valta assholes.

"I can't wait to get transferred off-planet," he said under his breath. "I didn't sign up to escape from the hell hole on Naiaid to end up in an even worse shit hole on Earth."

A couple of the monitors next to him chuckled in agreement. Mong just sniffed and continued staring at the collie. No doubt the kid probably felt insulted having to patrol with a bunch of monitors instead of running time salvages, which was what chronmen were supposed to do. The collie landed with a splat in the mud and the squad, exhausted and glad the day had ended without incident, made its way on board.

Mong looked Roman over and put his hand out. "Wipe yourself off first, damn it."

"Yes, Chronman." Roman sighed. "Just give me a . . ."

His voice trailed off as a dark flash arced up into the air. He squinted and raised an arm just in time for the object to thud into his shoulder, the impact knocking him on his back and once more into the mud. Roman groaned and stared in shock as a thick wooden shaft stuck out of his body. Another shaft sunk into the soft ground near his feet. He began to scream.

More spears rained down, bouncing off the collie's roof and sticking in the soft ground. There was a loud bang and Chaki fell, clutching at his leg. A blaster shot narrowly missed Renee. The rest of the squad scattered for cover, their wrist beams pointed outward at the ruins surrounding them.

A swarm of savages appeared, seemingly crawling out of every nook and cranny of the ruined buildings. They peppered Roman's squad with small arms fire, ranging from thick spears to primitive firearms to blaster rifles. Mong activated his exo and launched into the air. Most of the enemy attacks bounced ineffectually off his shield.

"Defensive positions around the collie," he roared. "Renee, get Roman. Gouti, suppression fire the building to the north."

Two kinetic coils appeared on both sides of Mong as if he had suddenly grown wings, and he barreled toward the main group of the charging savages head on. The coils cut the savages down as he swept through them, knocking a score of them off their feet. He changed direction and shot upward along the nearest building. Redirecting the coils into the opened windows, the chronman began to pluck savages out and drop them down into the streets below.

Roman whimpered as rough hands grabbed his injured shoulder and hauled him to his feet. "Come on," Renee said, dragging him toward the collie's opened hatch. A savage charged at them from the left, only to fall to her wrist beam. Another came from their right, which Roman was just able to hit before the savage could bury a hatchet into his face. More came from every direction, forcing Renee to drop him halfway to the ship so she could engage them.

Roman fell onto a knee and held his right arm with his left to steady his trembling body. His nerves screamed as he forced his arm up to aim with the wrist beam. He hit an old-looking savage in the chest and took out another that didn't even look old enough to shave. That last one came perilously close to sticking him with another spear. He watched, dismayed as the young savage fell at his feet.

An involuntary shudder coursed through his body. He had almost become dinner just now. At least that was the rumor among the monitors; these wasteland tribes were cannibals, and civilized people were a delicacy. He couldn't think of a worse way to go than roasting over a fire. He bet he tasted awful.

Gouti screamed at them from the collie's hatch. "Get your asses inside!"

Renee picked Roman up again and the two desperately tried to sprint to the collie. To his right, Baeth shot a charging savage point-blank in the stomach, then fell to a vicious club to the side of his face. Roman watched in horror as a savage woman towered over Baeth, ready to strike the killing blow. It never came. They must like their food alive when they cooked them. Those bastards. It was too late to help Baeth now. The rest of the team converged on the collie. Chaki was limping badly while Gouti desperately tried to provide covering fire.

Mong was still flying through the air, acting as a battering ram and launching his body at groups of savages, trying to keep them at bay to buy time for the rest of the squad. Roman, himself a failed initiate at the Academy, had often seen chronmen and auditors in battle. Mong wasn't one of the more skilled exo wielders, but he was getting the job done. Roman and Renee had almost fought their way to the waiting collie when it began to take off, jerking unsteadily into the air.

"We're not in yet!" Renee screamed, dropping Roman and sprinting toward the ship. It was too late. By the time she reached it, the collie was already five meters off the ground. Before it could speed away, something slammed into it, knocking it out of the air. It crashed to the ground on its side, almost crushing Renee and Roman as it slid down the slope. The two were just able to dive out of the way at the very last moment.

"Black abyss, no," Roman stared at a new figure floating in the air above him. It was the traitor, James Griffin-Mars. Before Roman could react, a coil wrapped around his feet, lifted him off the ground, and tossed him into the mud. Renee tried to flee down the hill but was pulled back and flung into the embankment next to him.

"Chronman," the traitor said, his voice echoing among the ruins. "Leave the Elfreth alone and face me."

When Mong, who was still busy tearing through scores of savages, didn't respond, the traitor shot forward in a streak of yellow and collided with the chronman. The two of them, exos flaring, slammed into the side of the hill, spewing mud and rocks into the air. A second later, they exploded out and crashed down at the bottom of the riverbank.

The men's coils were interlocked, but it wasn't difficult to tell who was winning. The traitor had the chronman wrapped in what looked like ten coils. Somehow, Mong was able to slip away and launch up into sky. Just as quickly, the traitor shot half a dozen coils after him. The chronman created four of his own coils to fend them off, but it was obvious the former Tier-1 was much more skilled than the Tier-5. The traitor's coils tied up Mong's coils, and then the remaining sank into his shield and dragged him back down to Earth. As much as Mong tried, he couldn't get away a second time.

"Go ahead, you abyss-plagued traitor," Mong spat. "Finish the job."

By this time, the rest of the savages—and they numbered in the dozens—had the monitors surrounded. Most of his squad was beaten up pretty badly. Baeth had suffered a concussion and was awake but woozy. Blood poured down Chaki's leg, and Roman still had this stinking spear sticking through his shoulder. Two of the savages were carrying an unconscious Renee up the embankment. The remaining monitors—Gouti and Caud—were being rounded up. A few seconds later, the pilot of the crashed collie was pulled out of the wreck and also joined the prisoners. Roman squeezed his eyes shut. This was when the savages would decide which one of them looked the most delicious.

Roman had been with ChronoCom for almost fifteen years, and nothing made the hair on the back of his neck stand up more than savagery, either from the pirates along the Ship Graveyard or the commies on Venus or these primitives here on Earth.

The traitor suspended Mong in the air. "Release your bands to me and I will spare you and your people."

"How about you go fuck yourself," Mong replied.

"Actually," Caud said. "That's not a bad trade."

The chronman shot him a glare. "Be quiet."

"Give him the stupid bands," Gouti said.

"Shut up, monitors," Mong snapped.

"Just give him the fucking bands!" Roman screamed.

The rest of the squad joined in with their pleas. Mong looked furious, but Roman didn't care. It was better to give up the stupid bands than become dinner. Chronman or not, this kid was risking their lives for no reason.

"Fine," Mong snarled. "You want the bands? Here you go."

He held his hands out, and with a snap, all his bands broke in two.

Roman's legs gave way and he collapsed to the ground. That fool. Now they were all going to be dinner. He felt his pants grow warm as he wet himself. This time, his body shook from fear instead of pain. He couldn't decide what was worse, being boiled alive or roasted over a fire.

He flirted with the idea of pulling the spear out of his body so he could bleed out. Roman gripped the shaft with his working arm and took a couple of deep breaths. He gritted his teeth and willed his arm to push the spear through his body. The stupid thing wouldn't budge; his arms felt like noodles. He tried once more, and again, his hands felt so weak, he could barely hold the shaft, let alone push it through his body.

Roman just couldn't do it. He was too frightened to kill himself. That was why he had failed to tier at the Academy. He was good enough, everyone said so. He had surprised his teachers by failing. And now his stupid cowardice was going to get him killed in the worst way possible. His frustration and the tension in his body built up, begging for a release. Roman's arms shook as he stared at his own blood sliding down the shaft and dripping onto the ground. He did the only thing he could think of at this very moment. He began to laugh. All eyes turned to him as Roman mixed his laughter with sobs.

Caud leaned in to him. "Pull yourself together."

"Please . . . please don't eat me," Roman sniffed loudly. "I'll taste terrible."

A buzz spread through the crowd of savages. It seemed a few of them understood what he said and translated to those who didn't. A chorus of laughter erupted. Several of the savages began rubbing their bellies. An apple bounced off his head. Even the traitor was masking a smile.

The traitor floated Mong to the rest of the squad and picked up the broken bands, examining them one by one. He sighed and tossed them to the ground. "You're making my life a lot harder than it has to be."

Mong stuck his chin out defiantly. "Just get it over with and kill us."

"Speak for yourself, "Gouti grumbled.

"If we had wanted you dead, you'd be dead," said James.

Roman looked over at the rest of his squad. He hadn't realized this at first, but it was true. All of them were alive, and it probably wasn't a coincidence. In fact, these savages took extra precautions, at the risk of their own lives, to not kill any of them. Why?

The traitor motioned to a group of savages standing nearby. "You have seven minutes. Get to work."

Roman watched open-mouthed as two dozen savages swarmed the collie, like burn ants over a corpse, and began to strip it bare. To his shock, they moved efficiently, as if they knew what they were doing. These were primitive savages. How could this be possible? However, within minutes, many of the collie's modules were dismantled. All that remained was its frame, engine, and structural components.

"Wrap it up," James said. "Co-op forces will be here any minute."

Just as quickly as they appeared, the savages disappeared back into the ruined city. The only one left was the traitor. He surveyed the sky and then the squad. "Your people will be here soon."

Mong looked confused. "Why not just kill us and be done with it?"

"Shut up before he changes his mind," Roman hissed.

The traitor studied Mong's face. "How many years out of the Academy, Chronman?"

Mong hesitated before answering. "Five months."

The traitor nodded. "You use the exo well for a Tier-5. You'll make a fine chronman one day. Just make sure you live long enough to make a difference."

"Why are you letting us go?" asked Mong.

James sighed. "Because at the end of the day, you're just trying to do the right thing, and so am I." Then he shot into the air in a streak of yellow and was gone.

Five minutes later, a Valta Valkyrie appeared, followed by three collies. The area was soon flooded by monitors. Roman looked in the direction he had last seen the traitor as he and the rest of his squad were led to safety. This was the first time he had seen the traitor, this James Griffin-Mars. He had to admit he was surprised. All the intel had described the man as an unstable, greedy, self-serving lunatic. This man seemed anything but that. He glanced over at Mong, whose troubled face spoke volumes as well.

Roman crawled into the medical collie and was soon in the air. His last thought before he passed out was that now that he was injured, did he still have to wait two days to shower?

ABOUT THE AUTHOR

WESLEY CHU is the recent winner of the John W. Campbell Award for Best New Writer. His debut novel, *The Lives of Tao,* earned him a Young Adult Library Services Association Alex Award.